Scourge

To my very patient and supportive family: my husband, Larry, and my children, Kyrie, Chandler and Cody. You make these books possible.

Chapter One

A HEAVY IRON candleholder slammed against the wall, just missing Corran Valmonde's head.

"Son of a bitch!"

"Try not to make her mad, Corran."

Rigan Valmonde knelt on the worn floor, drawing a sigil in charcoal, moving as quickly as he dared. Not quickly enough; a piece of firewood spun from the hearth and flew across the room, slamming him in the shoulder hard enough to make him grunt in pain.

"Keep her off me!" he snapped, repairing the smudge in the soot line. Sloppy symbols meant sloppy magic, and that could get someone killed.

"I would if I could see her." Corran stepped away from the wall, raising his iron sword, putting himself between the fireplace and his brother. His breath misted in the unnaturally cold room and moisture condensed on the wavy glass of the only window.

"Watch where you step." Rigan worked on the second sigil, widdershins from the soot marking, this one daubed in ochre. "I don't want to have to do this again."

A small ceramic bowl careened from the mantle, and, for an instant, Rigan glimpsed a young woman in a blood-soaked dress, one hand clutching her heavily pregnant belly. The other hand slipped right through the bowl, even as the dish hurtled at Rigan's head. Rigan dove to one side and the bowl smashed against the opposite wall. At the same time, Corran's sword slashed down through the specter. A howl of rage filled the air as the ghost dissipated.

You have no right to be in my home. The dead woman's voice echoed in Rigan's mind.

Get out of my head.

You are a confessor. Hear me!

Not while you're trying to kill my brother.

"You'd better hurry." Corran slowly turned, watching for the ghost.

"I can't rush the ritual." Rigan tried to shut out the ghost's voice, focusing on the complex chalk sigil. He reached into a pouch and drew a thin curved line of salt, aconite, and powdered amanita, connecting the first sigil to the second, and the second to the third and fourth, working his way to drawing a complete warded circle.

The ghost materialized without warning on the other side of the line, thrusting a thin arm toward Rigan, her long fingers crabbed into claws, old blood beneath her torn nails. She opened a gash on Rigan's cheek as he stumbled backward, grabbed a handful of the salt mixture and threw it. The apparition vanished with a wail.

"Corran!" Rigan's warning came a breath too late as the ghost appeared right behind his brother, and took a swipe with her sharp, filthy nails, clawing Corran's left shoulder.

He wronged me. He let me die, let my baby die— The voice shrieked in Rigan's mind.

"Draw the damn signs!" Corran yelled. "I'll handle her." He wheeled, and before the blood- smeared ghost could strike again, the tip of his iron blade caught her in the chest. Her image dissipated like smoke, with a shriek that echoed from the walls.

Avenge me.

Sorry, lady, Rigan thought as he reached for a pot of pigment. *I'm stuck listening to dead people's dirty little secrets and last regrets, but I just bury people. Take your complaints up with the gods.*

"Last one." Rigan marked the rune in blue woad. The condensation on the window turned to frost, and he shivered. The ghost flickered, insubstantial but still identifiable as the young woman who had died bringing her stillborn child into the world. Her blood still stained the floor in the center of the warded circle and held her to this world as surely as her grief.

Wind whipped through the room, and would have scattered the salt and aconite line if Rigan had not daubed the mixture onto the floor in paste. Fragments of the broken bowl scythed through the air. The iron candle holder sailed across the room; Corran dodged it again, and a shard caught the side of his brother's head, opening a cut on Rigan's scalp, sending a warm rush of blood down the side of his face.

The ghost raged on, her anger and grief whipping the air into a whirlwind. *I will not leave without justice for myself and my son.*

You don't really have a choice about it, Rigan replied silently and stepped across the warding, careful not to smudge the lines, pulling an iron knife from his belt. He nodded to Corran and together their voices rose as they chanted the burial rite, harmonizing out of long practice, the words of the Old Language as familiar as their own names.

The ghostly woman's image flickered again, solid enough now that Rigan could see the streaks of blood on her pale arms and make out the pattern of her dress. She appeared right next to him, close enough that his shoulder bumped against her chest, and her mouth brushed his ear.

'Twas not nature that killed me. My faithless husband let us bleed because he thought the child was not his own.

The ghost vanished, compelled to reappear in the center of the circle, standing on the blood-stained floor. Rigan extended his trembling right hand and called to the magic, drawing on the old, familiar currents of power. The circle and runes flared with light. The sigils burned in red, white, blue, and black, with the salt-aconite lines a golden glow between them.

Corran and Rigan's voices rose as the glow grew steadily brighter, and the ghost raged all the harder against the power that held her, thinning the line between this world and the next, opening a door and forcing her through it.

One heartbeat she was present; in the next she was gone, though her screams continued to echo.

Rigan and Corran kept on chanting, finishing the rite as the circle's glow faded and the sigils dulled to mere pigment once more. Rigan lowered his palm and dispelled the magic, then blew out a deep breath.

"That was not supposed to happen." Corran's scowl deepened as he looked around the room, taking in the shattered bowl and the dented candle holder. He flinched, noticing Rigan's wounds now that the immediate danger had passed.

"You're hurt."

Rigan shrugged. "Not as bad as you are." He wiped blood from his face with his sleeve, then bent to gather the ritual materials.

"She confessed to you?" Corran bent to help his brother, wincing at the movement.

"Yeah. And she had her reasons," Rigan replied. He looked at Corran, frowning at the blood that soaked his shirt. "We'll need to wash and bind your wounds when we get back to the shop."

"Let's get out of here."

They packed up their gear, but Corran did not sheath his iron sword until they were ready to step outside. A small crowd had gathered, no doubt drawn by the shrieks and thuds and the flares of light through the cracked, dirty window.

"Nothing to see here, folks," Corran said, exhaustion clear in his voice. "We're just the undertakers."

Once they were convinced the excitement was over, the onlookers dispersed, leaving one man standing to the side. He looked up anxiously as Rigan and Corran approached him.

"Is it done? Is she gone?" For an instant, eagerness shone too clearly in his eyes. Then his posture shifted, shoulders hunching, gaze dropping, and mask slipped back into place. "I mean, is she at rest? After all she's been through?"

Before Corran could answer, Rigan grabbed the man by the collar, pulled him around the corner into an alley and threw him up against the wall. "You can stop the grieving widower act," he growled. Out of the corner of his eye, he saw Corran standing guard at the mouth of the alley, gripping his sword.

"I don't know what you're talking about!" The denial did not reach the man's eyes.

"You let her bleed out, you let the baby die, because you didn't think the child was yours." Rigan's voice was rough as gravel, pitched low so that only the trembling man could hear him.

"She betrayed me—"

"No." The word brought the man up short. "No, if she had been lying, her spirit wouldn't have been trapped here." Rigan slammed the widower against the wall again to get his attention.

"Rigan—" Corran cautioned.

"Lying spirits don't get trapped." Rigan had a tight grip on the man's shirt, enough that he could feel his body trembling. "Your wife. Your baby. Your fault." He stepped back and let the man down, then threw him aside to land on the cobblestones.

"The dead are at peace. You've got the rest of your life to live with what you did." With that, he turned on his heel and walked away, as the man choked back a sob.

Corran sheathed his sword. "I really wish you'd stop beating up paying customers," he grumbled as they turned to walk back to the shop.

"Wish I could. Don't know how to stop being confessor to the dead, not sure what else to do once I know the dirt," Rigan replied, an edge of pain and bitterness in his voice.

"So the husband brought us in to clean up his mess?" Corran winced as he walked; the gashes on his arm and back had to be throbbing.

"Yeah."

"I like it better when the ghosts confess something like where they buried their money," Corran replied.

"So do I."

The sign over the front of the shop read *Valmonde Undertakers.* Around back, in the alley, the sign over the door just said *Bodies.* Corran led the way, dropping the small rucksack containing their gear just inside the entrance, and cursed under his breath as the strap raked across raw shoulders.

"Sit down," Rigan said, nodding at an unoccupied mortuary table. He tied his brown hair into a queue before washing his hands in a bucket of fresh water drawn from the pump. "Let me have a look at those wounds."

Footsteps descended the stairs from the small apartment above.

"You're back? How bad was it?" Kell, the youngest of the Valmonde brothers, stopped halfway down the stairs. He had Corran's coloring, taking after their father, with dark blond hair that curled when it grew long. Rigan's brown hair favored their mother. All three brothers' blue eyes were the same shade, making the resemblance impossible to overlook.

"Shit." Kell jumped the last several steps as he saw his brothers' injuries. He grabbed a bucket of water and scanned a row of powders and elixirs, grabbing bottles and measuring out with a practiced eye and long experience. "I thought you said it was just a banishing."

"It was *supposed* to be 'just' a banishing," Rigan said as Corran stripped off his bloody shirt. "But it didn't go entirely to plan." He soaked a clean cloth in the bucket Kell held and wrung it out.

"A murder, not a natural death," Corran said, and his breath hitched as Rigan daubed his wounds. "Another ghost with more power than it should have had."

Rigan saw Kell appraising Corran's wounds, glancing at the gashes on Rigan's face and hairline.

"Mine aren't as bad," Rigan said.

"When you're done with Corran, I'll take care of them," Kell said. "So I'm guessing Mama's magic kicked in again, if you knew about the murder?"

"Yeah," Rigan replied in a flat voice.

Undertaking, like all the trades in Ravenwood, was a hereditary profession. That it came with its own magic held no surprise; all the trades did. The power and the profession were passed down from one generation to the next. Undertakers could ease a spirit's transition to the realm beyond, nudge a lost soul onward, or release one held back by unfinished business. Sigils, grave markings, corpse paints, and ritual chants were all part of the job. But none of the other undertakers that Rigan knew had a mama who was part Wanderer. Of the three Valmonde brothers, only Rigan had inherited her ability to hear the confessions of the dead, something not even the temple priests could do. His mother had called it a gift. Most of the time, Rigan regarded it as a burden, sometimes a curse. Usually, it just made things more complicated than they needed to be.

"Hold still," Rigan chided as Corran winced. "Ghost wounds draw taint." He wiped away the blood, cleaned the cuts, and then applied ointment from the jar Kell handed him. All three of them knew the routine; they had done this kind of thing far too many times.

"There," he said, binding up Corran's arm and shoulder with strips of gauze torn from a clean linen shroud. "That should do it."

Corran slid off the table to make room for Rigan. While Kell dealt with his brother's wounds, Corran went to pour them each a whiskey.

"That's the second time this month we've had a spirit go from angry to dangerous," Corran said, returning with their drinks. He pushed a glass into Rigan's hand, and set one aside for Kell, who was busy wiping the blood from his brother's face.

"I'd love to know why." Rigan tried not to wince as Kell probed his wounds. The deep gash where the pottery shard had sliced his hairline bled more freely than the cut on his cheek. Kell swore under his breath as he tried to staunch the bleeding.

"It's happening all over Ravenwood, and no one in the Guild seems to know a damn thing about why or what to do about it," Corran said, knocking his drink back in one shot. "Old Daniels said he'd heard his father talk about the same sort of thing, but that was fifty years ago. So why did the ghosts *stop* being dangerous then, and what made them *start* being dangerous now?"

Rigan started to shake his head, but stopped at a glare from Kell, who said, "Hold still."

He let out a long breath and complied, but his mind raced. Until the last few months, banishings were routine. Violence and tragedy sometimes produced ghosts, but in all the years since Rigan and Corran had been undertakers—first helping their father and uncles and then running the business since the older men had passed away—banishings were usually uneventful.

Make the marks, sing the chant, the ghost goes on and we go home. So what's changed?

"I'm sick of being handed my ass by things that aren't even solid," Rigan grumbled. "If this keeps up, we'll need to charge more."

Corran snorted. "Good luck convincing Guild Master Orlo to raise the rates."

Rigan's eyes narrowed. "Guild Master Orlo can dodge flying candlesticks and broken pottery. See how he likes it."

"Once you've finished grumbling we've got four new bodies to attend to," Kell said. "One's a Guild burial and the others are worth a few silvers a piece." Rigan did not doubt that Kell had negotiated the best fees possible, he always did.

"Nice," Rigan replied, and for the first time noticed that there were corpses on the other tables in the workshop, covered with sheets. "We can probably have these ready to take to the cemetery in the morning."

"One of them was killed by a guard," Kell said, turning his back and keeping his voice carefully neutral.

"Do you know why?" Corran tensed.

"His wife said he protested when the guard doubled the 'protection' fee. Guess the guard felt he needed to be taught a lesson." Bribes were part of everyday life in Ravenwood, and residents generally went along with the hated extortion. Guilds promised to shield their members from the guards' worst abuses, but in reality, the Guild Masters only intervened in the most extreme cases, fearful of drawing the Lord Mayor's ire. At least, that had been the excuse when Corran sought justice from the Undertakers' Guild for their father's murder, a fatal beating on flimsy charges. Rigan suspected the guards had killed their father because the neighborhood looked up to him, and if he'd decided to speak out in opposition, others might have followed. Even with the passing years, the grief remained sharp, the injustice bitter.

Kell went to wash his hands in a bucket by the door. "Trent came by while you and Corran were out. There's been another attack, three dead. He wants you to go have a look and take care of the bodies."

Rigan and Corran exchanged a glance. "What kind of attack?"

Kell sighed. "What kind do you think? Creatures." He hesitated. "I got the feeling from Trent this was worse than usual."

"Did Trent say what kind of creatures?" Corran asked, and Rigan picked up on an edge to his brother's voice.

Kell nodded. "Ghouls."

Corran swore under his breath and looked away, pushing back old memories. "All right," he said, not quite managing to hide a shudder. "Let's go get the bodies before it gets any later. We're going to have our hands full tonight."

"Kell and I can go, if you want to start on the ones here," Rigan offered.

Corran shook his head. "No. I'm not much use as an undertaker if I can't go get the corpses no matter how they came to an end," Corran said.

Rigan heard the undercurrent in his tone. Kell glanced at Rigan, who gave a barely perceptible nod, warning Kell to say nothing. *Corran's dealing with the memories the best way he knows how*, Rigan thought. *I just wish there weren't so many reminders.*

"I'll prepare the wash and the pigments, and get the shrouds ready," Kell said. "I'll have these folks ready for your part of the ritual by the time you get back." He gestured to the bodies already laid out. "Might have to park the new ones in the cart for a bit and switch out—tables are scarce."

Corran grimaced. "That'll help." He turned to Rigan. "Come on. Let's get this over with."

Kell gave them the directions Trent had provided. Corran took up the long poles of the undertaker's cart, which clattered behind him as they walked. Rigan knew better than to talk to his brother when he was in this kind of mood. At best he could be present, keep Corran from having to deal with the ghouls' victims alone, and sit up with him afterward.

It's only been three months since he buried Jora, since we almost had to bury him. *The memory's raw, although he won't mention it. But Kell and I both hear what he shouts in his sleep. He's still fighting them in his dreams, and still losing.*

Rigan's memories of that night were bad enough—Trent stumbling to the back door of the shop, carrying Corran, bloody and unconscious; Corran's too-still body on one of the mortuary tables; Kell praying to Doharmu and any god who would listen to stave off death; Trent, covered in Corran's blood, telling them how he had found their brother and Jora out in the tavern barn, the ghoul that attacked them already feasting on Jora's fresh corpse.

Rigan never did understand why Trent had gone to the barn that night, or how he managed to fight off the ghoul. Corran and Jora, no doubt, had slipped away for a tryst, expecting the barn to be safe and private. Corran said little of the attack, and Rigan hoped his brother truly did not remember all the details.

"We're here." Corran's rough voice and expressionless face revealed more than any words.

Ross, the farrier, met them at the door. "I'm sorry to have to call you out," he said.

"It's our job," Corran replied. "I'm just sorry the godsdamned ghouls are back."

"Not for long," Ross said under his breath. A glance passed between Corran and Ross. Rigan filed it away to ask Corran about later.

The stench hit Rigan as soon as they entered the barn. Two horses lay gutted in their stalls and partially dismembered. Blood spattered the wooden walls and soaked the sawdust. Flies swarmed on what the ghouls had left behind.

"They're over here," Ross said. The bodies of two men and a woman had been tossed aside like discarded bones at a feast. Rigan swallowed down bile. Corran paled, his jaw working as he ground his teeth.

Rigan and Corran knew better than most what remained of a corpse once a ghoul had finished with it. Belly torn open to get to the soft organs; ribs split wide to access the heart. How much of the flesh remained depended on the ghoul's hunger and whether or not it feasted undisturbed. Given the state these bodies were in—their faces were the only parts left untouched—the ghouls had taken their time. Rigan closed his eyes and took a deep breath, willing himself not to retch.

"What about the creatures?" Corran asked.

"Must have fled when they heard us coming," Ross said. "We were making plenty of noise." Ross handed them each a shovel, and took one up himself. "There's not much left, and what's there is... loose."

"Who were they?" Rigan asked, not sure Corran felt up to asking questions.

Ross swallowed hard. "One of the men was my cousin, Tad. The other two were customers. They brought in the two horses late in the day, and my cousin said he'd handle it."

Rigan heard the guilt in Ross's tone.

"Guild honors?" Corran asked, finding his voice, and Ross nodded.

Rigan brought the cart into the barn, stopping as close as possible to the mangled corpses. The bodies were likely to fall to pieces as soon as they began shoveling.

"Yeah," Ross replied, getting past the lump in his throat. "Send them off right." He shook his head. "They say the monsters are all part of the Balance, like life and death cancel each other out somehow. That's bullshit, if you ask me."

The three men bent to their work, trying not to think of the slippery bones and bloody bits as bodies. *Carcasses. Like what's left when the butcher's done with a hog, or the vultures are finished with a cow*, Rigan thought. The barn smelled of blood and entrails, copper and shit. Rigan looked at what they loaded into the cart. Only the skulls made it possible to tell that the remains had once been human.

"I'm sorry about this, but I need to do it—to keep them from rising as ghouls or restless spirits," Rigan said. He pulled a glass bottle from the bag at the front of the wagon, and carefully removed the stopper, sprinkling the bodies with green vitriol to burn the flesh and prevent the corpses from rising. The acid sizzled, sending up noxious tendrils of smoke. Rigan stoppered the bottle and pulled out a bag of the salt-aconite-amanita mixture, dusting it over the bodies, assuring that the spirits would remain at rest.

Ross nodded. "Better than having them return as one of those... things," he said, shuddering.

"We'll have them buried tomorrow," Corran said as Rigan secured their grisly load.

"That's more than fair," Ross agreed. "Corran—you know if I'd had a choice about calling you—"

"It's our job." Corran cut off the apology. Ross knew about Jora's death. That didn't change the fact that they were the only Guild undertakers in this area of Ravenwood, and Ross was a friend.

"I'll be by tomorrow afternoon with the money," Ross said, accompanying them to the door.

"We'll be done by then," Corran replied. Rigan went to pick up the cart's poles, but Corran shook his head and lifted them himself.

Rigan did not argue. *Easier for him to haul the wagon; that way he doesn't have to look at the bodies and remember when Jora's brother brought her for burial.*

Rigan felt for the reassuring bulk of his knife beneath his cloak—a steel blade rather than the iron weapon they used in the banishing rite. No one knew the true nature of the monsters, or why so many more had started appearing in Ravenwood of late. Ghouls weren't like angry ghosts or restless spirits that could be banished with salt, aconite, and iron. Whatever darkness spawned them and the rest of their monstrous brethren, they were creatures of skin and bone; only beheading would stop them.

Rigan kept his blade sharpened.

Chapter Two

"WE'VE BEEN TRACKING the ghouls and we think we know where their lair is." Trent met Corran as he entered the cellar in the abandoned building.

"You think they're the same creatures that killed Ross's cousin?" Corran asked.

Trent shrugged. Dark haired and dark eyed, he was a butcher by trade, skills that came in handy now that there were other, more dangerous uses for knives. "No way to tell. Ghouls all kind of look alike. But whether they are or not, they'll kill again—unless we stop them."

"Lead on." Corran followed Trent into a small room. Eight other men, all roughly Corran's age, murmured greetings as they entered. Corran crossed to the chest that held his equipment and readied himself for the night's work. He already wore his steel sword in a scabbard on his belt. Wearing a sword in public risked trouble; the Lord Mayor's guards took a dim view of weapons larger than knives. *Not that the guards themselves do much of anything to protect us, gods know*, he thought. He already risked a beating—or worse—being out past curfew. And if they were caught hunting monsters, they would earn a noose, not a jail cell. Monster hunting was the official purview of the city, not the business of unruly citizens.

The only creatures more feared than monsters were the Lord Mayor's corrupt guards. Corran's father had died at their hands, along with so many others. While monsters came and went, the guards remained a constant threat. Bribes only went so far in assuring safety. Beatings, extortion, and rape kept Ravenwood's residents compliant—excesses that the Guilds and the Lord Mayor chose to ignore. The guards needed no infraction of the law to earn their ire; merely being in the wrong place at the wrong time sufficed. Any slight, real or imagined, presented cause for swift, brutal retaliation. Corran never learned what caused his father's fatal beating, since any witnesses feared to speak out and the guards did not explain themselves.

"I'm surprised you didn't bring Rigan with you," Trent said.

Corran shook his head. "Not going to happen. I want Rigan and Kell kept out of this. Bad enough we lost Papa to the guards and Mama to one of those things. I won't lose my brothers, too."

"Didn't you say Rigan's banishing magic is stronger than yours?" Ross said. "Might come in handy—"

"No," Corran said in a flat, hard voice. "They don't know I'm here, and they aren't going to. I told Trent that when I agreed to hunt."

Ross raised his hands in appeasement. "All right. I get it. Just thinking we can use all the help we can get."

"Get the help somewhere else, then. Keep my brothers out of it."

Monsters returned time and again to Ravenwood, and when they did, tradesmen became hunters. The guards' ineffectual protection forced residents to take matters into their own hands, even at the risk of a beating—or worse—if caught.

Groups of hunters—bound by blood, grief, or friendship—formed in secret, fought, and disbanded on their own, without central authority, rising up when necessary and fading away into the night once the threat had been neutralized. Most people became hunters because they had lost someone to the monsters, doing what they could to ensure no one else would feel that pain.

Corran pulled on a padded jacket and slung a bandolier of knives—iron, steel, and obsidian—across his chest. In his rucksack, he had plenty of the salt and aconite mixture he used in the banishing ritual. He straightened, ready for the hunt. "All right. What's the plan?"

Mir, the blacksmith's son, pointed to several glass bottles on a battered table. "It's not as much of the green vitriol as I'd like, but it's damnably difficult to make, and I didn't want Father asking questions."

"If it takes more than that, we've got bigger problems." Calfon, a lamp merchant, stepped away from where he had been leaning against the wall. His sandy hair was shorn close, and his muscular body testified to his vigorous training. "Six ghouls are enough of a problem as it is."

"Six?" Bant echoed. He was a tanner, and the smell of his trade never completely left him. Given his skills with a blade, they forgave the odor. Even so, Pav, one of the weaver's sons, and Jott, a carpenter by trade, stayed upwind of him.

"Yeah. Don't know if it's the only nest, but it's close enough to the farrier's barn. It's a good bet they're the ones who killed those folks," Calfon said.

Ross stood to one side, near Allery, the potter's eldest son. Ross kept clenching and unclenching his fists, readying himself for the fight. Corran knew that, for him, tonight was personal.

Corran blinked, trying to shut down the memories of another hunt, another night, when it had been *his* vengeance the hunters sought; vengeance and something near enough to justice for Jora. What happened that night never strayed far from his mind, waking or sleeping.

* * *

"SURELY YOUR FATHER will come around." Corran's lips brushed Jora's ear. He kissed her gently, and felt her shiver.

"I don't know," Jora whispered, leaning into him. "He always said he wanted me to marry into the Guild, to keep the business in the family."

Corran buried his face in her long, dark hair, and kissed her neck. "You have brothers. They'll inherit the business. Where will that leave you? But if you marry me, I'm the eldest, the one in charge. And undertakers are guaranteed steady work."

Jora chuckled and pulled him close, returning his kisses. She slid her hand across his back, then let it tangle in the dark blond curls of his hair. "Is that a proposal, Corran Valmonde?"

"You know it is."

"Then I accept."

Corran kissed her, long and slow. "I'm glad to hear it. The question is, when do we go to your father?"

"Later," she whispered, pulling him into the shadows, where fresh hay would make a comfortable trysting place. "There's no rush."

A strange, scratching noise made them freeze. "What's that?" Jora said, digging her fingers into Corran's arm.

"I don't know," he replied, glancing around. The stable should have been empty. Jora's father had taken their horse on his trip. The scratching sounded again, closer. A low, guttural wail sent a chill down Corran's spine. He strained to see in the dim moonlight filtering through cracks between the boards, which left much of the stable in shadow.

"Stay here," Corran breathed. He grabbed a solidly-built rake with iron tines from where it leaned against the wall.

"Forget that." Jora reached for a shovel. Whatever made the scratching noise blocked the way out.

"Probably just rats," Corran said, trying to sound hopeful.

"Big rats." Jora sounded unconvinced. She looked as spooked as

Corran felt, although she'd never admit it. With two older brothers, Jora knew how to hold her own.

The creature barreled into Corran, knocking him to the floor before he could get in a good swing with his rake. The thing that attacked him looked like a withered corpse, but moved swiftly and fought savagely. Sharp teeth snapped just inches from his throat; a bony hand pinned his left arm, digging its nails through his shirt and deep into his flesh.

"Get out of here, Jora!" Corran yelled, twisting to evade the creature's snapping teeth. He thumped the ghoul hard on the head with the handle of his rake, and brought his knees up into its belly.

Jora swung the shovel with all her might. The iron blade came down hard on the ghoul's back, with enough force to break bone. The creature shrieked, but it did not release its hold on Corran.

"Go get help!" he shouted.

"I'm not leaving you." Jora swung again, and the blade of the shovel clanged against the creature's skull.

Corran gritted his teeth as he ripped his arm free and rolled out from beneath the ghoul. He swung his rake, sinking the sharp metal tines into the creature's side.

The ghoul grabbed Jora's arm and threw her aside with inhuman force, before backhanding Corran hard enough to blur his vision and set his ears ringing. Jora scrambled to her feet, coming back at full speed, swinging her shovel for a killing blow. The ghoul wrenched the shovel from her hands, grabbed her by the throat, and twisted. Her neck snapped with a sickening crunch and her body fell to the ground.

Fear and anger burned through Corran, and he stepped toward the monster, scything the rake. Blood ran down his left arm, hot and sticky. He forced himself past the pain and brought the rake up as the ghoul sprang at him, catching it in the jaw and opening a wide, bloody gash in its face.

The monster paid no attention to its injuries, stalking Corran with hunger in its eyes. It sprang forward, and Corran barely escaped the worst of its bite as its yellowed teeth dug a bloody furrow in his thigh. He bit back a cry of pain and swung his rake again, bashing the solid iron tines against the creature's skull.

Icy hands threw Corran to the ground, breaking the rake's handle, and he thrust the broken shaft up like a stake. It caught the monster in the ribs and the thing howled, tearing free and leaving a bloody trail.

Pain and blood loss made Corran light-headed. He could no longer feel his left arm, and the gash in his thigh burned unbearably. He tried to get to his feet, but his injured leg gave out on him. The ghoul picked him up and threw him across the floor, knocking Corran out.

Corran awoke to witness the ghoul ripping at Jora's still-warm corpse with its teeth. Corran staggered to his feet and advanced, gripping the blood-slick broken rake. With a feral cry, the creature launched itself at Corran. In the same instant, the stable door slammed open and a man stood silhouetted in the moonlight. Corran heard a whirring noise and saw a flash of steel. The ghoul landed on top of Corran, and he braced himself for teeth to close on his throat.

"Still alive?" Trent spared a worried glance at Corran before he hauled the ghoul clear. He withdrew his knife from the ghoul's back, then sawed it across the monster's neck, severing the head. Trent pulled out a flask and poured a stream of green liquid that sizzled and burned when it hit the ghoul's flesh, then took a vial from the pouch on his belt and sprinkled powder over the monster's corpse.

"Jora—" Corran managed. Blood soaked his shirt and slicked his skin; his own and that of the monster. He rolled onto his good arm and started to crawl toward where the monster had thrown his lover.

"Corran?"

"We never saw it before it was on us," Corran said, gasping in pain.

Trent knelt beside Jora's savaged corpse. "I'm sorry, Corran."

"Oh, gods," Corran moaned, cradling his head in his hands, unable to look at the damage the creature had done.

"She's gone, Corran. I'm sorry. I've got to get you out of here, before the guards come. Both of us need to be far away from here."

"Jora—"

"Jora's dead." Trent wiped his knife on the ghoul's ragged shirt. "If you're found here, odds are her brothers will blame you. And if the guards find me, I'll hang."

"Corran?" Calfon said. "Are you with us?"

"Sorry," Corran muttered, shaking himself out of the memory. "I'm ready."

"Let's go," Trent said, leading the way out of the cellar and into the night.

According to the Guilds and the Lord Mayor, curfew protected residents by encouraging law-abiding folk to be indoors, safe from the criminals and monsters that roamed the streets at night. But curfew's sole function, as far as the city's residents could tell, was to provide one more excuse for the guards to rough up whomever they pleased with impunity. Earn the ire of a guard for any reason, no matter how insignificant, and they need not even invent charges of theft. Curfew violation alone could excuse a beating severe enough to leave a man hobbled, or dead.

Wrighton, the neighborhood of Ravenwood that was home to most of its skilled tradespeople and artisans, was empty and silent. No one but the Lord Mayor's guards should be abroad at this time, but the guards didn't care to risk their skin to put down monsters, so that left the hunters dodging two groups of predators, both equally deadly.

Trent and Calfon led the way. Mir, Pav, and Bant brought up the rear, with Corran, Ross, and Allery in the middle. They slipped through the shadows and into a narrow alley, keeping tight to the wall of a building, stepping over garbage as rats squealed and skittered out of their way.

Trent's hand snapped up in warning and they froze, backs against the wall, making themselves as still and silent as possible. Bootsteps sounded around the corner, and voices carried in the dark. *The night patrol*, Corran thought.

"You there! Stop!"

Corran felt cold fear slip down his spine. Ross laid a hand on his shoulder and gave a sharp shake of his head. No guards were silhouetted in the alley entrance; the command was not meant for them.

Running footsteps sounded, then a cry of fear, and the unmistakable sound of fists meeting flesh. Beside Corran, Ross flinched at the sound of the beating.

Calfon shot a warning glance at the hunters gathered behind him. *Intervene now, and we lose our shot at the ghouls.*

"Don't hurt me!" a man begged.

Corran gritted his teeth. *Did the guards that beat Papa to death make him beg? Did they even give him a chance to?*

"Curfew began a candlemark ago."

"I'm sorry! My daughter is sick with fever. I had to go out to fetch a healer."

"So?"

"Please. I'll pay you whatever you ask, just let me help my daughter."

"Turn out your pouch. Let's see what coin you have."

"Take it. I need to bring the healer."

"This won't buy me two tankards of ale!" one of the guards complained.

"It's all I have. Please—"

Corran heard the man cry out as he slammed against the wall.

"Not enough," the first guard said. "What else can you offer?"

"Let me bring the healer to my house, and you can take me to the jail," the man bargained. "I'll serve my sentence."

Corran and Ross exchanged a glance. A night in jail or a hefty fine would more than suffice as punishment for violating curfew—and often did, unless the guards were looking for an excuse for violence. The Lord Mayor's soldiers grew bold in the certainty that their excesses would be overlooked, while Ravenwood's residents learned to fear the guards' caprice.

"There might be one thing you could give me in payment," the guard replied. "I let you take the healer to your house, and in return, I come back in a week and spend the night with your daughter."

"Mercy! She's only fourteen! Please—"

"Just one night. Probably not her first toss. And if you don't get the healer, she won't see fifteen."

Corran closed his eyes and clenched his fists. Ross dug fingers into his shoulder. "Stay out of it," he whispered. "We can fight ghouls, but we can't take on the guards, too." Corran's eyes flashed in response, and he saw the same anger and revulsion on Ross's face.

"You want to heal your daughter, and we want a little something for pretending we didn't see you out here," the guard continued in a smug tone that made Corran want to throw up. "Now what's it gonna be? Dead or borrowed?"

"One night," the desperate man bargained. "And you'll take care with her—"

"We take care with all the ladies, don't we?" the guard said to his companion, who guffawed.

"Yeah. We take care of them. No complaints outta any of them."

"All right." Defeat resonated in the father's voice. "Just let me get to the healer."

"Go right ahead," the first guard mocked. "We're coming along. Keep you out of trouble. Need to know where you live, after all, if we're going to come calling."

None of the hunters moved until the guards and their victim moved off. By then, Corran shook with rage, and his nails had cut red half-moons into the palms of both hands.

"We fight one kind of monster, and let another run loose," he growled as Calfon clapped a hand on his shoulder.

"And what would you have us do?" Ross asked quietly. "Take on the guards?"

I wanted to put a knife in that bastard's back and slit his friend's throat, then serve them up as ghoul bait, Corran thought, still seething. He shook off Calfon's hand and glowered at Ross. "Let's move. If I hadn't been ready for a fight before, I am now."

"Hurry," Calfon urged. One more block brought them to the dilapidated warehouse Calfon had identified as the ghouls' nest. Far removed from the usually bustling harbor front, buildings this close to the old city wall were less desirable, and often, at least temporarily, abandoned; the warehouse looked deserted. Nothing moved at the dark windows, and no lanterns lit the interior.

Bant and Allery watched the street. Calfon and Mir took point, easing open the double doors, swords at the ready. Ross and Pav followed right behind, weapons drawn. Corran and Trent came next, armed and carrying green vitriol and salt.

Calfon signaled the others to follow, and Ross lit a lantern, keeping it tightly shuttered, allowing just enough light to escape to let them get their bearings inside the decrepit warehouse.

The stench hit Corran as he entered, like an abattoir in summer. If he had any doubts that the ghouls had made their lair here, the smell dispelled them. "Get moving," Calfon ordered, and the hunters fell to their tasks.

Mir lit another lantern and lifted it high while they made a sweep of the large, open space. The bloodstains on the floor told Corran that the ghouls had brought their dinner home with them on more than one occasion, and he swallowed hard at the thought.

Bant and Allery kept watch, staying just out of sight behind the edge of the door. Mir unloaded the bag with the salt-aconite and the green vitriol.

Now we wait, and see how long it takes for the ghouls to smell our blood, Corran thought as he flattened himself next to one of the windows. He saw a shadow slink around the warehouse and signaled the others. Bant gestured from his post at the opposite wall, alerting them to a second ghoul. Corran strained to hear anything that might clue him to the location of the other creatures.

The scrabbling on the roof sounded like hail, until Corran remembered the clear night. He looked up at the darkness above the wooden beams, and realized with a creeping dread that he could see stars through the broken shingles.

"They're here!" he shouted, as the shadows in the rafters began to move. Ghouls flowed upside-down across the ceiling like gaunt, long-limbed spiders, thin as famine victims despite their distended bellies. The joints in their elbows and knees looked too pronounced, their skulls too large, eyes sunken and dark. Corran wanted to tear his gaze away, but was fascinated by the ghouls' macabre dance. Shaking himself into action, Corran raised his sword in one hand, and a long knife in the other.

"We're down here, you bastards! Come and get us!"

A ghoul sprang from the shadows, its bony fingers barely missing Corran's arm. Corran backed up, one step at a time. The ghoul stalked him, head down, eyes focused on its prey.

A second ghoul appeared from the back door, training its gaze on Trent. Bant squared off with the newest adversary, circling carefully, waiting for an opportunity to attack.

Four on the ceiling, one at each door. Eight of us. Not bad odds.

"Two more over there," Mir said.

I liked it more when we outnumbered them.

Four ghouls dropped from the ceiling and hit the ground running. One of the creatures sprang at Allery, catching him by surprise and knocking him over. Allery and the creature wrestled, rolling over and over, the ghoul struggling to get a grip on Allery's throat as he fought to bring his knife up to land a killing strike.

Corran's opponent hesitated and he took advantage of the opening, launching himself at the ghoul. The creature hissed as it saw the steel blade coming and dodged aside, letting the sword slice down through its shoulder and ribs instead of taking it through the neck. Dark blood slowly oozed from the shattered chest and the ghoul's right arm swung limply from the useless socket. The wound would have had a living man on his knees, overcome with pain and shock, but Corran saw calculation and naked hunger still burning in the creature's dead eyes.

The ghoul knocked aside Corran's sword and lunged forward, jaws wide, going for his neck.

Corran staggered backward. His world had narrowed to the maw snapping inches from his throat, and the sharp nails ripping through his shirt. The ghoul threw him against the warehouse wall, following with uncanny speed to make the kill, pinning him against the wood as its fingers tightened, cutting off his air.

Corran bucked, getting his feet up between himself and the ghoul and kicking the creature away. He sagged to his knees, gasping for air, but when the ghoul came back at full speed, he met it in a crouch. He raised his sword in both hands, and the ghoul's momentum drove it down the blade, black blood washing over his hands. The creature's good arm came up fast, opening gashes in Corran's cheek even as he wrestled the blade up into the chest cavity. The monster shuddered, its jaw working open and closed, ichor spilling from its blue lips. Corran was still trying to shift his grip when silver flashed through the air and the ghoul's head toppled from its shoulders. Corran kicked the body free from his blade and looked up as Mir extended a hand to help him to his feet.

"Come on. There's more where that came from."

Corran took in the scene as he got to his feet. Three ghouls were down, hacked to pieces. Five still battled the hunters, and if the ghouls felt fear at the sight of their fallen nest-mates, it did nothing to slow their attack or blunt their hunger.

Sharp claws raked down Trent's arm and he cried out. The butcher's blade sank deep into the ghoul's shoulder, but blood ran down his arm, and the wounds made it difficult for him to keep a firm grip on his sword. As Corran ran to help Trent, Mir circled behind the ghoul still evading Ross's blade.

"I've got you!" Corran yelled.

"I'm all right! See to your own!" Trent managed, not daring to take his eyes off the ghoul. The creature moved right; Trent mirrored it, but not fast enough, as the ghoul shifted at the last moment, opening new gashes with a swipe of its bloody, clawed fingers. With a fierce cry, Corran lurched into the ghoul's path, slashing at its side and belly with his blade and slitting it open. The ghoul dropped with a howl, splattering Corran with blood. He swung his sword again, sending the ghoul's head rolling.

"Shit!" Calfon's curse made Corran turn. Three battered ghouls faced off against their opponents, as Mir and Allery beheaded the fallen monsters and sprinkled their corpses with green vitriol and the salt-aconite mixture.

Trent held his own against his opponent, keeping his bloody left arm tight against his chest. Bant ran to join him, and together they cut down a ghoul and severed its head. Ross bled from gashes across his chest, the sword in his hand slick with monster blood. Before Corran could provide any assistance, Ross launched himself at another ghoul with a two-handed strike that cut the creature in half through the waist. A second strike tore through the ghoul's neck and spine with enough force to send the head rolling across the floor.

Pav circled one of the remaining ghouls. Blood soaked his shirt and ran down his arm. He was tiring, and as Corran closed the gap between them, the ghoul sprang forward.

"Pav, watch out!"

The ghoul attacked, maw open wide, claws bared, ready to take the weaver to the ground. Pav swung and missed, and the ghoul sank its teeth deep into his shoulder. The hunter screamed, struggling to get free. He shoved his dagger into the ghoul's belly at almost the same moment Corran slashed down through the creature's neck. The monster's headless body fell backward, but the head remained, jaws tight on Pav's shoulder.

"Gods, Corran! Get it off me!"

Corran swallowed bile as he shoved his sword into the ghoul's mouth, prying the jaws apart; they snapped open and the bloody head dropped to the ground. Corran kicked it toward the center of the room, and Pav collapsed to his knees, eyes wide with sheer terror.

"It's over," Corran said. He frowned as he looked at the deep bite and the blood staining Pav's shirt. "We need to get you out of here and clean that wound." He helped Pav to his feet and turned toward the center of the room.

"That's all of them—for now." Calfon stood with his hands on his hips, surveying the damage. Mir and Trent used poles they had found somewhere in the old warehouse to push the ghouls' corpses toward the center of the floor, while Bant and Allery scavenged bits of broken crates and splintered boards to stack against the pile of bodies. Once Corran had assured himself that Pav was not going to pass out, he went to help, trying to ignore how his hands shook now that the fighting was over.

"Hurry it up; we really don't want company," Calfon urged, going to retrieve more of the green vitriol and the salt. Corran brought the rest, and together they doused the bodies, standing back as noxious smoke rose from the burning flesh. Salt, amanita, and aconite came next. Mir and Trent joined them, carrying the lanterns. Mir and Trent used their candles to light the dry wood piled around the bodies. The flames caught quickly, and the smell of the burning ghouls made Corran gag.

"Come on," Calfon said, once the blaze was underway. "We all need patching up, and it'll be dawn soon. Let's get out of here, while we still can."

Chapter Three

"SHE'S NOT LOOKING at you," Rigan Valmonde said, as he and his friends, Wil and Donn, hunched over a table at The Lame Dragon, nursing their tankards of ale.

"I'm sure she winked at me," Wil said, his eyes on the pretty dark-haired serving girl.

"She had something in her eye," Donn replied. "Or maybe she was trying not to cry at the sight of your ugly face!"

Rigan and Donn laughed, while Wil bore the teasing with a long-suffering sigh. "You're both just jealous," he retorted, but he had more ale than fight in him.

"I suspect she gets a dozen marriage proposals a night from the fellows in here," Rigan said, "and turns them all down."

"That's because she's got high standards," Wil sniffed. "She's been holding out for the best."

"Well, then, you're completely out of luck, my friend," Donn said with a laugh.

"I don't see either of you courting anyone," Wil sulked, glaring at his two friends.

"That's because we're working, mate. I only got away from the shop because they needed me to run some errands," Rigan said, holding up a bag full of pigments and powdered plants. *I'm not going to tell them about Elinor. She said she'd go walking with me. Now I just have to work up the courage to ask.*

Rigan was eighteen, old enough to marry—an eligible bachelor in a respectable trade. Corran, two years his senior, was among the few men in the Guild his age who wasn't betrothed or already married. But the losses of the past year had pushed marriage from the minds of both brothers. *Corran would have been married to Jora by now, if she'd lived. And Mama would have been happy to see it.* Rigan pulled himself from his thoughts, returning his attention to the conversation.

"Speak for yourself," Wil said. "We finished up with the horses early, and I got sent over to bring back a bucket of ale, with spare coin to enjoy a little for myself." In the warm press of bodies inside The Lame Dragon, the distinct smell of horse clung to his clothing, an unavoidable part of being the farrier's apprentice.

"I have to agree with Rigan. There's not much chance for courting when we're this busy at the shop; there's a ship in port and orders to fill," Donn said, and sighed. He was apprenticed to the potter, and the stubborn clay on the wheel was to blame for his rough, reddened hands.

"Then here's to some well-deserved time off!" Wil lifted his tankard in salute. He waved to the serving girl, motioning for her to come over.

"What are you doing?" Donn said.

"Getting another round of ale," Wil said, balancing uncertainly on the chair.

Rigan shook his head. "That's your second—or third—already, isn't it? And I can't. I'm late enough as it is. Corran will have my head if I come home drunk."

"*Pfft.* We're close to home, and you hold your ale well. Come on—"

Donn pushed Wil's hand back to the table. "I can't either, and neither should you. Why don't you get that bucket of ale and we'll all head back—before you drink the inn dry."

The serving girl came over and Donn did the talking, ordering the bucket of ale and sorting out their coins to pay for their drinks. Wil tried to catch the girl's eye, but she managed to ignore him.

"At this rate, I'm never going to get married," Wil lamented as she left without a glance in his direction.

"Mate, at this rate, you're not even going to get a roll in the hay before you're an old man," Donn laughed. "Let's go." It took both Rigan and Donn to get Wil out of the tavern without him making another attempt to get the poor girl's attention, and he had sloshed part of the ale from the bucket before they even reached the door.

"We'll drop you off on our way back," Donn said, steering Wil in the right direction once they got to the street.

Rigan heard the tower bells chime and cringed; he had been out much longer than Corran expected. Still, letting Wil loose on his own in this condition was a really bad idea. "Let's move. I need to get back."

Halfway to Wil's house, Wil stopped and leaned against a wall. "I don't feel too good," he said in a woozy voice.

Rigan looked both ways, keeping an eye out for the guards, while Donn guided Wil into the nearest alley. They barely made it around the corner before Wil retched, and dropped his bucket of ale in the bargain.

"Dear gods, watch your boots!" Donn hurried out of the way as Wil emptied his stomach.

Footsteps from the street made Donn and Rigan turn. "What's the problem?" Three of the Lord Mayor's guards blocked the mouth of the alley.

"Our friend just got a little sick, sir," Donn said, managing a pleasant grin. "We're seeing him home."

"Is it the bloody guards again?" Wil said, staggering as he stood up, wiping his mouth with his sleeve. "Piss off. We're not doing any harm."

Rigan grabbed Wil's arm. "We need to get him home. He's not feeling well."

Wil took a swing at Rigan, who ducked, and the blow nearly struck the guard behind him. The guard hooked a fist at Wil, who dodged out of the way and returned a punch of his own, this one catching the guard on the chin. Wil stared in stunned silence, finally realizing what he had done, before taking off running. Donn and Rigan sprinted after him with the guards in close pursuit.

"Split up!" Donn shouted as they came to an intersection. Wil moved remarkably fast considering his condition, though fear seemed to have tempered the alcohol. Donn went one way, Wil another, while Rigan veered to the right.

One pair of boots pounded behind him. It seemed the guards had separated to follow the three young men. Rigan knew the alleys and ginnels of Ravenwood better, he hoped, than the guard. A wooden fence blocked the end of an alley and he ran up to it at full speed, jumped and caught hold of the top, then rolled over it, landing in a crouch before starting to run again.

Footsteps behind him told Rigan the guard had followed him over the fence. "Shit." Rigan dodged piles of garbage and pools of chamber pot refuse as he wound through the back alleys of Wrighton.

"Stop, in the name of the Lord Mayor!"

He paid no heed, running as fast as he could to lose his pursuer in the maze of darkened alleys.

Rigan managed to get half a block ahead of the guard, but then he turned the corner to a long, straight stretch with no crossings, and despaired of getting away. A battered wooden door stood ajar in a filthy doorway, and for lack of other options, Rigan darted inside and carefully closed the door after him.

The dark, dank building smelled like rats and squatters. Rigan edged several steps back from the door, keeping against one of the walls, hoping the guard would give up the chase.

A minute passed without discovery, and Rigan let out a long breath of relief. Then the door jerked open and the guard dodged inside, grabbing Rigan by his collar before he had a chance to move.

"You're in a lot of trouble, boy." The guard threw Rigan back against the wall, knocking his head hard against the bricks.

"We were just trying to get home," Rigan said, forcing himself not to fight back, fearful of making the situation worse.

"I ought to drag your ass to jail. It would serve you right for causing trouble."

"Please, we meant no harm," Rigan protested. "I won't cause you any problems."

"No, you won't. Because I'm going to teach you a lesson you won't forget." The guard's fist lashed out, catching Rigan hard on the jaw and sending him stumbling.

The guard was older and stronger, while Rigan had little experience fighting beyond wrestling with his brothers.

"Please—" Rigan started, but a fist to his gut doubled him over and another blow to the side of his head made his vision swim.

We're completely alone here. No one would know if he killed me. He could get away with murder. Corran might not even find my body.

Rigan stumbled away and the guard came after him with a growl. His punch went wide, and the guard seized him by the shoulders, throwing him against a wall, hard enough that dust fell in a fine powder onto Rigan's face and hair.

"Good-for-nothing troublemakers." The guard closed one of his big hands around Rigan's throat. Rigan gasped as the guard's fist tightened.

I'm going to die.

He punched the guard's arm in vain, trying to loosen the man's grip, while his right hand pressed against the man's ribs, attempting to push him away. The guard's hold grew tighter, and Rigan's vision narrowed as he struggled for breath. Fear flooded through him as he thought of never seeing Corran and Kell again, and as the fingers dug into his throat, a desperate energy welled up inside, rising from the core of his being, making his heart pound. A jolt like lightning ran down his outstretched arm and through his palm, then blasted into the guard's chest.

The guard's grip faltered and his hand fell away from Rigan's throat as he clutched at his own chest, eyes bulging. His breath gurgled as he tried to speak. The soldier sank to his knees, staring at Rigan in disbelief and fear, then toppled forward and lay still.

Rigan collapsed against the wall. His heart pounded so hard he could barely breathe. The guard did not get up.

Oh, gods! Oh, shit, oh, shit, oh, shit! What did I do? Is he dead? Mortal fear turned into stunned horror as he realized that he had somehow killed the guard. He squeezed his eyes shut. *I'm going to hang. Oh, gods. I killed a guard. People don't just fall over dead like that. Sweet Oj and Ren, take my soul! I don't know how I did what I did, but they'll hang me anyhow.*

Rigan's hitching breath broke the silence as he tried to regain control. He felt weak and dizzy, as if whatever happened had bled him dry. His skin prickled as the temperature dropped, and when Rigan opened his eyes, he saw a translucent figure watching from the shadows.

I'm really not up to banishing anything right now. Please just go away.

Hear my confession.

This is really not a good time. Rigan had never denied a spirit confession before, but right now, alone and dying, Rigan barely had the energy to fight for consciousness.

My time has run out.

Duty won out over desire, even though he did not know how much time he had left himself. *What do you need to confess?*

My name was Rocard. I hunted the monsters. I bested them—all but one. One mistake was all it took for me to end up a ghost in this deserted building. Rigan felt something shift painfully inside him and knew that the guard had done real damage.

Sounds like you were a hero, Rigan told the ghost.

I'm not ashamed of what I did, Rocard's spirit replied. *But I went to my grave knowing something that must be shared.*

Rigan hated this part of the process the most—when the departed shifted the weight of whatever guilt held them to this world onto his shoulders. Presumably, the dead moved on, unburdened. Rigan could wash the taint of a corpse off his skin, but he'd never found a way to remove the stain of the confessed betrayals and harm done from his memories. *And who's going to hear my confession when I pass? It won't be long now. I'm fading.*

Someone is controlling the monsters, the spirit said.

Who?

I never found out. But I'm certain they're being controlled, and I think that's also why there are more vengeful ghosts than usual. I believe that someone suspected I knew—and had me murdered to keep me silent.

I finally get a valuable bit of information, and I'm probably not going to make it out of here to tell anyone, Rigan thought, feeling his consciousness slipping away. To the ghost, he said, *Go in peace.*

Rocard's spirit dissipated like smoke in the wind and Rigan closed his eyes, leaned back against the wall, and waited to die.

"You've got to get away from here."

He barely registered the voice, overwhelmed by pain and terror. It slowly dawned on him that a living stranger stood before him now.

"Who are you?"

"Do you want to hang, or do you want to live long enough to find out what you did to the guard and how you can control it?" Shadows obscured the stranger's face, but Rigan made out the silhouette of a tall, thin man. "I can get you to safety. But you've got to come with me, now. Can you walk?"

"Of course—" Rigan tried and failed to get to his feet. His head swam, and he felt as if he might pass out.

"I didn't think so," the stranger said, reaching out a hand.

Too stunned and scared to argue, Rigan accepted the hand up and struggled to stand, leaning heavily on his rescuer, who put one shoulder under Rigan's arm to hold him up. "What about—him?" he asked, with a nod toward the motionless guard.

"Leave him for the rats. Follow me."

A dim light glowed, and Rigan realized the man had opened the shutters on a small lantern. It enabled him to get a good look at his rescuer—a man probably ten years his senior, with sharp features and flint-gray eyes.

Terror filled Rigan. *What does he want with me?*

The man led him through the rubble of the ruined building, picking his way with confidence, as if he had done this many times. They passed through a door into another, equally decrepit building, then down a flight of stone steps into a cellar that extended farther than the lantern could illuminate.

From there, Rigan and the stranger went through an old brick tunnel, then down an ancient flight of worn stone steps and through another passage before emerging at the edge of a huge underground room. Lanterns and torches lit the cavernous area, which bustled with people. Merchants hawked their wares from tables and stalls, musicians played and the babble of conversation echoed from the rock walls.

"Where are we?" Rigan asked, awed by what lay before him.

"Below."

Out of the cauldron, into the fire.

Most residents of Ravenwood had never been Below, though stories about the underground city abounded, each more terrifying than the last.

"Don't believe everything you hear," the stranger said, noting the fear on Rigan's face. "It's just a place, like any other place."

Rigan doubted that. 'Below' spanned a subterranean warren of tunnels, old cellars, and built-over streets long-forgotten by those who dwelled on top. In Ravenwood's long history, fires, floods, and other calamities had destroyed parts of the city many times. Rebuilding often meant covering over entire streets, along with the shops and homes, and erecting new buildings and roads above them as if the old structures had never existed. Most people forgot the old city, but for those who needed a hiding place, Below provided a sanctuary.

"Please, I don't have any coin on me," Rigan said, realizing he was still carrying the bag of items from his errand, clutched in a death grip. "I'm not worth robbing, and there's no money to pay a ransom. Just let me go."

The stranger chuckled. "In your current state? How far do you think you'd get? You have no idea how you killed that guard, do you?"

"I didn't kill anyone. I don't know what made the guard fall down, but it wasn't me. I couldn't have—"

"You could and you did. And if you know nothing about your abilities, then you're a danger, and we need to fix that."

"Fix?" *Oh, gods, he's a madman.*

Any thought of escape died when Rigan attempted to stand on his own. Whatever had happened with the guard, it had sapped his energy, leaving him as weak as if he had just risen from a long illness. Light-headed and sick to his stomach, Rigan would collapse before he got ten steps away from the stranger.

If he meant to kill me, why didn't he do it in the cellars, with no one around to see? He could have easily picked my pockets and left my body, or thrown me down a hole. Why bring me here, with so many people?

Rigan tried to remember what he had heard about the people who lived Below. Criminals and outcasts made the tunnels their homes, along with all manner of shady dealers and those on the run. *And people with magic,* Rigan thought.

The stranger led Rigan away from the more crowded areas. *They say witches live down here. Is that what he is? By Ardevan and Eshtamon! Maybe he means to sacrifice me.*

"I'm not going to rob you or kill you," the man said quietly. "You're hurt worse than you know, and if I don't get you to a healer, you just might die. Quit fighting me; you don't have the energy to waste."

Die? Rigan's jaw throbbed and his throat ached from the guard's assault, and his gut hurt from the punch he had taken. *Would I know if the punch had opened something inside me?* As an undertaker, he knew well enough that a hard punch in the wrong place could set a man bleeding to death without breaking the skin. *Is this how it feels? Am I dying?*

"How did you know where to find me?" Rigan asked.

"When you killed that guard, your magic flared as bright as a beacon. You're just lucky I got to you before anyone else did."

"I don't understand."

"That's part of the problem."

Somewhere along the way, Rigan lost consciousness.

When he woke, he lay on a comfortable cot, covered with a blanket. He recognized the sharp smell of liniment mixed from medicinal plants, and realized that both his neck and jaw had been bandaged. A lantern hung from a bracket on the ceiling, giving enough light to let him get his bearings. *A kindness,* he thought, *since they could have left me in the dark. But what do they want with me? And why would they care who found me?*

"How do you feel?" the stranger said from the doorway.

"Not dead," Rigan croaked. His throat hurt on the inside as much as his bruises did on the outside, and a dry mouth made swallowing painful.

"Drink this," the man said, handing Rigan a tankard. "We didn't want to risk drowning you by trying to pour it down your throat when you were unconscious."

Rigan hesitated before deciding that poisoning was the least of his worries, and drank thirstily; it tasted of ginger and honey, and soothed his raw throat. "Thank you."

The stranger pulled up a chair and sat beside the bed. "You can call me Damian."

"I'm Rigan." Given the situation, Rigan had little to lose by giving his real name. "What are you going to do to me?"

Damian chuckled. His deep voice and gentle manner were reassuring, though his eyes were guarded. "Heal you, if all goes well. Warn you, since you have no idea what happened back there. And if you'll agree to it, train you, so you have a better chance of surviving."

"Are you Wanderers?" Rumor had it that the nomadic clans of tinkers, peddlers, and fortune-tellers could do forbidden magic. That, along with an unfortunate reputation for theft, made the Wanderers unwelcome throughout the League. Even so, they found their way into the cities. Rigan knew for a fact that the rumors about their magic were true: his mother had Wanderer blood, and it was from her Rigan had inherited his ability to confess the dead.

"Witches, yes. Wanderers, no," Damian replied, amused.

Rigan digested that for a moment. "Maybe that guard cut off my breath longer than I thought, but I don't understand." He reached for the tankard and took another sip, buying himself time to think.

"What do you think happened, with the guard?"

Rigan lay back down, spent by the effort of raising himself up. "He attacked me, pushed me into the wall, choked me. I couldn't get loose. He was too strong. I put my hand out, to push him away."

He paused, straining to remember. Something *had* happened. "I was scared and angry. He meant to kill me. And then... it felt like lightning flowed through my body, and the next thing I knew, the guard grabbed at his chest and fell over." Rigan sighed. "I think I passed out."

"You stopped the guard's heart," Damian said. "Your magic protected you."

"I'm an undertaker, I help ghosts cross over and dispel restless spirits. I can't *kill* people."

"Do you have another explanation?"

"I've never done anything like that before."

"Has anyone ever tried to kill you before?" Damian asked with a faint smile.

"No. I'd never even been in a real fight before tonight."

"Your magic tried to protect you," Damian said. "Unfortunately, magic of that sort is against the law in Ravenwood—at least, for people like us."

"You said I was dying."

Damian leaned forward with his elbows on his knees. "I know this is strange for you, but hear me out. Your magic rose up, unrestrained and unfocused, to fight off an attacker. Because of your lack of training, it drew from your own life energy to do that, and it nearly drained you dry."

"What would have happened, if you hadn't found me?" Rigan asked.

"You'd have been caught by the guards, I expect; you weren't in any shape to outrun them. But assuming you made it home, you would have probably been dead by morning."

Despite the room's warmth, Rigan felt a chill. "How long have I been out?"

"The healer sat with you all night, helping you regain your life energy," Damian replied. "Then you slept quite a while. It's been nearly a day since I found you."

"A day? Corran will have my hide!" Rigan tried to rise from the cot, only to fall back, too light headed to stand up.

"Who is Corran?"

"My brother. He'll be worried sick—and then he'll be angry that I made him worry." Rigan slumped against his pillow and closed his eyes. "I am in deep shit."

"The healer assures me you are mostly recovered. You're weak from hunger. I'll have food brought, and when you're able, I'll lead you back to the surface."

"Thank you," Rigan said. He looked at Damian. "Why? Why bother saving me?"

"There are many people who have a flicker of magic and are able to hide it, even from the guards. Your magic is much stronger. I didn't want you to fall into the Lord Mayor's hands. You would be conscripted to serve him, or be killed. That's still a real risk, if you try to pretend none of this ever happened. But there is another option."

"What?"

"We can train you. You can return to us and we will teach you how to use—and conceal—your magic."

"I've heard about the witches of Below," Rigan replied. "They say that you gain your power from killing people."

"And yet you're not dead." Damian chuckled. "Don't believe everything you hear. It serves our purpose to be feared, since even the guards hesitate to come looking for us."

"I can't stay here. My brothers depend on me," Rigan argued. "I can't leave them and move Below."

"If the Mayor's guards discover what you are, they're likely to kill you *and* your brothers."

Rigan looked away. "It's just the three of us. Corran and Kell need me. I can't run off."

"The rituals you use to prepare the dead have power so old, no one thinks of them as magic anymore," Damian replied. "Done by someone with true power, they rival anything the priests can do."

Damian paused. "Your power is strong. Without training, it will grow harder to control. You'll kill again, without meaning to, and perhaps next time, the target won't deserve it. Your brothers maybe, or someone who just got in the way. That's one reason magic is so tightly controlled. It's dangerous." He stood. "You'll be recovered enough to go home in a candlemark or so. I'll lead you out. I can show you how to find me, to get the training you need. Think about my offer, and tell me what you decide." He left Rigan alone with his thoughts.

By the time Damian returned, Rigan had eaten and his head had cleared. He would have bruises from his struggle with the guard, but as the pain faded, he felt his strength gradually returning.

"Ready?" Damian asked.

Rigan rose and followed him from the room, pausing to glance around. The inside of the house looked utterly normal, except for its age and for being below ground.

"I didn't get to thank the healer."

"I'll pass along your gratitude to Aiden," Damian replied. "Did you consider my offer?"

Rigan had thought of little else in the time Damian left him alone. *I can scarcely believe it's true that I have that kind of power, but I can't explain what happened any other way. And I don't want to be a danger to Corran and Kell—or anyone else. I certainly don't want to be hunted by the guards. What choice do I have?*

"I accept," Rigan replied. "Tell me how to find my way back here, so I can learn what I need to know. There are enough monsters up above already, I don't need to be one of them."

Chapter Four

"Where's Rigan? He never misses dinner." Kell set a bowl of boiled cabbage, potatoes, and pork in front of Corran, and fetched a warm loaf of crusty bread from the oven. Since their mother died, Kell had taken over the cooking and shopping and most other errands so Rigan and Corran could see to the work downstairs.

"I don't know, but I'm ready to give him a good thrashing when he shows up," Corran replied with an ill-humored edge to his voice, tucking his napkin under his chin. "We've had five new bodies come in today, and I need the pigments and powders I sent him to get."

"Bet he stopped off at the Dragon with those friends of his and forgot the time."

"He won't forget it again, once I'm done with him." Corran stabbed his fork into the meat, more comfortable with anger than with the fear gnawing at his stomach. *Rigan's dependable. He's never this late. I don't begrudge him a drink or two with his friends, or a chance to go see that girl he's sweet on—gods know, all we do is work—but something's not right.*

Kell often regaled Corran and Rigan with the gossip he heard during his rounds. He'd go to market early to get food, then take the cart through Wrighton, gathering the bodies of those who'd died in the night and could pay for proper preparation and burial. He embellished his tales shamefully for his brothers' entertainment, and reveled in the telling. Kell's silence tonight told Corran that he worried about Rigan, too.

Three months had passed since Jora's death; six since their mother died, the last time monsters surfaced in the city. Since then, there had been too many silent evenings. Kell and Rigan alternated between trying to jolly Corran out of his mood, which never worked, and leaving him to his thoughts, which was worse. Corran doubted that the ache of Jora's loss would ever really leave him. Hunting the monsters that killed her helped, but it wouldn't bring her back.

Halfway through dinner, a pounding on the back door roused them.

"I'll go see who it is," Corran said, finding his appetite gone. "Maybe Rigan lost his key."

Donn stood in the doorway looking flushed. "Is he here?"

"Who?" Corran asked, his heart sinking.

"Rigan. Did he make it back?" Donn peered past him into the workroom.

"I think you need to tell me what's going on," Corran said, grabbing Donn by the arm and pulling him inside. He shut the door and motioned for Donn to sit. Kell stood halfway down the stairs, watching worriedly.

"What's going on?"

"That's what Donn's about to tell us," Corran replied, hands on hips.

Donn licked his lips nervously. "We didn't mean to get in any trouble," he said, looking from Corran to Kell. "I ran into Rigan after he finished his errand, and we stopped off for some ale at The Lame Dragon. Wil had already drunk a pint or two—or three—before we joined him. Rigan said he had to get back, so we left."

"When?" Corran demanded.

"About two candlemarks ago. Wil got sick, and we ran into some guards, who decided to be bastards about it. They started pushing us around, and Wil was drunk. He took a swing at one of the guards, so they came after us. We ran."

Corran and Kell exchanged a worried glance.

"We split up, and one guard went after each of us. I picked up two more. It took me a while to shake them; I almost didn't get away." Donn's hands shook. Scrapes bloodied his arms, and blood oozed from a gash on his pale forehead.

Kell went back upstairs and returned with a cup of hot tea, which Donn accepted gratefully, though his hands trembled so much that he nearly spilled it on himself.

"I hid in an old shed when I couldn't run anymore," Donn said. "I didn't expect them to chase us so far. Figured they'd just put the fear of the gods in us and that would be it." He shook his head. "But they didn't let up. I thought I was going to die."

A cold chill settled into the pit of Corran's stomach as Donn talked. *Rigan's never been in any trouble, but that wouldn't stop the guards from giving him a beating if they thought he'd crossed them.*

"Do you think the guards knew who you were?" Kell looked as worried as Corran felt.

Donn shrugged. "No. Maybe. I don't know." He paused to sip his tea and take a deep breath. "I don't think so. I'm guessing they were just in a black mood about something and we crossed their path. We were an easy target."

"What about Wil?" Corran asked. The more he heard, the more he worried. *I don't think Rigan's ever even thrown a punch that wasn't meant for me or Kell. He* hates *fighting, and Kell's a faster runner. If Rigan couldn't talk his way out, he'd be in big trouble.*

Donn looked up miserably. "I haven't seen him. I hoped he and Rigan made it back here." He set the empty cup of tea aside and buried his head in his hands. "By Qel! What do we do?"

"Stay here with Kell," Corran told Donn. "I'll go to the farrier and see if Wil got home safely, and if he did, whether he knows where Rigan is. If he's safe, I'd rather not draw attention by asking around at the jail."

"It's after curfew," Kell warned. "And the farrier's a distance away."

Corran met his brother's gaze, and saw his worry reflected in Kell's eyes. "What choice do we have? If Rigan's lying hurt somewhere, we need to go find him." *And if he's dead, we need to bring his body home.*

A rap at the door made them all jump.

"Hide," Corran hissed at Donn. He waited until Kell had hidden Donn in the cupboard under the stairs before he opened the door, hoping to find his brother waiting in the alley.

"Please, help me." Rendan, the farrier, stood in the darkness, holding a limp, bloodied body in his arms. "Wil's dead."

Corran looked both ways in the alley, checking for guards, and ushered Rendan into the workroom. Donn and Kell joined them a moment later.

"He's dead," Rendan repeated, tears running down his cheeks. Rendan was Ross's father, and Corran knew the family well. That just made the loss keener.

Corran helped him lay Wil's body on one of the tables. The young man's face was bloody, beaten badly enough to break bones. Just from the way Wil lay, Corran could tell that an arm and a leg were broken, likely ribs and a shoulder blade, too. Bruises and cuts marred his skin. The body smelled of ale, piss, and bile.

"I'm so sorry," Corran said, his heart in his throat. *What if they've done the same to Rigan?*

"*Why?*" Rendan asked in a strangled voice, looking up as if beseeching the gods. "He was my sister's son. I took him in when she died of fever. Wil was a good boy, a hard worker. He didn't cause trouble. I just want to know, why?" He broke, down sobbing. Corran glanced to Kell, who poured a glass of whiskey and handed it to Rendan.

"Where did you find him?" Corran asked, gently. Donn stood behind Kell, staring at the corpse in shock.

"A man came to the door and said they'd found him in one of the alleys halfway across Wrighton," Rendan said. "Someone recognized him and brought him home. He was already dead." Rendan's throat seized up and it took him a moment to speak again.

"Ross was so angry, I thought he would go out looking for Wil's killers, and I would lose two of them in one night," Rendan sobbed. "I made him swear not to go anywhere." He sniffed and blinked, trying to regain control. "I didn't want my wife or the others to see Wil like this. I can't imagine what he went through." Ross bowed his head, taking Wil's bruised hand. "Please, give him a good burial. Full Guild honors. I don't know who did this or why, but I do know Wil deserved better."

Corran and Donn exchanged a glance. *He deserves to know.*

"I know what happened—up to a point," Donn said quietly. Kell fetched him a whiskey to fortify him as he prepared to recount the awful tale, then poured one for himself, Corran and Rendan.

Kell barely held back tears as Donn recounted what had happened. Corran had not seen his brother weep since the night their mother died.

"Since when is it a killing crime for a young man to drink a bit too much ale?" Rendan cried when Donn finished. "By Jorr and all the gods of the Guilds, it's gone too far!"

"Both of you had better get home. And be careful; if the guards catch you, you'll be joining him," Corran said. He looked over at Rendan, covered in Wil's blood. "Kell, go fetch some water so Rendan can clean up." He turned to Donn. "Where did you last see Rigan?"

Donn told him. "If he ran like I did, he could be anywhere."

Corran's heart sank. *I can't just leave him out there. I've got to bring him home.*

"See that's Wil's taken care of, please," Rendan said. He took Wil's hand again, then crossed the young man's arms over his chest and bent to kiss his bruised forehead. Donn put an arm around the older man's shoulders and guided him to the door.

"I'll walk him home," Donn promised. "It's not far out of my way. And if I hear anything of Rigan, I'll come back as soon as I can."

Corran nodded. "We'll take good care of Wil. Full honors."

As the door closed behind them, Corran shut his eyes, mustering the strength to do what had to be done.

"We've got to go find Rigan. We can't let the guards get away with this!" Rage reddened Kell's cheeks, but his eyes were utterly blank.

Corran put a hand on his brother's shoulder. "Don't make this any worse. I'll go look for him."

"I'm coming with you."

"No, you're not." He held up a hand to stall Kell's argument. "Someone needs to be here in case Rigan comes home. It's after curfew—bad enough for one of us to be out. I'll be back to work on Wil's body. Anything you can do to get the preparation started will be a help." He sighed. "Neither of us are going to get much sleep tonight."

"Do you think Rigan's alive?" Kell's voice had deepened of late and he usually tried his best to keep it from cracking, but now it sounded thin and reedy, like a scared boy. Corran put a comforting hand on his brother's arm.

"I don't know. If he is, I'll find him. And if he isn't—well, I'll bring him back so we can do right by him. Do what you can to get Wil ready. Anything we need for Farriers' Guild honors we can get in the morning. If we can prepare his body tonight, we can bury him early. The fewer questions asked, the better."

"I'll do it," Kell promised as Corran grabbed his cloak off a peg, and, after a moment's thought, reached for a long knife from the worktable. "Be careful, Corran."

Corran nodded and headed out.

* * *

Trying to follow Rigan's trail posed more of a challenge than Corran had expected. He had no difficulty finding the place where Donn said the three young men had split up, trying to outrun their pursuers, but every block further out meant more paths Rigan might have taken, to say nothing of the cellars, abandoned buildings, and walled yards.

Maybe if I had a bloodhound, I could pick up his trail, Corran thought. His chest tightened at the thought of Rigan, hurt or dying, alone in the dark.

Rigan and Kell depend on me. Mama and Papa expected me to carry on after they were gone. And I've failed.

If Rigan had left a trail, the dim light in the alley hid it, and by daybreak, foot traffic would obliterate any clues. *He's out there, somewhere, and if he's alive, he's counting on me to find him.*

For all that Corran worked with the dead, helping them to their rest, he thought little of the gods from day to day. Doharmu, the god of undertakers, was a dark and fearsome presence, not the kind of deity whom one beseeched for good luck and reassurance. For that, the common people still turned to the other Elder Gods, the old deities now fallen out of fashion with the rise of the new gods of the trades. Doharmu was the only Guild god that was also an Elder God; death was a constant, whatever the pantheon.

Kell usually took care of the offerings and feast day rituals, delivering the required gifts to the temple, offering prayers on their account—one more task he had taken over when their mother died. But tonight, bereft and at a complete loss, Corran had no other choice but to beg the Elder Gods for help.

Oj and Ren, Forever Father and Eternal Mother, hear me. Bring Rigan home safely to us. Doharmu, god of darkness and death, if it's too late for him to come back to us, make his passage swift and his journey easy, And by the Old Ones, by Ardevan and Eshtamon, by Balledec and Colduraan, if his life is forfeit, let me see vengeance done.

Chapter Five

THE SUNSET CAST the streets in gold as Rigan made his way across Wrighton. He kept to the alleys, fearful of encountering the companions of the guard he had killed. But as he got closer to home, a new fear filled him. *I've been gone for a night and a day. Corran's gonna have my ass. Have Donn and Wil made it back? Do Corran and Kell have any idea what happened? If I'm a danger to them, would it have been better for me to stay Below?*

All of those concerns paled in comparison to his real fear: what to do about the lethal power he could summon.

If Corran and Kell ever find out, what will they think? Will I become one of the monsters in their eyes?

He thought again, briefly, about just staying 'dead' and going back to find Damian, but he forced himself to keep going.

It's not fair for me to leave Corran and Kell with all the work. It's hard enough to make ends meet. I'll figure out a way to live with this, to keep the power under control, I have to. If Damian's right and the Mayor's guards suspected I had unsanctioned magic, they'd kill me—and probably Kell and Corran too. Gods! What have I gotten myself into?

Rigan slowed as he neared the shop. Damian had given him fresh clothing to replace his torn, bloodied shirt and pants, as well as a cloak with a collar and a hat with a wide brim that hid his bruised face and neck. Aiden had spent his power saving Rigan's life, replenishing the energy tapped dry by the burst of magic, and had not concerned himself with less urgent matters, so every muscle ached.

He paused in the alley behind the workshop and saw a light in an upstairs window. *Kell's probably making dinner. Corran's likely working, and mad about having no help. I am in so much trouble, and I can't even tell them the whole truth.*

He steeled himself, took a deep breath, and opened the back door, to see Corran working on a body. His brother turned, holding a bloody knife. When he saw Rigan, the blood drained from his face and the knife clattered to the floor.

"Sorry I'm late," Rigan said, knowing the apology was wholly inadequate. He held out the bag with the items from his errand. "Here. I got what you needed."

Corran rushed toward him, crushing him in a hug that made Rigan wince. In the next moment, his brother had pushed him away and grabbed him by the shoulders, knocking the hat from his head.

"Where in the name of the gods have you been? We've been searching for you for more than a day!"

"I stopped at The Lame Dragon for a drink with Wil and Donn, and Wil got drunk. There was trouble with some guards and they chased us. One of them caught me and roughed me up. Knocked me out. It took this long for me to feel decent enough to try to make it home." He hated lying to Corran, but Damian had impressed on him the need for secrecy. *What he doesn't know can't be gotten out of him by the guards. He's safer this way.*

"Wil is dead," Corran said, eyes blazing. "Donn came here, to see if you'd returned. He told me what happened."

Rigan felt suddenly weak and sank down into a chair. "Wil's dead? He was way ahead of the guards the last time I saw him."

"Yeah, well, there were more guards. I buried him this morning. Dammit, Rigan! I spent the night and half of today looking for your body, figuring I was going to have to bury you too."

"I'm sorry."

"*Sorry?* If I wasn't so glad to see you alive, I'd kill you myself for what you put us through! Don't do that to me again."

"Where's Kell?"

"Out looking for you, while he does his usual rounds," Corran replied, running a hand back through his hair. "Where were you?"

"I tried to hide in an abandoned building, but the guard found me and knocked me around pretty hard." Rigan let the cloak fall, exposing his neck. Corran stared at the bruises on his throat and jaw.

"I passed out. When I woke up, I tried to find my way through the cellars, and ended up Below. I really must have taken more of a beating than I thought, because I passed out again. I had to sleep it off and eat before I was up to making it back." *That's almost what happened.*

"I don't know what's worse, trying to outrun the guards or being fool enough to go Below." Corran shook his head. "But I'm glad you're back."

"So am I. Tell me what happened to Wil."

Corran recounted Rendan's story, as well as Donn's harrowing escape. "Kell and I took turns looking for you," Corran concluded. His gaze lingered again on Rigan's throat. "Kell can make a poultice for those bruises. And then there's the regular work to catch up on, since I went out looking for your sorry ass instead of taking care of the dead."

"Getting back to work would be really good," Rigan said, glad for the distraction. "I might not move as fast as usual, but I can get started on that right away." He paused. "Thanks for looking for me."

Corran clapped him on the shoulder, and Rigan winced. "You

might not be so grateful after Kell gives you a piece of his mind. Where did you get those clothes?"

"Stole them," Rigan replied, hanging the cloak and hat on a peg. "The guard made a bloody mess of my clothing." He winced as he brought his arm down. "Ribs aren't in great shape, and my throat hurts like a son of a bitch."

"Well, we'll take it easy," Corran said. "Now, let's get to work."

Rigan fell into the familiar routine—an old man with a bad heart; a trader who had choked on a piece of meat; an elderly woman felled by a stroke; a dock hand who had fallen into the harbor and drowned. None of them violent deaths, all mourned by someone able to pay the burial fee.

Rigan wished that the rhythm of the work would help to keep his thoughts from replaying the past two days, but he could not banish his anxiety. *It could have been me on this table, like Wil. I know what it cost Corran and me to prepare Mama's body, when she was killed. I wouldn't have wished that on my brothers, having to do the same for me.*

The back door opened a candlemark later. "Nothing," Kell said, not bothering to look up as he entered. "Didn't find a damn thing."

Corran cleared his throat, loudly.

Kell raised his head, and stared at Rigan as if he had seen a ghost. He tried to remain stoic, but a broad grin spread across his face even as tears brimmed in his eyes. "You're back? You're alive!"

"A little worse for wear," Rigan admitted.

Kell eyed the livid bruises on his throat and face. "Guards?"

Rigan nodded. His brother looked torn between taking a swing at him and embracing him in overwhelming relief. He stood still for a moment, then headed upstairs without another word.

"You're in for it now," Corran said with a sideways glance. "The last time Kell looked that angry, he didn't speak to me for two weeks."

Rigan glared after Kell. "Am I supposed to be sorry I'm not dead?"

Corran's hand came down on his shoulder so hard Rigan froze, expecting a blow. "Don't say that, ever. Kell helped me with Wil's body, and he thought I didn't see him crying. Last night hit him hard. Give him time; he really thought you were gone."

Rigan looked up the stairs after Kell, struggling against a wave of remorse. *I shouldn't have left Wil, even if he looked like he was doing all right. Maybe if I'd stayed with him, I could have made a difference. Maybe he'd still be alive.*

He roused himself from his thoughts, realizing Corran watched him with an appraising stare.

"If you're feeling guilty about Wil, stop. What happened to you three wasn't right. You should have been able to get home safely. And if you'd stayed with him, you'd be dead for sure."

Rigan looked away, certain Corran could read too much from his expression. "Part of me knows that," he said in a rough voice. "But the rest of me thinks that part is lying."

All his life, Rigan had watched and helped with the preparation of the dead. He had watched his father and uncles work their grave magic, sending spirits into the After and dispelling restless ghosts. He and Corran had long ago learned the rituals for themselves. That kind of magic felt second nature to him, but he had never considered the idea that the power could take any other form. Now, as he helped Corran ready the corpses, he wondered how he had ever been so blind.

Rigan focused on their preparations. Ancient lore and ritual dictated every step, and undertakers fulfilled a priestly vocation in helping the departed safely reach the Golden Shores. Rigan could feel the magic thrumming in every syllable as he spoke over the dead, crackling along his raw nerves like lightning, burning through his veins. He had never felt so acutely aware of anything in his life, and it terrified him.

He fetched the basin of herb-infused water Kell prepared for them every morning. As he bathed the corpse, the smell of hyssop and rosemary, lily and mint filled Rigan's nostrils and he thought back to his apprenticeship. *Corran knows my magic is stronger than his—that's why he fights the ghosts and lets me handle the wardings. Mama worked with me on the rituals, teaching me how to make the banishing circle. She told me once that her grandmother was a Wanderer witch-woman, but swore me to secrecy. Did Mama know my magic could do more? And if she did, when in the name of the Dark Places did she intend to tell me?*

Guilt flashed, white-hot and searing. *She didn't expect to die young. Probably thought she had plenty of time to ease me into it. And Kell—he's only fourteen. My ritual magic didn't even come to me until I was a little older than that. So there's no way to tell if he'll inherit her abilities, too. And if it's Wanderer blood that's given me this, could they*—would *they—teach me to handle it so I don't kill someone by accid—*

"I said, hand me the pigment."

Rigan started and looked up to find Corran staring at him. Concern, not anger, filled his brother's gaze, but Rigan felt his face flush and he ducked his head, hurrying to comply. "Sorry. Just a little... preoccupied." Thankfully, Corran let it go, and Rigan struggled to keep his concentration on the task at hand.

Marking the bodies with sacred symbols on the face and torso came next. Their father had explained it once as a signal to the gods, a way for the spirit to find its path, and to be welcomed. Kell mixed the pigments fresh each morning, depending on the number of bodies to be prepared. Corran and Rigan daubed the sigils on the corpses with their thumbs, using a brush where needed to avoid contagion.

Blue woad, black soot, white chalk, and orange ochre. As Rigan drew the sigils, he felt a frisson of magic, an echo of the terrible power that had welled up inside him and burst forth with lethal strength. Once the bodies had been marked, Corran and Rigan wrapped the corpses in shrouds. Regardless of how plain or elaborate the shrouding, the process again followed strict steps, accompanied by ritual and chanting. The latter fell to Corran, as the oldest. Rigan had never minded, since he always thought his brother had a better voice for it. Tonight, the chants sent a shiver down his spine, connecting with something deep inside him that threatened to well up—powerful and volatile. Rigan clamped down on the power, terrified of what might happen if it slipped his grasp.

I'm a danger to everyone like this. I've got to figure out how to get back Below and train, but I can't imagine my brothers are going to let me out of their sight for a long while.

Damian said I nearly died because I drew on my life force. That blast took a lot of power, but these markings need just a flicker. Is that what we're really doing in these old rituals, sending off the dead with a last, faint flicker of borrowed life? No wonder we're so tired by the end of each day. Gods above! And I thought it was from digging graves!

Rigan and Corran were finished with their work by the time Kell called them to supper. Stewed chicken with carrots and parsnips had never smelled better, and Rigan's stomach growled as he watched his brother ladle the food into bowls.

"I heard that Wil's uncle went storming up to the Guild Hall today," Kell said. "From what people are saying, Rendan demanded that the Farriers' Guild bring a formal complaint to the Lord Mayor, and press murder charges against the guards."

Corran sighed. "That probably didn't go well."

Kell shook his head. "If Rendan wasn't so highly thought of within the Guild, he'd have probably ended up in the Mayor's dungeon. As it happened, the Guild had him escorted from the premises and made noises about him being 'mad with grief.'"

Rigan could just imagine the hotheaded farrier demanding justice. The Guild could not risk doing anything that might offend the Merchant Princes or run afoul of the Lord Mayor, who brokered the trade negotiations with the other city-states in the League, the agreements on which they all depended for their livelihood.

"It's just like the monsters," Rigan said. "A few people dead here, a few more there, but so long as it's no one wealthy, Lord Mayor Machison and the Guild Masters have more important things to do."

"Did you hear something?" Kell asked, asked with feigned confusion. "For a moment there, I thought I heard a voice."

"Stop it, Kell," Corran chided. "You're being childish."

Kell fixed him with a black look. "*I'm* being childish? He runs off and nearly gets his damn fool self killed and scares us both half to death, and I'm just supposed to *get over it?*" Kell smacked his hands down on the table with a flushed expression, like he might explode with rage or burst into tears.

"We didn't go looking for trouble," Rigan said, abashed at how his absence had affected Kell. "It's not a crime to get drunk. Wil didn't deserve what happened to him. None of us did. You know how the guards can be."

"They're fearsome warriors, except when there are monsters to be fought," Corran muttered.

"How many bodies have we buried of people who got on the wrong side of the guards, Rigan?" Kell said. "I saw what they did to Wil. I helped Corran prepare him—"

"Kell—" Rigan began.

"And you know what, Rigan?" Kell shouted. "I didn't see Wil on that table. I saw *you.*" Tears glistened in his eyes; anger and fear made him tremble. "So I don't care whether or not you and your friends have a right to be out. You have a *responsibility* to stay alive." The fury had run its course, and Kell suddenly looked young and frightened. "Please, Rigan? I don't want to go through that again."

Rigan looked down. "I'm sorry. I really am. I'll be careful—I promise."

Liar, Rigan's thoughts taunted. *You haven't told them you killed someone with your magic. Or that if you don't want to become a monster, you're going to have to keep sneaking away to Below. Who's going to catch on first to the lies? Kell and Corran... or the guards?*

Chapter Six

"STOP, THIEF!"

Kell Valmonde didn't bother glancing behind him as he wove through the press of the marketplace crowd, intent on escape. He squeezed around a vendor, nearly toppling his stall in the process, and then dodged behind a heavily-laden cart horse. Screened from view, he quickly pulled a hat from his pack and jammed it on his head, tucking his hair underneath, and turned his jacket inside-out.

The fact that Kell had not committed any crime would make no difference to the guards. Nor would they believe that the cranky merchant was just angry that Kell refused to pay his exorbitant prices. Regardless, if he was caught, he risked a beating or worse.

But if he could elude the guards, all would be forgotten by the time he returned to tomorrow's market. Kell debated who enjoyed the blood sport more, the merchant or the guards.

He grabbed his pack and kept moving as the shouts of the Mayor's guards echoed around the marketplace. Short, thin, and wiry, Kell could move through the maze of stalls, rickety pushcarts, and wandering hucksters with ease. The market buzzed with voices in a jumble of languages: friends called out greetings, merchants haggled with buyers, and whores promised paradise. Goats bleated, chickens squawked, dogs barked, and horses whinnied.

Kell plowed right into a heavyset man in the whites of a cook from a noble house, nearly taking them both off their feet. "Sorry, pardon," he muttered as he veered away, ignoring the man's oaths. He turned sideways, taking advantage of his slim build to weave his way between shoppers.

"Over there!" a guard shouted, signaling to a second guard, who searched the crowd with a puzzled expression. The cook yelled and gestured towards Kell, setting the guards back on his path.

Kell slipped on a piece of garbage that nearly sent him sprawling, before righting himself and hurrying on.

"In here!" hissed Betan, the fishmonger, waving Kell over, and he dodged behind the long wooden table wet with sea water and fish entrails. He tore his hat and jacket off and shoved them into his pack, then grabbed a knife and started gutting fish, whistling nonchalantly when the guard came by. Kell kept his head down as the man barked a question at Betan. The fishmonger shrugged, palms raised, and replied in his thick southlands dialect. He smiled and offered the guard a fresh fish. The guard cursed and walked away, shaking his head.

"You're pretty good at that," Betan said when the guard was out of sight, gesturing to Kell's handiwork. "Maybe I'll give you a job someday."

"And maybe someday I'll take you up on that offer," Kell said, setting the knife aside. "Right now, I need to get home and cook dinner. My brothers are cranky when they're hungry."

Betan chuckled. "No doubt. Here." He handed Kell a large fish. "Take this. I still owe you on Catiana's burial. Tell your brothers it was caught fresh today; worth two crowns on my debt."

Kell put the fish in his bag. "Looks good. Thanks."

Betan shrugged. "Hey, a good deed is never wasted. Figure it helps maintain the Balance, right? Your brothers did me a good turn, I pay my debts. Now go, before the guards come."

Kell slipped out the back of the stall, staying in the shadows of a narrow alley. Ravenwood's wynds and closes wound maze-like around the Old Market, dirty and full of garbage. Strange sigils chalked on the walls suggested that Wanderers came this way. He paused to look at one of the chalked symbols and wondered what it meant. *Do the Wanderers use them to mark safe routes? Is it some kind of message, or a way to indicate territory? Why do they bother?*

"It's not for you."

Kell startled, wondering where the old woman had come from. Bent and wrinkled, skin weathered by the sun, she had the look of one of the Wanderers.

"What's not for me?" Kell asked.

"The message in the sigils. Not for you." The old woman came a step closer, squinting closely at Kell. "Yet you have the blood, don't you, boy?"

"I don't know what you're talking about."

A crafty smile touched the old woman's lips. "Wanderer blood. I can smell it in you. Not strong; half-breed or less." She frowned, concentrating. "But you don't have the power, not yet. Though it's touched you. Clings to you like dust. Maybe when you're older."

"Are those curse signs?" Kell got up the nerve to ask.

The old woman croaked a laugh. "Curse signs? Sometimes. Depends on the message to be sent. Not always." She gave him a canny look. "Some are, some aren't. The less you know, the better for you."

"Then let me pass."

Kell hoped his voice sounded defiant. He saw the Wanderers often in the marketplace, selling an assortment of wares. Some of them played music and danced for the coins thrown by passers-by, while others read omens from cards or tea leaves. The guards drove the Wanderers off, but they always came back.

The old woman cocked her head, taking his measure. "I see fire and loss in your future, boy. Best you take care."

"Let me pass."

"As you wish. Mark my words."

Kell waited until the old woman had hobbled away, before checking that the alley was clear. He climbed a trellis up the wall of a house to a balcony, and then hoisted himself onto the roof. Kell stayed low as he maneuvered to the edge of the rooftop to get a clear view of the harbor.

From up here, Kell could look out across the water and imagine what it must be like aboard one of the ships berthed at the crowded wharves—tall-masted trading ships unloading their cargo; fishing vessels setting out before first light, returning heavy with their catch. At a particularly opulent dock, the pleasure barges of the nobles and Merchant Princes sat awaiting their leisure.

Kell pulled off his cap and ran his fingers through his long blond hair, enjoying the breeze, breathing the fresh, salty air. In the crowded streets of the market, food vendors hawked sausages, bean patties, and spiced ale. Smoke from the cooks' wood fires rose in the air, joining the fug from the blacksmiths' furnaces. The scents mingled into a heady miasma that Kell would always associate with home.

Sunlight glittered on the water of the bay, spreading out in a shimmering pathway that called Kell to follow it. *Maybe someday,* he thought with a sigh, as he shouldered his pack.

He thought of Betan's comment about maintaining the Balance. *Everyone talks about it, but no one knows what it is. Do they mean a birth for every death? A win for every loss? Are the gods keeping tally? Somehow, I doubt it works like that.*

Kell kept to the backs of the rooftops, out of sight of the busy main market street, as he leaped from roof to roof on his way home. When he felt like he'd put enough distance between himself and the market, he climbed back down to the ground.

His rooftop route had taken him across the invisible boundaries of several of Ravenwood's neighborhoods—from the bustling shops of Market and into Wrighton, where the tradespeople of the city worked and lived. He tipped his hat to the cobbler on his way and spoke to the tailor, hurrying past the potter's workshop and wrinkling his nose as he passed the brewery at the tell-tale smell of a fresh batch of mash.

At the edge of Wrighton stood a large stone arch celebrating the one hundredth anniversary of the Bakaran League, the economic heart of the Kingdom of Darkhurst. The ten supporting pillars represented the League's ten city-states, of which Ravenwood—the walled city itself and the lands beyond its gates—was one. A Crown Prince ruled each city-state for the King, and beneath him were Merchant Princes who saw to the management of the lands and raw materials. Guild Masters in each city-state oversaw the trades. But the real power as far as Ravenwood's residents were concerned lay with the Lord Mayor, who brokered the trade agreements on which their livelihoods depended and who commanded the guards who wielded the power of life and death.

The cobblestone road that fronted the harbor and wound through the marketplace became hard-trod dirt a few blocks into Wrighton; the shopkeepers and tradespeople were located near the front of the neighborhood, convenient to patrons and customers. Kell's family's business was in the back, where people could forget it existed. When necessity forced them to look for the Valmonde brothers, they would come.

Kell ducked through the back door of the workshop, grabbing a few pieces of firewood on the way. He climbed the stairs to their living quarters over the shop, shrugged out of his pack, and stoked the fire, fanning it until the embers glowed. A bucket of water sat where he'd left it, drawn from the pump before his trip to the marketplace. He set the iron cauldron over the flames, then dusted off his hands and turned to the treasures in his pack.

One fresh fish, courtesy of Betan. A chicken for the pot and a loaf of bread. Six potatoes, an onion, and two heads of cabbage.

Kell snatched down the worn, stained apron from a peg by the door and tied it around his waist, then took a knife from the drawer, gave it a few licks on the whetstone, and took out his frustrations on the vegetables. He would never admit it to his two older brothers, but the apron gave him comfort. It had belonged to their mother. Even now, memories of her made his eyes tear in a way that had nothing to do with the onion he was chopping. Bittersweet as the memories were, Kell hoped they didn't fade, like his recollection of their father. Sometimes Corran and Rigan told him stories about Papa, but Kell had been so young when he'd been killed that he only remembered bits and pieces—a glimpse of a face, a man's voice, the smell of the oil he used in his hair. Every year, those grew fainter; soon, they'd be gone.

Kell began to whistle, trying to lift his mood. He diced the onion, cubed the potatoes and sliced the cabbage thin, tossing the vegetables into the simmering water. He reached up to the bundles of dried herbs hanging from the rafters and crumbled a few stalks in his palms, dumping the powder into the cauldron along with some salt.

He did his best to get all the pinfeathers off the chicken, and checked that the butcher had properly gutted the bird, then washed the cavity clean. He had neglected to do that once, and his brothers still teased him about the night they'd eaten 'shit stew' for dinner; once was enough, especially when food was so dear and money so short. Many of those who died in the city lacked funds for anything more than a basic burial, and some could not afford even that. Undertakers were guaranteed steady business, but not always sufficient pay.

Kell cleaned and seasoned the fish, an unexpected bounty, and put it in a covered iron pan, which he shoved among the hot coals. He could not be certain what tomorrow's dinner might be, but tonight, they feasted.

They also had plenty of ale. Kell had brokered an agreement with Prendicott, the tavernmaster at the Lame Dragon; a bonus in return for tending to any who passed on his premises, no questions asked and no tales told.

He cut a loaf of bread into chunks and sniffed at the butter to make sure it hadn't gone rancid before he put it on the table. Then he filled a pitcher with ale from the barrel, set out a bowl of pickles from the crock, and laid three battered tin plates and cups at their places. Kell glanced at the cauldron, checking on the stew.

"Will the swill be ready soon?"

Corran's voice made him jump. "About a candlemark, unless you like your chicken raw. There's fish, too, from Betan. He said to put it against his bill."

"Too bad the tailor's family is in good health. I could use a new pair of pants," Corran said, smiling at his own grim joke.

"You want me to bake him some of that mushroom tart that gave you visions?" Kell said. "The old man might have a weak heart after all." He smiled, recalling an unfortunate meal some months ago. Since that time, Kell had steered clear of the mushroom vendor in the marketplace.

"Nah. Things aren't that tight—yet." At twenty summers old, Corran had inherited the family business and responsibility for his two younger siblings. Kell knew his brother felt that burden keenly; he rarely saw glimpses of the good-natured humor he remembered. "If I thought we were that desperate, I'd have you give the recipe to Prendicott at the Dragon." He managed a tired smile.

"Trouble at the market?" Corran asked, gesturing to a fresh graze on the back of his brother's hand.

Kell shrugged. "No more than usual. Old Wrigley thought it sport to call me a thief for refusing to pay his ridiculous prices. Good thing the guards are fat and the market was crowded."

"Didn't I tell you not to buy from him? You know what the guards might have done if they'd have caught you."

Kell bristled. "Yeah, well, they didn't catch me. And I know all about Wrigley, but he's got the best cabbage in the market."

"I don't give a damn about the cabbage. I forbid you to buy from him."

Kell flipped Corran a rude gesture. "I looked at the other farmers' cabbages before I went to Wrigley. Theirs had worms."

"Then we do without."

Kell turned away and rolled his eyes so that Corran couldn't see him. "Let me remind you of that when you're hungry."

Corran grabbed him by the shoulder and spun him around. "You think this is a joke?" he said, color rising in his cheeks.

Kell and Corran glared at each other. Kell shook off his brother's hold. "I can take care of myself, Corran. Been doing it long enough."

"Stop it. Both of you." Rigan had come up the stairs while the two brothers were arguing. Now, he stood with his hands on his hips, glaring at them, and something about the tilt of his head and the way his dark hair hung in his eyes reminded Kell so strongly of their mother that he had to look away rather than let his brothers see the tears in his eyes.

"Wrigley set the guards after Kell," Corran said.

"Corran's worrying about nothing," Kell retorted.

Rigan looked from one to the other. "Really? With all the work there is to do around here, you've got time to fight?"

Rigan took after their mother, slender and dark-haired with fine, angular features. Corran and Kell took after their father, or so Kell had been told. They had the same blond hair that fell in loose curls and similar broad features. Corran stood half a head taller than Rigan, with a more muscular build. Kell hoped that he would catch up in height and bulk, but he might have to wait a few more years at least.

"He started it," Kell muttered.

"You're the one who bought cabbage from that ornery son of a bitch," Corran snapped.

"Enough!" Rigan yelled. He paused and sniffed the air. "Fish—and chicken?"

"Betan gave me a fish toward his debt," Kell replied. "It won't keep, so I'm cooking it. I'd already bought the chicken."

Rigan grinned. "Keep bringing home bounty like that, little brother, and I'll be on your side in any argument."

"Don't encourage him," Corran grumbled.

"I'll check the pot," Kell said, eager to get away from Corran. Rigan drew Corran over to one side. They spoke in low tones, but Kell could make out some of the conversation.

"*—too hard on him.*"

"*—you've seen the bodies.*"

"*—not a child.*"

"*—live long enough to grow up.*"

Despite the argument, Kell smiled as another memory came to mind. He'd seen his mother take Corran to task more than once for disobeying her, when worry fueled her anger. Much as Corran grated on him, he understood his brother's anxiety. In their business, they saw firsthand what happened to the ones who got caught. The Lord Mayor could hide details from the public, but not from the undertakers. Few secrets went to the grave, and fewer still escaped the confessions of the dead.

A candlemark later, they sat down to eat. The chicken was scrawny, but the fish surpassed their usual fare, testament to Betan's gratitude. There had been hungry nights before and there would be hungry nights again, but tonight was not one of them.

"More edible than usual," Rigan said, wiping his mouth. "I think Kell's cooking is improving."

"That would be a pity. I thought of hiring him out to send us more customers from the people who'd eat his food," Corran replied, but his tone took the sting from his words.

Kell rolled his eyes. "Burn one cabbage, and no one ever lets you forget it."

Rigan raised an eyebrow. "The house smelled like burned peelings for a week. And we still had to eat the damned stuff. And don't forget the 'shit stew'—"

"Any time the two of you want to take over the cooking—and standing in line at the market—be my guest," Kell retorted.

He realized their comments were mostly in jest. They knew as well as he did that without Kell to do the cooking and haggle with the sellers in the marketplace, Rigan and Corran wouldn't be able to get enough bodies buried to keep a roof over their heads and pay off the guards, the Guild and the taxes. And although he expected to help with the family business when he got older, Kell was in no hurry.

Corran laughed, then turned serious, laying a hand on his brother's shoulder. "When you're finished in the kitchen, make the rounds and see if you can drum up some more business," Corran said, pausing before he headed down the steps. "We're behind for the month, and the guards will be by for their due in a few days."

After dinner, Corran and Rigan headed back to their work. Kell stripped off his apron and scrambled down the rickety wooden stairs. He paused in the alley behind the shop and looked up at the afternoon sun. *If I hurry, I can make the rounds of the taverns, surgeons, and rooming houses, hunt up Widgem, and get back before curfew.* Just in case, he had slipped a large knife in his pack.

Kell took up the handles on the cart and set off. Many things might get stolen, but the body wagon figured low on thieves' list of desirables. He maneuvered the cart down the alley and out to the main street, wishing yet again that they could afford a mule. Passersby hurried out of his way as he approached, averting their eyes and drawing their skirts and cloaks toward themselves, as if death might rub off.

Finding dead bodies in Ravenwood wasn't a problem. The challenge lay in finding people willing and able to pay for the proper preparation of their recently departed, and for a grave to be dug in blessed ground. Kell cleared his throat and called out, "Bring me your dead! Valmonde Brothers bury them right!"

Agatha, the old weaver, stopped him before he had gone far. "Boy! Over here. I've got a body for you." Kell pulled the wagon up beside her shop. Age stooped Agatha's back, but her nimble hands still flew across her loom, and her sharp eyes never erred in tracking the complex patterns she wove.

"Brissy died in his sleep," Agatha said. "Not surprised. He'd been coughing something fierce and off his food. Found him last night in the kitchen, still at the table. I've already said my prayers and bid him goodbye. What will you charge me to take him and give him a proper burial?"

Kell quoted her an amount, dropping it a little because he liked the old woman. Agatha grimaced, then dug in her purse and pulled out a handful of coins. "Here. Now help me carry him—I can't move him by myself."

Kell had no idea what the customs were in other city-states, but in Ravenwood, most people mourned their dead in private. Family and friends gathered to bless the departed and say their farewells before the undertaker took the body. No one but the priests and the gravediggers went to see the body interred.

He followed Agatha past the loom and through to a small kitchen. Brissy, her manservant, lay slumped across the table. He was likely older than Agatha, Kell thought, and he marveled that the man had not died years ago. His body had gone cold and stiff, making it hard to wrestle him from his seat. "Mind you don't knock over the table," Agatha warned as they struggled with the corpse out to the cart.

"You won't have to bury him that way, will you?" she asked. Brissy was still in a seated position.

"We'll work with it," Kell assured her. Together, they hoisted the corpse onto the wagon.

"You have any more of those amulets?" Agatha asked. "Like the one you sold my neighbor? I feel a need for a bit of protection, what with a death in the house."

Kell dug into his bag and withdrew a charm made of bone, pottery and bits of colored twine. "It's protection against ill fortune," he said in his most serious tone. "Made by The Ones Below," he added, not needing to say more.

"How much?"

Kell named his price, and Agatha dug into her purse for the coins.

"You're sure it works?" she asked, eyes narrowing.

Kell held up a hand in pledge. "I have it on the best authority. You know what everyone says about... Them." He did not have to mention either the legendary witches or the the tunnels of Below.

Agatha nodded conspiratorially. "Aye. It's a dodgy business, selling these, Kell Valmonde, but I reckon it does good."

"Let's keep it our little secret," Kell whispered, collecting his money. "Some folks wouldn't understand," he added, and they both knew he meant the guards and the Guild. *And neither would my brothers, if they ever found out about my 'side business.'*

Agatha touched the tip of her nose to let him know she got his point. Kell put the coins away and took up the handles to the cart.

"Brissy'll have a grave out in the Oak Field, if you care," Kell added. "Don't you worry, we'll do right by him."

Agatha shook her head. "I'm not of a mind to visit the dead. I figure the Balance is kept more by what you do for the living, than by dwelling on those who have passed. But I appreciate you taking good care of him. He was good company, for a long time."

"You can count on us," Kell replied. Agatha's neighbors gathered for a look at the corpse, peering out their windows or coming out on their stoops. Kell gave them all a wave. "Anyone else got a body for me?" he called out in a chipper voice.

The neighbors shook their heads and gradually disappeared back into their shops and houses. Kell picked up the shafts of his cart and went on his way.

"Kell!" Kell turned to see a boy running toward him; he figured Tek might be eight years old, though he had been aged by life on the streets. "There's been an accident over where they're building the new wall on Trundle Street. You can be the first undertaker on the scene if you get a move on. I'll take you, for a bronze."

Kell grinned, and flipped a bronze coin to the boy. He had spent time cultivating a network of informants and lookouts; his eyes and ears in the back streets. Kell paid for information, and on occasion dished out sweet biscuits—which often won more loyalty among the urchins than the coin. "What do you hear?" Kell asked as he hauled the cart alongside Tek.

Tek glanced around to make sure no one else could hear him. "Old man Janus nearly cut off one of his fingers yesterday, down at the butcher shop. He let me see the cut, after Mistress Sally stitched it up for him."

"Exciting," Kell replied in a voice that suggested the opposite.

"They hanged a couple of pirates down by the harbor day before yesterday."

"No interest to me. Constable doesn't pay the undertaker for hanged men. Just cuts them down and throws them in a pit at the dump."

"Arcad took a beating from the Mayor's guards last night. Roughed him up good before they hauled him to the jail. No one's seen him since."

"Oh, yeah?" It was wise in Ravenwood to keep track of who the Mayor's men were beating and for what. "What did they say he did?"

"Fought monsters."

Kell turned to look at him. "Really?"

Tek nodded vigorously. "That's what the Mayor's guard says, anyhow. Caught him out at night with weapons."

Kell thought of the big knife in his pack, and shifted its weight on his shoulders. "You think he was? Fighting monsters, I mean."

"Probably. Been some attacks down toward Skinton, over on Barker Street. Ghouls, I hear. Folks are sick of it, you know? Mayor says his guards will handle it, and the soldiers kill a few monsters, but they don't ever get them all. I think the guards are as scared of the monsters as anyone."

"Maybe so."

Tek frowned. "You think it's true, what they say? That the monsters come when the Balance is off-kilter?"

Kell snorted. "You think the gods have nothing better to do than chalk off lives and deaths like the score in a dice game?" He shook his head. "I don't know where the monsters come from. Can't be anywhere good. Don't care, so long as they go away again."

They turned the corner, and Kell could see the site of the accident. Three walls of a brick building were still standing, but the fourth had collapsed into rubble. Workers crawled over the rubble while the foreman shouted orders. Kell saw a man's foot protruding from the wreckage.

"Looks like you might need an undertaker," Kell said as he strode towards the foreman. Tek vanished into the crowd.

The foreman looked up, scowling. "You don't waste any time, do you?"

Kell grinned. "Valmonde Brothers, the hardest working undertakers in Wrighton."

"The *only* damn undertakers in this part of Wrighton," the foreman grumbled. There were other undertakers in Ravenwood, but the Guild Masters governed their number and location, and the areas they served.

"The only—and the best. You need some help?"

"No." The foreman watched with a grim expression as the workers uncovered the crushed remains. "What will it cost me to see him buried well?" he said, gesturing to the corpse. "He was one of our senior masons."

Kell quoted a figure twice what Agatha paid. The Masons' Guild had money, and they thought highly of themselves. Guild members paid into an account to handle burials and accidents, so Kell had no compunction about making a profit. *They'll give a stipend to his family, so I'm hardly taking bread from his widow.*

"That's extortion," the foreman grumbled, but he dug into his vest for his money pouch and counted out the coins into Kell's palm. "I expect a burial worth the price. A proper preparation, with honey and myrrh, clean winding sheets, and homage made to the Old Ones as well as the Guild gods."

Kell gave a respectful bow. "As you wish, sir," he said, hiding his glee at getting such a good price. He kept a suitably melancholy expression as the unfortunate worker's colleagues loaded the smashed remains into his wagon. The metallic tang of blood and the odor of shit and entrails assaulted his nose. "I'll have my brothers work on him right away," Kell promised, eager to be on his way before the foreman reconsidered the terms.

I'll have to be sure to pay Tek an extra bronze when I see him. That's enough to keep us fed for most of the month.

RONDU, THE OWNER of The Hound and Hare, paid Kell double the standard vagrant fee to haul away the body of a man killed in a knife fight, with a few coins more to say nothing to the Mayor's guards should they make enquiries. Mistress Glimph, the owner of one of the better kept tenements, flagged him down for the body of a tenant whose heart had failed him in the night. Two families hailed Kell on his rounds with fever victims; Kell pulled his scarf up over his face, and sprinkled those bodies with quicklime to prevent contagion.

Still, a good run, Kell thought. The quicklime brought an extra fee, and Mistress Glimph paid nearly as much as Prendicott at The Lame Dragon, the last stop on Kell's regular route before heading home.

Kell thanked the gods for the cool day, since it kept down the smell and the flies. Hot summer days were the worst, drawing maggots and making the corpses bloat faster. Digging the graves in winter was hard work, but Kell much preferred cooler temperatures when collecting bodies.

He cursed under his breath when he found his way blocked by a crowd just a few streets from the pub. Kell could hear voices, but could not see over the people blocking the road, so he climbed up and stood on the back of the body cart.

"It's a *sign!* A sign that the gods are displeased with our tribute. The monsters walk among us because we have turned away our faces and hardened our hearts!" The speaker paced up and down as he spoke, gesturing and lunging with the force of his words. His beard and hair were shot through with gray, and his thin body and hollow cheeks—along with the stained and ragged robe that barely covered his unwashed body—suggested an ascetic, or a madman.

"Look to the old stories!" the prophet cried. "As it was in the days past, so it is again, to call us to give the gods their due." He thrust a bony finger at a man in the front of the crowd.

"You! Do *you* remember what befell our ancestors before the sea rose and the crops died? The gods tried to warn us. Do you *remember* the stories?"

The man stepped back, either from fear that the gnarled finger might poke out his eye, or perhaps to dodge the spittle flying from the prophet's lips. "Monsters, each kind a judgment for our sins," he stammered.

The legends were part of what every child learned about the gods of Ravenwood. Kell knew the stories, though now that he was older, he wondered about their truthfulness.

"*Judgment!*" the prophet shrieked, throwing up his arms. "An army of *ghouls*, robbing the dead of their rest, because of their *unfaithfulness* to the worship of the gods. *Snake-monsters* from your worst nightmares, two-mawed and twice-fanged. *Beetles* that eat flesh and drink blood, *mortifying* the body. Great *beasts* that come in the night and hunt their prey through the streets, to remind us that we are *nothing* compared to the power of the gods! *Corpses* animated by vengeful spirits because the *wicked* will never know rest. And *worms*, a plague of *maggots*, because Doharmu, the god of death, *will not be mocked!*"

The crowd murmured in dismay, caught up in the spectacle. Kell had to admit the prophet put on quite a show. His cynical side wondered when the old man would pass the hat.

"*You!* Gravedigger!"

Kell's eyes widened as the crowd turned to look at him. Kell realized he stood head and shoulders above them on the body cart. "Don't mind me—"

"*All* of you should beg his pardon!" the wild prophet shouted. "*Beg him* for deliverance to the After. Because *he'll* be the one who sees your wretched flesh to its final rest, who lowers your rotting corpses into the wet dirt. *Beg* the gods for deliverance and the undertaker for confession, and turn from your sins so we may be *delivered* from the cycle of monsters that the gods have brought down upon us!"

Kell's mouth was dry and his hands were shaking, but he managed his best cocky smile. "Just making my rounds," he said, feeling his cheeks flush scarlet from the unwanted attention. "Don't mind me. Clear the way." He put his head down and picked up the cart handles, resolutely refusing to look up until he was past both the prophet and his followers.

A wooden sign with a picture of a dragon holding a crutch heralded The Lame Dragon, a wattle-and-daub building with a steeply sloping thatch roof. The smell of sausages from the inn made his stomach rumble. As had been agreed, he came around to the back. Two stable hands loafed by the corner, smoking their pipes. Polly, one of the cook's helpers, smiled when she saw him.

"You come looking to see if we have a stiff for you?" she called, merrily.

Kell grinned. Polly was close to his own age, and he liked how her red hair bobbed when she moved. "That, and more," he said with a wink that made her blush. A kitchen girl could do much worse than a boy from a Guild, even one in his trade. *Corran and Rigan are slow to take wives,* Kell thought. *But when I'm of age, I want a lass like Polly, one who can cook and make me laugh.*

"I heard a riddle when I took ale out to the common room," Polly said, glancing over her shoulder as she emptied her bucket of scraps into a slop tray for the hogs.

"Tell me."

"'What I build, I build stronger than the mason, the shipwright, and the carpenter. What am I?'"

Kell thought for a moment, then shook his head. "Don't know."

Polly laughed, her eyes sparkling. "Silly! The undertaker, because the houses of the dead last forever!"

Kell laughed, but sobered when he saw the bruise on her cheek. His gaze fell to a fresh cut on one arm, and he noticed the handle of a small knife tucked into the apron ties around her waist.

"What happened?" His voice deepened with anger.

"Nothing." Polly looked away.

"Prendicott needs to keep his eyes open and have a care."

"Please, don't," Polly begged. "I need this job. That sort of thing happens—" Kell guessed what she didn't say aloud. *—in a place like this. To a girl like me.*

Kell's teeth ground together. "Polly—"

Polly met his gaze and moved a step closer. "I stopped him, Kell. Don't ask for details." He saw a dark line beneath her fingernails that might have been dried blood. "After a while, you learn. It's just the way of things."

Kell swallowed his anger. "I won't say anything. I wish I could get you away from here."

Polly kissed him on the cheek. "You're sweet. Keep thinking that way. Maybe in a few years—"

Just then, the kitchen door opened and the stern-faced cook leaned out. "Polly! Get in here. There's work to do."

Polly winked at Kell before slinking back into the kitchen.

The cook eyed the undertaker. "I'll tell the tavern master you're here," she said, wrinkling her nose in disgust as she glanced at the wagon's contents. The door slammed behind her, leaving Kell in the cold.

Prendicott came out a few moments later. "There's a man's body in the barn," he said. "Found him in there this morning. No idea who he is; he wasn't staying at the inn, and he's not one of the regulars. Looks like he got a knife between the ribs. There's a second body, too, and from the way it's been chewed on, he ran into some monsters and crawled in there to die. Don't want anyone catching sight of either of them. Bad for business." He paid Kell his usual fee. "Throw a piece of burlap over them so the gossips don't see, or there'll be no end to the tales. Things are bad enough as they are."

As Kell hauled the cart towards the stables he glanced up: almost sunset, and he still had a distance to go to get home. *Best be back before dark if I don't want to end up like the fellows in the barn. Corran would skin me alive for taking the risk.*

The first corpse looked to have been a few years older than Corran, with bruises on his face and upper arms. *Like a slap to the cheek might make, or where punches would land if you were holding someone's arms.* Kell felt his temper rise. Only one wound marked the body, a thin cut where a small knife had slipped between the ribs and into the heart; a knife much like a kitchen girl would carry.

I'm glad Polly killed you, you son of a bitch. I'll fix it so the gods will never accept your soul. People forget that undertakers get the last word. He threw the body into the cart, making no attempt to be gentle, and went to look for the other corpse.

He found it in the back of the barn on a blood-soaked pile of hay. Deep claw marks had gashed the dead man's chest and opened up his belly. One arm looked as if it had been gnawed by something with a disconcertingly human bite. *Ghouls. So it's true—they're back.* Kell braced himself and dragged the corpse by its feet until he was close enough to shoulder it into the wagon, trying to get as little of the dead man's blood on him as possible.

This wasn't the first time he had retrieved a monster kill. He was no stranger to the many ways men died, and the particular horrors of each. More than once, Kell had seen the hanged man's purpled face and swollen tongue, the rope bruise fresh around the throat and the head flopping at an odd angle on the broken neck.

He had seen bodies green with rot and contorted from poison, and mangled from fall and accident. Drowned men with their fish-pale waterlogged skin and murdered women with throats slit were all in a day's work, along with the old, the sick and, at times, the plague-ridden.

But the monster kills were the worst, the corpses most likely to haunt Kell's dreams. Unnatural creatures roamed the streets and alleys of Ravenwood. No one knew where they came from, or why sometimes they would disappear for months at a time, only to return hungry and more vicious than ever. That's what made the rantings of the old prophet so appealing to his audience. Angry gods could be appeased, sins atoned or avoided. Mad or not, he offered an explanation, something better than random chance and bad luck. His wild tales were not the only theories Kell had heard for the return of the monsters: some said it followed a pattern, while others blamed a shift in the Balance, though Kell doubted that.

Do they even know what they mean when they mention the Balance? Or is it just something they tell themselves because any reason—however flimsy—is better than no reason at all?

Once, Kell had glimpsed one of the creatures savaging its victim in the street outside the shop. Corran and Rigan had ordered him away from the window. Rigan stayed with him, while Corran joined the other men who took to the street with whatever tools might double as weapons to protect their families. That alone would warrant a beating if the Mayor's guards caught them, but the guards, as usual, were nowhere to be found.

Dead is dead, Kell thought, taking two burlap grain bags from a heap in the corner to cover the corpse. But though he tried to convince himself, he knew the truth—not all deaths were equal.

Chapter Seven

WIDGEM'S FAVORITE PLACE to conduct business was a seedy tavern called The Muddy Goat. Kell's cart full of corpses looked right at home beside the disreputable tavern, and the couple of drunks passed out in the gutter might almost have fallen from it.

No one gave Kell a second glance when he walked in, stepping carefully as his soles stuck to the grubby floor. The tavern was more popular for its low prices than the quality of the watered ale. An off-key minstrel caterwauled in a corner, but most of the patrons were too consumed by their card games or too deep into their cups to care. The smoke wreathing the tap room did little to mask the smell of unwashed bodies and old vomit. Worn-looking trollops cozied up to clients who looked to have a few coin to spare.

The Goat stood on a back street in Wrighton, far enough from the harbor that only locals congregated here. Farriers and blacksmiths favored the place, assuring enough strong men in the tavern to keep the peace so the barkeeper seldom needed the assistance of the Mayor's guards; that the guards were not welcome here went without saying.

Kell found Widgem in his usual spot: a table in a shadowed nook where business could be transacted with some degree of privacy.

Widgem's massive, rolling belly strained at the buttons beneath a dirty shirt and a torn jacket worn thin at the elbows. The tankard in front of the big man was likely not his first, but, even in his cups, nobody could get one over on the old codger.

Widgem looked up as Kell approached.

"What do you have for me today?" Kell asked. He glanced around, then perched on a stool on the other side of the table, making sure to keep his back to the wall. Widgem dug a pouch from beneath his jacket and put it on the table.

"As you requested," Widgem said, his voice unctuous. "I made the very dangerous trek Below to get these from the witches down there." He gave an exaggerated shudder. "Terrible place, Below. And those witches—"

"I make it worth your while, don't I?" Kell replied without looking up. Widgem's acting was worse than the amateurs on the stage in the city green, and Kell did not fall for it.

Kell dumped the bag's contents onto the table between them. A motley collection spread out: good-luck charms of dubious value, a 'lucky' ring of uncertain provenance, a worn set of prayer beads, a few carved worry stones.

"Let me see the money," Widgem said, his rheumy eyes lighting up as Kell held a few coins up, then withdrew them again. Kell gathered the pieces toward him and picked them up and examined them, one after the other.

"The amulets are nice," Kell said. "But the beads look like the ones I saw on the peddler's cart for three bronzes. The worry stones will sell." He raised an eyebrow. "You didn't steal them, did you?"

"Can't steal from witches, boy. I'd be a dead man." Widgem chuckled, a wheezy sound that ended in a coughing fit.

"Well?" Kell asked.

"Ten bronze," Widgem replied.

Kell laughed. "Take me for a fool? They're not worth more than five."

Widgem's eyes narrowed. "I'll give them to you for six, and not a bronze less."

Kell grinned. "Done!" He dug the coins out of the pouch tied around his neck. "Here," he said, sliding them toward Widgem and gathering the items with a sweep of his arm. "Now, how's business?"

Widgem shrugged. "Been busy. What do you hear?"

"What do you know about that street prophet filling people's head with nonsense about monsters and gods?"

Widgem gave him a measured look. "Who's to say it's nonsense? The monsters are back—and more than what should be. Why're they here? Where do they come from? Why now, and why so many?" He shook his head. "Maybe he knows something we don't."

Kell snorted. "I'd think the gods could find a better mouthpiece than the likes of him, if they had a message to send. What else do you hear?"

Widgem looked around, dropping his voice. "I heard that the price of bread is going up. And that the Merchant Princes are worried about the trade negotiations with Garenoth. Have to fix the contract for the next while, you know."

"Couldn't care less about the Merchant Princes, or trade agreements. None of my business. We don't import dead people. Anything else?"

"Couple more people gone missing, a few more hunters dead or dragged off to jail. Some folks took sick, down near the harbor. They say witches did it."

"Magic like that's illegal in Ravenwood."

"Lots of things are illegal in Ravenwood," Widgem said with a crafty smile. "Don't mean they aren't going on."

"You think it's true?"

"What do I know? People say all kinds of things. Easier to blame witches than the gods. More to the point is what the guards believe. And I've heard there've been some accusations."

"Of witchcraft?"

"Aye. There'll be a hanging or two, mark my words."

"Any other news?"

"Trania, the fortune teller, says the monsters will return within a fortnight; more this time, hungrier. And she says grief will come to witches and Wanderers." He daubed the sweat dripping of his face with a filthy kerchief.

"The monsters always come back sooner or later, so that's a safe prediction for Trania, *and* that crazy prophet," Kell said. "As for the witches and Wanderers, the guards are always causing problems for them. Maybe something worse this time?"

"Can't tell you more, boy. That's all the lady said." Widgem leaned back and grinned. "You'll do good business selling those charms," he said, patting his bag. "Just remember—I'm the one who risks going down in that vile place and dealing with those witches—and I always give you the best prices." He hesitated. "About the fortune teller. I think she's right this time—be careful."

"Yeah. Don't worry. I know how to watch out for myself."

Kell wove back through the crowded inn. The cart sat right where he'd left it, and a quick glance assured him no one had pawed over the bodies looking for clothing to scavenge. A thin stream of blood still poured from the crushed man. *Maybe that put off any robbers,* Kell thought. He grabbed the cart's shafts and headed back across town.

Kell maneuvered the cart through two more blocks before he heard shouting. He left the cart against the side of an alley and carefully eased closer, staying against the wall to remain out of sight. He reached the corner and peeked around. One of the Mayor's guards towered over the kneeling form of Jacen, the baker. Jacen's bloodied mouth and swollen eye told a tale.

"Please! I swear I'll pay you the rest next week," Jacen begged.

The guard cuffed the baker on the ear. "Your portion was due today."

"My wife's sick. I had to pay the healer. She couldn't work this week. She's better now. We'll make it up. I promise."

"Your excuses don't interest the Lord Mayor." The guard aimed a kick at Jacen, who scrambled to avoid the blow.

"I'll have coin to pay you in a few days."

"Not my problem."

Bleeding and bruised, the baker got to his feet and returned a few moments later with a few coins, probably all the money he had left. "Here. Take it."

"I'll be back for the rest," the guard said, shouldering past.

Kell eased back into the shadows as the guard stalked away. He waited several minutes before he continued on his way.

The guards get bolder every day, and there's naught to be done about it. If the gods are concerned about the Balance, why don't the monsters go after the bloody guards?

Troubling thoughts churned in his mind the whole way back to the undertaker's shop.

"What took you so long?" Corran glared at Kell.

"There's at least half a candlemark until nightfall." Kell shrugged out of his jacket. "The seer at The Muddy Goat says there'll be more monsters within the fortnight," he reported. "She also predicts there'll be trouble for witches and Wanderers. Couple more people have disappeared, and Arcad's been arrested as a hunter and taken to the Mayor's jail."

Rigan and Corran both stopped still at that.

"Oh, and the dead guy with the knife wound? We've been paid extra to bury him with the wrong markings outside holy ground." *I'd have dumped the body in the sewer if I didn't think he'd float. Someone might have recognized him.*

"Doesn't take an oracle to predict more monsters," Corran muttered. "Or trouble for Wanderers and witches. I think the seer is a fraud." Something in Corran's tone sent a shiver of worry down Kell's back. Rigan turned away, looking troubled, but said nothing.

Rigan and Corran laid the bodies out on wooden tables. On one wall hung joiner's tools, for making caskets. On another were the embalmer's supplies: honey, juniper, cedar, cinnamon, vinegar, wine, and salt. A jar of aconite and one of amanita powder sat on a shelf, for the binding rituals. Winding sheets lay in a pile, for those who could not afford a coffin but wanted more than plain burlap.

A table in the back held the knives and saws, above which were shelves filled with pots of ochre and soot, chalk and woad, all used to prepare bodies for their journey into the After. Shovels leaned against the corner of the workshop, ready for the next trip to the burying ground.

They set the bricklayer's body on a table off to one side, so that they could first see to the clients for whom more expensive arrangements had been made. Rigan and Corran used leather gloves to lift the fever victims' bodies while Kell threw a length of burlap beneath each of them, which doubled back to cover the front of the bodies and gathered along each side with a drawstring. They would add more quicklime at the cemetery.

Brissy's corpse took up a table on the right, toward the better quality preparations, while the lodger with the bad heart went on a slab to the left, with the cheaper materials. The monster-savaged body also went to the left, for the minimal preparations Prendicott's payment covered.

Rigan stood looking at the man Polly had stabbed. "Someone actually paid you extra for us to send this bloke to the Darkness?"

"Uh huh." Kell didn't look up.

"Don't go offering that sort of thing," Corran grumbled. "Bad for us if the Guild hears."

"You did real good," Rigan said, looking out over the bodies as he tied on his work apron and pulled on the leather gloves blessed to protect against contagion. "The Guild body and the one from The Lame Dragon more than make up for the slim payment on the others."

Corran eyed Kell. "What did you promise Agatha about Brissy's body?"

"I just said we'd do right by her."

Corran swore under his breath. "Well, there go a few more coins to the priest for his prayers."

Rigan glared at Corran. "Something's really got up your nose today, hasn't it? Mama always said Agatha was good to her when she was a girl. That's worth something. For Mama's sake."

Rigan did not catch Corran's grumbled response, but he shot Kell a victorious smile when Corran wasn't looking, certain the matter was settled.

"Since the stew's already simmering, you can stay and watch, maybe lend a hand, Kell," Corran said. "The Guild won't let us officially apprentice you for another year, but they can't stop you from learning the ropes in the meantime. Mind you're careful with the blades. It only takes a poke and you're as dead as the corpse. That's how Uncle Rem died."

Kell bit back a response and fetched the leather work belt. A hammer, saws of several sizes, and pliers were part of preparing the body for its journey to the gods. A row of pottery jars sat against one wall, ready for the more elaborate preparations.

The brothers began work on the mason first. "There's not much left of him, is there?" Rigan remarked, looking at the crushed body.

"We can't do much about removing his innards, since they're smashed to jelly, but at least the head's in one piece," Corran replied.

"Go prepare the wash," Corran ordered, Kell went to get one of the full buckets of water that the brothers drew early in the day. Long practice meant Kell could go down the row of bottles quickly, pouring out just the right amount of the expensive spices and tinctures into a cup carved with runes and sigils sacred to the gods. He made a hurried sign of blessing over the cup, and then dumped the contents into one of the buckets.

He brought the bucket and rags to Rigan and Corran, and went to fetch the shroud and winding sheets.

"This is not going to work well," Rigan observed, looking at the shattered remains of the mason.

"Do what you can," Corran said. "The Guild paid well and the gods will appreciate the effort."

Kell mixed the pigments—ochre for the gods of the earth; woad for the gods of the sea; chalk for the gods of the sky; soot for the gods of fire. Corran motioned for Kell to bring the paints closer. There were songs to be sung over the departed, and ways in which even the humblest corpse had to be readied to present itself to the ancient spirits. Corran sang in the old language, and his clear baritone sent chills down Kell's spine. Rigan took the palette and put his thumb into the ochre, drawing a complicated sigil as best he could on the dead man's crushed abdomen. Next, he marked in chalk on what remained of the chest, making another symbol in woad across the lips, and finally drawing one more rune in soot on the forehead. Corran lifted the battered corpse onto the bottom sheet of a linen shroud, and wrapped it in clean strips of cloth. The shattered corpse jiggled disturbingly as they worked. Corran made a motion in blessing.

"That will have to do," Corran said once they were finished. "I'll ask the priest to say some extra blessings at the grave site."

Brissy's body received the same treatment, despite Agatha's meager payment. Next was the old man with the bad heart.

"How much did Mistress Glimph pay you?" Corran asked Kell.

"As little as she could."

"All right," Corran said. "Sprinkle his body with water. We're not preparing a fresh wash when she's barely paid enough for the shroud. Don't use more of the pigment than you have to. No winding sheets, either. We might make a few bronzes on him if we keep it simple."

Working together, the three brothers quickly prepared the old man's body. Corran and Rigan then stepped outside and saw to the two wretches in the cart, though Rigan used a brush to paint the symbols on the shroud instead of on the bodies themselves. Once they'd finished, Corran turned to body of the man from The Lame Dragon.

"Looks like someone stuck a knife in this one," he mused, pulling away the bloody shirt. He eyed the other bruises. "Seems he might have had it coming."

"He did," Kell muttered. Rigan gave him a sidelong glance, but did not say anything.

"What?" Corran asked.

"I imagine he did... have it coming," Kell said, covering his slip. "No other reason someone would pay for a curse now, is there?" *Even if I paid the extra from our grocery money.*

If Rigan suspected that Kell had a personal stake in the matter, he said nothing—at least not in front of Corran. "Looks like a sailor," Rigan said, taking a closer look at the stained shirt. "Guess he pushed his luck a little too far." Corran turned to get more pigment, and Rigan took something out of the dead man's hand: several strands of red hair, clutched in the corpse's stiffened fingers. He hesitated for a moment, then dropped the hairs to the floor and reached for the paints. "This won't take long."

A mere lack of burial or rituals wasn't enough to curse the dead; the curse was a combination of mismarking the runes and then burying the body beyond the hallowed ground of the burial yard.

Rigan didn't like doing the curse runes, but tonight he made no comment. "There," he said, finishing the runes and then carefully washing the pigments from his hands with the clean, blessed water Kell had prepared. "That should do it. We won't lose money on him without a shroud or a priest's fee, or a coin to the burying yard."

The savaged body was the last one left. "I guess the seer was wrong about the monsters not coming back for a fortnight," Rigan said, looking down at the corpse. "Looks like ghouls have been at them."

"We wouldn't have these problems if the guards did their job," Corran muttered. He shifted as if his shoulder hurt him, and Kell watched him closely, wondering what he had done to injure himself.

"I saw one of the guards beating Jacen, the baker," Kell said. "He didn't pay his full portion."

Corran swore under his breath. "A pox on the guards, and the clap as well."

Rigan glanced at him. "They'll be by here in the next day or so. Can we pay ours?"

"Yeah, but there's not much left over afterward, even after a good day. That chicken in the pot upstairs might be the last one for a week or so, unless more folks than usual take sick."

"We'll get by," Rigan said. An odd look crossed his features as he looked down at the corpse. *Does the body make him think of Mama?* Kell wondered. *Is that how she looked?*

Even now, his memories of that awful night were a jumble. His mother had gone to visit a friend, not far away. She never made it back. Kell had heard her scream from the street outside their shop. Corran was the first to realize what was happening; he'd shoved Kell into the upstairs bedroom and locked him in. Rigan and Corran would never tell Kell exactly what they did next. He'd heard the door slam behind them and watched from the window until they were out of sight.

A candlemark later, when Rigan came to let him out of the room, both brothers were covered with blood. Rigan had been the one to take Kell aside and break the news. Corran was down in the workroom, tending to their mother's body, making preparations, saying prayers to the gods. Corran had forbidden Kell to see the mangled corpse. He knew his brother meant it as a kindness, but Kell had never had the chance to see her face again, and was left saying his goodbyes to a shrouded body. *And I'm supposed to believe the gods took her to keep some kind of Balance no one can explain? So I lose my mother, and that cancels out something somewhere else? No. It's just another lie.*

As if Rigan could guess the direction Kell's thoughts had taken, he nudged his brother gently in the ribs. "Hey, we can handle this one. Why don't you get cleaned up and see to dinner? Pour us each a glass of whiskey while you're at it. I think we've earned it today."

Kell eagerly made his escape. He washed up in the horse trough outside, shivering since the evening had grown cool. Then he went upstairs, and lit the kitchen lanterns.

The bread hadn't risen right, and the stew was too thick. "It'll have to do," he murmured. "It's hardly like Mama got the chance to teach me to cook—or thought I'd need to know." He told himself that it was the smoke from the kitchen fire making his eyes tear up.

"That smells good—even for your cooking." Rigan came into the kitchen, Corran right behind him. They sat at the table as Kell set out the meal. He had already poured them each a generous measure of whiskey.

As they ate, Rigan recounted the gossip he had heard from some of the other tradesmen that day.

"I've got to go to a Guild meeting," Corran said when the meal was finished. He tossed back the last of his whiskey.

"It's not safe to be out this late," Rigan cautioned.

"I won't go unarmed. There's no helping it, and the meeting isn't far."

"Why are they holding meetings after curfew? That's asking for trouble."

"Because we all have to work, to put food on the table. It's the only time everyone could get together. Special project for the Guild Master."

"I could go with you, as back-up," Rigan volunteered.

Corran shook his head. "No need to put both of us in danger. I'll be fine. Really. You stay here with Kell."

A look passed between the two older brothers, and Kell could see Rigan was not happy with Corran's plan.

"All right, then. Watch yourself," Rigan said.

Corran gave a curt nod and went downstairs.

Once Rigan and Kell had tidied away the supper things, Rigan poured them both a good measure of whiskey.

"Corran will have something to say if we go through the bottle too fast," Kell said. "Good whiskey's expensive."

Rigan merely smiled and walked over to the window, opening the shutters. The night air was cool. From here, they could see down to the harbor, and beyond to a sky full of stars.

"Corran doesn't mean to be so gruff, you know," Rigan said.

"You could have fooled me."

Rigan's lips twitched in a sad smile. "All right. He knows he's being gruff. But he wasn't ready to take over the business so soon. He's got his hands full, trying to make enough to pay the King's taxes, the Guild's fee, *and* the Mayor's portion, and still make ends meet. It's not like we have a choice about what we do for a living. Corran worries himself sick over keeping us both safe." He sighed. "And I gave him good cause this week. Damn."

"What would you do, if you had a choice? If you weren't tied to the job?" Kell asked.

"I'd travel," Rigan said wistfully. "Do you see those ships in the harbor? I want to know where they go. I want to see what's on the other side of the ocean. I'd be happy just to see what's outside of Ravenwood."

Ravenwood was one of the larger, wealthier independent principalities in the Bakaran League. Beyond the city walls lay the farms and vineyards of the Merchant Princes, as well as smaller towns and villages. Further out were the other nine city-states, and the distant kingdoms people within the League referred to as 'The Unaligned.'

Rigan sighed. "How about you? What would you do?"

"Well, I wouldn't be a cook," Kell replied, and they both chuckled. "I don't rightly know what else I'd want to do. But if I had to pick, it might be nice to work with the living."

Rigan laughed. "I'm not sure about that. Have you been around many of them? At least the dead are polite."

They watched the moonlight on the ocean in silence for a few moments. Finally, Kell said, "I'm afraid I'm forgetting them, Rigs. Mama and Papa. I know, with Mama, it's only been six months. But sometimes, when I try to remember their voices, it's hard. I can see their faces in my mind, but what if that fades too? I don't want to forget."

Rigan took a long breath before he answered. "Sometimes, I wish I could. The night Mama died... there was a reason Corran locked you in your room, Kell. He didn't want you to see her, how—how she was at the end."

Rigan and Corran had prepared their mother's body for burial, seen to the rituals themselves, and paid the priests extra coin. Corran, who had always been bossy, grew moody and snappish. Rigan tried to mediate, but often ended up walking out in disgust when they could not stop arguing. After that, they had been so busy keeping body and soul together that there wasn't much time for talk.

"Do you think the Mayor's guards will ever get rid of the monsters?" Kell asked. "And if they don't want to, why don't they just let the hunters do it? Surely that couldn't be a bad thing?"

Rigan raised an eyebrow. "Do you really suppose the Lord Mayor and the Guild Masters want tradesmen organizing into armed fighting groups? Once we finished off the monsters, we might come looking for them."

"What about the Balance? Do you think that's real?"

Rigan snorted. "People don't have any idea what they're talking about. Do I think bad things have to happen to cancel out good things, to make the gods happy? Sounds stupid to me." He shook his head. "I think it's either something people made up to explain why bad things happen out of nowhere, or they've got it wrong. But no one's likely to explain it to the likes of us, so I wouldn't worry about it."

"There was a prophet in the street saying that the monsters come because the gods are angry with us," Kell said quietly.

"He's full of shit. The gods had no reason to be angry with Mama. Or with Wil. Or Jora. He'd better not say that kind of trash where Corran can hear, or he'll end up with a fat lip."

"Do you think witches are real?" Kell blurted. "I mean, people who work magic outside what the Guilds allow."

Rigan frowned. "Where did that come from?"

"Widgem said there's been a fever, down by the harbor. Some people died. Said they're blaming it witches. There've been arrests—"

"Bad stuff happens when people start talking about witches," Rigan said, and something in his voice sent a chill down Kell's back. His brother slugged back the last of his whiskey and turned away from the window. "It's been a long day. I'm going to get some sleep. Don't bother waiting up for Corran. He'll come back in his own time."

Kell watched him go. He stayed where he was, looking out at the harbor, sipping the whiskey and enjoying the fuzzy-headed calm it brought. He looked at the dark sea with the shimmering moonlight path stretching out to the horizon. *I didn't want to say so to Rigan, but if I could do anything, I'd be on one of those ships. I'd take Polly with me, leave Ravenwood and its monsters, and never come back.*

Chapter Eight

"TELL US ABOUT the hunters." Lord Mayor Ellor Machison stood over the prisoner and flexed his hands. Two guards stood by the door, making certain the prisoner posed no danger, despite the many coils of rope that bound the man to his chair.

"Don't you have hired dogs for this kind of thing?" The man looked up at his tormentor through swollen, bloodshot eyes.

Machison planted a solid punch on the prisoner's jaw. Blood darkened his knuckles. "I'm a fortunate man. I enjoy my work. Hate to delegate when I can do it better myself."

Blood dripped in a slow, steady trickle from Arcad's split lip. Machison was just warming up. He had enjoyed sparring during his military service, long ago—or rather, he liked the release of tension that came with handing out a beating. He delivered three more hard punches in quick succession.

One caught Arcad on the cheek and snapped his head to the side, hard enough to make him black out briefly. The second sank into Arcad's gut, which would have doubled the man over had the ropes not kept him upright. The third blow caught him beneath the jaw, throwing him back hard against the chair, almost toppling it.

A sheen of sweat rose on Machison's forehead. He felt limber, powerful... alive. That rush of energy was the reason he preferred to interrogate prisoners himself when time allowed, though his guards were certainly capable.

"How many hunters are there?"

"Go to the Dark Ones."

Machison dug his knuckles deep into the man's side, making him cry out. "Maybe you should be worried about seeing the Dark Ones yourself. Now, we can do this the hard or easy way. Tell me what I want to know and I'll give you a quick death."

"May Darkness take you."

The toe of Machison's boot drove into the vulnerable flesh between Arcad's legs. "Are the Guilds assisting the hunters?"

Arcad sagged. "The Guilds have nothing to do with it," he muttered thickly.

Machison chuckled. "I knew you could be reasonable. Not that I believe you, but it's a start." He looked to one of the guards. "Reward him with a little water."

The guard heaved a bucket of cold water into Arcad's face, and the prisoner sputtered for breath. "Tell me about the other hunters," Machison urged.

"I've told you already," Arcad slurred. "I hunt alone. No one else. Never has been."

Machison pressed one broad hand against Arcad's throat, pushing him against the high-backed chair, his thumb against the man's larynx. "I can have a healer repair the damage so we can start over again," he whispered next to the prisoner's ear. "Or just enough to keep you from dying, for as long as we want. As long as it takes to get useful information. As long as we're enjoying ourselves." He tightened his grip on Arcad's throat until the man's breath came in harsh gasps. "Names."

"There are no others."

Machison responded with a barrage of strikes, each more

powerful than the last. A wheeling kick snapped the man's head to the side with enough force to break his neck, sending the chair over backward, and the mayor followed him, his boot connecting with Arcad's ribs with a cracking of bone. The beating ended with Machison crouched, sweat-covered and blood-spattered, breathing hard, almost giddy with release, finally sated.

"Shall we call for a healer?" The guard asked as Machison wiped the blood from his hands.

"No need. He knew nothing of value." He glanced down at the body. "Call a servant to run me a hot bath and have one of the girls brought to my room." He spared a backward look at the dead man. "And then take out the trash."

TWO CANDLEMARKS LATER, Machison pulled on a clean shirt and drew in a deep, satisfied breath. The hot bath had eased his sore muscles and washed away the worst of the blood, and the woman brought to his bed from the cells below had met his needs. He looked back at her cold body, staring blankly at the ceiling, throat purpled where his hands clenched during climax. *Pity I don't often get more than one use out of them,* he thought. *But there's more where she came from.*

He looked forward to the prospect of a good dinner, and the decanter of brandy that awaited him in the parlor.

As bells rang eight times in the tower, a knock sounded at the outer doors. "Enter," Machison called.

Hant Jorgeson entered the room, closing the door behind him. No one who saw him would mistake Jorgeson for anything except hired muscle. He was tall and strongly built. A scar cut through his left eyebrow and cheek, and the notch in his left ear suggested fights long past.

"What do you have for me?" Machison asked, leaning back in his chair.

"The ship bearing Ambassador Jothran from Garenoth has arrived," Jorgeson replied. "You'll be having a private dinner with Ravenwood's ambassador Halloran and Merchant Prince Gorog tomorrow night."

"And the other ambassadors?"

"The rest of the ambassadors from the League will arrive shortly. I think you can be certain they will want to keep an eye on the trade negotiations."

Survival in the Kingdom of Darkhurst was a never-ending, dangerous game; a constant, merciless winnowing where only the strongest and wiliest survived. Darkhurst's King Rellan paid little attention to the details of ruling, so long as the taxes were paid on time and revenues rose. Rellan accepted the dubious allegiance of the Crown Princes who oversaw the ten city-states of the Bakaran League, all of which constantly vied for favor and backstabbed for gain.

The hereditary nobility invested in the Companies whose fleets supported the Bakaran League's trade, and bankrolled the Merchant Princes who controlled the vineyards, forests, mines, and farms. The Guilds of each city-state represented the traders and crafters, and while they did not answer to the Merchant Princes, they were beholden to them for the raw materials of their work.

Economic necessity bound the Guilds and the Merchant Princes together tighter than any chains: the Princes needed the Guilds' skilled tradespeople, and the Guilds needed the Merchant Princes' commodities and their trade ties. Saying the resulting relationship was 'stormy' understated the reality by quite a bit.

And in the middle of everything, tasked with keeping the bloody mess running and profitable, were the Lord Mayors of the city-states. Machison and his peers walked a dangerous line that required finesse and ruthlessness, the acumen of a moneylender and the morals of a cutpurse. Crown Prince Aliyev ran Ravencroft for King Rellan. It was to Aliyev that the three Merchant Princes—Gorog,

Kadar, and Tamas—ultimately owed their allegiance. Machison owed his position to Crown Prince Aliyev, but Merchant Prince Gorog, currently the most powerful of his peers, had bought and paid for Machison's loyalty long ago.

The ten city-states of the Bakaran League vied for favor like the spoiled children of a wealthy, capricious father. Treaties and negotiations held the League together, with each of the city-states bound to the others for mutual protection and trade benefits. Negotiating those treaties fell to the Lord Mayors of the city-states and the ambassadors. Old grudges ran deep, wariness and suspicion tinged every interaction, and individual greed warred with mutual self-interest. The negotiations hadn't started yet, and Machison already felt weary just thinking about the squabbling diplomats.

"We have to make sure that Ravenwood retains its favored status with Garenoth," Machison said. He took a sip of his drink. "And you can bet the other ambassadors will be armed with plenty of ideas and fat bribes to sway the discussions in their favor."

"Surely Gorog has taken measures of his own to make certain the talks go in his favor," Jorgeson replied.

"Assuredly. And just as certainly, Tamas and Kadar will attempt to skew the agreement to benefit themselves. What benefits Ravenwood does not necessarily benefit each of its Merchant Princes equally, and by all accounts, Gorog's had the best of the deal in the current agreement—for Ravenwood and himself." Machison let out a long breath. "Gorog expects me to ensure his position remains unchanged."

"We wouldn't have these problems if every city-state had equal resources," Jorgeson said with a sigh.

"A stronger king might have done away with the city-states altogether," Machison replied. "But we all know that the Crown Princes and the Trading Companies are the real power."

"Ravenwood has good soil for farming. We don't have to be quite so dependent on Garenoth for imported food."

"The only way Ravenwood could grow enough food to feed its people on its own would be if Kadar gave up some of his precious vineyards. And we both know that's not going to happen."

"And that's just the point, isn't it?" Jorgeson said. "Ravenwood's got the lumber, and we can't just plant trees elsewhere and have them grow overnight. Grapes won't grow as well in Itara and Ostero. Tamas's farms can't feed everyone, and even if they could, exporting what he grows is more profitable. Even if we didn't have city-states, we'd have the same problem with alliances and agreements to get the goods where they're needed."

Merchant Prince Tamas owned the farms closest to the city, which produced corn as well as beef, pork, and lamb. Some of that bounty fed the city-state, but much of the grain went to the distilleries and breweries; Ravenwood's beers and spirits sold well both locally and abroad. Kadar owned Ravenwood's vineyards and Gorog's lands produced the lumber used in shipbuilding, carpentry, and barrelmaking. In theory, all the Guilds owed their allegiance to the Crown Prince, but in practice each cozied up to whichever Merchant Prince's holdings most directly contributed to their own trades. Machison walked a dangerous line, needing to keep all the factions off-balance enough to control without letting the whole thing collapse into infighting.

"Do you think Kadar has the backing to obtain more favorable terms for himself?" Jorgeson asked. "Ravenwood as a whole has done well with the current treaty, even if it did favor Gorog. We've had the best of Garenoth's harvest, and plenty of it. No one's gone hungry in a long time. I don't like the idea of losing that."

Machison sighed. "Better food makes for more productive workers, which means more trade and profit. And a higher ranking in the League means we don't bear the brunt of the Cull to keep the Balance. Gods know, that demands enough deaths as it is."

"But Gorog's worried about Kadar?"

"Gorog believes it's possible for Kadar to muck things up

somehow." *I feel like a bone pulled between two dogs.* "The treaty is a ten-year agreement. Whoever benefits most from the final terms will keep the upper hand for a decade. It would make our lives miserable if the terms were to change."

Machison's position was secure even if Kadar gained power; he owed his appointment to Crown Prince Aliyev. But Kadar knew Gorog had purchased favors from Machison, and so while ultimately they would have to find a way to work together, Kadar could make negotiations as difficult as possible. Machison had witnessed Kadar's spitefulness, and did not look forward to being on the receiving end of it. Kadar pushing too ruthlessly to increase his own advantage could damage the talks and hurt Ravenwood's chances of retaining its favored status with Garenoth. Kadar might not think about long-term consequences, but Machison could not afford to ignore the risk.

"I assume you have a plan," Jorgeson said, watching Machison closely.

Machison tossed back the rest of his drink. "Of course I do."

For Ravenwood's three Merchant Princes, commerce was a never-ending pissing contest, a way to vie for position, score points with the Crown Prince and King Rellan, and bring each other down a peg. Any advantage in terms for one Merchant Prince's commodities and trades meant a disadvantage, a coup, against the others—with retaliation a certainty. Revenge was usually taken by proxy, striking at the men who served the major players, not at the highborns themselves. Machison's fealty to the Crown Prince protected him from the worst of the proxy strikes, though Kadar rarely missed an opportunity to make a cutting comment or a petty snub.

Machison poured himself another drink. "Enough talk of the Garenoth agreement. What other news?"

"The witch finders have been busy these last few days," Jorgeson said. "Two hedgewitches taken, though they turned out to be of middling power. A few more wretches disappeared from the Skinton area after their neighbors blamed them for casting the evil eye on fever victims. Not our doing, but it serves to keep the commoners on edge." He gave a snort of derision. "Probably ended up at the bottom of the harbor."

Machison chuckled. "I suspect you're right. What's being said about witches down in the city?"

Jorgeson shrugged. "A little more than the usual, as we hoped. What with a fever going around, the rabble are nervous. They'd likely hold a feast for the witches if their magic reliably healed the sick or raised the dead, but since it doesn't, they're all too happy to blame them for every bit of bad luck—real or imagined."

"Nicely done."

Jorgeson inclined his head, accepting the rare praise. "It doesn't hurt that the monsters are afoot, and the witches don't seem to be able to do much about them. Since the commoners see no value in the witches, they're quick to find them responsible."

"We need to make certain the Cull is large enough to satisfy the Balance. I've advised Blackholt to make certain the monsters strike hardest against the Guilds and merchants most beholden to Kadar, and make up the rest from the Wanderers and vagrants along the harbor."

With the wealth that came from a favorable treaty with Garenoth came other benefits, like more money to pay guards to protect the wealthy areas of the city. And while few knew it, proving profitable to the Crown Prince and the king brought another, darker benefit: a reduction in the Cull required from that region's residents.

Jorgeson tensed at the mention of Machison's blood witch. "I don't trust Blackholt."

"Neither do I," Machison replied with a shrug. "But he is useful. We need him to maintain the Balance."

"You're certain that the Balance isn't just a fairy tale dreamed up by the aristocrats to keep us in line?"

"As certain as I am of anything. On many things I doubt Blackholt's word, but not when it comes to the Balance. The Crown Prince confirmed it himself."

Of all the things he wished he didn't know—and there were a lot, in the League's sordid politics—the Balance sat at the top of the list.

Three hundred years ago, Darkhurst was embroiled in a bitter civil war over the crown. King Rellan's ancestor, the warrior-king Strawn Athorp, had emerged victorious, but owed his triumph to the help of a blood-sorcerer, and to an unholy bargain with the dark powers.

The entity with whom the blood sorcerer made his pact demanded tribute in blood and death. Athorp and his descendants consoled themselves with the belief that the payment was preferable to the unrelenting carnage a continued war might have caused, even as successive generations of their blood witches called monsters to the farmlands and city-states to cull the population, honoring the old debt with fear, pain, and death.

Over time, men like Gorog and witches like Blackthorn learned how to turn the Cull to their advantage, use it against rivals. They also discovered that fear of the Lord Mayor's guards, and the death dealt at their hands, helped to maintain the precious Balance as much as blood shed by monsters. More to the point, they realized the benefits of the enormous power they could draw from blood magic, but were frustrated by the requirement to personally repay the power-debt through their own life energy. The Cull became a way to 'delegate' the consequences by reaping the fear, death, and pain of those killed by the monsters.

"And *are* we maintaining the Balance?" Jorgeson asked.

Machison made a vague gesture. "So Blackholt assures me. Our status in the League helps. Pay more in gold with taxes, and less in blood for the Cull. The Crown Prince lets me know if we fall behind, reminds me that the King keeps a close eye on such things. But as often as I've asked, I've never gotten a suitable answer as to why the Balance seems to require more at some times than others, or how it can go for months at a time without needing monsters, and then needs them to Cull nearly continuously at another time."

"Or what, exactly, would happen if the Balance were not maintained?"

"I'm given to understand the outcome would be... catastrophic."

"Perhaps these are things one is better off not knowing, then."

Machison glared at him. "I have no conscience left to speak of, and I gave up expectations of a good night's sleep when I accepted this position. No, knowledge is power, no matter how repugnant the truth is."

Those who knew the truth about the Balance were a hand-picked few, sworn to secrecy on peril of dire consequences. It would not do for the Guilds and commoners to know that the same leaders who made such a show of protecting them from the monsters were the very ones who sent the scourge upon them.

The rabble were none the wiser. Talk of a cosmic 'balance' found its way into the temples from priests paid to please their masters, its essence diluted to a vague mystic tit-for-tat, a leveling of the scales of good and evil, life and death. Machison supposed the concept provided a little comfort, letting the bereaved believe that their lives and losses actually counted for something.

Machison's expression darkened. "Which brings us to the matter of the godsdamned hunters."

"The guards watch for them, arrest them when they're discovered. Like the one you interrogated. Enough of them disappear, the people won't think them so heroic."

"I want them stopped for good," Machison replied, pouring himself a measure of whiskey. "They're interfering with the Cull. Frame them for crimes; make them just a different kind of monster. We need the creatures to keep the rabble frightened. If we don't make the quota for the Cull, it'll be worse for us. Aliyev's not a merciful patron."

Jorgeson's lip curled. "The body count and the disappearances should be enough, even for Aliyev. And you can report that the Guilds have surrendered their hostages for the duration of the trade negotiations." He raised an eyebrow. "They were surprisingly agreeable."

Machison let out a harrumph. "Of course they were. They know it keeps their rival Guilds from trying to undermine the process."

"We have them safely under guard in the Tariff House, where they'll be kept in accordance with their rank—so long as the Guild Masters know their place."

The Guilds had no direct voice at the bargaining table to renegotiate the trade agreements. The actual negotiation fell to the Lord Mayors and ambassadors of the League members involved. But the Guilds and their members did control the ability of a city-state to meet its trading quotas. Forty years earlier, irate Guild Masters had called for a work stoppage, hoping to force through concessions in the negotiations to benefit individual trades. The resulting chaos had nearly scuttled the trade talks, cost a Lord Mayor his title, and nearly cost the Crown Prince his title. Since then, taking hostages from the Guilds to ensure the continued support of their members had become tradition.

Machison snorted. "That's assuming the Guild Masters give a rat's ass about the hostages they gave you. I'm not holding my breath, not when there's gold on the line and favors to be won. Probably just sent us their annoying relatives, hoping we'll get rid of them."

"You won't hear any argument from me on that, m'lord."

For a few moments, the two men fell silent as Jorgeson watched the glowing embers in the hearth and Machison nursed his whiskey. "What else?"

"My men stopped two assassins from entering the palace just this week," Jorgeson replied. "We think one of the other city-states might have been behind them, trying to scuttle the negotiations. Our suspects are pretty much everyone *except* Garenoth and Ravenwood."

Machison wasn't egotistical enough to think his own importance in the grand scheme warranted two assassination attempts in one week, or the many before that. No, the strikes were really warnings to his patron, Aliyev, or his favored partner, Gorog. *It's all a damn proxy war, fought so the highborns don't get blood on their brocade waistcoats.*

The threat of assassination came with the job; proxy strikes were the way business was conducted in the League. Some were meant to kill, others to wound—body or pride—always with the certainty that the strike could have been deadly had that been the assassin's intent. Machison reminded himself that the perks countered the dangers of his appointment, most of the time. "It would embarrass Aliyev if I were killed in the middle of negotiations."

Machison leaned back and closed his eyes for a moment. *Gods! League politics is exhausting, a game for jaded and wealthy men. Playing people like chess pieces and meddling in affairs of state, as easily as gossips trading dirty secrets over the back alley fence.*

"Any news from your spies in the other League city states?" Jorgeson inquired.

Machison nodded. "Kasten has fallen into chaos. Solencia is struggling. If Ravenwood succeeds in pressing for favorable terms with Garenoth, we keep second place in the League. So Kasten and Solencia have the most to gain if we lose our spot. They might haggle for better terms for themselves if we fell a few notches. I hear that the Cull's gone very hard on both Kasten and Solencia—paying in blood what they can't in gold."

"Kadar and Tamas and their Guilds want to tweak the terms in their favor at Gorog's expense—though we all come out ahead, retaining our place with Garenoth," Jorgeson sighed. "Greedy bastards."

Machison ran a hand over his face. Maneuvering among the competing interests was like dancing on a gallow's trap door. It was tense and tiring, but he was very good at this game. He already had the gears in motion to make sure Ravenwood came out on top, and that the agreement still favored Gorog where it mattered. If he could throw a bone to Kadar and Tamas, he would.

Crown Prince Aliyev cared only that the agreement would maintain their League ranking and keep food and gold flowing. The King cared even less—so long as he got his due. Aliyev's patronage provided advantages—like the powerful blood witch who presided over the dungeons beneath the Lord Mayor's palace. He paid little if any attention to the minutiae unless something went wrong. Machison intended to cement his plans by keeping the Guilds off-balance so that they did not tangle up the negotiations with petty bickering and pointless work stoppages.

The hostages were one means of securing cooperation, but so were carefully planted rumors. If the Guilds were busy suspecting one another of trying to get the upper hand, they paid less attention to the maneuverings of Machison and the ambassadors, where the real power lay. Should the Guilds ever put aside their differences and present a united front, they could dictate terms to the Merchant Princes, maybe even to the Crown Prince himself. Machison had every reason to ensure that did not happen.

"The Vrioni situation is well in hand," Jorgeson said. "Everything will proceed as you've planned."

"Good. The Carpenters' Guild has been causing too many distractions from the negotiations. We'll set the Guilds back on their heels and take the wind out of Kadar's sails, all in one move—nicely deflected from us."

"No one will trace it back to you. I've made certain."

"You'd bloody well better have," Machison snapped. "We can't afford a mistake."

"There won't be any mistakes," Jorgeson assured him in a cold voice.

"See that there aren't."

For just a second, Machison thought he saw annoyance in Jorgeson's eyes before the security chief's expression shut down.

"You should know, Wanderers have been seen near the harbor."

Machison cursed under his breath. "Get rid of them. Send them back to where they came from."

Jorgeson snorted. "Gladly—as soon as someone figures out where that is."

Aptly named, the nomadic clans traveled the countryside, roaming from one city-state to another as each in turn drove them out, only to see them return a few months later. The Guilds railed against the Wanderers as unregulated peddlars, thieves, and whores, but the rest of the residents laid their money down without reservation.

"In due time. But m'lord, if we play this right, the Wanderers can provide us an advantage in the short term."

"Oh?" Machison's tone made his skepticism unmistakable.

Jorgeson's expression was cagy. "Let them stay a while. Long enough for the merchants to start complaining about losing business, and the madams to scream that they're taking away clients, and everyone else to blame them for missing children, fever, and hens not laying. The Merchants' Guilds will complain that the Wanderers are engaging in unauthorized trade. We can stoke the fear. Plant the seeds, feed the rumors. Wanderers, witches, and monsters—it's a perfect storm. The city stays on edge. The Guilds are distracted by a phantom threat. Once we're done with the negotiations, our men will round the Wanderers up and get rid of the vermin."

Machison chuckled. "I knew there was a reason I kept you on payroll," he replied. He poured a glass of whiskey for Jorgeson, and slid it in his direction, then raised his own glass in a toast.

"To the future."

"Will it work?" Machison eyed the amulet skeptically. The carved bone and dried sinew lay on his desk, attached to a thin leather strap. It looked like something a child might piece together from scraps rather than a powerful talisman.

"It'll work," the blood witch said curtly. "Should keep the nightmares from actually harming you, maybe even reduce the frequency of the dreams—unless they're being sent by a *very* powerful mage."

Machison's skepticism extended to the witch who stood in front of him, a man he knew only by his alias, Kane Valdis. "That's the best you can do?"

There was a faint, knowing smile on Valdis's lips. "I assume there's a reason you asked for my help, instead of Blackholt?"

"My reasons are my own. And my need for you—and Blackholt—are not open for discussion." He paused. "What about the wardings?"

"I'll renew them. Salt, aconite, and amanita powder along the windows, doors, and hearth, to ward against evil." Valdis pulled out a pouch and started working, carefully pouring the mixture around the edges of the room. "I'll make another circle around your bed, but take care you don't smudge it, or it's for naught."

"Don't patronize me," Machison snapped.

"No offense intended."

Arrogant bastard. If he weren't so damned good at what he does, I'd entertain him in the dungeon. Maybe see how deep that arrogance goes.

Valdis walked widdershins around the bed, laying down another line of the salt mix and muttering under his breath. "Tell your servants to mind they don't disturb the lines," he added. "Everything I'm doing can be made useless by one overzealous wench with a broom."

When he finished the second circle, Valdis moved to the windows. Machison had recently reinforced the locks with heavy iron bolts, but he knew better than to trust in mundane protections which could be bested by a clever thief or skilled witch. He watched Valdis drive nails into the window frame and hang two rough charms, like the one Machison now wore around his neck.

"I can't promise this will hold against *all* witches, or a skilled thief with a powerful relic," Valdis said. "But it should slow down even the best attackers. You understand that the increased hauntings, more powerful ghosts, dangerous poltergeists—they're all side-effects from the blood magic? No one's been able to draw power from blood without riling the spirits. It's an unfortunate—and unavoidable—consequence."

"Then you need to figure out a better way to protect against such things. I would have thought you valued your own safety more highly," Machison said. "Since it is directly dependent on my continued good health."

Valdis's eyes narrowed. "I find that the people who are most certain about what magic can and cannot do are those who possess none of it themselves." His voice was even, his tone conversational, yet the rebuff was clear.

"I expect results," Machison replied. "I pay for them, I reward them. And I punish failure. It's a simple system, but it serves me well."

The cold glint in Valdis's gaze suggested that the witch did not fully trust him to keep his word. *The feeling is mutual.*

"I was clear about my abilities when you chose to retain me," Valdis replied with a shrug. "I've never represented myself as more than I am—and while I am not quite an equal to Thron Blackholt, I *am* faithful to the one who pays me."

It was a qualified loyalty, subject to terms and conditions, but Machison expected nothing else. *That's more than I get from Blackholt, even if we share the same patron.*

"I remind you to say nothing of these preparations to anyone—especially Blackholt," Machison warned. Blackholt might have been a gift to Machison from Crown Prince Aliyev, but the Lord Mayor had never really liked or trusted him. Hence Valdis, a blood witch of Machison's own choosing: a little insurance on the side.

"You purchased my discretion along with my loyalty," Valdis answered. "I have no plans to discuss your requirements with anyone, and certainly not Blackholt. I assure you that I trust him no more than you do."

Bodyguards and retainers knew the vulnerabilities of their employers; Machison saw no way around that truth. Simply by providing their services, they bore witness to the very weaknesses they covered. So he hired guards to watch his guards, a witch to protect him from his witch.

Machison held no illusions about the ability to be *truly* safe. Such a thing did not exist, certainly not within Ravenwood, or in any of the League lands. Yet bets could be hedged, odds might be nudged more in one's favor, and loopholes closed. Survival in the upper echelons of Ravenwood required constant maneuvering and the instincts of a master gamesman.

"Before you go," Machison said as Valdis gathered his materials to leave, "check the protections on my ring. I can't always have my food taster beside me." He slipped the bulky ring from his finger and passed it to the witch. The large gold signet carried the crest of the Lord Mayor's office, and it also served as his seal. Only Jorgeson, Valdis and his guards knew that the ring was enchanted to detect poison. Given the constant storm of attacks and retaliations between principals and proxies, poisonings were just another hazard of doing business.

"I've refreshed the spell," Valdis replied in a bored tone, handing the ring back. Machison slipped it onto his finger and thought he felt a frisson of energy when it touched his skin. "It will darken in the presence of all known poisons."

All known *poisons*, Machison thought. *Always wiggle room for error, but still better than nothing.* "What do your portents tell you, of the trade negotiations, and Gorog?" Machison asked as Valdis turned for the door. The witch froze.

"I'm not a seer, m'lord."

"Perhaps not, but I know you have some power of foresight. So answer the question. What do you see?"

Valdis did not turn. "Turmoil, m'lord. From whence the source, I do not know. The resolution is murky, hidden in smoke and darkness."

"Can you see who is standing when resolution comes?"

"No, m'lord. I see only flames, but what that means, I do not care to guess."

"Leave me." Machison watched Valdis go and bolted the door behind the witch. Alone, he let out a long breath and poured a measure of whiskey into a glass. It burned down his throat as he knocked it back, but did nothing to loosen the knot in his gut.

Machison refilled his glass and sat in a chair beside the fireplace, watching the embers.

In his dreams, he would often find himself running headlong toward an unknown goal. Death was on his heels, though when he looked behind him, he could see nothing but darkness. Yet the certainty of impending, inevitable doom pounded in every heartbeat—in his labored breathing, in the beat of his running footsteps. An old Wanderer woman stepped out the darkness. "It's coming," she said with a cruel smile. "The dead never forget, never forgive. Slipping through your grasp, all of it. All for naught." He pushed past her, running for his life, desperate to find his way back...

Machison swore under his breath and took another sip of his whiskey, anger rising deep in his gut.

The nightmares are likely sent by a rival's witch, meant to undermine my confidence, wear down my resolve, he thought. *I have worked too hard for too long to get where I am to be cowed by dreams and portents—especially from the likes of Wanderers. Every decision shapes the future, so surely its course is not fully set. I can alter it—I will forge it to my advantage and anyone who gets in my way will suffer for it.*

* * *

The Lord Mayor's palace glittered atop the Vista hills within the city walls of Ravenwood. Only the palaces of the Merchant Princes and Crown Prince Aliyev were more opulent. Within the banquet halls, reception rooms and salons, power-brokers transacted the business of Ravenwood, negotiating treaties, maneuvering for advantage in trade agreements, wheedling favors, and delivering veiled threats.

Deep below the palace, the dungeons concealed a world of darkness and pain. Prisoners vanished. Condemned men and women gave up their secrets to the torturer's craft, and blood witches worked the spells that summoned monsters to the neighborhoods of Ravenwood in sufficient quantities to sate the Balance.

Political prisoners filled the cells, along with men and women taken as a surety to prominent merchants and the most profitable ship's captains, all in the name of Ravenwood's fortunes. Common criminals awaited the noose in cramped, barred rooms. Unfortunate wretches were crowded into cages, useful only for their blood, which provided the energy for the cadre of witches who answered to Machison's commands. And then there were his special ones, those he found appealing to his needs, pretty and untried, perfect to quench the hunger that consumed him.

Machison hustled down the stone steps, paying the prisoners no heed. He was bound for the deepest level, the oldest part of the palace, carved out of caves and tunnels that existed long before Ravenwood was more than a small settlement on the harbor. There, Thron Blackholt worked his magic to enthrall the soul of the city-state and bring its most powerful men and its nameless rabble alike to their knees.

Breathing through his mouth blunted the worst of the stench as Machison descended the steps. As he neared Blackholt's domain, the smells changed from the odor of death and captivity to a noxious mix of potions and blood. *Running a city-state is a lot like making sausages. There's no going back after you know how the process really works.*

"What a pleasant surprise," Blackholt said as Machison entered his workroom, in a voice that said the interruption was anything but.

"Watch your tone," Machison snapped.

Blackholt had not bothered to turn as he entered. "Or?" Just a single word, in a neutral tone, but that he said it at all spoke volumes. Defiance. Indifference. Arrogance. Power. In the palace above, no one would dare speak to Lord Mayor in such a manner, but here in the depths both of them knew who held the real power. "What do you want?" the blood witch said testily.

"I've come to hear about your monsters. Are they sufficient?"

Blackholt did not temper the scorn in his expression. "Of course they are."

Machison feigned boredom. "Anything new? You've gotten rather predictable of late—ghouls, big red-eyed dogs, walking corpses. Surely you can find creatures that are a bit more… entertaining."

"This isn't theater," Blackholt snapped. "There's a reason I choose those monsters. They're efficient. They require less energy to summon. And they're stupid—and therefore easier to control."

"I've heard tales of much more frightening creatures in the lands beyond the city wall," Machison countered. "Ones that show more imagination."

"There are monsters that occur naturally," Blackholt replied with strained patience. "They're relatively few, but they tend to be smarter—able to do more than eat and fight. In some cases, as smart as a person—with more strength and teeth. I can't pull that kind of monster from the Rift, and I wouldn't if I could. Too hard to control; too much damage if they get free."

"If you don't change things up a bit, the people may learn how to fight back. Oh, wait. They already are." Machison made no attempt to hide his disdain.

"I've already thought about that," Blackholt replied with a cruel smile. "I ripped up a man's mind and filled it with the ravings of a lunatic. He's a 'prophet' now, proclaiming that the monsters herald the end of all things, sent from the gods to punish a wayward people. Nice touch, don't you think?"

"How does that help?"

"I gave him his 'script' when I imprinted my will on his mind," Blackholt said. "His head is full of the ancient tales and legends, with a twist of my own. As we speak, he's out there telling everyone who'll listen that each of the types of monsters represents a different judgment by the gods." He smirked. "That should keep the rabble cowed a while longer."

"It had better," Machison snapped. He paused. "You've heard from Aliyev?" Blackholt was the Crown Prince's creature, as was Machison, and it was Aliyev who had decided that they would be stuck with each other. *Gifts from patrons are always shackles in disguise. It takes creativity to forge a sword from chains.*

"Yes."

"And?"

"He's concerned about the Balance," Blackholt replied tonelessly. "He's as single-minded as you are about the damned monsters."

"And I've assured him that we will have the deaths he requires," Machison returned.

"It's not just about what is required in Ravenwood," Blackholt said. "This is a kingdom-wide danger—all of the city-states are at risk. The King's sorcerers draw their power from fear and death. Without sufficient energy to tap into, they won't be able to protect Darkhurst from its enemies—those outside our boundaries, and rivals to the throne from within. The Balance must be maintained. Without it, I fear the Rift may become unstable. The land itself could be poisoned. And those monsters you so love might come through on their own accord."

"How can the Balance be kept when it's not just the King's sorcerers using death magic?" Machison countered. "If Aliyev has given me you, then we can be certain that at least some of the other Crown

Princes also have death mages, maybe even some Merchant Princes. How can any kind of Balance be maintained against that draw of power? And if it fails—or if we end up killing all our subjects to sate the Balance—what then? Do we preside over a kingdom of the dead?"

"A bit dramatic, even for you," Blackholt chided. "But you're not entirely wrong. Death magic works best when worked rarely. But the secret is out now, to those with the money and ability to hire the talent. No changing that, though we're lucky that very few have the means to buy the services of a blood witch, and even fewer the ability to work the magic."

Blackholt called the source of the monsters 'the Rift' and refused to explain further, except to tell Machison it was a breach torn by the working of blood magic itself. Machison lacked Blackholt's knowledge of the arcane, but he was a keen observer: when the Balance faltered, there were nasty repercussions, including more and stronger vengeful spirits—like the ones that haunted his dreams. He had no desire to find out what might happen if the Balance ever actually failed.

"Anything else?"

"Not at the moment." Blackholt moved to turn away, and then stopped. "You and I may not always agree," the blood witch said, "but we have common cause: this goes beyond politics. The Cull must continue aggressively. Culling maintains the Balance, and without the Balance, everything dies."

Chapter Nine

"THIS IS ONE of my dumber moves," Rigan muttered as he wound through back alleys. He had left the workshop to run an 'errand'; if all went well, he would be back long before curfew.

Lately, counting on luck seemed like a dangerous thing to do.

Rigan looked around warily, and his hand went to his knife. This area of Ravenwood was dodgy at best. It was no place for a young man from a Guild trade to be wandering alone, magic or not. Rigan had not come looking for trouble. He came looking for answers.

He picked his way through the garbage-strewn alley, sidestepping the worst of the pools of piss and horse shit fouling the cobblestone. The buildings looming on either side of the street had seen better days, as had the desperate men and women watching from doorways and broken windows. Not for the first time, Rigan cursed his foolhardiness, but after his experiences Below, he had new questions he doubted the witches could answer. Maybe the Wanderers would.

He saw them ahead, a group of twenty or so, clothing and faces smudged with the dirt of the road. They were camped in a run-down plaza. Cracked tiles and broken plaster marred the central fountain, and weeds struggled from between the worn paving stones. Sigils chalked on the walls caught Rigan's attention. He had seen the Wanderers' marks here and there in the city, and had often wondered at their purpose. Up close, they looked similar to the symbols he and Corran marked on the dead, although the runes drawn here were unfamiliar. Maybe they were a secret code, directing their companions to safe shelter or homes generous with a hand-out.

"You're a long way from home." The voice, low and deep, sounded behind Rigan's left ear as the cold edge of a knife rested against his throat.

A hand slipped around to relieve him of his weapons, and then a firm grip locked onto his bicep as the man behind him walked them both into the plaza.

"Found someone spying on us," his captor said as the others looked up.

"Not spying," Rigan protested, raising his hands "I came to ask questions."

A broad-shouldered man rose from beside the fire. He had the dark hair and eyes of his people, and the dust on his clothing spoke of a life lived outdoors. He looked to be late in his third decade, with gray just starting at his temples. From the way the others hung back, Rigan guessed the man was one of the clan's leaders.

"We're easy enough to find down on the wharves all day," the big man said, his tone clearly unfriendly. "Find us there and pay your coin, and you can have plenty of answers. We don't like strangers in our camp."

"My mother had Wanderer blood," Rigan said, very aware of the blade that brushed his throat as he spoke. "Wanderer magic. It passed to me. I need to know what to do with it, how to manage."

The man's hard gaze raked Rigan up and down. "If she left us, then she left everything. She's dead to us."

"Please, I want to understand how to keep my magic—her magic—from hurting anyone."

The big man moved a step closer. "Go home. Forget you found us. We have no need of outsiders."

"Hush." An old woman made her way alongside the leader, and laid a hand on his arm. "That's enough, Zahm."

Rigan stared at the newcomer. She stood barely taller than Zahm's elbow. Many layers of clothing engulfed her petite form. Deep wrinkles lined her leathery face, but her eyes danced with amusement, and glittered with curiosity. Rigan doubted that the crone had the strength to stop Zahm from doing anything, yet the man stilled with a word.

"You're Alaine's boy." She met Rigan's gaze and he felt as if she could into see his soul.

"You knew my mother?"

"I knew *of* Alaine. I knew her mother well." She turned to the others and spoke in a language Rigan did not understand. Zahm did not look happy with the old woman's words, but he made no move against her.

"Why did you come here?" she asked, returning her attention to Rigan.

"I'm an undertaker. But I have more than grave magic. My mother told me once that I'd inherited her ability, but she died before she could tell me more. I... it's... slipped out. I need to know what to do. I thought you could—"

The old woman shook her head. "Our ways are not for outsiders. You don't keep our ways."

"Please. I don't want to accidentally hurt anyone."

Zahm said something under his breath, and the old woman made a curt reply that caused Zahm to close his mouth and take a step back.

"You fear your magic?" she asked, moving closer.

"I'm afraid of what could happen if I can't control it," Rigan admitted. "I mean you no harm. I'll leave—"

The old woman snapped an order, and the man behind Rigan

dropped his hand, removing the blade from his throat. A thin trickle of blood slipped down Rigan's neck from a shallow cut.

"What do you wish to know?"

"Is my magic—the Wanderer magic—different from what the witches Below can do?"

The old woman considered him for a moment before answering. "Yes and no."

"Is this power the reason I can hear the confessions of the dead?"

The woman tilted her head, looking up at him and paused as if she were listening to something only she could hear. Rigan had no doubt that she was one of the clan's seers, probably a powerful witch herself. *If she decides I'm dangerous, will she just have her man finish me off?* he wondered.

"So *you're* the one," she said quietly. She looked up at Zahm and spoke again in their language. Zahm frowned and argued back. Whispers moved through the group behind him. "What would you do with your magic, if you could control it?" she continued.

"I don't mind hearing the confessions of the dead—it helps them find peace—but I hurt someone by accident and I don't want that to happen again."

The old woman gave him a shrewd look. "Would you fight monsters?"

Rigan stared at her, surprised by the question. "I'm not a hunter. I just bury people."

"Do you know why your grandmother left our people?"

"Mama never talked about her family... about anything from before she married my father."

"One of the Lord Mayor's guards raped your grandma, boy. Her parents weren't the forgiving kind. She ran away, ashamed, afraid the clan wouldn't accept her child. I tracked her, kept an eye on her, but she wouldn't return to us, though she let me help when your mama was born. Kept body and soul together as a bar maid, and your mama did, too, when she got old enough. 'Tis how she met your father."

Rigan's face reddened. "She never said—"

"Of course she didn't. But her mother, Netana, had a goodly measure of magic. Seems like it bred true in Alaine, and in you."

"I guess so." He hesitated. "If they had magic, why didn't they defend themselves?"

"I don't know," the old woman replied. "Can't do magic if you're drugged or unconscious. Maybe threats were made, against others. We won't ever know."

Or maybe they had control I don't, and refused to kill. "Can you help me?" Rigan asked.

"It's not for stubbornness that I can't train you," the woman said, her voice softening a little. "The magic we work is very old. It comes from Eshtamon himself. What we do in the marketplace, telling fortunes, reading palms, that's but a shadow of the power."

Zahm chided her and she silenced him with a glare and a sharp word. "The old magic struggles to keep the Balance. But it's magic we must work as a clan. I can't tell you more than that. You would have to leave your life behind and come with us, forever."

"I can't do that. My brothers need me."

She nodded. "That is why I can't train you," she went on. "Your path follows a different road than ours. Train with the witches Below, but be careful; things are not always as they seem. I can aid you, in my own way."

"Thank you," Rigan managed, trying to hide his disappointment. He glanced warily at Zahm. "Will you grant me safe passage from here? And may I have my knife back?"

The old woman chuckled and spoke to the man behind Rigan, who handed back his dagger and stepped to one side to allow Rigan to go.

"Do not come back," Zahm said. "For your safety, and ours. Go, and may the Elder Gods go with you."

Rigan only realised how badly his hands were shaking when he was halfway home. He had been careful not to run; he didn't want to attract the attention of the guards. Now he fell back against a filthy wall and let the tremors wrack him.

Gods, what a chance I took! And for nothing. He knew from the start that he was likely on a fool's errand. *What if they'd slit my throat? That would have left Corran and Kell in the lurch.*

"Of all the stupid, reckless things to do!" Damian's voice shook Rigan from his thoughts, and he looked up to see the witch striding toward him.

"What are you doing here?" Rigan managed.

"Watching out for you! Baker had a premonition, and I came up to check on you. By the time I found you, you'd already gone to the bloody Wanderers. What possessed you to do such a thing?"

"My mother's people—"

"And you've seen how much that matters to them," Damian cut him off. "Didn't I promise to train you? Haven't I saved your life once already?"

"I just thought—"

"You obviously *didn't* think. You put yourself in danger, and for nothing."

"I'm sorry," Rigan said, swallowing hard. Corran would be annoyed at him for being gone so long, and would have questions about the cut on his throat. Now he'd jeopardized his one chance to gain control of his magic and possibly alienated his teacher.

"Good. That's a start." Damian pulled him away from the wall and hustled him toward the main thoroughfare. "We're close to an entrance to Below."

"I can't—"

"This isn't a game," Damian said, jerking Rigan around to look at him. "Do you want the guards to take you to the Lord Mayor? To have him force you to serve him? Because stumbling around with that sort of power, untrained, is going to land you in the dungeon. Either you're going to kill someone, or you're going to get snatched. It's time you took this seriously."

Rigan shook his head, pulling away. "I *am* taking this seriously. But I can't leave my brothers. I'm sorry. Please, I'll come back as often as I can. Just... train me. I don't want to be a danger."

Damian glared at him, before herding Rigan down the steps of a nearby cellar. "Come on. We have time for a training session before curfew. The night won't be a *total* loss."

Rigan followed, fighting back his shame. Damian said nothing more until they reached the house of the witches. Baker met him at the door and Rigan hung back.

"You found him?"

"He was lucky," Damian replied. "One of them had a knife to his throat."

"You were right to go after him," Baker said, laying a hand on Damian's forearm. She looked past him to Rigan, worry clear in her eyes, then gave Damian's arm a squeeze. "Leave him with me tonight."

Rigan did not catch Damian's response, but he walked away, shaking his head. Baker waited until he was gone before she motioned for Rigan to enter. "He'll get over it," she said.

"I didn't mean to do anything foolish," he said, eyes downcast, feeling shame burning his cheeks.

"You're not reckless. I've seen enough of you to know that. Come talk with me in the kitchen. I'll make tea."

"Shouldn't I be training?" Practicing his magic was the last thing Rigan felt up to doing, but he desperately wanted to atone, to regain the witches' trust.

"Training takes many forms. Follow me."

Rigan did as she bid him. The kitchen looked remarkably mundane. More bundles of dried herbs than most homes, perhaps, but otherwise, nothing about it suggested that the inhabitants were witches. Baker took a pot from the coals in the fireplace and poured them two steaming cups of tea.

"Drink. There's little that can't be helped by a good cup of tea."

Rigan let the tea's fragrance soothe him. "I thought the Wanderers could help me," he said finally. "I thought they might know more about Mama's magic."

"And they do. But they don't share outside their clans."

Rigan gave a self-deprecating snort. "Yeah. Found that out."

"Why did you go to them instead of coming back to us?"

He looked down into his cup for a moment before answering. "I thought that sharing their blood would count for more," he said quietly. "Mama never told us how her grandmother left the clan. Maybe she didn't know the truth herself. I know it seems foolish now, but I thought there might be something particular about her magic that was different from what you do down here."

"The magic we practice—that we'll teach you—comes from the energy of the world around us, the natural currents of power," Baker replied. "Blood magic comes from death; a primal, destructive energy. From everything I have observed, the Wanderers' magic has the same source as ours. Intent is also key. Magic used for greed or in vengeance corrodes the soul and will eventually destroy the witch."

"Then I'm doomed. Because I've killed with magic."

Baker shook her head. "Self-defense is not the same as vengeance. I speak of cold retribution, hatred nurtured over time."

"She said that her people serve Eshtamon, and that they try to preserve the Balance."

Baker raised an eyebrow. "Did she, now?"

"What does the Balance have to do with magic? People talk about it like it's the gods balancing fortune and misfortune, as if something good happening in one place has to cause something bad to happen elsewhere."

Baker snorted. "The same fools blame witches for bad ale and the moon for spoiled cheese. *I* know that the Balance is real, and that currents of power flow through this world that few understand and fewer still can control. Perhaps the witches of the Crown Princes and the King understand such things, perhaps not. I've concerned myself with more practical magic. If you're looking for insight into the Balance, I don't think any of the witches Below have that kind of knowledge. Maybe the monks did, back before the monasteries fell. But not now."

"Is it a secret, or a mystery?" Rigan asked.

"In a way, all magic seeks a balance. There is equilibrium in not drawing more power from your life force than you can sustain, in learning to tap into the air, water, earth, and fire around you, enough to achieve your purpose and not harm yourself. You have to understand when to use magic and when to not to, when to intervene, and when to let things take their course." Baker smiled at him. "Perhaps you should worry about actually *using* your magic before you ponder the unknowable."

"I didn't mean to make Damian angry, and I didn't intend to seem ungrateful for all you've done." Rigan kept his eyes averted.

"You're young and curious, burdened with a power you've only just discovered and have yet to harness. These are dangerous times, and you fear for your family. Your decision might have been unwise, but it was made for sound reasons."

"So you'll still train me?"

Baker chuckled. "Yes. In fact, I've got just the thing to start us off." She pushed the cup of now-cool tea toward him. "Magic isn't always about power. Most of the time, finesse is more important. It would be easy to use your magic to smash the cup, but I want you to use it to warm the tea."

Rigan's eyes went wide. "I don't know how!"

"Power flows from intent. Think about warming the tea. You don't have to make it boil. Just... make it warmer."

Rigan stared at the cup, utterly at a loss. He closed his eyes and took a deep breath, thinking about holding the cup in his hands, feeling the smooth sides against his fingers, imagining how it would tingle in his grip if the tea were hot.

"That's it," Baker encouraged. "Just a little more."

Rigan realized he had squeezed his eyes shut and pursed his lips in concentration, willing warmth into the amber liquid. All of a sudden, Baker yelped and Rigan's eyes flew open. Steam rose from the tea, and Baker shook her hand.

"Nicely done. You see? Learning to control your magic isn't always about grand gestures and big displays. The most powerful magic often requires delicacy. You've done well tonight."

"Damian won't throw me out?"

Baker shook her head. "Give him a few days. He'll get over it. Nothing has changed. You're welcome here, and it would be best for everyone if you come often. But now I think you'd best get back to your brothers. I'll walk you to the nearest passage to the surface."

"Thank you," Rigan replied, setting his empty cup aside. "For everything."

Chapter Ten

"IF YOU WANT additional protection, you'll have to pay for it." Machison leaned back in his chair and folded his hands across his ample stomach.

Dagan Sarca, Master of the Smiths' Guild, was not ready to let the matter rest. "Our members pay their taxes. Surely those taxes should entitle us to protection by—and *from*—the Lord Mayor's guards?" Sarca was slim, with sharp features and cold dark eyes that missed nothing.

"Maintaining the Guards is expensive," Machison countered. "It all costs money. Our League ranking already earns Ravenwood additional money from the King for defense—one of the benefits of keeping that favored agreement status with Garenoth, need I remind you."

"And we know that those guards keep the villas safe from monsters and assassins," Sarca shot back. "Wheareas down in Wrighton and Skinton and Harbordon, where the rest of us live..."

"Monsters go where they go," Machison said with a shrug. "And there are plenty of guards in the lower city. But there won't be, if these negotiations don't succeed. We need the Guilds in support.

All of the Guilds. Must I remind you about what we stand to lose? Right now, our preferred terms with Garenoth gets Ravenwood the first, best shipments from their farms. Fresh produce, not the rotting left-overs. Those go to Kasten and Solencia. We pay half the import fees as well, keeping materials cheap enough for *you* to turn a profit. Lose our favorable terms, and your goods get too expensive for people to buy them."

"Then see to the godsdamned agreement and let us get on with our business," Ragh Lazin snapped. He was Master of the Vintners' Guild, and his temper was as wild as his white hair. "And I've noticed that for all your talk, the guards have not rid us of Wanderers, which are the worst of the vermin."

Lazin didn't have to elaborate; the other Guild Masters saw the nomads as he did. They suspected them of making wells run dry, chickens stop laying, and children to fall ill. Merchants hated them for their unlicensed peddling, and the Guilds despised them for providing services without membership. Only the wharf rats drew more ire.

"Forget the Wanderers. What good is the new trade agreement going to do *us?*" Raston Zabak, the representative for the Artisans' Guild, demanded, half-rising from his seat in indignation. He was perpetually red-faced, with a large, florid nose and broad, pig-like features. "The artists of Ravenwood produce one-of-a-kind treasures for patrons. Will the agreement get us better prices on the pigments we import?"

The Council of Guild Masters had convened in the palatial Guild Hall, and had invited the Lord Mayor to dine with them. Machison had accepted the invitation fully aware that it was likely to end in a brawl. His bodyguards stood behind him, visibly armed, just in case anyone was tempted to be rash. A delectable meal and a goblet of the finest wine went untouched in front of him, though the others ate and drank with relish. While his ring assured him the food and drink were not poisoned, he was not hungry enough to test his luck.

"How do you think we feel? The Garenoth agreement isn't going to import the dead," Harb Orlo, Guild Master of Undertakers, retorted. "And we pay the same fees you do. We deserve better for our coin," he added, fixing Machison with a stare. "We don't benefit from trade, so the least you could do is ensure enough guards to keep our people safe from monsters."

"Kasten and Solencia lost their favorable agreements with their trading partners a year ago," Machison said. "Look what's happened. The King reduced their allotment of guards and criminals took to the streets, killing as many residents as the monsters they claimed to hunt. Their city-states get the last of the harvest; and there wasn't enough to go around last time, so they went hungry. The prices of their materials went up and they had to charge more for their goods, so no one buys from them. It's bad enough that there's talk of carving up both territories and giving the bits to neighboring states."

He did not share with them that some of the hardship befalling Kasten and Solencia came from bearing a heavier toll from the Cull, since their residents and merchants were more valuable to the King dead than alive.

A shocked gasp went round the table. "The Crown Princes wouldn't allow it," Sarca challenged.

"They'll allow what the King requires. The situation got bad enough that King Rellan himself had to get involved, and he doesn't like that," Machison replied. "Now do you see why we can't let your bickering get in the way of this agreement?"

"This meeting isn't about the agreement, it's about the monsters." Aviano Vrioni, head of the Carpenters' Guild, rarely spoke, but when he did, others listened. He was tall and spare, with a long face and mournful eyes. "Don't forget our purpose." He slapped his hand on the table. "We are here to demand that the Lord Mayor spend more of the Guild taxes we pay him to protect us. We accomplish nothing if we fight among ourselves."

Machison watched the conversation with an unreadable expression born of long experience. *Oh, you accomplish a great deal if you argue. You remain divided, which makes my job so much easier.*

Part of his role as Lord Mayor of Ravenwood was to broker peace among its various constituencies. The commoners required little negotiation; the strong presence of the guards ensured their compliance. But many residents were tradesmen and merchants, and while they had little power as individuals, the Guilds kept alive the economy of the city-state, and gathered as a council, they had significant commercial power. If they ever stopped sparring with each other, they might present a serious threat. The Lord Mayor spent a good bit of his time and energy assuring that the Guilds always remained at odds.

Yet during the touchy negotiations between Ravenwood and Garenoth, Machison could not afford ill-timed remarks or aggressive maneuvering by the Guilds. Hence the hostages; a guarantee that the Guilds would remain on a short leash, complaining as always, but effectively defanged.

"The smiths pay more than their share," Sarca continued. "We pay tax on the wood for our forges and smelters, and we have to pay *another* fee to have our goods loaded onto ships."

"So charge more for your bloody iron," Lazin snapped. "Vintners pay a tax on our land and a barrel assessment. Our prices reflects that."

"Don't blame the coopers," Vrioni argued. "We have nothing to do with the tax. We pay fees of our own, for over-priced iron barrel hoops and nails."

"If you don't like the price of iron, do without it," Sarca returned. "We pay taxes and fees that you don't. It has to come back to us in the price."

"I'm tired of hearing the lot of you whine," Vrioni growled. "Carpentry's hard work—not like squeezing a few grapes," he said, glaring at Lazin. "Dangerous work, too."

"Especially if your members are the ones doing the building," Taj Ruci retorted. "So drunk they can't build a wall straight."

"The only thieves worse than the merchants are the whores," Vrioni replied, his lip curling in a sneer. "I knew it was a mistake attending this meeting. A complete waste of time. Five of the Guilds didn't even bother to come." He looked to Machison. "I've suggested more than once we split the Council—half for the real trades, and the other half for everyone else."

Machison sighed. Vrioni's views were well known, and he repeated them as often as anyone would listen. In his mind, only the 'muscular' trades like carpentry, smithing, ship building, and tanning were Guild-worthy. The rest—glassmakers, shopkeepers, tavern masters, distillers, weavers, potters, cobblers and tailors, chandlers, artists, and others—he viewed as too pedestrian for Guild status. It was an opinion that did not win him friends on the Council.

"I can't see where the artisans gain any advantage from the negotiations," Zabak insisted. "We pay a premium for our pigments and a fee to import rare materials, but we won't gain foreign patrons from the Alliance."

"You eat, don't you? Nice to have enough plenty of food of all kinds on a regular basis that's not full of worms when it comes off the ships," Sarca challenged. "And while I'm all for getting more guards, I've got no desire to lose the ones the King sends us, or have to charge so much for our goods that we're beggared when no one can buy."

Machison had learned long ago that if he allowed his antagonists to do the talking, they would fight his battles for him. He struggled to keep a satisfied smile from his lips. *There's only one harbor in Ravenwood. There's nowhere else to take their precious trade. Prices only ever go one way—up. It's the way of the world.*

"We came here to talk about the trade agreement with Garenoth. Continuing the current arrangement serves the Merchant Princes, but the terms aren't equally favorable to all the Guilds, and it's time to fix that. Another ten years of those terms will put some of us in the poor house, even given our favored status with Garenoth—and there is no trade at all without the Guilds to make what goes into the holds of those ships!" Lazin growled. "We want a say in the negotiations."

"The agreement isn't fair to the smaller Guilds," Zabak argued. "That has to be addressed."

"You bring in less of the money, account for less of the trade," Vrioni shot back. "So you get less of the profits, and have less of a voice."

"The Guilds get better terms in some of the other city-states," Zabak persisted.

"Those city-state have different resources," Sarca practically shouted. "Different Guilds get favored because their trades bring in the most money. That has no bearing on our agreement."

"This meeting isn't about the Garenoth agreement," Orlo repeated. "It's about getting our due for the fees we pay for the guards. It's about having the guards do their jobs and kill the monsters—instead of their own people. And if they won't do their jobs, then they need to leave the hunters alone."

Machison stirred at that. He leaned forward. "Make more money, and the King will send more guards. Are you alleging that my guards are derelict in their duty?" His voice was low and level. "That's a very serious charge. I hope you have proof. Doubly so, if you're supporting brigands like the hunters."

Machison had no doubt that guards demanded more than the merchants and tradespeople were required to pay, or that they pocketed the difference, or that they roughed up whomever they pleased to reinforce who was in charge. Just another cost of doing business. But proof would be impossible to find. No one would be foolish enough to bear witness—or survive long if they did.

"I was making a comparison, m'lord," Orlo backtracked, reddening. "I did not mean to accuse."

I'm quite sure you meant every word, Machison thought, enjoying Orlo's discomfort. *But you also know not to make an enemy of me. Let's see you get out of this one.*

The sound of an empty goblet clanging like a bell against the edge of the table silenced them all.

"My Lord Mayor," Candra Pask, the head of the Weavers' and Dyers' Guild, said. The authority in her voice silenced the others; none wanted to fall victim to her sharp tongue. "We fear for our safety. People go missing. Unspeakable creatures hunt our alleys. We pay our fees for the protection of the guards. Give us the security we've paid to receive." Pask crossed her thin arms over her chest and gave Machison a steely glare.

"My good lady," Machison said, mustering as sincere a smile as he could manage. "You've gotten to the heart of the issue. The guards that are now in Ravenwood—and patrolling the boroughs of Wrighton and Skinton—are exactly what you have paid for, plus those allotted from the King. If you want more protection, I'm afraid it will require higher fees."

Pask's expression made clear her thoughts, but she said nothing. Taj Ruci spoke up instead. "I have been asked to speak on behalf of the Shopkeepers' Guild as well as the Taverns and Distillers. Guild Master Pask is right, Ravenwood is beset with disappearances and plagued by monsters. People will risk the possibility of having their pockets picked to do their shopping or go to a tavern, but they won't come if they fear for their lives."

"Surely you exaggerate," Machison said smoothly. "I hear no such dire news from the guards who patrol the streets long into the night. A few incidents, yes; there are always runaways and stowaways, or those who leave to seek their fortunes outside the city walls. As for the 'monsters'—feral animals taken with fever can be vicious and behave strangely. You mustn't let wild talk affect business."

Vrioni leaned forward as if to speak, and then froze. He toppled from his chair with a grimace. He convulsed, and vomited with such force that those seated near him scattered to avoid being soiled. The Guild Masters gasped and drew back in fear.

Lazin turned to Orlo. "You're the undertaker. Do something!"

Orlo gave him a withering glance. "He needs a healer, not a gravedigger." He glared at Machison. "Call one now!"

Machison motioned to one of the guards, gave a hushed order, and sent him on his way.

Vrioni had grown deathly pale. His eyes were wide, pupils dilated. He moaned and clutched his abdomen, rolling in pain. He had emptied his stomach and voided his bowels, and the smell was overpowering.

"The wine! Someone's poisoned the wine!" Candra Pask exclaimed. She rounded on Lazin. "You're the vintner. What's wrong with your wine?"

"Nothing!" Lazin argued. "We all drank from the same bottle—even me. So you can take back your slander!"

"If someone meant to make an end to all of us, we'd be on the floor already," Sarca said. "There might have been something in Vrioni's wine, but it didn't come from the bottle."

Machison called to another guard. "I want to know which servers poured the wine. Get them in a room and don't let them go until we can get to the bottom of this." He even managed to look outraged, with just the right degree of unsettled surprise. *A good performance, if I do say so myself.*

The second guard went to do the Lord Mayor's bidding. It was several minutes later when the first guard returned with an older man, somewhat out of breath, with long grey hair and the robes of a healer. "What's wrong with him?" Machison demanded, pointing at Vrioni.

The healer regarded Vrioni without getting close enough to soil his robe. He closed his eyes and stretched out one hand over the Guild Master's writhing form. "Arsenic," he proclaimed a moment later, opening his eyes. "It's likely he's been poisoned with it for weeks. It builds up in the body's humors. What he consumed today pushed his body to its limits." He looked to Machison. "There's nothing I—or anyone—can do for him. It's just a matter of time until he's dead."

"Was it the wine?" Pask had regained her composure. "That's his goblet," she added, pointing at the cup where Vrioni had been seated.

The healer walked over and once again let his palm hover above the vessel. "Arsenic," he said. "Definitely not accidental."

The surviving Guild Masters traded glances. "Lazin's right: if it were in the bottle, we'd all be dead," Orlo said.

"Not necessarily," Sarca replied. "Arsenic takes time to kill. Maybe someone's been poisoning Vrioni for a long while and a large final dose just did him in. We could have all drunk poison, and the effects don't show—yet."

"Tell us," Pask said, looking to the healer. "Was the poison in all the wine?"

The healer moved around the table, holding his hand in turn over each goblet. Finally, he shook his head. "There was no arsenic in any cup but his," he replied with a glance toward Vrioni.

Vrioni lay still, eyes closed. The labored rise and fall of his chest was the only indication that he was still alive. "He's not going to wake up," the healer said. "It might take a day or two for him to die, but the damage is done."

"Move him to one of the unoccupied rooms, and get someone in here to clean up the mess," Machison ordered. "Make him as comfortable as you can."

Two of the guards bent to pick up Vrioni, and carried him from the room. Servants began mopping up the vomit, while others cleared away the goblets.

"Is that all, m'lord?" the healer asked.

"Watch over Guild Master Vrioni until he dies. If you can ease his suffering, do so. When he passes, notify the undertakers to come for the body. Whatever the cause, he is entitled to a burial befitting his rank." *And the bill will be sent to his Guild.*

"We still don't know how the poison got into his goblet," Pask said. "Or who put it there. Or why someone wanted Vrioni dead badly enough to make a move *here* of all places."

"I have no idea why Vrioni was murdered or who did it, but the fact that the killing was done here, on neutral ground, should be a warning to all of us. We're not safe until the guards find the murderer," Lazin added.

"Look to the trades that use arsenic," Orlo commented, studiously avoiding eye contact with anyone. "Everyone knows it goes with smelting—and glassmaking. I've heard artists use it in their paints." He shrugged. "That should narrow it down."

"Are you suggesting that I or my members had anything to do with this?" Sarca shot back indignantly. "Because if you are, I'll see you on the dueling grounds!"

"Orlo is talking out of his ass." Zabak's face was red with anger. "Of course he's suggesting we killed Vrioni. I am outraged at such an allegation against the honor of the Artisans' Guild. We had nothing to do with killing that horrid man. Nothing!"

Pask rolled her eyes. "Don't flatter yourselves," she said. "We all know Vrioni's fondness for cheap whores and expensive mistresses. I doubt it's about business, but he's left such a trail of wronged lovers it might take all year to interview the suspects."

"Given the circumstances—and the fact that not all of the Guilds have been represented here—I'm going to table this discussion until a later time," Machison interposed. "After all, the Carpenters' and Coopers' Guild will need time to select a replacement, after the days of mourning are completed."

"By then, the Merchant Princes will have already gotten their way over the trade alliance," Lazin grumbled.

"Seemly or not, we want to be at the table for the negotiations," Morina repeated. "And we are prepared to make it worth your while."

After all the shouting was finished, it always came down to money.

"What did you have in mind?" Machison asked.

"A man is dead!" Cela objected. "Surely this discussion can wait?"

Morina rounded on him. "Vrioni wanted to change the Garenoth agreement to give more favorable terms to the vintners and distillers, because the coopers raised a hue and cry. More wine and spirits means more barrels, and more money for the coopers. Without his objections, we might be able to work out a compromise that works for all our members. Our livelihoods depend on this being handled correctly."

"The shipwrights would say that, of course," Orlo said. "You win by default if trade increases."

"And so do you if more ships bring more sailors and traders, some of which will die in Ravenwood," Morina shot back. "Plenty do."

Unspoken beneath the tension in the room lay the fact that some Guilds—and Merchant Princes—wanted a bigger share of the profits in the new agreement, whittling Gorog's advantage, while those who currently benefited had no desire to see the terms change. While the Coopers and Carpenters relied on Gorog's timber for their trade, Kadar's vineyards and Garenoth's distilleries and breweries played an oversized role in the Coopers' profits, and other Guilds that felt squeezed out wanted a bigger piece of the action. Lazin, representing the Vintners' Guild, was definitely loyal to Kadar and coveted more of the profits.

Yet what was good for individual Guilds did not always work in Ravenwood's overall favor. Machison, more than the Guild Masters, was mindful that what mattered to Crown Prince Aliyev—and ultimately, to King Rellan—was the total amount of gold brought in by trade, not the share that each Guild took. In the background as the Guilds quarreled, the other League city-states watched and waited, standing to gain if Ravenwood lost its favored status, which provided a powerful incentive to meddle.

Morina gave Lazin a cold look. "You and Vrioni were the only two opposed to the agreement. He's dead. You would stand alone on this, against the interests of the other Guilds and Ravenwood? That might be... unwise."

Lazin paled as the implication of the statement and Vrioni's sudden reversal of fortune sank in. Machison saw a flicker of fear in his eyes.

"My good Guild Masters," Machison interposed. "I suggest that we table this discussion until tempers are quieted. There will be time enough to sort things out later." While the meeting might not have gone in the direction the Guild Masters had desired, for Machison's own purposes, it had been quite productive.

ONCE HE LEFT the quarrelsome Guild Masters, Machison returned to the Lord Mayor's palace, where he retired to his private chambers. Hant Jorgeson arrived a few minutes later.

"Well done," Machison said, pouring them both a glass of whiskey. "Plenty of suspects; no tears shed. The arsenic was a nice touch."

Jorgeson nodded, accepting the praise. "You want arrests made?"

"Vrioni was a pain in the ass. Plenty of other people felt the same way. Question suspects, but spread the blame widely. Let the rest of the Guild Masters stew in their own juices, wondering who the killer is. The more time they spend pointing fingers, the less time they have to be a thorn in my side."

"I have spies in all the Guilds," Jorgeson replied. "I'll keep you apprised of what is said, who's falling under suspicion."

"And make an example of the guards who were supposed to be protecting me," Machison added. "Let them think I was rattled by death striking so close. The guards were sloppy; make sure the next ones are more diligent."

"Yes, m'lord."

"Your plan is working. The Guilds are starting to complain about the Wanderers," Machison said, changing the subject. Dragging the Wanderers into his plans had gone against his best instincts: he mistrusted their secretive manner and rogue magic as much as he hated their dirty faces and thieving ways. *And my dreams about a crazy old Wanderer woman threatening my life certainly don't help.* Still, it seemed to be bearing fruit.

"We've been running off the Wanderers too, but not in earnest yet, until their usefulness is done. They'd only come back again, like roaches. A few of the ship's captains are willing to take the fit prisoners off our hands and pay us a pretty price for them. That might do for some of the Wanderers. Might actually put the fear of the gods in them, with all their talk of loving freedom: being chained up in a ship's galley." He chuckled at the thought. "We'll hang some of them, once we go after them in earnest, and just finish off the rest." He shrugged. "Hang too many people too often, even vagabond scum, and the locals get uncomfortable."

"And they don't when people just disappear?" Machison replied. "Cut off some hands or put a few of the thieves in stocks—that's a good deterrent too. If you hang *every* dishonest man in Ravenwood, there'll be no one left to pay taxes."

Jorgeson chuckled. "I will make sure the men limit their sport, m'lord." He paused for a moment, as if he wanted to ask a question, then thought better of it.

"The guards are going to need to be a bit more visible when the monsters attack," Machison said. "I know they keep the creatures out of the better areas, and the Merchant Princes pay us well for that, but the Guilds are starting to make noise about not getting the protection they're paying for, so order your men to be seen more in Wrighton killing monsters. Be smart about it; we can't risk jeopardizing the Balance, but we can't completely antagonize the Guilds and the commoners. If the guards put on a good show, make it look like they're risking their lives to protect the residents, it'll be harder for the rabble to lionize the hunters. Proves you did your part, and, after all, you can't be everywhere at once."

"It will be done, m'lord."

"Oh… one more thing. Vrioni had daughters. The younger one—dark hair and bright eyes—it would be a shame if she were to disappear in this difficult time. But sad things happen during times of grief."

"Yes sir. It certainly would add to the tragedy of these difficult times," Jorgeson responded with a smile.

Once Jorgeson was gone, Machison moved aside a tapestry by the fireplace, revealing a concealed door, then lit a lantern and descended the hidden stone steps.

The air smelled of torch smoke and charred flesh, with the coppery tang of blood above all.

"I wasn't sure you had the balls to come back to me so soon." Blackholt's sneering tone reflected his certainty that the Lord Mayor posed him no danger.

Machison gritted his teeth, and reminded himself of Blackholt's value. As for the mage's confidence that he was untouchable, Machison was working intently to change that fact, and perhaps if Valdis proved himself, he might soon be rid of Blackholt, permanently.

Thron Blackholt presided over the dungeons as if he believed he was Doharmu himself. Many of the unfortunates who disappeared from Ravenwood's streets ended up here, their blood used in Blackholt's dark rites.

One of those wretches lay bound and spread-eagled on a table, eyes wide with fear, chest hitching with panic. Deep cuts had opened the veins in the man's forearms and inner thighs. Bright red blood drained from the wounds into the grooves on the table, funneled into bowls set at the corners. From the pallor of the victim's skin and his glazed eyes, Machison guessed the man had only minutes left before he bled dry.

"What do you want?" Blackholt said.

"We need to maintain the Balance. The Guilds are looking to upset the trade talks, so I want you to direct the monsters to punish them. Start with the Coopers and the Vintners. We can't allow the Guilds to find common cause, or the city dwellers to unify."

"I told you that I would see to that, and I will." Blackholt's self-assurance set Machison's teeth on edge. "You have seen evidence of my handiwork." The blood witch picked up one of the bowls of blood, barely glancing at the dying man, and took it to his work table, where he poured a measure into a glass sphere and set the rest of the bowl aside.

"I'm not sure that what you're doing is enough," Machison said.

"There is a fine line between terrifying people into submission and pushing them to the point where they have nothing to lose, making them reckless and dangerous. We risk everything if we go too far." As Machison watched in sickened fascination, Blackholt swirled the blood around the vessel until the entire sphere was coated, before holding it up between them.

"Behold."

At Blackholt's word, the sanguine film rippled. In the scarlet orb, Machison saw creatures that might have been ghouls ripping their way through an alleyway and the lower levels of a house. As he watched—fascinated and horrified—the creatures tore into their victims, rending them apart, and feasting on the bodies before the last of the blood pumped from them.

"Three monster attacks tonight, targeting the most troublesome Guilds," Blackholt said. The image in the blood vanished, and the dark witch set the crimson-stained orb aside. "Sufficient for your purposes, don't you think?"

"When I get the results I want, that's when your work is 'sufficient,'" Machison snapped.

"Have a care how you address me. I serve your master, not you."

"You were *given* to me, not loaned," Machison shot back. "Have a care yourself. We rise or fall together."

"And if the Balance breaks? What then? A new King? Return to civil war?"

"Unpleasant and undesirable, but survivable," Machison countered. "You've got to make the monster attacks count—make certain they're targeting the right people. We can only kill so many of the residents before the rest rise up against us."

"What the Balance holds at bay is far worse." Blackholt made no attempt to disguise the contempt in his voice.

"If the commoners storm the palace and burn us for our sins, we will be dead; and if the Balance does not hold, we will be dead," Machison countered. "We have an equilibrium of our own to maintain."

Blackholt snorted. "If the Balance doesn't hold, death is not the worst of it. Right now, the monsters do our bidding. Their numbers are manageable, and the creatures we summon are not the worst of their kind. If the Balance is not maintained, the walls between our world and the Dark Places will grow thin. Breaches will occur. We will be consumed."

Machison regarded Blackholt. "I've heard many a warning about the end of the world," he said. "None have come true. But push men too far, give them nothing to lose, and they rebel. On that, you can be assured. I worry more about what's likely than what's possible."

"Spare me." Blackholt turned away. "I will increase the diversions—but in my own way and as I see fit. If you don't like that, I suggest you take it up with Crown Prince Aliyev."

"Your service is appreciated," Machison ground out through clenched teeth. He cast a disapproving glance toward the corpse on the table. "Try not to decimate the population before they can pay their taxes."

He has got to die, and soon. Valdis must work more quickly.

* * *

Later that night, long after curfew, the guards announced that Guild Master Sarca had come to pay a call. "Bring him to my library," Machison ordered. He straightened his collar and smoothed a hand over his thinning hair, checking his reflection in a mirror. Sarca's appearance this late could only mean that the Guild Master had information, or business he did not wish to discuss in front of the full Council. Machison smiled. *He's running late. I expected to hear from him a candlemark ago.*

"Come in," Machison replied when the guard knocked on the library door. He rose from a chair near the fireplace as if he had just been at leisure.

"Guild Master Sarca," he said, affecting a tone of mild surprise. "What can I do for you, at this hour? Please, come in. Would you like a whiskey?"

Machison poured liquor for both of them, and gestured for Sarca to sit in a chair near the fire. They both knew this was not a social call. A hardness in Sarca's eyes told Machison that his guest understood and resented the advantage the Lord Mayor gained by meeting on his own territory.

"Vrioni's death leaves a void," Sarca said. "The Guild is meeting tomorrow to elect a new Master. They don't want to be left out of the talks."

"Interesting. And do you know who the candidates are?"

Sarca licked his lips nervously. "Two names have come up: Inton Throck and Hess Stanton. They're among the most senior members of the Carpenters' Guild's inner council."

"Continue."

"Throck is Merchant Prince Kadar's favorite to succeed Vrioni, from what I hear. He's seen as tough, and willing to fight for what Kadar wants. That means trying to rewrite terms and shortchange the rest of us. He could get in the way of a new agreement with Garenoth. He'd be good for the carpenters—and a headache for the rest of us."

"And Stanton?"

"He's the preference of the rest of the Guild Masters. Easier to work with, less dogged, and happy with the deal the carpenters get under the current agreement with Garenoth. He won't get in the way with the negotiations, and he's well-liked by the members."

"So Stanton favors Gorog?" Machison asked. Old alliances and long-standing treaties meant that no one was completely his own person, not the Guild Masters or the Merchant Princes—or even the Lord Mayor himself.

Sarca shrugged. "Yes. Throck's a cooper, with a long-standing association with the Vintners' and Distillers' Guilds, like Vrioni before him. He's sure to side with their demand to renegotiate. Stanton's a carpenter; he'll side more with the Shipwrights' Guild and the Masons' Guild. Internally, though, the joiners and furniture makers will have his ear. Throck's got the stronger personality, but Stanton comes from the side of the Guild with the most members and the most influence."

"Which would be the most easily swayed?" Machison asked.

"Stanton's made furniture for Gorog, so he's liable to favor whoever Gorog tells him to support. Throck's coopers supply the vineyards Kadar's invested in, and Tamas' breweries and distilleries. He's going to be owned by them."

"Weaknesses?" Machison asked.

"Stanton's better at making furniture than making money. He's in debt. That's always good for leverage. Throck runs a profitable business, but he has a weakness for pretty women and beautiful men. It hasn't been difficult to supply him with lovers who'll turn pillow talk over. I'm told he pockets some of the fees that are supposed to go to the temple."

So he's likely cheating the tax collector and skimming off Guild fees too, Machison thought.

"You've done well, telling me this," he said. He reached beneath his vest, pulled out his velvet purse and removed two gold coins.

"Consider this a down payment on a large order for new pikes and stirrups for the guards. I'll have my exchequer come by with the specifics tomorrow."

"Thank you, m'lord," Sarca said, pocketing the bribe. "I'd best get back."

"Take the back lanes. Make sure you're not seen." He did not rise to see Sarca out, knowing his guards would see him on his way.

When he was certain the man was gone, he rang for Jorgeson.

"M'lord?" the chief of security asked as he answered the bell.

"Send an assassin for Inton Throck. Make a sloppy job of it, and leave something to implicate Kadar's people."

Jorgeson raised an eyebrow in surprise. "When?"

"Before dawn. He must not live to attend the Guild vote tomorrow." Machison met Jorgeson's gaze. "If Throck is elected Guild Master, he'll find a way to jam up the negotiations with Garenoth to please Kadar. We can't afford that. We've got to ensure that the negotiations run smoothly."

Outside, the tower bells tolled twelve times. "I have just the person for it," Jorgeson said. "Consider it done."

Machison tossed back the rest of his drink. "I never *consider* anything done until it's done. Too much can go wrong. Bring me word when Throck is dead."

"Yes, m'lord." Jorgeson closed the door behind him, leaving Machison by himself. He poured himself another whiskey and returned to his chair by the fire, staring into the flames.

The Merchant Princes play the Guilds for pawns and the Guilds fight each other for bronzes. If Blackholt does his job, we'll keep the commoners occupied, maintain the Balance, and send the Guilds chasing their tails while we cinch the agreement with Garenoth.

These trade negotiations are going to turn out just fine—for Ravenwood, and for me.

Chapter Eleven

"YOU'RE EARLY." CORRAN eyed the Lord Mayor's guard warily. "Payment's not due for another week."

The guard gave an ugly grin. "Payments are due when we *say* they're due, and I say they're due now."

Arguing would just make things worse. Corran reached beneath the counter and found the small money pouch. "Take it."

The guard made a show of emptying the coins into his hand and counting them. "How's business?"

"Middling," Corran replied. "Thanks to you, it'll be a cabbage week."

The guard chuckled. "Well, then, you won't starve. Don't let us catch you hurrying anyone along to get more business." He laughed heartily at his own joke, and bounced the money bag in his hand. "See you in a few weeks. Try to stay out of trouble."

From a friend, it might have been taken as a joke. But coming from one of the Mayor's guards, it had an ominous edge to it that made Corran uncomfortable.

He didn't leave his place behind the counter until the guard was out of sight. Kell had taken the cart to make the day's rounds, and

Rigan to fetch the priest; Corran had shooed him out the back door as soon as he spotted the guard.

Corran went back to the workroom. At least five generations of Valmondes had labored over the dead here. It was honorable work. He looked up as Rigan came through the back door.

"Old Saunders will meet us in the graveyard in half a candlemark," he said. "We'd better get moving."

The bodies they'd prepared the night before were cold and stiff, so loading them was not too difficult. Rigan pulled the cart, while Corran pushed as they moved along the dirt streets. A fence of stone and iron marked the limits of the burying grounds. Corran was never sure whether the wall was meant to keep animals out or to keep restless spirits in.

Lavish monuments marked the sections of the cemetary reserved for particular Guilds. Funeral expenses were part of what Guild fees went to pay for, along with training apprentices, maintaining the Guild hall and the temple of the Guild's patron god, and offsetting the Lord Mayor's expenses for guards to protect members from the monsters. The Guild into which a person was born set the course for the rest of his life, and into the After.

"Took you long enough," Saunders grumbled as they pulled up. "What did you bring me today?"

"One bricklayer and one weaver," Corran replied. "They'll require the usual service." The other two bodies would not receive the ministrations of the priest.

"You know the fee."

"Understood," Corran said. He dropped the coins into Saunders' arthritic hand.

"Go ahead and lay them out," the priest said. "I trust you'll take care of the digging part once I'm done."

Corran and Rigan lifted the bodies out of the cart and carried them to where they would be buried. Brissy would be interred in the plot reserved for the Weavers' Guild, while the crushed bricklayer went to the Masons' Guild's plot on the opposite corner. The others, including the nameless victim of the monsters, went along the back wall into a common grave. The stabbed man would go outside the wall, beyond the protection of hallowed ground; Corran and Rigan would take care of that themselves, once Saunders was gone.

Saunders might be an old sot, but he does the blessings right, Corran thought. The brothers began digging right away, though they were unlikely to have even the first grave completed before Saunders finished his work. The priest's voice was melodious, blending with the bells, chimes, and drumming with which he accompanied the prayers.

He could rush through, but he doesn't, Corran thought, as the strike and shuffle of dirt made a counterpoint rhythm to the chant. *I could almost believe he cares.*

Saunders packed up the ritual items and slung his pack over his shoulder before walking to where the brothers were filling in the first grave. "Just so you know," he said, with a glance over his shoulder, "the head of our Order doesn't want us saying the ritual over anyone killed by the monsters."

Rigan and Corran both stopped what they were doing to stare at the old priest. "Why not?" Rigan demanded.

Saunders raised a hand. "I don't make the rules. I suspect it's connected to what that prophet in the marketplace is saying, about the monsters being the vengeance of the gods. But if the bodies are shrouded and wrapped, and properly marked, I don't make it my business to peek inside. I just thought you'd want to know about the change. I've also heard talk that the Guilds might bar the victims of monsters from their plots."

Corran took a deep breath and bit back the retort that came to mind. *Saunders is doing us a favor by telling us,* he reminded himself. *Don't blame the messenger.*

"And the priests are all right with that?" Corran asked.

Saunders shrugged. "Apparently so."

The priest headed back toward Wrighton, leaving Rigan and Corran to finish their task. Corran tried to channel his anger into his digging, plunging his shovel deep into the ground and quickening his pace.

"You're thinking of Jora."

Corran did not reply immediately. Rigan could read him better than anyone except maybe Kell. Rigan had left him the space to grieve those first days after Jora's death, and then made sure he was on-hand when he needed him.

Corran stabbed his shovel into the dirt. "Yes, it's about Jora. Those bastards would have denied her a proper burial for something that wasn't her fault. Mama, too. All because some crazy prophet decides that the people the monsters kill deserved to die?"

He gestured toward the city. "Instead of getting rid of the monsters, they levy a curfew. They say it's for our protection, but if they did their jobs, we wouldn't have to hide inside. I swear it's more about controlling us than protecting us." His fist clenched in frustration. "It's wrong, dammit, and the Guilds are backing them up."

Rigan took a deep breath and pulled his shovel free. "Come on. One more to go."

The sun was low in the sky by the time they dug the last grave. They were just lowering the corpses into the common grave when Corran froze. "Did you hear that?"

Rigan was in the grave, laying the bodies down as Corran handed them in. "Can't hear anything except you. Why?"

The hair on the back of Corran's neck rose. He scanned the wall, trying to locate the noise, and thought he caught a glimpse of something dark moving behind the stones.

"We've got trouble!" Corran shouted as the monster hurtled the cemetery wall in one mighty leap. The beast was the size of a large wolf, but thin enough that bones showed under gray skin stretched tight. Every movement rippled sinew beneath the flesh. Lean muscle flexed in its haunches, and long claws dug into the ground, propelling it forward. Powerful shoulders rose to a muscled neck and a grotesque head. Its face was bat-like, with a wide, flared nose and pointed ears lying flat against its skull. Its wrinkled snout rose to a ridged brow. Red eyes, like glowing embers, fixed on their prey. But what had Corran's full attention were the jaws, wide-hinged and powerful, filled with glistening rows of long, pointed teeth.

Corran fell into a fighting stance, holding his shovel like a stave. He grabbed a rock and hurled it as hard as he could, striking the monster between the eyes, stunning it for a moment. The monster bellowed, then fixed its red eyes on Corran and charged. Sharp talons swiped at him and he dodged, but one claw caught his sleeve and sliced into his forearm. Corran brought the shovel down, clubbing the monster over the head with the iron blade. The metal clanged against its bony skull and Corran leaned forward, putting his weight and momentum behind the blade, driving it into the monster's head. The creature roared and sprang at him, blood streaming from the ragged gash, the wound deep enough to show bone.

"Corran! What's going on up there?"

"Stay down!" Corran swung the shovel again. The monster staggered, then leaped, pushing off with its powerful hind legs, landing so close that Corran had to scramble backward. This time the claws ripped through one of Corran's pantlegs and gouged bloody trails into his thigh.

He bit back a cry of pain, and shifted his weight to his good leg before charging with his shovel leveled like a lance, ramming the edge of the sharp iron blade into the monster's face. Warm blood spattered Corran. He circled the shovel above his head and slammed it down hard enough he feared the blade might crack. The monster reeled, then rallied with a growl and the snick of teeth, close enough for Corran to smell its fetid breath.

Powerful claws ripped the shovel from Corran's grip, and the creature knocked him flat on his back, pinning him to the ground. Corran twisted, evading the snapping teeth, wildly searching for a weapon. He reached over his head, and touched one of the pieces of rock left from digging the graves. Corran gripped the hunk of stone and brought it down hard onto the monster's skull, splitting the furrowed ridge of bone and sending a sheet of dark blood into its crimson eyes.

He brought the rock down again, slamming it into the creature's face, breaking its wrinkled nose. The monster bucked, nearly pulling out of reach before Corran gave one more desperate swing and felt its skull give way completely. Blood ran down Corran's arms and gushed from the monster's mouth. The red eyes lost focus and, with a shuddering groan, the creature collapsed. Corran wriggled out from under its weight, heart thudding, amazed to be alive. The whole fight had taken only seconds. Rigan was just hauling himself out of the grave, and he looked at his brother in horror. Blood soaked Corran's torn clothing.

"By the gods, did you kill that thing?" Rigan said, wide-eyed. He advanced warily on the monster, and gave it a cautious poke with his blade.

Corran leaned forward, hands on thighs, trying to get his breath. "I guess I have good reactions," he lied, hoping Rigan wouldn't think too hard about Corran's fighting skills.

"What was it?"

"No idea. Never seen anything like it before."

"We can't leave it here," Rigan protested, "the guards will ask questions."

"Throw it in the hole."

Rigan raised an eyebrow. "In the grave with the bodies?"

"The dead won't care," Corran said. "And I want to keep on living. So let's get rid of that thing and get on our way before someone comes by."

That's a new kind of monster, one the hunters haven't seen before. I've got to let Calfon and the others know.

Chapter Twelve

"RIGAN VALMONDE! YOUR jokes are so bad, you must practice them on your customers!" Elinor, the dyer's apprentice, rolled her eyes.

"Why not? They're at least as lively as the regulars down at The Lame Dragon."

Elinor chuckled and turned away. Rigan's gaze followed her every move. She was the reason he volunteered to pick up the order of dyes and pigments.

"I didn't know undertakers were allowed to have a sense of humor," Elinor teased.

Rigan sighed. "Actually, it helps. If we couldn't make some pretty dark jokes about the work, we'd probably crack."

Elinor went to mix up the pigments. Parah, the head dyer, was busy with another customer, and Rigan wondered if she had caught on that Elinor preferred to handle this particular order.

Rigan came around to watch her blend the leaves in the mortar and pestle.

He liked the smell of the dried herbs and powders, and the regular pulse of the grindstone. But mostly, he enjoyed Elinor's company. Just being in the same room with her made him feel like he'd drunk too much ale.

"I'm sorry," Elinor said quietly.

"Come again?"

"I'm sorry—about Wil. I haven't seen you since, well... since all that happened." Elinor did not look up, and her cheeks flushed.

"It was a bad night," Rigan replied. "I still can't believe he's gone."

"You and Donn were lucky," Elinor said, still keeping her eyes on her work. "There are some guards around that are just plain trouble."

Rigan looked at her, surprised. "From what I heard, most people got told it was monsters."

She glanced up at him then. "There's what people got told, and what people believe. There are all kinds of monsters, some of them wear uniforms."

It had taken Rigan a week to heal before he felt up to venturing outside their workshop. Today was the farthest afield he had gone other than the cemetery, though he had plans for something more tonight, something he might only have the nerve to do if he did not think on it too long.

"I can't argue with that," Rigan replied. "I'm just sorry that Donn and I couldn't have protected Wil better."

Elinor clunked the pestle back into the mortar. "Rigan Valmonde! You listen to me. There are some things you can change, and some you can't. Allery saw a little of what happened, and he told Jacen, who figured I'd want to know."

"Oh?" Rigan said, raising an eyebrow. "Why's that?"

She reddened. "Never you mind. What I'm saying is—once a wheel gets to turning, it's hard to stop. And that wheel started turning for Wil when the guards roughed him up. Do you think it would have changed a thing if you and Donn had stood your ground and fought? You'd all three be dead."

Rigan looked away. "That's what Corran and Kell said, although they swore a little more."

Elinor chuckled. "Then why aren't you listening? Bad things happen. Some you can stop, and some you can't. Sooner or later, I believe the wheel of the gods will grind those guards just like I grind these leaves. That's why people still pray to the Old Ones, to Ardevan and Eshtamon. They pray for vengeance, for the powerful to get brought low and the wrongdoers to get what's coming to them." Elinor stole a glance toward where Parah was talking with a customer on the other side of the shop. The two older women had their backs to them, and were deep in discussion.

"Because Wil's not the only one," she added in a low voice. "Same kind of thing killed Parah's youngest son eighteen years ago. That's why she goes to the temple of the Old Ones and makes offerings."

"She's been praying all that time and nothing happened?"

A cold smile crept across Elinor's lips. "Oh, she didn't wait eighteen years. Not how she tells it, when you can get her to say. The guard responsible got caught stealing from the Guild, and was hanged a few months after she made her plea to the gods. She still goes to the temple to give thanks for justice that wouldn't have come any other way."

Justice. Vengeance. I want both—for Wil's sake, and for Papa's. If I can't get rid of this new magic, maybe I can use it to help.

"You're quiet, all of a sudden." Elinor laid a hand on his arm. "You can't keep blaming yourself for what happened. It's like when the fever comes through: some die and some don't. It's the way of things. It's a waste if you survive and don't go on enjoying life."

Rigan managed a smile. "I'll keep that in mind."

She poured the mixture into a pottery jar, and their fingers brushed as Rigan reached for it. He felt a spark, so brief he figured that he imagined it, except that Elinor's eyes widened, just a bit, as if she felt it, too. *Not just attraction. A bit of magic? Could it be?*

"Thanks for mixing this up," he said.

She did not snatch her hand away.

"Thanks for coming by," she replied with a hint of a smile.

Parah and her customer had turned back toward them, and Elinor withdrew her hand, though she did not hurry to drop her gaze. "You'll have to see if Kell will let you come more often."

"Definitely."

Parah hurried over. "Don't you have somewhere else to be, Rigan? I've got a shop to run, and Elinor has orders to fill." Her tone was tart, but the amusement in her eyes softened her words.

"Just leaving," he said, withdrawing his coin purse to pay. "Many thanks."

Kell drew up with the cart of the day's dead just as Rigan returned home. "Good. You're back," he said. "Help me with these bodies. We've got four today, and one of them is a heavy son of a bitch." He glanced at the burlap bag Rigan carried. "You got more pigment? We're going to need it."

Rigan helped Kell heft the dead weight of a man who probably outweighed the two of them together. "By the gods, he's heavy!" Kell groaned as they shuffled their way into the workroom. "On three. One... two... three!" They heaved the body onto the nearest table.

Rigan was about to comment when he heard raised voices from the front of the shop. He lifted a hand to silence Kell and they crept forward, toward the door that divided the business office from the workroom.

"That's a silver more than you demanded last month!" they heard Corran protest.

"The Guild fee's gone up," another voice said. "You want more guards to go after the monsters; the Lord Mayor raised the fee, so our contribution goes up. Otherwise, there'll be more of those hunters taking the law into their own hands, not much better than the creatures they're hunting."

Kell's face flushed with anger, and Rigan felt his own heart pound. But Corran's voice was calm, though Rigan heard the strain it took. "We always pay our fees: to the guards, the Guild, and the gods. Take it and go. I've got work to do."

"I don't imagine your customers mind when you make them wait," the man said, and guffawed.

Kell looked spitting mad, but Rigan grabbed his arm hard and gave him a stern look to remain silent. "The dead might not, but their families expect prompt burial," Corran said. "Now if you'll excuse me—"

The Guild collector grumbled something Rigan did not catch, right before the door to the street banged shut. Rigan and Kell were back into the workroom, working on another corpse when Corran stormed in. "You two are late!"

"Just that kind of day," Rigan replied. "We carried in the heavy one already—the rest shouldn't take long."

"We'll be up all night at this rate, and I've got a Guild meeting later." Corran went out to the wagon, heaving one of the remaining bodies over his shoulder.

"Tonight? I didn't hear anything about a meeting," Rigan said, as he and Kell went back for the next body.

"It's a special group that Guild Master Orlo has brought together. To discuss how all the undertakers in Ravenwood are charging for services."

"They should know better than to hold late meetings," Kell complained. "Tempting fate to have you out past curfew."

Corran shrugged. "I'll be fine. But I don't fancy being up at dawn doing work that could be done tonight, so let's get to it."

Kell bustled around the workshop, mixing up pigments and preparing the ritual bath. Kell told Rigan what each family had paid for, and Rigan fetched the appropriate shrouds.

"Do you want me to help down here, or feed you?" Kell asked after mixing the pigments and setting out the bucket of prepared water.

"I want to eat!" Rigan voted. Corran shrugged. Rigan and Kell exchanged a glance.

"I vote with Rigan," Kell announced. "I'll call you when it's ready." He headed up the steps. A few moments later, they heard Kell banging around in the small kitchen.

Corran's silence weighed on Rigan as they worked. "A copper for your thoughts?" Rigan said, bringing over the bucket.

"Nothing to tell. Just tired."

He was like this for months after Mama died. He hasn't been himself since Jora's death. Corran was preoccupied, and if Rigan didn't know better, he would have guessed his brother was torn between fear and anger. "Something go wrong today?"

Corran shook his head. "No more than usual. The Guild raised our fee." He snorted. "They've become quite the cutpurses."

"The Lord Mayor likely gets a piece of that."

His brother merely nodded.

"Did the collector give you a hard time about the fee?"

"Bloody bastards," Corran muttered. "Wouldn't be so bad if they actually did anything useful." The tirade did not surprise Rigan—it occurred every time the collector came for their money—but his brother's mood was grimmer than usual.

Corran was quiet all through dinner. Even Kell's wildly embellished stories did not get a reaction. Kell and Rigan shared a look, and Rigan shrugged.

Outside, the bell in the city tower rang eight times. "I need to get going to the Guild meeting." He still did not meet Rigan's gaze. "Stay and finish things up. I'll be back."

"Well, what do you make of that?" Kell said after the door shut behind Corran.

"No idea. I haven't seen him that upset in a long time. Come on. I'll help you clean up." Rigan hesitated. He didn't want to lie to either Kell or Corran, but telling them about his newfound magic or his training Below was not an option if he meant to keep them safe.

"Donn stopped by, earlier," he said. "I didn't want to mention it to Corran. But Donn's having a hard time of it, since Wil died. He asked if I could come over and play some cards. We'll be at his house, not the tavern. I figured I'd stay the night, so I don't have to worry about curfew." He licked his lips. "I think he could use someone around."

Kell shrugged. "Sure. I'll let Corran know." Kell turned away, cleaning up the dishes. Something in his voice let Rigan know that the lie had not been entirely successful. "Thanks," Rigan said. *I'd be putting them at risk if they really knew where I was going. I won't do that, no matter how mad Corran gets at me for being gone.*

Rigan got his cloak and slipped outside, making his way through the shadows to an entrance to Below.

How can I learn magic a few candlemarks at a time? And with the mood Corran's in, I'll be in for real trouble if I'm not back early in the morning. At least I let Kell know. At least they won't be out looking for my body. Rigan remembered the naked relief he had seen in his brothers' faces when he had returned after going missing, and reflected how hard that night must have been for them.

He found the old warehouse, picking his way across the litter-covered floor, wincing as ruined floorboards creaked beneath him. Rigan let out a sign of relief when he reached the other side of the room. Steeling his nerve, he found the hidden door and slipped through to Below.

Rigan descended the dirty stone steps leading deeper underground. A long-disused cellar led to a passageway in a forgotten part of the city that at one time had been open to the light. The air smelled of lamp oil and smoke, of cooking fires and roasting meat. Corran had always teased him about being good with directions; now, Rigan was glad that he could remember his way. He emerged from a side tunnel into the crowded marketplace, loud with the babble of voices as buyers and sellers haggled. *How many come here because they need to get out of someone's way?* he wondered.

Damian was waiting for him at the entrance to the witch's residence. "I had a feeling you'd be back."

"I don't really have much choice, do I? The odds aren't in my favor trying to figure this stuff out on my own."

Damian chuckled. "You always have a choice, but some options are better than others. Come with me."

"I can only stay until morning," Rigan blurted. "If I'm gone too long, my brothers will come looking for me."

"You haven't told them about your magic?"

Rigan shook his head. "I'm not going to put them in danger. This is my burden. They have enough to worry about."

"You see your magic as a burden?"

"What else would it be?"

"It saved your life. Some might consider that a gift."

Rigan let that pass without comment. "Where is everyone?" he asked as Damian brought him into a large room.

"Busy. There's more to life here than just magic. We still have cooking and cleaning and mending to do, just like everyone else."

"Can't you just use magic for that?"

Damian laughed. "Only if we wanted the chores to take twice as long and leave us thrice as tired. Power takes a toll."

Rigan looked around. Dozens of candles lit the large room. A few worn cushions lay on the floor, and to one side sat a chalice, a bowl of salt, and several pieces of charcoal. Smaller bowls contained pigments of various colors.

"Sit here," Damian said, indicating one of the cushions. Rigan sat. Damian walked in a circle, leaving a thin trail of salt behind him, leaving enough room for one or two people to join Rigan inside the area of protection.

A plump old woman with short gray hair emerged from a doorway, and Rigan recognized Baker. "Ah, I see you're back," she said.

"Can you sense his power? It rolls off him too easily," Damian said.

Baker nodded. "That's not good. No wonder he's had difficulty containing it." She peered at Rigan, as if seeing down to his bones. "Better if you stayed here Below. Safer for everyone."

"I can't do that," Rigan replied. "My brothers need me."

"Humpf." Baker sat quietly for a moment, putting a small brass bell on the floor between them. "Move the bell."

Rigan reached out a hand, and Baker smacked him on the knuckles. "Not with your hand. With your magic."

Rigan looked at her as if she were daft. "I don't move things with my mind," he replied. "So far, I've only buried the dead, banished ghosts, and killed someone."

Baker shrugged. "You warmed the tea that night with your magic. You've got more control than you think. A knife can cut food or slit a man's throat; it's just a tool. So is magic. What matters is intent—and control. So... move the bell."

Rigan took a deep breath, focused on the bell, and imagined sliding it to the right. Nothing happened. He tried to remember what he had done to warm the water in the tea cup. He leaned forward, staring intently at the bell, brow furrowed. This time, he visualized moving the bell to the left. Nothing.

"Maybe I don't have the kind of magic that moves bells," he said, sitting back with a sigh. "Maybe I'm better at stopping things than starting them."

"Nonsense," Baker snapped. "There isn't such a thing as 'bell ringing magic' or 'killing magic.' Magic is magic. I want to see what you can do."

"I'm not sure that's a good idea—"

Before Rigan could finish his sentence, Baker sprang at him. She was faster than he expected, and bowled him over, one hand going for his throat.

Rigan reacted before he thought. His arms came up reflexively, and the same thrum of power he had felt before surged through him, hurling Baker away, sending her flying a few feet through the air. An iridescent curtain of power cushioned her fall as she landed at the edge of the circle of protection.

Rigan's cheeks flushed with shame, and he sprang up. "Are you all right? Gods, I've killed her!"

Baker chuckled. "It takes a lot more than an untrained pup like you to kill me." She turned to Damian. "I am grudgingly impressed."

"I told you he had power."

Baker snatched up the bell and hurled it at Rigan. It hit him in the forehead. "Ow."

"But he's going to need a lot of work," Baker observed, drily.

"Maybe he wasn't afraid of the bell killing him," Damian replied. "Right now, his power only seems to surge when he fears for his own life."

Baker crossed her arms. "Perhaps that's a good thing," she mused. "If he can stay out of trouble, it might keep him from the attention of the Lord Mayor's mages." She cocked her head as she looked Rigan up and down. "Still, that's not something we can count on. I think he can do better."

Rigan lost track of time as Baker set him one test after another, assessing his power, trying to determine the limits of his control. His head ached and his stomach knotted. Finally, when it felt as if Baker had been drilling him forever, Rigan slumped forward onto his hands and knees, trying to hold on to consciousness.

Baker helped him to lie down, still within the warded circle, then rose and stepped carefully over the wardings. "Stay here," she said. "I'll be back."

When Baker was gone, Rigan turned toward Damian. He felt as if he had put in a hard day's work. The room felt wobbly. "Am I doing well enough?"

"I think you actually impressed her."

"Do you think she's right? I mean, about my magic being good for something besides banishing ghosts and killing people?" Rigan tried to keep the hope he felt from coloring his voice.

"Do you go around killing people with the knives and saws you use in your trade?"

"Of course not!"

"Not even when you're angry?" Damian pressed.

"It's not the same thing. I can control what I can do with a knife. The magic just comes out of nowhere."

"Actually, the magic came from inside you, not out of 'nowhere,'" Damian corrected, "and you controlled it quite well under duress. Many men, when faced with a fight for their lives, can't defend themselves with a knife or a sword, even with practice; with no experience, you not only summoned your power, but sent it specifically against the person who endangered you. You didn't blow him to bits. You didn't kill everyone on the whole block. You killed your tormentor by making his heart stop. That's rather remarkable."

Maybe there's hope that I won't turn into a murderer, Rigan thought, cautious but relieved. *After all, soldiers train how to kill in battle, but they don't slice their neighbors to bits. At least, not often.*

Baker returned and stepped inside the circle, then stopped, raising a hand, palm out, toward Rigan. "If I concentrate, I can feel a flicker of magic from him," she said. "Damian?"

"Yes. I feel it too."

Rigan managed to sit up. His head pounded and he was drenched in sweat, but he took pride in managing to stand without assistance.

"Take this." Baker dropped an amulet of wood, metal and bone on a leather strap into Rigan's outstretched hand. "Put it on."

Rigan tied the strap loosely, so that the talisman lay against his collarbone. Once again, Baker stretched out her hand. This time, she nodded approvingly. "Better. Damian?"

"Muted and diffused," Damian replied. "Harder to be certain it comes from him."

"How does it work?" Rigan asked, touching the amulet.

"It's not going to hurt you," Baker said with a chuckle. "The design won't attract attention—it's a style often worn by those who worship the Old Ones. It won't give you away, if that's what you're afraid of. The magic is subtle. It's a mild distraction enchantment, but the beauty of it is that the spell distracts from its *own* existence as well."

"What effect will it have on others around me?" Rigan asked. "It's not going to be much good if no one can keep their mind on their work if I'm in the room."

Baker laughed. "No, lad. Only a mage will be distracted, and not from everything. Unless a witch truly focuses with intent, their attention will just skim past you. You'll be present, but unimportant. They won't notice the distraction, or the latent power beneath it."

Baker stepped forward, uncomfortably close to Rigan. "Now listen. This is important. If you draw attention to yourself, the amulet won't make you invisible. If someone *knows* about your magic, they can sense it; they'll know where to look. If they're suspicious enough, they'll find you out. So stay out of trouble, don't go out more than you have to, and for the love of all that's holy, steer clear of anyone in the Mayor's entourage that might be a witch. Do you hear me?"

Rigan nodded, hoping he did not look as utterly overwhelmed as he felt. "Yes. I will. Thank you." He staggered, and Baker caught his arm. Damian came around the other side, holding him up.

"You need to rest. We've pushed you hard," Damian said as he and Baker got Rigan to bed.

"I'll bring a healer," Baker promised as they eased him down. "It's only midnight. You should be able to go home in the morning. But mind that you come back within the week. Your power is too strong to leave untrained."

She might have said more, but Rigan did not hear her as he fell into a deep sleep.

* * *

RIGAN HAD A moment of panic as he tried to get his bearings. A shuttered lantern on the table beside to the bed gave him enough light to realize he was still in the house of the witches. *What time is it? Still dark?*

He chuckled ruefully as his mind cleared. *Of course it's still dark. I'm underground.*

"We need to get you home," Damian said from the doorway. "Baker was right, though; come back as soon as your strength is regained. Training is your best protection."

"What if the training makes my power stronger?" Rigan asked. "What if I can't hide it?"

"Then we will deal with that when it happens. It's morning. You'd best be on your way. Go, and may the Old Ones guard you."

Rigan thanked Damian, then retraced his path to the surface. Cool morning air greeted him when he stepped out of the warehouse and back into the street. The city bells began tolling eight just as he reached the back door of the workshop. He let himself in, bracing for a dressing down. To his relief, the workshop was empty.

Worry followed the first flush of relief. *Corran would have noticed I was missing if he went upstairs to bed. He's usually up by now—unless he didn't come back until very late. Odd for a Guild meeting to run so long. Something's up.*

With luck, I can get the water drawn and prepared for washing the corpses and the pigments ready before Corran comes down. Explanations can wait.

But not for long. Rigan felt that certainty in his bones. Not for long.

Chapter Thirteen

Rigan pulled the hood of his cloak over his head and slipped out the back door of the undertaker's shop. A week had passed since his last journey Below, and he was filled with questions and worries. Another late Guild meeting had taken Corran from the workshop, and Kell had gone to bed. Rigan had told Kell that he was taking a room at The Lame Dragon for the night, that he'd 'found a girl in town he wanted to court.' Kell had given him a look somewhere between encouragement and doubt, and told him to make sure he was back early, before Corran was up. *I wish what I told him were true. I wish I were going to see Elinor.*

Rigan had gotten up the nerve to ask her to go walking. She had agreed, and more importantly, Parah had consented. That boded well. *Until she finds out I'm a witch.* They had talked about everything and nothing, and at one point he had taken Elinor's hand. He could have sworn he felt a tingle, like touching wool on a dry day. Elinor's eyes widened, but she didn't pull away. For an instant, Rigan saw a flicker of hesitation in her eyes, and then the smile was back.

I'd give anything to be courting Elinor tonight, instead of this.

Rigan flattened himself against a wall and held his breath as two guards passed only an arm's length from where he hid. He let out a ragged sigh after they were out of earshot, and kept moving.

He passed through the darkened alleyways like a ghost. When he was almost halfway to the entrance to Below, a man stepped out of a doorway, blocking his path. Another man turned into the alley behind Rigan, trapping him between them.

"We don't want any trouble," the man in the front said. "Just give us your money."

Rigan could not make out their faces. As the second man closed in, he slipped his knife into his hand. "I don't have any money. You're wasting your time."

The man in front gave a cold chuckle. "Give us what you have, and you can go on your way."

Rigan strongly doubted that was true.

"Take it." He emptied his pockets of a few coins, letting them clatter to the ground.

The thieves moved in unison. Rigan was quick, and he had grown up wrestling with two brothers. He still hoped to find a way to outrun the bandits, but when steel glinted in the taller man's hand, Rigan knew he would have to stand and fight.

He dodged the blade, grabbing the tall thief's arm and bending it backward as he dodged out of the way, throwing the man off balance. The short thief had a knife, also, and he came at Rigan fast, slicing his forearm.

The short thief swung his knife for Rigan's throat, and he ducked and wove, before burying his blade in the thief's thigh. The brigand howled, slashing again and lancing open Rigan's side; he left his knife—still stuck in the thief's thigh—and dove out of the way.

The tall thief went for the kill now that Rigan was unarmed. "You could have done this the easy way. It would have been quick. Now, it's gonna hurt. A lot." He lunged, grabbing a handful of Rigan's cloak, and shoved him up against the alley wall, blade pressed against his throat.

Pain, anger, and fear welled up in Rigan, and his half-finished training came to the fore—more instinct than experience. Fire blasted from his palms, catching quickly in the brigand's clothing. The tall thief screamed as he burned and staggered backward, tripping over his wounded companion, setting him ablaze too. The smell of burning flesh and cloth filled the air. Their screams echoed. Fire spread to the old rags and broken crates littering the alley.

Wounded, bleeding, and terrified, Rigan ran. The cut in his side gave him a hitch in his gait. A warm trickle ran down his hip, and blood from his slashed forearm made his left palm slick. He gritted his teeth and kept moving, focused on putting enough distance between himself and the burning thieves to evade capture or retribution.

Rigan stumbled on a cobblestone and crashed through a pile of crates, scrambling back to his feet and careening down the alley, then dodging into a side street. He ran until he could run no more, putting several blocks between himself and his assailants, before staggering to a halt, leaning heavily against the alley wall. Washing hung on a line above him and Rigan snatched down a dark shirt. He ripped off the sleeves and made a rough bandage for the wound on his side, then tore another strip to staunch the bleeding on his forearm. Only then did he realize how badly his hands were shaking.

I'm halfway across town, no one knows where I am, and I'm hurt. And that son of a bitch got my knife. But I killed them, I burned them alive.

Rigan turned to one side and retched. He wiped the vomit from his mouth with the edge of his cloak and took a deep breath, trying to pull himself together. *I can't stay here. I've got to keep moving, got to get Below. Those men won't have been the only ones looking for an easy mark. I drew too much on myself again, I've got to get off the street before I collapse. I hope Damian and the others know I'm coming. He'll know what to do. I'm too far gone to turn back now.*

No one knew how many entrances existed to Below. Their location—and safety—changed almost daily. An entrance might be passable one day, bricked shut by the guards the next, and busy as ever by the end of the week. Below was Ravenwood's shame and obsession. Some went there to disappear. Others sought the protection of the subterranean world, fleeing their lives Above.

In his haste to lose the guards, Rigan realized he had also lost his way.

"You shouldn't be here."

The voice startled Rigan, and he drew back, ready to fight or run, knowing he was too weak to do much of either.

"Looks like you got the worst of it, didn't you?" An old woman stepped from a doorway, regarding him with curiosity. She was dressed like a Wanderer, but she was not the woman he had met in the plaza.

"Leave me alone. I don't have any money," Rigan stammered, weak with blood loss.

"You've got Wanderer blood. I can see it in your eyes. Feel it in your magic."

"I'm hurt. I need to get out of the street."

"Follow me. I know a way Below from here." She gestured to him and stepped back into the doorway. "I mean you no harm. The enemy of my enemy is my friend."

"Who is your enemy?" Rigan asked warily, seeing no option but to follow her.

"Maybe you'd best be asking, who are *your* real enemies?" the crone replied, leading the way into a dark, stinking cellar. She lit a candle and slipped through a gap in the wall.

Rigan followed. *Hope it's not too far. I don't think I've got it in me for a long hike*, he thought. "I don't understand."

The old Wanderer woman chuckled. Her hoarse, rough echoed in the darkness. "It's not the monsters who are your enemy, boy. It's the monsters' masters."

"What do you know of the monsters?"

"I know enough of magic to know that their presence in Ravenwood is no accident, and that what you've been told about the Balance is rubbish."

Gradually, the tunnel grew lighter. Torches in sconces and hanging lanterns lit the rest of the way. In the distance, music played. The smell of lamp oil mingled with cooking odors. The narrow pathway opened up into one of the large chambers of the underground city.

As far as Rigan knew, no one had ever fully mapped the miles of natural and man-made passageways that ran beneath Ravenwood and past it, to the mountains beyond. In many places, the stone walls of the corridors were worn smooth from the touch of hands over centuries. Some sections that were now Below had once been street level. Time, floods, and fires meant that sections of Ravenwood had been built over, adding to the underground warrens.

"Can you tell me about the Balance? About what those sigils mean?" Rigan asked, following the woman to an archway. The rooms were better lit beyond the arch, and he could hear the bustle of people.

"My people survive by keeping our knowledge to ourselves," she snapped. "We help keep the Balance—the *real* Balance—in our own way. The sigils help us do that. You don't need to know more." She paused. "Now, you need a healer. But this one thing I will tell you before I go: call upon Eshtamon and the power in your blood. If it is His will, your eyes will be opened." The old woman pushed him toward the arch. "Go."

Rigan pushed through the crowds, all too aware of the strength draining from him. He navigated through open rooms where vendors had set up booths and musicians played tunes that echoed from the cavern walls. Most of the people here wore either masks or cowls, hiding their faces. The business and pleasures to be found Below were not the sort one wanted to admit to. Criers called out to passersby, extolling their wares or services. Street vendors fanned the aromas from their food carts to lure hungry customers, while the taverns drew a thirsty, appreciative crowd.

Nearly everything for sale Below was forbidden above. The whores in Below would agree to practices even the most sullied trollop Above refused; the liquor here was laced with potent substances banned by the Guild; the foods violated the dietary laws of all of the city's major religions; the business agreements settled here were almost certainly illegal elsewhere. Most people found what they wanted here and returned Above. Some never left.

Rigan clutched his cloak around him and looked straight ahead, fixed on his goal.

"Beautiful women—sure to best your wildest dream!"

"Banned liquor—get it here!"

"Anything you want—guaranteed."

The voices were too loud, the odors pungent, the music overwhelming. He headed down a side passage and stopped to catch his breath. *Not much farther.* His world spun, and Rigan gasped for breath as he staggered. He managed to reach the door before his knees buckled.

"Baker had a premonition that you would come, but we expected you sooner. We were afraid something happened to delay you." Damian caught Rigan as he fell, supporting his weight.

"I was attacked."

"Here, Below?"

Rigan shook his head. "On the edge of Wrighton."

"We'll see to you. Come with me."

Rigan's legs felt like jelly. The blood pulsed in his ears, and his vision was tinged red. "I've done something terrible."

"Then you've come to the right place," Damian replied. "So has everyone else. You'll fit right in."

Rigan wanted to make a reply, but no words came. Safe at last, he lost consciousness.

* * *

RIGAN WOKE TO the dim light of a single candle, reflected from a polished tin sconce. Memories returned, and with them, shame.

"How are you feeling? You lost a lot of blood," Damian said.

Rigan's hand felt for the wound in his side, only to find the skin smooth. The slash in his forearm had been healed as well. "I feel... tired. How long was I out?"

"A couple of candlemarks."

Rigan winced. "Less time than before." *I would have thought killing two men would take longer to recover from.* His body might have healed but the loathing he felt for himself was unabated.

"Aiden was able to speed your recovery from the blood loss. The magic also drained your life force, and that took longer to heal. But you're stronger than before, and you recovered faster." Damian paused. "You said you needed to confess something."

"I used magic to defend myself. Again." Shame colored his cheeks. "In the alley, when I was attacked. There were two thieves with knives. I had a knife as well, and I tried to avoid the fight, then I tried to fend them off, fight them the normal way."

"What happened?"

"I stabbed one of them, but the other pinned me," Rigan recounted. "He was going to kill me. My knife was gone. He meant to cut my throat. And then I..."

Damian waited. The silence stretched on, unbearable.

"I was scared," Rigan said in a voice just above a whisper. "I reacted. The power just came from within—it was like a wave. I couldn't stop it. It poured out of me and burned them."

Damian's head cocked to one side. "You forced the bandits back with fire?"

"I set them ablaze like kindling." Rigan steeled himself for a rebuke, and glanced up when one was not forthcoming.

"How interesting," Damian said finally.

"I'm afraid."

"Of what?"

"I'm afraid that next time, I'll rely on the magic instead of trying to avoid using it."

"All weapons have their role. There's no shame in using a sword when a sword is called for."

"But what if I reach for a sword because it's easier than using my fist, when a fist would do?" Rigan asked, struggling to put his fears into words. "You've got to help me learn to control this. What if I stop feeling regret? What if I can do even worse? And what if I come to *like* it?"

"If that is what frightens you, then I don't believe you pose a threat," Damian replied. "And the more you train, the more control you'll have. That's the real risk: once again, you have drained yourself badly."

"How can I keep hiding something like this? If the Mayor's guards found out—"

"Your training will help you to control your power, and repress it when it needs to be hidden. The amulet will help shield you. Rest a while longer, then we'll train."

"I need to be home not long after dawn," Rigan said.

"There's time. For now, rest."

When he woke again, Aiden was leaning over him, checking his pulse. Rigan startled and the healer laid a reassuring hand on his shoulder. Aiden was a little shorter than Rigan, perhaps a few years older than Corran, with brown eyes and dark blond hair.

"Thanks," Rigan replied. "Whatever you did worked. Will I be able to... heal myself, once I get better at magic?"

Aiden shrugged. "I don't rightly know. Some can and some can't. Magic and healing don't always go together, if that's what you mean. It just happened to be what I'm good at."

Rigan heard footsteps, and glanced over to see Damian enter the room. "Come. If you're well enough to walk, you're well enough to train. Learning to deal with the effects of using your power is a lesson in itself."

Rigan rose from his bed, surprised to find his legs steady. He flexed his left hand; only a thin scar remained as proof that the wound had ever existed.

Rigan followed Damian into the training room where a hunched old woman was waiting for them. "Call me Granmam," she said to Rigan. "You have used magic to kill. This bothers you?"

"Shouldn't it? I burned both those men."

"And if you'd been a more experienced knife fighter and won through skill with your blade? Would that have bothered you?"

"Probably not, or not as much. It would be a fair fight."

Granmam eyed him appraisingly. "Fair, yes, of course. But magic is a skill. One you practice, just like a swordsman practices parries and footwork, or a boxer fights his shadow. The only thing that is not *fair* is that some are kept from using the talent born to them, because of the Lord Mayor's laws. It's like coming bareknuckled to a swordfight. Talent is not *fair*."

Rigan looked around the room, which looked like it might once have been part of a temple. Elaborately carved arches rose to the vaulted ceiling. Torches flickered in iron sconces along the walls.

"Show us your elements," Damian instructed. It was part of the lesson they had gone over the last time, something he had practiced.

Rigan took a deep breath to center himself. *Let's start with water.* He focused his will and held out his hands, palms down, eyes closed.

Rigan's palms grew moist. He focused on harnessing his power, bringing it up through his body and out into his hands. Sweat became droplets. In another few minutes, liquid began to drip from his hands.

"Enough!" Damian's voice had a strange edge to it. "What are you doing?"

Rigan opened his eyes, feeling woozy as he released the power and it sank down through his body, into the ground. "You wanted water."

"Look at your hands," Granmam said.

Rigan turned his hands palm up. They were wet with warm blood.

"How—" he stammered.

"From where did you summon your power?"

"I thought about water. I focused my concentration on water. And then I reached inside myself and pulled—"

"And manifested your body's own liquid," Damian finished for him. "Your power took from your body because you tried to draw the power from inside yourself."

Granmam brought him a towel and Rigan wiped the blood from his hands. "It could have been worse," she whispered.

"Try again," Damian instructed. "This time, summon wind."

Rigan closed his eyes, and concentrated on the scents he could make out in the air around him: incense, soap, sweat, candlesmoke, dust and damp rock. He focused on each breath, mindful of the air filling his lungs and rushing back out through his nose. He felt a cool draft of fresh air, and the heat of the torch flames. At last, he thrust deep inside his mind, and down through his body, and outside himself. Rigan felt the air, claimed it, and channeled it, holding his hands out in front of him, palms just a few inches apart.

A blast of wind knocked Rigan flat on his ass. Dust rose around him in a blinding cloud before howling away through the doorway.

Rigan lay on the floor, gasping. The blast of wind might not have been as dramatic as droplets of his own blood, but it tore the breath from his lungs and seemed, for an instant, to suck the air out of the room. He drew in the cold air gratefully.

Once, long ago, he had nearly drowned. He would never forget how it felt to suffocate, how his lungs had burned and bloody pinpricks had danced in his vision as his ears popped and his body screamed for air.

"Interesting," Damian said, as he and Granmam regained their footing.

"Interesting?" Rigan croaked, staggering to his feet. He was covered with dust. "That's all?"

"Promising, then. Is that better?"

Rigan slapped his hands against his pants and shirt, beating away the dust. "I pulled from outside myself, and look what happened!"

"You did well," Granmam said. "Had you used that much force drawing from your own lungs, they would have ruptured."

Now *you mention this?* "Then I guess I got lucky. How do I keep from smothering us... next time?"

"You must build in limits to your commands," Granmam replied. "If you call to all the air, you will attempt to summon *all* the air. So you must contain the scope of your power."

"I think I've already proven I can call fire—and a little more forcefully than I intended."

"Give us one last attempt. Call to the ground."

If I do this wrong, do I end up with a handful of shit? "You want me to gather dirt into my palm?" Rigan asked, beginning to suspect that the success of magic lay in precisely defining the request.

"If you can," Granmam replied. "This will require finesse. Look at the walls around you and the ceiling overhead. They are made of stone, which is from the ground. Bedrock is beneath the floor. Pull too hard on the 'ground' and you may cause a quake, bring the ceiling down onto our heads."

No pressure at all, then... Rigan tamped down on his misgivings and tried to center himself. He was aware of the fear that tinged his thoughts, and the quickening of his heartbeat. He forced himself to breathe slowly and deeply, and as his breath grew more stable, his heart slowed. When he was ready, Rigan cast his power down through his body, through his legs and feet, through the soles of his shoes. He held the image in his mind of his power sinking through the mosaic tiles and stone floor, to whatever else lay beneath them, into the pure, clean soil long buried beneath the ancient structure.

Rigan paused, aware that the ground went so much deeper. Soil lay atop bedrock, and beneath bedrock were even older strata, down into the bowels of the world, where tale-tellers swore melted rock coursed through hidden tunnels and sometimes burst up through broken mountains. He had never seen such things himself, but his magic bore witness to them, seductively offering to let him touch them, harness them, call to them.

He resisted the temptation, and drew his power back, leaving the deepest places untouched. This time, Rigan's mental image was precise and limited. *I want a handful of dirt. Not my own shit, not hot melted rock, not bedrock. Just dirt.*

Without bringing everything down on top of us.

He felt a tremor beneath his feet. He fought down panic, and kept steady focus on his gift, imagining it was a rope tied to the dirt, pulling at it with gentle, even pressure. The tremor subsided, though dust and plaster trickled down from the ceiling as the old structure trembled.

Easy, he thought, as if comforting a skittish colt. *Easy, now. Steady as she goes. That's it. Good. Almost there.*

Rigan held out his hand, eyes closed, and willed his power to fulfill his command. Magic coursed through him like sullen lightning, reluctant to bend to his will. And then, he felt the damp heaviness of *something* in his hand and was afraid to look.

"Very good," Damian said. Rigan opened his eyes. In his palm lay a handful of fresh, rich dirt.

"I think that's all I can do tonight," Rigan said and felt proud of himself that, while he slumped to his knees, he still remained conscious.

Chapter Fourteen

"YOU UNDERSTAND THE delicacy of the situation," Crown Prince Aliyev said as he walked with Machison in the garden of his villa. From here, they could see clear to the harbor, over the rooftops of Ravenwood.

"Of course, Your Highness," Machison said. "We can handle this discreetly."

Three Merchant Princes divided the spoils of Ravenwood's commerce among themselves, after paying Guilds and the hefty portion due to Crown Prince Aliyev, who passed on a share to King Rellan. The Merchant Princes, in turn, had patrons among Ravenwood's nobility, which invested in overseas trade expeditions the way lesser men gambled on horses. Their fortunes depended on the trade agreements with their League neighbors, as much as the tradesmen and the common people's lives depended on the quantity and quality of food and materials, and the severity of the Cull that were a direct outcome of the agreements.

"I am not blind to the fact that the current agreement favors Gorog, and that you benefit from that," Aliyev said. "Your favoritism persists at my sufferance, because, ultimately, it benefits Ravenwood as a whole."

"I am aware, my lord."

"I am also quite aware of the maneuvering by Kadar and Tamas to improve their profits," Aliyev continued. "And I am not averse to it—up to a point." He turned to fix Machison with a look. "Let them win a percentage point or two to stoke their vanity. But permit nothing that threatens Ravenwood's favored status."

"No, of course not, my lord."

"Nice work with Vrioni and Throck, by the way. Well done." Aliyev chuckled. "Vrioni would have been too much of a wild card during the negotiations, too much of a potential threat. Stanton will serve us much better, although I imagine Kadar is sweating by now. Good. Let him stew. Serves him right. He forgets himself when he seeks his own profit over Ravenwood's."

Machison cleared his throat. "The evidence left with the deaths suggests Kadar's hand, but remains sufficiently... ambiguous." *Jorgeson knows his business. The best evidence damns without being easily gainsayed. Kadar can't completely refute the connection, which is almost as good as admitting it, and we covered our tracks well on Vrioni. Gorog plays Kadar; Kadar plays Gorog. Round and round it goes.*

"Ambiguous!" Aliyev echoed. "Not to anyone who has been paying attention. Everyone knows Vrioni allowed the coopers to raise the prices of their barrels. It was going to cut into Kadar's profits from his vineyards. That's what they'll all see."

"That may be true," Machison allowed, "but it wouldn't be enough to prove he had Vrioni killed."

"Prove? No. But certainly enough to cast suspicion." Aliyev waved his hand to dismiss the argument. "Throck's death is harder to pin on Kadar, since he was Kadar's man. Kadar may even blame Tamas."

Machison shrugged. "Jorgeson's spies have spread rumors that Throck had angered Kadar, disappointed him. And they made certain that a bloody gold coin struck by Kadar's mint was found," he said, smiling. *A good move by Jorgeson. Nicely done.*

Kadar's coin might have come into Throck's possession legitimately, but its presence lent itself to uncomfortable questions, given the timing. That left Kadar denying culpability without any way to prove his innocence, and gave critics all the evidence they needed while stopping short of anything actionable.

"Make sure Stanton sticks to the plan," Aliyev said. "Vrioni knew the way these things work, but Stanton is new, and going into an important trade negotiation. He'll need to tread lightly. We want to make sure he does his part so we don't lose the advantage we already have. And remember: while it is in my benefit to somewhat favor Gorog and remind Kadar of his place in this matter, all three Merchant Princes owe me fealty, and I am their lord. They must all benefit from this process in the long run to keep the peace."

Gorog will interpret Stanton's promotion as favoring him. From where I stand, with Vrioni dead and an untested Guild Master at the negotiating table, it destabilizes Kadar and Tamas. Gives me more leeway to influence the outcome of the negotiations. The Merchant Princes have less chance to force an agreement to the detriment of the Guilds, and the Guild Masters won't be quite as brash in their demands. Together they're still strong enough to broker a good outcome for Ravenwood with Garenoth.

"You understand how important it is for this agreement to go well?" Aliyev said. "Your games with the Merchant Princes aside, we will have to live with the outcome for the next ten years."

"Of course, my lord." Machison had aligned himself with Gorog because he was the strongest of the Merchant Princes, contributing the most to the Crown Prince's revenues. With Aliyev and Gorog as his patrons, a rise in Machison's fortunes seemed likely. Perhaps a promotion to the Crown Prince's court, and from there, Machison could woo the attention and favor of the King himself.

"What about the hunters?" Aliyev said, changing the subject as he turned away to look out over the city. "You know we can't allow them to continue—and you know why. Blackholt's been as precise as possible about targeting members of unruly Guilds and their neighbors, enough to keep the fear constant. It will all be for naught if the people believe their 'hunter heroes' will save the day."

"I interrogated a hunter this week, my lord," Machison replied. "The guards have orders to find and capture them, and—I'm quite proud of this—to pin their disappearances on hunters. The families won't dare come forward and refute it; they would have to admit their men *were* hunters. And it all helps to vilify the so-called 'heroes'." He paused.

"We have to keep up the pressure on the rabble. Disappearances, monsters, rumors of witches—or have your own witchlings stir up a little bloody mayhem and blame it on the Wanderers. The Balance is fragile right now, we don't dare allow it to tip."

"As you wish, my lord." *What threat is so great that the Crown Princes—and King Rellan himself—are drawing so much power? Or are they* creating *a threat out of their petty sniping, using blood magic against their political enemies when a mortal assassin would do?*

"What of the distraction we discussed, once the ambassadors are assembled?" Aliyev asked without turning to look at Machison.

"It's been arranged. My witches have done their part, and the scenario will play out as we desire."

"See that it does," the Crown Prince snapped. "It must go exactly right to have the effect we want. Kasten's hungry to gain back its status in the League, which makes them dangerous. If we play this smart, we can weaken Itara and Sarolinia."

Sarolinia, in particular, posed a threat to Ravenwood that Machison wanted to neutralize. The Sarolinian Merchant Princes were young and aggressive, a new generation in power, eager to expand their fortunes.

"Everything is ready, my lord," Machison confirmed. "Just as we discussed. I assure you; the negotiations will run smoothly."

"They had better." Displeasing the wrong people at the wrong time had cost past Lord Mayors their position, and their heads, and Machison knew it.

"You have my word on it," Machison replied.

THE CARRIAGE LEFT Aliyev's villa and headed into the heart of the city. Guards rode on horseback in front and to the rear of Machison's vehicle, outfitted to give the impression of an honor guard. *Wouldn't want anyone to think I'm worried about anything.* Machison could not shake a feeling of dread. *Ridiculous. I'm letting my imagination run wild. I'm still among the villas. No one would dare strike here.*

A loud *thud* shook Machison from his thoughts, and the carriage lurched forward, accelerating to breakneck speed. He clung to the carriage strap to keep from being thrown from his seat. He did not need to ask the cause for the driver's alarm; the sound of an arrow striking the carriage frame was reason enough to flee.

Lovely. Now was that arrow meant for me, or the Crown Prince?

By the time they reached the Lord Mayor's palace, Machison's fear had become rage. "Report!" he barked as he alighted, safe within the gates of his compound.

"A lone archer took a shot as the carriage left the villa," the senior guard replied. "One of our men gave chase, but we considered it more important to get you to safety."

"What of the archer?" Machison snapped.

"The guard hasn't returned. We're not sure whether the attacker intended to shoot at you, or thought it was the Crown Prince in the carriage."

Certainly that's the way I'll have my people tell the tale, especially after Vrioni's death. Yes. Someone is trying to destroy the trade talks, unnerve the participants, kill Aliyev. Enemies of Ravenwood. I can use this.

"Give the arrow to Captain Jorgeson," Machison ordered. "I want to know where it came from." Then he turned and strode calmly into his home as if nothing had gone awry, intent on giving no appearance of weakness or fear.

Several candlemarks later, Jorgeson stood before him in his office. "The arrow could have come from anywhere," he said, dropping the missile on Machison's desk. "Nothing special about the workmanship or the fletchings. In fact, I suspect that's why it was chosen. There's no way to trace it."

"And the archer?"

Jorgeson shook his head. "Gone without a trace."

"Is it possible he thought he was shooting at Aliyev?"

Jorgeson shrugged. "Hard to say. Is that how you want us to explain it?"

Machison shared his thoughts, and Jorgeson nodded.

"That can work to our advantage. Heroic of you to risk yourself to protect the Crown Prince," Jorgeson added, raising an eyebrow so the sarcasm was not lost. "Puts him in your debt."

"Damn right. But we'd be in a stronger position if we knew whose faction fired that arrow."

"Agreed, but right now there are too many suspects. The Guild Masters and the Merchant Princes all have reason to remove rivals from the negotiations, or set them on edge. Even Itara or Sarolinia, or one of the other city-states, hoping to benefit if Ravenwood falters. Or it could be Kadar's assassin, warning that he knows you're supporting Gorog and reminding you that he wants in on the spoils." Jorgeson paced as he speculated.

Machison scowled and settled himself into the chair behind his desk. "Keep digging."

"In light of recent events are you planning to cancel the party tomorrow night?"

"Cancel? No! Let's see who has the balls to show up. Whoever's behind it won't dare not attend. They would look weak—or guilty. Especially if something did happen. Besides, everything's set. Blackholt's done his part, and my 'witchlings' have seen to theirs.

We won't have another chance like this, and I want to make sure it's done right."

"It's a dangerous game."

Machison gave a cold smile. "This whole negotiation is a dangerous game—and one I intend to win."

"Do you want additional guards at the party? To reassure the guests?"

"I want all the guards we have on duty. Keep your eyes open."

"Very well," Jorgeson replied. "What of the street patrols?"

"Keep a few men around this house and the road to the palace. Just make sure none of those damn hunters are about."

"One more thing, m'lord," Jorgeson said. "I received word that Merchant Prince Gorog said to expect him at ninth bells. Something urgent he wished to discuss."

Machison swore under his breath. "I'll be ready."

Gorog arrived on time. Machison received him in his parlor, the most private place in the palace. Two glasses of whiskey sat ready on the table beside a decanter.

"I know Aliyev summoned you," Gorog said, wasting no time in preliminaries. "What did he say?"

Machison pushed one of the glasses toward Gorog, and took the other himself. "He wants assurances the negotiations will be handled carefully. He approved of the Vrioni affair, but urged caution. Kasten's got him worried—he figures they're desperate and dangerous."

"They are."

"And we have made plans to handle that," Machison reassured him.

"Did he say anything about Kadar and Tamas?" Gorog pressed. His thin, dark hair barely covered all of his scalp. Good food had softened his prominent jawline and thickened his waist, but he carried himself like a man who could hold his own in a fight, and Machison knew that at heart, the Merchant Prince was a brawler.

"He's in a conciliatory mood," Machison replied with a pointed glance. "Wants to keep the peace among the three of you, even if it means giving up a percentage or two, though he has no objection to you retaining your edge."

"That's a load of shit," Gorog muttered. "Kadar and Tamas don't contribute as much to Ravenwood's wealth as my Guilds and exports do. Why should I give them a larger share of the profits? They'll only want more next time, and for less on their part." He shook his head. "No. We keep to the plan. If you handle this carefully, I'll maintain my favorable terms and you'll be well-compensated for your trouble, Kadar will be reminded his place, and Aliyev will be none the wiser."

"We risk much, for relatively little," Machison said.

"A point or two over ten years, with revenues as they are, is a fortune. One I'm not willing to hand over to Kadar or Tamas. Infuriating upstarts."

"Garenoth may have something to say in the matter. If it's true Kadar has invested in Garenoth's vineyards, they may see an advantage in rewarding him. After all, their own vineyards were failing until they had a sudden—and mysterious—turnaround."

"All the more reason to block Kadar," Gorog growled. "Investing in the infrastructure of other city-states, even friendly ones, is a dangerous business. Shouldn't be encouraged."

"It's not technically against League law," Machison mused. "I looked into it. How far we dare push may depend on how cozy Kadar has made himself with the powers in Garenoth."

"I don't care!" Gorog's fist banged on the table, sloshing the amber liquid in the decanter. "If Kadar gains in these discussions, he'll want more the next time, and he'll forget himself, forget his place. Tamas will watch what works for Kadar, and he'll do the same, and then I'll be losing ground twice as fast."

He shook his head. "No. We stop this before it starts, before they start thinking too highly of themselves and their cleverness. We don't give up anything. In fact, we press for more, so that if we keep what we have now, Kadar and Tamas can be grateful they didn't lose what they had. I'll see those two slimy sons of bitches kneel, before this is over."

Machison smiled and lifted his glass in salute. "I like how you think."

"Spare me the sycophancy. You stand to benefit—*richly*—from my good fortune. Win me this, and Aliyev will most assuredly bestow some of Kadar's or Tamas's lands to me as a reward. And as I rise, so do you."

"Everything is as we discussed. The pieces are all on the gameboard."

"Don't leave it all up to the negotiations," Gorog said, knocking back the last of his whiskey. "We can use the monsters against Kadar. Keep him busy, distracted, handling problems from his Guilds. Keep Blackholt targeting the Guilds that owe their loyalty to him. Kadar will know that he and his interests are the real targets."

"I believe he is already quite clear on that matter," Machison said. "Someone put an arrow in my carriage as I left the Crown Prince's villa tonight. Not meant to do real harm, or he'd have hit my horse or driver." Machison shook his head. "No. It was a warning, though my people will tell it as a foiled attack on the Crown Prince. I believe it was Kadar, giving me a heads up that I'd best not leave him out in the cold."

Gorog regarded him for a moment. "That's unacceptable. I'll retaliate in kind, against one of Kadar's proxies. Let him know his message was received and rejected."

Machison's left hand balled into a fist. *I am tired of being anyone's proxy.* "I thought you'd want to know," he said in a carefully neutral voice.

"I'll take care of it," Gorog said, moving toward the door. "And I shall look forward to hearing how tomorrow's reception goes. Remember—your fortunes are tied to mine. You know what I expect of you. See that it happens."

"Yes, my lord." Machison watched Gorog stalk from the room. His stomach knotted in a mixture of predatory anticipation, and a vague uneasiness. He understood Gorog's desire to punish Kadar and his insistence on keeping his rivals not merely weakened but humbled. But it was Gorog's greed that left Machison uneasy, though he stood to benefit. *Easy enough for Gorog to give orders. He doesn't have to handle the negotiation. Garenoth may not be so easy to persuade.*

Then again, I'm in so deep, I have no choice. We will rise—or fall—together.

"As always, the Lord Mayor of Ravenwood is a fine host." Ambassador Jothran's voice held warmth his eyes lacked. "Quite a nice touch, having the Crown Prince show up to greet us. In case we might have forgotten that he is your patron."

"Always an honor to have Crown Prince Aliyev grace us with his presence," Machison replied smoothly. "And how could he not, given the importance of the upcoming negotiations?" Machison was certain that the servant attending Jothran was, in fact, a hedgewitch in disguise, brought along to watch for poison. The news of Vrioni's death had quickly spread. "I hope the wine is to your liking, and the food to your taste?"

"Quite." Jothran's ample girth and heavy jowls suggested that he refused few indulgences. His frock coat was trimmed in gold, and golden rings gleaming with gems adorned his fingers. Machison wondered if beneath the finery, he also wore a light mail shirt, just in case.

"I hear you keep a clear head in chaotic situations," Jothran added. "That's commendable."

"All part of the office," Machison replied. *Comes with practice.*

"The Itaran ambassador doesn't seem to be having a good time," Jothran said, inclining his head toward a thin, hawk-faced man standing with a few others off to one side. Ambassador Kiril always looked as if his dinner had disagreed with him.

"Any time there are negotiations, there will be worries about terms and favoritism," Machison replied with a shrug. While the Lord Mayors of the negotiating city-states and their ambassadors handled the actual agreement, the League's dignitaries descended on the event for the chance to lobby for their own interests. And, should talks run into difficulty, other ambassadors would have no hesitation about rushing in to offer their 'advice.'

"Some have more cause to worry than others," Jothran said. The allied city-states traded with each other, and pooled resources to mount trading expeditions to unallied kingdoms. While the League members benefitted from their alliance, they were also jealous of any advantage or preference. That push-pull dynamic led to the League's founding long ago—formalizing the understanding that working together, the city-states had all the resources they needed, but opposing each other, they would quickly fall to ruin.

"Tell me, is there truth to what I've heard? That Itara and Calvot are at odds?" Machison asked. The reality of the situation was that for nearly all of the League's two-hundred-year existence, only its members' greed surpassed their aggression. Without the League, the city-states might well have battled each other into ruin.

Jothran rolled his eyes. "Is it a surprise? Those two states fight like they were a badly arranged marriage. And yet, they remain within the League because they know the benefits they reap." He shrugged. "Let them quarrel. While they're distracted, the rest of us gain business."

Machison looked around the room. Barring an epic failure or exceptional public disgrace, each of the ambassadors would hold his or her position for life. The strength of the alliances among the League often depended more on long-standing personal bonds than on the formalities of treaties and contracts. Knowing they would be dealing with one another for decades tempered the ambassadors' reactions—most of the time. *Meaning that the real warfare among them is carried out by proxies, like assassins and witches, a carefully orchestrated system of tit for tat.*

"Has the Osteronian ambassador had much to say about the upcoming negotiations?" Machison asked. "Theirs will be the next treaty up for renewal."

If the new agreement between Garenoth and Ravenwood retained its current, mutually favorable terms, the other League members would have to jostle with each other to improve their own standing. But if Ravenwood's terms with Garenoth worsened at all, or the negotiations fell through, the other city-states all stood to improve their ranking. Murder had been done for less.

Jothran chuckled. "Oh, they'll be watching, all right. Ravenwood is a valuable trading partner, and Ostero's mines need buyers like your smiths."

"Certainly all of the League states benefit from Ostero's rich mines. And all have smiths of their own."

"None that rival Ravenwood's," Jothran replied. It was true. Osteronian ore was the purest mined in the League, but the skill of Ravenwood's smiths made their forgings worth double those of the other states.

"Ah, but Garenoth's farmers are the envy of the League," Machison said. "Along with types of timber that won't grow here."

Being the favored trading partner meant getting the first quality exports and assurance that quantities stipulated would be fully met before those of less-favored partners, even if that meant those lowest on the list did without.

Jothran had the good grace to feign humility. "That's what makes the League, isn't it? Each with its advantages, balancing our deficits." He dropped his voice. "One of the reasons we value our relationship with Ravenwood so highly. Your state is known for keeping its word. Unlike some."

This was where the true politics came into play, navigating the closely-woven web of conflicting interests, large personalities, petty grievances, and thwarted ambitions. Aside from the quality of its exports, Garenoth's favored-partner status was so highly sought-after because Garenoth prided itself on keeping to—or exceeding—its contractual obligations. In short, they were reliable in every way.

"Tell me," Machison said, discreetly steering Jothran to a corner where they might talk more privately. "Are any of the other states particularly situated to benefit if we fail to come to a successful resolution?"

Jothran took his meaning immediately. "Enough to kill, you mean?"

Machison shrugged. "Such passion is not unknown." *United by need; divided by greed.*

"If you're asking, 'Do I believe one of the other League states had a hand in the unfortunate death of your Guild Master,' I would suggest that historical rivals remain as dangerous as ever." Jothran paused and glanced around to assure himself that they would not be overheard. "A man in your position might want to take a closer look at his allies, before hunting for enemies." With that, the ambassador drifted into the crowd.

He's as much as said Kadar's to blame for the archer. Things are truly out of hand if the Merchant Princes' proxy skirmishes have become the gossip of our League rivals, Machison thought.

He made his rounds, greeting each of the ambassadors and making small talk.

"Tell me, Lord Mayor, what is Ravenwood's policy concerning the Wanderers?" Ambassador Arlan from the city-state of Morletta asked. "Have you guards enough to patrol all of the city?"

"You must have a reason for asking, beyond mere curiosity."

Arlan shrugged. "The Wanderers have seemed more active of late in Morletta, and in Kasten and Sarolinia, our neighbor states. We've kept their presence from impacting trade in Morletta by doubling the number of guards, driving them out of the city, killing the ones that refuse to leave. Still, having to deal with Wanderers is far better than what befell Kasten after their negotiations failed and their League rank fell. Surely you've heard that they've fallen behind in their tribute?"

"Oh?"

Arlan paused to sip his drink. "Meddling from witches and Wanderers and hunters has become a *scourge* in Kasten. Warehouses have been burned, a ship or two was scuttled, and orders went unfilled. Monsters have attacked in droves, if you can believe the stories, more than anyone has seen in years. Something of a bloodbath, I've heard tell. Many, many deaths. You can guess how that impacted Kasten's shipments. The League has given them six months to make good on their tribute and increase their exports, or they've threatened to carve Kasten up between Morletta and Sarolinia." A slight smile touched his lips.

"And what of Sarolinia? I assume they had problems with the… infestations as well."

"They saw Kasten fall into chaos," Arlan said. "I'm sure Sarolinia took their fate as a cautionary tale; their reactions to the monsters and the Wanderers appear highly effective. In fact, with Kasten's trade having fallen away, both Morletta and Sarolinia stand to benefit. The High Lords and Crown Prince of Kasten are under house arrest on order of the League. Confidentially, I'm amazed Ambassador Vittir hasn't been recalled and replaced." He chuckled. "It's been an interesting spectacle."

"Why replace Vittir?" Machison asked. "Wasn't he here in Ravenwood when the problems arose?" Vittir was unlikely to have been home to Kasten in months, perhaps a year or more.

"Vittir's raised a few eyebrows, making accusations," Arlan confided. "You'd think an ambassador would be more circumspect, but he seems to be taking the fall of Kasten's fortunes personally."

"What kind of accusations?" Machison pressed. Something about Arlan's story did not ring true.

The ambassador shrugged. "The kind a man concocts when he's desperate to deny the truth. He doesn't want to believe that the mayor they supported brought this all on them, so he sees conspiracies from the League, from other city-states, from foreign kingdoms—even the gods. Some noise about the monsters being sent because Kasten couldn't pay its gold, to keep the Balance." He shook his head. "Rubbish, all of it." He finished his drink and regarded his empty glass with a sigh. "If you don't have anything to add to the tale, I think I'll excuse myself and get another drink."

Arlan's words stayed in Machison's mind as he continued to mingle. Across the room, Vittir was hemmed in by the Torquonan and Calvottian ambassadors, who were besieging him with questions he obviously did not wish to answer. The drunken Potronian ambassador, in the meantime, was trying to seduce the serving wenches, and the Arlan and Sarolinian ambassadors had struck up a conversation with Halloran, Ravenwood's ambassador.

Machison looked out over the reception with a swell of pride. The room conveyed prosperity and order, the liquor was excellent, and the food was befitting of his guests' station. Jorgeson ghosted in and out of the room discreetly, checking to make sure everything was as it should be. Musicians moved to take their places on a dais at the side of the room. The Lord Mayor reached into a pocket and withdrew a soft lump of wax, rolling it between his fingers until it was warm and pliable, then separated it into two pieces and plugged his ears, in preparation for the magic that was to come.

Machison's thoughts drifted back to Vittir. *Who stood to prosper from Kasten's downfall? Morletta and Sarolinia. Were they just fortunate, or did their Merchant Princes and Crown Princes have a hand in causing Kasten's misfortune?* Machison felt certain that Kasten's sudden reversal of fortune had been helped along by the enemies of its rulers. *Whoever was behind Kasten's troubles, they've given us a gift, though I doubt that was their intention. Once we've secured the terms with Garenoth, Itara and Sarolinia will be weakened, and the rest of the ambassadors will go home with their tails between their legs.*

His guests drifted toward the musicians, though Machison could hear nothing with the wax in his ears. He glanced toward Jorgeson and the guards, standing toward the front of the room, and Jorgeson gave a minute nod to confirm that all was ready. Jorgeson and the guards also had ear plugs, as did the musicians, who were mages under Blackholt's direction.

The dignitaries fell silent, entranced by the music as the flute played a skirling descant. A few of the ambassadors swayed to the tune, while others tapped their toes. Even dour Kirill permitted himself a smile. The magic woven into the music worked its spell. Machison watched their expressions as all other thoughts fled the guests' minds, so that only the music remained. Nothing else seemed important. Nothing but the music and the compelling, beautiful flute with its hidden magic, which played on for at least a quarter of a candlemark.

Abruptly, the music came to an end. Machison removed the wax from his ears. A bloodcurdling scream sounded from the corridor beyond the reception hall. Another scream sounded, and the ambassadors and their staff came back to themselves with panicked expressions.

One of his guards came running up to him. "M'lord, come quickly! It's Ambassador Vittir. He's dead."

Chapter Fifteen

When the triple knock came at the back door of the workshop, Corran made his excuses to Rigan and Kell as quickly as he could, then took off to meet up with the hunters. His lies sounded thin even to his own ears; Rigan and Kell would not believe him much longer.

He wound his way through back alleys, keeping a watchful eye for guards. A movement in the shadows made him freeze, weapon at the ready.

"Put down your knife, boy. I mean you no harm." An old woman stepped out of the darknesss. A colored rag bound up her hair, though wiry gray strands straggled from beneath the covering. Her dark eyes flashed with cunning. "I just wanted to have a look at you."

"Why?"

"I've seen you in my dreams," the old woman replied, taking a step closer, undeterred by Corran's raised blade. Her utter confidence unnerved him, and the idea that a witch-woman recognized him made his gut tighten.

"What do I matter to you?" Corran maintained the distance between them, even as the woman stepped toward him.

"You have caught Eshtamon's attention; and we are his people. Our blood runs in your veins."

"My mother had Wanderer blood."

She nodded. "Yet our magic did not come to you. Such is fate. You chose the blade."

"I do what I have to do to survive."

"As with my people." She gestured to the sigil on the wall behind her, which began to glow.

"Is that a curse sign?" Corran asked.

She laughed, a dry, husky sound. "No, not a curse. The world is broken. We do what we can to steady the Balance."

"By killing people?"

She leveled her gaze at him, a cold smile on her lips. "Is that what you believe?"

"I don't know *what* to believe."

The old woman gestured, and the sigil faded. "We are an old race, Eshtamon's people, cursed to find no peace. Yet we endure. We cannot restore the Balance, but we can slow the drift."

"Right now, the Balance isn't my concern," Corran said. "I've got monsters to fight."

She did not appear surprised. "Take this." The Wanderer woman held out a jar. "Goat's blood, mixed with a special powder made from leaves and roots. You will need it to kill the *azrikk*."

"What's an *azrikk*?"

"The thing you go to fight," she replied, as he gingerly accepted her gift. "They have existed since time began, servants of the Dark Gods. Coat your blade with this mixture. It is poison to the *azrikk*. Without it, your fight will be harder, and far costlier."

"Why are you helping me?"

"Because you have a role to play," the old woman answered, stepping back toward the shadows. "I have seen it in my dreams."

The squeal of rats took Corran's attention for just a second, and when he looked back, the old woman was gone.

Corran kept a tight grip on the jar and tried to still his thoughts as he wove through the shadows and alleys to the meeting point.

"We've got to pick our battles or recruit more hunters. There aren't enough of us to fight everything," Corran grumbled as he caught up with Calfon and Mir. "I won't be able to lie to my brothers forever, and I need to spend some time doing my job if we're to eat."

Mir huffed in agreement. "I think we need two teams, so the same hunters aren't going out every time."

Calfon glared at both of them. "The more hunters there are, the more likely we'll get caught. I don't like it either, but I don't see any other way."

"What is it tonight?" Ross asked.

"Butt-ugly things I've never seen before," Calfon replied.

"*Azrikk*," Corran said, and the others turned to him as he withdrew the jar of blood from beneath his cloak. "A Wanderer woman stopped me on my way here. Said that we'd kill the things faster if we dip our blades in this."

Calfon and Mir eyed the jar warily. "Just out of nowhere, a Wanderer woman gives you a special potion on your way to fight a monster?"

Corran shrugged. "Maybe she's a seer. They're a strange lot. Don't see how it could hurt."

"That's it? Just coat the blades?" Allery sounded skeptical.

"No spell to say? Nothing to chant?" Ross asked, sounding a little spooked.

Corran shook his head. "No. If there's magic, it's already in the mixture."

"Here goes nothing," Calfon muttered, carefully opening the jar and thrusting in the tip of his sword. One by one, the others did the same. Corran wondered whether he would be able to tell a difference, but his blade felt unchanged; no thrum of power, no uncanny glow.

"These *azrikk* are fast and mean," Calfon warned them as they headed out. "Powerful, too. Watch the mouths. They've got two of them—inner and outer, two sets of fangs as well. Keep away from the tail. It's got a barb."

"This just gets better and better," Ross grumbled.

The *azrikk* were prowling a section of Wrighton near the forges. The smell of coal smoke hung heavy in the air, though the blacksmiths had banked their fires for the night. Mir and Ross led the way, as they were most familiar with the area near their homes and shops. The hunters covered their faces with kerchiefs: a scant disguise, but better than nothing. The hunters were not quite so easily identified, and residents could claim ignorance.

"This way," Mir said. He led them toward a building that might be home to a dozen or more families. Lights glowed in the windows, but everything was eerily silent. No muffled bickering or quiet conversations; no squalling babies or barking dogs.

"Where is everyone?" Calfon held his blade ready.

"Gone—if they were lucky," Mir replied. "Happened right before I sent the boy to rouse you. Folks just finishing up dinner when the things came at them."

Bant, Pav, and Jott remained outside to keep watch. The others slipped inside and paired up, with Corran and Mir going left while Trent and Ross went right. Calfon and Allery headed up the stairs, moving off into the rooms and hallways opening off the main entrance.

"Some of them didn't make it out," Corran observed, throat tightening as he saw three savaged bodies in the first room. One was a child, perhaps eight or nine years old; the other two might have been a mother and grandmother. Too much of the upper bodies were missing to be able to identify them. Corran's stomach lurched as he realized that the corpses looked as if they had been partially skinned, and he wondered if they had disrupted the *azrikk*'s dinner.

He heard the scrape of something hard and slick against wood and looked up to see a nightmare beast coming right at him. The *azrikk* had the body of a snake as thick as a young man's torso, rippling and muscular, and tapered to a thin, whip-like tail ending in a nasty barb. But it was the face that would haunt Corran's dreams.

Jointed, bony ridges like skeletal fingers framed the outsized head. Black, cold eyes fixed on the creature's prey, and fleshy, knobbed growths twitched on its snout as if scenting the air. A high-pitched whine grew louder as the *azrikk* fixed its attention on the hunters, head bobbing up and down as it sized up its prey. The middle of the snake-thing's muscular body was oddly distended, and he wondered how long it took for a man to be fully digested.

Corran and Mir exchanged a glance and separated to flank the beast, swords ready. The creature turned toward Corran and came at him in a rush, its body writhing with powerful undulations that propelled it across the floor faster than a running man. The *azrikk*'s misshapen head tilted up and its hinged jaw opened wide, revealing a double set of pointed teeth curved inward. The clawed, bony extensions around its mouth moved independently, and Corran realized with a sick lurch that they served to grip the *azrikk*'s victims and push food into the monster's mouth.

The whine grew louder, shrill enough to send pain through Corran's skull, making it difficult to think. He swung at the *azrikk*, a glancing blow as the monster twisted. Mir ran toward the rear of the creature, forced to dodge out of the way as the wickedly barbed tail lashed out at him with uncanny accuracy.

Corran slashed again, and the tip of his blade caught in the smooth scales behind the *azrikk*'s head. The whine rose to ear-splitting intensity and Corran grimaced, fighting the urge to cover his ears. The *azrikk*'s mouth opened impossibly wide, revealing a second maw inside—a circular hole surrounded by pulsing muscle and rimmed in yet another row of sharp, curved teeth.

Shutting out the pain in his head, certain his ears must be bleeding by now, Corran dodged to one side and thrust his blade into the *azrikk*'s gullet, spraying himself with blood.

The *azrikk* swung toward him, close enough that one of the bony claws ripped across Corran's shoulder, digging in and drawing him toward the gaping maw. Corran stabbed with his sword, but the angle was wrong for a killing stroke. He tried to use the long knife in his left hand, but without the witch's coating it glanced harmlessly off the creature's sturdy hide.

"Corran!" Mir took a flying leap and landed on the *azrikk*'s back, clamping his legs around the muscular body, riding it as he drove his sword down two-handed into its back. The screeching changed abruptly to an angry hiss, and the maw snapped toward Corran, close enough that the first row of razor teeth tore the sleeve of his shirt.

Corran ripped himself free of the teeth, but the creature now had him up against the wall. Certain he was about to die, Corran snarled a curse and raised his sword with both hands to shoulder height, then threw himself forward, nearly into the mouth of the beast, ramming his blade through the pulsing muscles of the inner maw and out the back of the monster's skull.

The *azrikk* thrashed, twisting its head so violently it pulled Corran off his feet. Blood sprayed everywhere, stinging his eyes, tasting foul on his lips. Mir kept his seat on the bucking creature, drawing his blade up and plunging it in again, slicing the beast open through to the ribs. Corran saw a skeletal hand fall through the gash in the *azrikk*'s side.

It took all of Corran's strength just to hang on, but he used his weight to his advantage, knowing that every time the *azrikk* flung him from side to side, his blade dug that much deeper into the wound through its skull. It also brought Corran perilously close to the double row of teeth, and the bony claws that ripped at his shoulders and back, trying to dig in tightly enough to forced him into the monster's gullet.

Shouting a curse at the top of his voice, Mir reared back and swung his sword with all his strength at the *azrikk*'s body, just below the head. The blade sank deep, cleaving all the way to the spine. The *azrikk* shook, tail thrashing, and Mir had to throw himself from side to side to escape the vicious barb, which narrowly missed him and stuck in the floorboards.

Gurgling blood, trembling in its death throes, the *azrikk* gave one final scream of rage that threatened to black Corran out. Then, with a spasm, the monster crashed to the floor and lay still.

For a moment, neither Corran nor Mir dared move. Corran finally ripped his sword free of the creature's maw, sliding warily to the side and out of range, never taking his eyes from the beast. Mir pulled his sword clear of the body and stood, then gave a kick and jumped back, waiting for the monster to rise. The two men stared at each other in fear and amazement. Just to be sure, Corran brought his sword down with all his strength, severing the beast's head from its neck. He stood back, panting from exertion and fear.

"We're a mess," Corran finally managed in a shaky voice. His clothes were soaked with blood, both the monster's and his own. From elsewhere in the house, he could hear thumps and thrashing, along with cursing and a cry of pain as the others in their party fought more of the creatures.

"Think that any of the tenants who stayed survived?" Mir asked.

"Pretty damn quiet if they're still here," Corran replied. Keeping their swords ready, he and Mir made a sweep of the remaining rooms, and found nothing but partly digested corpses. Just as they approached the stairs, trying to decide whether to join the fight above them, they heard a torrent of curses and a heavy thump.

"Clear the way!" Trent yelled an instant before the headless body of another *azrikk* tumbled down the stairs, heavy coils taking out the rail as it fell.

"Ours is down! Let's get out of here," Calfon shouted.

"Light them up," Trent ordered. "We don't know if the damn things can regenerate."

Corran and Mir sloshed lamp oil over the two dead *azrikk*

downstairs, and a few moments later, Calfon and the others joined them. "Go!" Calfon hissed. "We lit the one upstairs. It won't take long for the flames to spread or the guards to notice."

Bant's shrill whistle split the night, warning them that guards had been sighted.

"Run!" Trent shouted.

Bant, Pav, and Jott were already almost out of sight by the time Corran and the others burst through the back door.

They were halfway across Wrighton from home, and Corran had no idea how many guards the lookouts had spotted. He traded a worried glance with Mir, but they were running too hard to waste breath on speculation.

"We'll head right. You go left. With luck, the others went a third way," Trent said, indicating himself, Mir and Corran as one group, Allery, Ross, and Calfon as the other.

"Go home—the long way. Stay low. Gods go with you," Calfon warned as the groups split off.

Corran spotted three guards heading their way. Sprinting for all he was worth, Corran and his friends ran for their lives.

Chapter Sixteen

AMBASSADOR VITTIR LAY in a pool of blood in a servant's hallway, his throat slit. Jorgeson stood over him, looking solemnly at the corpse. "I'll handle this," he said quietly. "Go see to your guests, m'lord."

Machison made sure his expression was blank before entering the reception room, where the frightened ambassadors and their nervous entourages milled about, kept from leaving—for now—by the guards.

Halloran was waiting for him when he came back through the door. "I demand to know what's going on!"

"There's been an accident," Machison lied. "Ambassador Vittir is badly hurt."

A murmur passed through the crowd. "Vittir?" Halloran repeated. "What in the name of the gods was he doing in the servants' hallway?"

Machison took Halloran by the elbow and steered him away from the door, lest he get a glimpse of the slaughtered ambassador. "We don't know yet," he said under his breath. "But I need your help to keep things from getting out of hand if we want to save the trade alliance."

To his credit, Halloran rallied. He was in his fifth decade, a lifelong bureaucrat with a bald pate and a rim of closely-cut silver hair. He had an agreeable face with craggy features, and when he chose to be charming, could summon up a winning smile and twinkling eyes. Now, he looked like the schemer he was, and Machison could almost hear the cogs turning as Halloran calculated the political ramifications and how best to turn the situation to Ravenwood's advantage.

"Where is Ambassador Vittir?" A thin, nervous man elbowed Halloran aside. "I'm Belson, his attaché. Is he hurt? I must attend him!"

"My surgeon's with him," Machison said smoothly. Halloran did not miss a beat. He grabbed a glass of whiskey from the tray of a passing servant and handed it to Belson.

"Drink this. You'll feel better," Halloran assured.

The attaché knocked back half of the whiskey in one slug before turning back to Machison.

"Surgeon? How badly is he hurt?"

"I promise you, he's in the best of hands," Machison replied. "And we will let you know as soon as we've heard about his condition."

Belson looked nervous enough to collapse. "I told him it was a mistake to come. I told him it was dangerous."

"Did you have a reason to think the Ambassador was at risk?" Machison asked.

"I shouldn't have said anything. It's an internal matter."

"I'll stay with this young man," Halloran volunteered. "Why don't you see to the other guests?"

Machison headed back into the milling press of dignitaries. Halloran would tell him what he managed to pry out of Belson when circumstances permitted.

"What's going on?"

"I demand to leave, immediately!"

"I shall speak to the Crown Prince personally about this!"

Voices rose from all corners of the room as Machison climbed up onto a chair to be seen. "Your attention, please!"

The room gradually quieted and everyone turned toward him. "I regret to announce that Ambassador Vittir has been injured. My best surgeon is with him now." Murmurs spread through the crowd, and the faces that looked up to him were frightened and worried.

"Injured how?" Ambassador Kirill was the first to speak.

"My chief of security is investigating. But we believe it may be related to Kasten's recent reversal of fortune." *Jorgeson planted enough false leads to have them all pointing their fingers at each other, watching their backs for a long time to come, while sacrificing someone who stood to gain if Ravenwood lost its favored status. Vittir's become valuable in the only way left to him: as a cautionary tale.*

"How could this happen?" Ambassador Jothran fixed Machison with a glare.

"No one knows why the ambassador was in the servant's hallway," Machison replied. "He may have caught sight of a pretty girl." A nervous chuckle went through the room. "The guards are patrolling the grounds now, and as soon as we're sure it's safe to leave, we'll have your carriages brought up."

"How do we know we're not all in danger?" The Osteronian ambassador looked panicked.

"You'll have guards escorting you back to your embassies," Machison promised. "Please understand this is a Kasten issue. None of the rest of you are in any danger." He knew that the more often he repeated that, the less likely the ambassadors were to believe it. One or two of the ambassadors gave Machison a look that let him know they recognized the lie for what it was, but said nothing. Jorgeson arrived at the main doors with a dozen guards behind him. "Your carriages are ready, m'lords, as are your escorts. This way, please."

The ambassadors followed the guards like frightened children.

* * *

"EVERYONE IS SAYING that Vittir was killed because of the threat he posed to the trade agreement," Jorgeson remarked. He and Machison met in the Lord Mayor's private parlor, where they would not be disturbed. "They all know he was willing to do anything to improve Kasten's lot, and it was no secret he'd made some bold overtures to try to win over the ambassador from Garenoth for better terms." He mused. "So now the rest of the city-states see Kasten as a threat to their own treaties, and the ambassadors are all wondering which of the others killed Vittir."

"Which is as we planned," Machison replied. "His murder opens up so many delicious possibilities. Keeps the water muddy, and ensures the rest feel a bit less trusting."

"My spies tell me the Guild Masters are terrified they'll be next, especially the ones who trade with Kasten. Merchant Princes Kadar and Tamas are worried, but whether it's for their own necks or their treasuries, it's hard to say. We did find and interrogate a man about the arrow that struck your carriage. He was a small-time assassin; my bet's on Kadar being behind it, though there's no way to prove it."

"Was he after me, or Aliyev?" Machison asked. "Or after me, to send Gorog a message?"

"The prisoner did not know or care about the significance of the strike," Jorgeson replied. "Even the blood witches could get nothing more from him. I'm not surprised. He was just the weapon. So the incident is still open to interpretation, though the gist of the message seems clear."

"I want answers!"

Jorgeson was unfazed. "Yes, m'lord. And I will get you those answers—as soon as we learn something new."

"What else?" Machison barked.

Jorgeson frowned. "The infestation last night was worse than usual. Blackholt's gotten creative. He sent several *azrikk*. Dozens of people died before the creatures were destroyed."

"I trust the guards contained the monsters below the villas?" Machison asked, repressing a shiver.

"Indeed, and they made special patrols around the homes of the Guild Masters and Merchant Princes, as well as the embassies." Jorgeson paused. "We lost three guardsmen trying to send the creatures back down into the streets where they belong. Would've gone even worse if Blackholt hadn't told us what we needed to hold them off. Once those damned *azrikk* have killed enough to satisfy the Cull, it'll be a fight to put them down if Blackholt can't just send them back to where they belong. We had few soldiers to spare for the rest of the city. The hunters were out in numbers."

Machison swore under his breath. "Armed and past curfew?"

"Yes, m'lord."

"We can't have armed mobs running through the streets. If they get rid of the monsters too quickly, it endangers the Balance. And they might get *ideas*."

In all of Ravenwood's long history, there had only been a few uprisings, but those had been bloody enough to be seared into memory. Whether the riots began over food or monsters or taxes, they had all ended with armed residents storming the villas and palaces and exacting their revenge on those in charge. Two Lord Mayors had been murdered: one hanged and the other decapitated.

"It's bad for trade," Machison continued. "Merchants won't come to the harbor if armed mobs are on the loose."

"They're hardly likely to come if there are *azrikk*, either."

Machison glared at him. "We don't dare allow vigilantes to get it into their heads that they can disobey the law. And we need to make certain we keep the commoners frightened enough to control them without pushing them into rebellion."

Hiring more guards and raising Guild fees was, obviously, a smokescreen. Blackholt's blood magic summoned the monsters and determined their targets, and the Lord Mayor's soldiers targeted the men who disappeared from the street. Yet the ruse with the Guilds was necessary to deflect suspicion and retain the fiction that the guards existed to protect the people.

Machison cursed. "The Guild Masters care about nothing except their profits. It's to the survivors' advantage if the creatures kill off a few members—drives the prices up."

"The Merchant Princes don't care about the toll the Balance requires so long as there's someone to get the work done and the goods for export ship on time. If there are a few less tradespeople, it's not their problem."

"But it's *our* problem if mobs run wild in the streets. The hunters need to be stopped."

Jorgeson's smile was cold. "Would you like to help interrogate the three hunters we captured last night?"

"I'll be happy to join you. We need to make an example of them."

THE LORD MAYOR steeled himself for the descent into the cold, stinking depths. Few prisoners left the dungeons for any destination except the gallows. Stories about lawbreakers who entered the dungeons and were never seen again were not uncommon—and not exaggerated.

"These are the hunters," Jorgeson said, stepping aside so Machison had a better view.

Three young men slumped against the bonds that secured them to their chairs. Blood stained their torn clothing and seeped from fresh wounds. Swollen eyes, battered faces, and fresh bruises showed that they had already undergone a thorough interrogation.

"Have they confessed? Have they given up their comrades?" Machison asked.

Jorgeson shook his head. "Confessed? Their guilt was apparent. But they've told us nothing about the other hunters."

"Do we know their names? Are they members of Guilds?"

"Go to the Pit." The prisoner on the left stared at Machison with a look of contempt. His head snapped to one side as the guard backhanded him. His broken nose, split lip, and eyes swollen nearly shut suggested that this was not his first impertinent comment.

"That's the Lord Mayor yer speakin' to!"

"I know who he is," the hunter slurred. Blood flecked his lips. "We pay our taxes. We deserve better than being food for monsters." The guard struck him again, but the man's glare was undiminished.

"That one is Bant, from the tanners in Skinton," Jorgeson said. "The man in the center is Pav, nephew to the head weaver in Wrighton. The last one is Jott, a carpenter. Also from Wrighton."

Pav hung forward against the ropes, unconscious. His chest hitched raggedly as he strained for breath. Blood covered half his face and stained his tunic a deep crimson. Next to him, equally battered, Jott remained conscious, though blood ran from his ears and mouth.

"What do their Guilds have to say?" Machison asked.

"Their Guilds disavow them," Jorgeson replied. "We're free to deal with them as we see fit."

Machison walked down the row, eyeing the prisoners. He stopped in front of Jott. "Are there more hunters?"

"No."

The Lord Mayor chuckled. "Three men against the monsters?"

"It's more than your guards can manage," Jott said through swollen lips. The guard behind him cuffed him so hard that the prisoner swayed as if he might pass out.

"They're of no use if they can't talk!" Machison reprimanded. He turned to Jorgeson. "How many other hunters *are* there?"

Jorgeson shrugged. "Hard to say. It's likely the groups work separately. Safer that way."

"We need to break them," Machison said, eyeing the prisoners. "It shouldn't take much. Perhaps I should assist. When we're done, we'll hang them or put them in gibbets. As a warning."

"M'lord," Jorgeson said, pulling Machison aside. "I would be careful in the manner of their punishment. There is strong support for the men, especially since the attacks have increased in frequency."

"What do you suggest?"

"Only a few guards know we found the archer who shot at your carriage," Jorgeson whispered. "They're sworn to secrecy. Blame the hunters. Charge them with treason, not monster-hunting. Claim that they were found attempting to assassinate the Crown Prince and ambassadors."

"You didn't arrest them anywhere near the ambassadors, did you?"

Jorgeson shook his head. "No. But we don't need trouble with the Guilds—or with the tradespeople."

Machison glowered in frustration. "The Guilds. Look how quickly they dropped these men. I'm not worried about them."

Jorgeson frowned. "The Guild Masters are famously good at politics. What they say isn't usually what they think."

"Agreed. But disavowing the prisoners waives the Guilds' right to object to their trial and sentencing."

"What good would it do them to object? It wouldn't change the outcome." Jorgeson held up a hand to forestall Machison's protest. "Just a warning, m'lord. They may prefer quiet revenge to loud protest."

"Unfortunately too true. Well, let's see what we can get from these men," Machison replied, returning to the prisoners. "Has the fire been stoked?"

"Yes m'lord, it should be ready," the guard replied.

Machison looked through the assortment of tools and selected the longest iron tongs before carefully working them into the hottest coals.

"Let's start with the tanner. He seems a little bit full of himself. Strip him and hang him by his wrists. Just high enough that his toes still touch the floor."

"You can't—" Bant's words were cut off when the guard shoved a rag into his mouth.

Machison pulled the glowing red tongs from the fire and smiled. "Oh, yes, I can."

The blood curdling scream echoed from the stone walls, despite the gag.

"Sorry m'lord, he appears to have passed out," the guard said after Machison had worked on the prisoner for a while.

"No matter. He'll wake soon and we'll keep the iron hot for him. He might be more willing to talk now that we've softened him up. String up the other one, let's see if we can whittle away some of that carpenter's pride. Unless of course you'd like to share some names?" Machison turned to Jott as he picked up and handled the knives, making sure the carpenter could see each one.

"You can rot!"

"Let's see how you feel once I start carving. Or maybe you'd prefer I begin with your teeth?" Machison held up a pair of iron pliers. "You don't need all of them to talk."

The screams continued to echo in the dungeon for quite some time before Machison grew bored. "Finish them," he said, handing the bloody pliers back to Joregeson. "I don't think we're going to get anything from these men, and there isn't enough of them left to provide any real challenge."

"As you wish, m'lord," Jorgeson replied.

The Lord Mayor returned to his rooms to clean up and change into fresh robes, before slipping outside. Night had fallen, and he glanced around himself as he left the palace, trusting that the bodyguards behind him would follow.

The cool air cleared his head, even as his questions multiplied. He headed toward the Avenue of Temples. The white marble paving stones and temple walls glowed in the moonlight, seeming to shimmer in the otherworldly light. This was a place of gods and spirits, and mortals entered at their own risk.

Down the street, toward the temples of Oj and Ren, was the grand edifice to Toloth, patron god of the Lord Mayors of Ravenwood, and all of the Mayor's staff and household. Normally, Machison made his appearance in Toloth's temple only for the great holidays and the high feast days, when he brought offerings or food and flowers to lay before the sacred fire. But tonight Machison wanted answers of a kind he might only find here.

The Guild gods' palatial temples lined the street, one for each of the trades. Ravenwood's Guilds and their members had paid tribute to their patron gods for generations, but not forever. A century, perhaps more, marked the rise of the new gods, each overseeing a particular skill or profession. Long enough to feel as if they had always been there, a fiction the Guilds promoted.

Custom demanded offerings and honor be given to the Guild gods, and the city obliged. But in the small hours of the night, when hope was scarce and needs were great, it was to the temples of the Old Gods that people came.

At the far end of the avenue from the opulent temples to the High God and Goddess were the oldest buildings on the street. These were the temples of the Elder Gods, who formed the world from chaos and presided over birth and death, sickness and health, famine and plenty. Ardevan and Eshtamon, Colduraan and Balledec. Oj and Ren, and Doharmu the god of the grave. They had owned the devotion of men long before the upstart gods made themselves known. And it was to these primal, primitive beings that the common people still poured out their offerings and prayers.

The temples to the Elder Gods were modest by comparison with the massive structures the Guilds built to their patron deities. The old temples had been stained by time and weather, floors worn smooth by the steps of penitents, and they were smaller, more intimate, from a time when gods were said to walk among the people of Ravenwood.

Machison passed the old temples with disdain, intent on Toloth's far more impressive structure. When he reached the doorway, he felt his heart race and his mouth went dry. He motioned for his bodyguards to remain outside, and climbed the steps. While he privately doubted that the gods actually dwelled in these garish temples, he had no difficulty believing that *something* lingered in this place. Two torches burned within, providing just enough light for Machison to make out the vast statue of Toloth.

"Why have you come?" The voice was raspy with age and echoed from the shadows.

"I need your Sight," Machison replied. "I will make a generous offering." The only mages that would acquiesce to serving the Lord Mayor or the ruling powers—other than healers, who went where they were needed—were blood witches. The others hid themselves, pledged their service to the gods, fled the city-state, or died for their refusal. Machison did not doubt the power of blood magic, but he did doubt the truthfulness and loyalty of its practitioners, which left him seeking the counsel of an old woman whose service to a young god might be no more than a sign of madness.

He sensed, rather than saw, movement in the dark. "I am curious," the dry voice said. "Why do you seek me now?"

Machison dared move further into the temple. The flickering torchlight played tricks on his eyes, bringing the shadows to life. "There's much at stake, and much unknown. I want to know what you see."

"You are uncertain." The voice was more hiss than whisper.

"Perhaps. These are fearsome times. I need to know, will Ravenwood succeed in bettering the terms with Garenoth? Or merely retain the advantage we already hold?"

Machison heard sandaled feet on stone. "Leave your tribute between the torches," the oracle commanded. "And we will see what we will see."

Machison withdrew a pouch of silver coins from his waistcoat and laid them out at the feet of the statue of Toloth. He bowed his head, a litany of questions, rather than prayers, running through his mind. *Opportunities are already starting to present themselves for after the treaty is finalized. A few of the other city-states have accepted that Ravenwood's current position—or stronger—will be the reality, and they've made overtures. That's just the beginning. The others will fall in line, or risk being left behind. Aliyev and Gorog will reward me. But have I done enough to secure the trade negotiations succeeds? What of the hunters? Can we get them under control before they cause problems? And what of the Wanderer woman in my dreams? How do I ensure my safety from a vision?*

When he stood, he saw the oracle silhouetted by the torchlight. "Come."

Machison walked into the shadows, hoping he appeared more confident than he felt. He followed the woman to a fountain filling a deep obsidian basin. The water glistened in the darkness, black and depthless.

"Ask."

"Are my dreams certainties, or just possibilities?"

The oracle dipped a long, bony finger into the black water and watched the ripples. "Difficult to say." Her voice was dry as a winter wind through old leaves. "Some of the things you have dreamed are nearly upon you, almost impossible to deflect. Consequences, of actions long past. Others are yet a ways off. There may yet be time to change the course."

"The agreement with Garenoth—will we succeed in bettering the terms?"

Again the oracle stirred the waters. "Uncertain." The hooded head rose, and the face within was lost in the shadows. "You have not asked the one question you truly wish answered."

Machison hesitated. "Will the assassins strike again? Am I in danger?"

This time, the oracle peered into the dark waters for longer. Machison stared at the ripples, catching glimpses of images that were there and gone. "You have more to fear from the voices of the dead than the hands of the living," the oracle replied. "I see a drowning man in a rising tide. The rest is veiled, closed to me."

Not much to go on for the price I paid. How dare she try to frighten me! She's angling for more coin, or perhaps she's in Kadar's employ, with orders to weaken my nerve.

But if the end is still uncertain, as she says, then I can still come out on top. No outcome is yet fixed. I must be more careful, and more ruthless than ever.

I'll have Jorgeson watch the oracle, see who she's beholden to, and then we'll take care of her. Let her think she's rattled me. The situation with Garenoth is coming together as planned. I was unwise to want validation from the likes of her. Next time, I'll know to keep my own counsel.

"Thank you, m'lady," Machison said, forcing his tone to be gracious. "I'm sorry to have bothered you." He turned to leave.

"A Wanderer will be the death of you."

Machison froze. "Can you see the means? The time? *Anything?*"

"Go. Fate will find you."

THREE CANDLEMARKS LATER, after Machison was safely back in his sitting room, calming his nerves with a glass of whiskey, Jorgeson knocked on his door.

"M'lord. We have finished with the prisoners." Jorgeson's uniform was splattered with blood, and his jaw was set.

"And? Did they give up anything more?"

"No, m'lord. The weaver never regained consciousness. The tanner cursed us until his last breath, when we broke what was left of him on the rack. But he told us nothing of value."

"And the carpenter?"

"He said nothing of the hunters—he was hard to understand, after you'd finished with him—but we believe he swore to find a way to avenge his friends. He bled out rather quickly."

"I hope you saved the blood for the witches. And what of the bodies?" Machison asked.

"They'll all hang in gibbets as traitors tomorrow, and the captain of the guards will denounce their crimes against Ravenwood."

"Very well. Tell me when it's done. Levy a fine on the Guilds the traitors belonged to. And come up with a plan to get rid of those damned Wanderers. Make it a priority."

Chapter Seventeen

"GUARDS! RUN!" CORRAN yelled. Behind them, flames rose and the air smelled of smoke and burning meat. They'd gone after an *azrikk*, and the creature would haunt his dreams for the rest of his life.

Damn guards couldn't be bothered to fight the monsters, but set one *little fire—*

Corran, Mir, and Trent ran. Corran's boots pounded on the cobblestones. Adrenaline pumped through his veins, and his lungs burned. Shouts sounded behind them, and running footsteps echoed as the guards caught their trail.

Gods, is this how Rigan felt the night Wil died? Corran fought down panic. Mir was in the lead; he knew these streets best. Corran and Trent kept pace as their fellow hunter zigged and zagged through the ginnels. When the guards were far enough behind them to be out of sight, he pointed skyward, hauled himself up onto a balcony, and began climbing a drainpipe, heading toward the roof. Corran was the last up the pipe, and flipped over onto the rooftop just as the soldiers came into view below.

The three hunters lay flat, not daring to breathe or move. *There's no reason for them to look up,* Corran told himself. *The alley goes on.*

Please don't look up. He let out a silent sigh as the footsteps pounded past. Minutes crept by while they remained motionless, waiting. Mir dragged himself to the edge and looked over, then nodded.

In the distance, Corran could see the guttering flames and plumes of smoke drifting in the wind. *That was close. Too close.* They made their way across Wrighton using the rooftops, crouched low. When they finally reached the room they used for training, Corran realized his hands were shaking. Calfon and Ross were waiting for them.

Calfon shrugged out of his padded jacket and wiped the soot from his face with a rag. "Where are the others?"

"Probably hiding," Trent replied.

"You'd better all get home," Calfon said, dragging a hand through his hair. "Things should have died down outside. I'll wait for the rest of them here."

Corran and the others protested, but Calfon sent them away. Corran let himself through the back door into the workshop as the clock in the tower rang third bells, and leaned against the doorframe, ready to collapse.

I need to get cleaned up and get some sleep. The cold water in the bucket woke him as it sluiced the sweat from his face. He checked his arms and legs for snake bites, relieved when he found none. *That's one good thing. And it doesn't look like we've burned down the city. That's two.*

Corran almost missed the note on the table in Kell's scrawled handwriting:

Rigan's staying the night at the tavern. Said there's a girl. Back early.

Corran crumpled the note in his fist. Raw nerves and sheer exhaustion made his temper flare. *Rigan left Kell alone. We're going to have a word about this.*

* * *

When he woke, Corran could feel the ache of the fight in every muscle. *The drainpipe might have saved our lives, but I haven't climbed like that in ages. Damn, it feels like someone tried to rip off my arms.* Sun streamed through the bedroom windows. Kell rattled pots on the hearth, humming cheerily. The room smelled of fresh coffee and burned bread.

Corran pushed himself out of bed with a grunt of pain. "Where's Rigan?" He said as he entered the kitchen.

Kell turned. "Morning, Corran. Coffee's ready and—"

"Where's your brother?"

"There was a note on the table—"

"Isn't he back yet?"

Kell's smile slipped a little. "It's still early, Corran." He frowned. "You look awful. Get in a bar fight last night?"

Corran grabbed a burnt piece of toast and a cup of black coffee and headed down to the workroom, ignoring Kell's question. Part of him hoped Rigan had returned before dawn and was sleeping on one of the tables. When he saw his brother was nowhere in sight, Corran's mood darkened.

"It's not like he left without saying where he was going." Kell followed him partway down the steps. "And he planned to stay at the Dragon rather than break curfew."

"It was a bad night out there."

"Which is why Rigan did the right thing by staying at the Dragon," Kell repeated, as if speaking to a child.

"He shouldn't have gone out. He should have been here with you."

Kell glared. "I've been old enough to stay home by myself for a long time, Corran. The doors were locked. Nothing got in."

"He's still not back." Since the close call the night Wil died, Corran had been unhappy letting either Rigan or Kell out of his sight.

"He'll be home."

"He didn't tell me he planned to go out."

"Is that the new rule? Because that's not going to go well," Kell warned, starting to lose his patience. "Gods, Corran! Do you think I didn't hear *you* come in just shy of dawn? How can you be angry at Rigan—who stayed over at the damn tavern—when you took a crazy fool risk like that?"

Corran bit back a reply as Kell's anger registered. *He knew where Rigan was. He didn't know where I was, and I didn't come home.* Before he could say anything, Kell stomped back up the steps and began crashing the pots and pans around as he started the soup for lunch.

The door opened to the alley. Rigan froze in the entrance, realizing Corran had beat him home.

"Where were you?"

"I let Kell know," Rigan snapped.

"You left your brother alone."

"So did you."

Rigan had not wanted the fight, but he wasn't going to back down now. Corran knew he should be relieved to his brother safe, but the storm of fear—for Rigan's safety and from last night's hunt—had already worked into a full-blown rage.

"Don't you dare do that again without asking me."

"You'd have to be home to ask."

It went downhill from there, although, later, Corran couldn't remember exactly what they had said—screamed—before the pounding on the door got their attention. With a glare toward Rigan, Corran walked around his brother and opened the door to find Mir standing in the alley.

"We need to talk," Mir said, and Corran's heart sank.

"Get started on those bodies," Corran ordered Rigan before he shut the door behind him and stepped into the alley.

"Bant, Pav, and Jott have been captured. Gods, Corran, what if they tell?"

Corran felt his heartbeat quicken. He put a hand on Mir's shoulder. "Captured, not killed?"

"Calfon found out this morning. If they break, the guards will be after all of us. By the Dark Ones! They might have already given our names. The guards have had them all night."

"If we run and Bant and the others didn't break, we've admitted our guilt."

"Yeah. Lousy choice. Stay and risk capture; run and confess."

"I'm going back to work," Corran said. "What about the others?"

"Everyone else checked back in after last night."

Rigan was already mixing pigments when Corran let himself back into the workroom. Normally, Rigan would have asked about Mir's visit, but after their argument, he kept his head down.

Just as well, Corran thought. *There's nothing I can say that isn't a lie. Gods! I started hunting the monsters to keep my family safe; but if the guards find out, I'll have destroyed us.*

Usually, they talked as they worked. Corran was too consumed by his own worries to press the matter, especially if it led to another fight. Kell made his opinion clear by leaving their lunch on the kitchen table to grow cold, before heading out without a word to make his rounds.

"Hand me the knife." Corran did not turn to look at his brother. He held out his hand, and Rigan placed the knife, hilt-first, in his grip. Footsteps told him Rigan had moved to the other side of the workshop to fix more of the mixtures.

Kell's got a reason to be angry, Corran admitted to himself. *I don't think he believes the story about Guild meetings anymore. But where in the name of the gods was Rigan? Is he really that taken with a girl?* A possibility occurred to him: *Maybe, after what happened to Jora, Rigan doesn't want to say anything if he's courting someone.*

Jora's death still haunted his memories, and probably always would. *We should have run instead of trying to fight. I didn't know anything about fighting monsters. I should have pushed her out the door and let the creature get me instead.* Too many nights his dreams played out all the other ways that evening could have gone.

Training or patrolling with the hunters let him fall into an exhausted sleep, a small mercy. And killing the creatures satisfied a little of his need for vengeance, something Corran suspected was a bottomless well.

Loud noises from the front of the shop interrupted his thoughts. He froze. *Is it the guards? Have they come for me?* "I'll go see what it is," he said, peeling off his gloves before Rigan had a chance to move.

He opened the door to find a crier in the square loudly ringing a bell. "Hear ye, hear ye! By order of Lord Mayor Machison, there's to be a gibbeting in the town square at fourth bells. The bodies of three traitors will be displayed for their attempt on the lives of the Bakaran ambassadors and Crown Prince Aliyev. The traitors are Bant the tanner, Pav the weaver, and Jott the carpenter. Their Guilds have disavowed them. Know this, all of you."

The crier walked off, heading for the next block, where he would repeat his message. Corran stood motionless on the front step, barely aware of the buzz of conversation around him.

"Corran?" Rigan's voice seemed far away.

How did they get blamed for trying to kill those people? What in the name of the gods is going on? Corran wondered. The crier's words sank in, and he realized something else. *He called them 'traitors,' not 'hunters.' Maybe they didn't break. Maybe the guards aren't coming after the rest of us.* He felt momentary relief, and then guilt washed over him. *It could have just as easily been any of us. If they died protecting us, their blood is on our heads.*

Rigan took his elbow and steered him back inside, watching Corran worriedly. "What do you think they did?" he asked.

Now I absolutely can't tell Rigan or Kell about the hunters. He had almost gone with Bant and Pav, only to switch to Mir's team at the last minute. *If I hadn't changed teams, if I had gone with them, it would be me in one of those gibbets.*

"Corran?" Rigan was staring at him, and Corran realized he had missed answering a question.

"I'm just stunned," Corran replied, looking away. "I knew all those men, grew up with them. I can't believe they'd do something like that." *I know damned well they didn't. So what game is Machison playing?*

"I'm sorry," Rigan replied. "I knew them, too. Are you going to go to the square?"

"I don't think—"

"They didn't do it." Rigan met his gaze. "I don't know what the guards are up to, but Bant, Pav, and Jott were not traitors. Maybe we should go. We were their friends."

Or maybe it will just make it easier for the guards to round up the rest of us. We don't know for certain what Bant and the others told them, if anything.

"Maybe you're right," Corran replied, feeling like he'd been punched in the gut. "I need to think about it. Come on. Let's get back to work."

JUST BEFORE FOURTH bells, Corran lingered at the edge of the crowd in the town square. He hated gibbetings and executions. They were common enough that many people considered them entertainment. *I get enough of death every day. I don't need to watch it for sport,* he thought. The size of the crowd sickened him. *How many of you are alive right now because we fought the monsters that were going to kill you? And this is the thanks we get?*

Corran stayed well back, out of sight of the guards. He didn't want to see any more of the ghastly show than necessary. A gallows stood in the center of the town square. The crowd jeered and shouted, calling for the prisoners, hungry for blood.

The prison wagon rolled into the square and the crowd cheered. Corran swallowed back bile, knowing the bodies of his friends were in that cart.

"Hear the sentence of Lord Mayor Machison!" One of the guards climbed onto the gallows platform, shouting to be heard. "These three men—Bant, Pav, and Jott—have been condemned for the crime of high treason, and for the attempted murder of the League ambassadors and Crown Prince Aliyev. Their bodies are to be gibbeted so all may take heed of their folly, and they will not receive burial. Their names have been blotted out from the ranks of their Guilds, which disavow their treason. This is the word of the law."

Corran swallowed hard and forced himself to watch as the guards dragged the bodies of the three men from the cart. Blood covered their faces and bodies, and the angles of their arms and legs suggested broken bones. *They've been tortured. How could they possibly endure that, and not turn the rest of us in?* He remembered the moment their groups went in different directions. *If we had gone left instead... if I had stayed with them instead... that would be me. And if they had taken me, would* I *have been able to keep from betraying my friends?*

The crowd pressed forward, anxious to see the spectacle. Guards held the bodies upright while the executioner fitted them into the iron cages hanging from the arm of the gallows. The cages swung when the doors clanged shut, creaking on heavy chains.

That ended the spectacle, so the crowd dispersed. Corran remained, bearing witness from a distance. He turned his back when the ravens descended.

Chapter Eighteen

"HEARD THEY CAUGHT a witch." The comment was offhand, just casual gossip, the kind Wrighton's merchants relished sharing.

For a heartbeat, Rigan froze, then tried to cover for his lapse with a neutral expression.

"What happened?"

He'd volunteered to run an errand when Corran had remembered a few things they needed for the workshop after Kell was already on his rounds. Corran was in a foul mood, and Rigan was glad for a break.

"Might be the one who caused the fever down near the harbor," the storekeeper remarked, gathering the salt and honey Rigan requested. "Won't be causing anyone any more trouble."

Rigan's stomach did a slow flip. "The guards caught her?"

"Nah, the folks who live down there did. It was the seamstress's apprentice. She'd made clothing for five of the people who died just before they took sick. And if that wasn't enough, I heard they went back and looked at the clothes, after they caught her, and found some strange patterns in the stitches."

"Does that prove she's a witch?"

The shopkeeper gave him a look. "She had dealings with five of the victims. Made something personal for them, something they wore—with those weird witch threads. And I heard they found black feathers in her room." He said the last with an emphatic nod, as if the feathers provided all the evidence needed.

"Did they give her to the guards?" Rigan looked down, counting his coins, so that he did not have to meet the shopkeeper's gaze. *It doesn't sound like any kind of witchery I've seen. Just bad timing and bad luck.*

"She didn't last that long. The folks who caught her had lost loved ones. They weren't inclined to be patient. Tried to make her confess to her crimes. But you know what they say, the Dark Ones are liars, through and through. The fellows that killed her, they'd lost family, and they wanted a little revenge."

The shopkeeper warmed to his subject. He had no other customers to serve, and a captive audience in Rigan. "She was a tough one. Wouldn't talk when they broke her fingers, or after they'd tried holding her head under water. Couldn't beat a confession out of her, either. So they burned it out, and I guess that worked just fine."

"Burned?" Rigan's mouth was dry.

"That big bonfire last night, down by the harbor? Guess you didn't catch the way the wind smelled. Roasted witch," the shopkeeper said with a laugh. "Oh, I guess once the fire got started, good and hot, she confessed to everything."

Who wouldn't? "So the fever's gone now?" Rigan focused on not being sick.

"Better, but not over yet. They're pretty sure a couple more witches are loose. They're monsters, just like all those creatures that show up. Worse, because the witches look human, but they ain't."

"Thanks," Rigan said, taking the bag.

"You look a little green around the gills," the shopkeeper called after him. "Thought an undertaker would have a stronger stomach."

"Breakfast didn't set well," Rigan lied. "I'd better be going. We've got a lot of work to do."

"Yeah, sorry they didn't save the witch for the undertakers, but there wasn't much left when the fire was done."

Rigan clenched his jaw and headed back to their workshop, taking deep breaths, trying to slow his racing heart. *They tortured her. Tried to drown her. Burned her.*

He swallowed hard. *Where were Damian and the others? Why didn't they do something?* But as soon as he thought the question, he knew the answer. *Because she wasn't a real witch. And because there are a lot more townspeople than there are witches. There's not enough magic to fight everyone on the harbor front, and I bet witches burn the same as regular people.*

Rigan took the long way home, knowing that if he showed up now, Corran would notice something was wrong, and in the mood his older brother had been in lately, that was likely to lead to another argument. *No one said anything about the witch's family. If anyone discovers what I am and comes after me, maybe they won't hurt Corran and Kell. That's why I have to keep what I'm learning Below a secret. That's why they can't know. Safer that way.*

Corran looked up when he finally walked through the door. "Where in the name of the gods have you been? There's work to do."

Rigan turned his back as he shut the door, willing his hands to stop shaking, hoping he could steel his expression to not give away his fear. "I had to go all the way to the shops near the harbor."

"Come on, give me a hand. Kell brought us some new bodies, and I'd like to be able to take them to the cemetery tonight. I hear there's a storm heading this way."

Rigan tied on his apron and got his gloves. He had stopped shaking, though he still felt like throwing up.

Corran looked his brother over. "Are you sick?"

Rigan shrugged. "I don't feel well. It's nothing. Probably something I ate."

Corran turned back to their work. "Watch yourself. Kell says there's a fever going around. If you're sick, get some tea when you see the herb woman."

The Chirurgeons' Guilds of the League held crown monopolies on healing magic. Those who could not afford Guild fees treated ailments with herbs, teas, poultices, and potions administered by midwives or herb women schooled in plant medicine. Or they braved the trek to Below, where magic and cures could be bought for a price. A 'miraculous' recovery without Guild intervention was more likely to be attributed to illicit magic than to favor by the gods.

"I'll go as soon as we're done," Rigan promised. "It'll be fine."

The fever victims were outside in the cart, and Corran had already quicklimed them. "Who do we have today?" Rigan asked, trying to distract himself.

"A woman who died in childbirth, a boy who died of fever, a traveler from the tavern who choked on his meat, and a suicide we've been paid extra to treat as an accidental poisoning."

"Suicide?"

"The family told me she used the wrong leaves in her tea. But look." Corran held up the corpse's forearm. Old scars, long and deep, ran almost wrist to elbow. "There's another set on the other arm. And an old scar on her throat. This wasn't her first attempt."

"So what did you tell them? Saunders said the Guild won't let the priests bless the passage of a suicide."

"The priest doesn't have to know, and the gods can figure it out for themselves. There's a mass in the corpse's abdomen the size of a melon. Probably damn painful. I'm not going to judge her choices, and I've never seen a priest look beneath a shroud."

Rigan mixed pigments in silence.

"You're awfully quiet tonight," Corran said.

He managed a weak smile. "Just letting my mind wander a bit, I guess. How was the Guild meeting?"

Corran looked up. For an instant, Rigan saw guilt in his brother's eyes before his face became impassive. "Boring. A total waste of time."

"They've been meeting more often lately."

"You know how the Guild is. Too much politics."

He's hiding something. Rigan clearly remembered Papa telling stories about the Guild meetings he attended. He'd vent over the arrogance of the Guild Master, or recount a ridiculous new rule to be implemented, or repeat something amusing that had occurred. The meetings had never been secret until just a few months ago, when Corran began attending more often.

Now that Rigan got a good look at his brother, he saw that a fresh bruise marked his cheek, and he walked with a slight limp. They weren't the first new injuries Corran had returned with after his evening meetings, but every time Rigan or Kell expressed concern, he either cut them off or tried to explain the damage away. A new, and frightening, possibility occurred to Rigan.

He took the gibbetings hard. Corran knew the men, but I didn't think he was close to them. Not close enough for the reaction he had when they died. He only gets that angry when he's afraid. Oh, gods. Is he a hunter? As soon as the thought came to him, he knew it to be true. *All these nights he goes out; he's been hunting monsters.*

"You'd best get going to the herbalist if you want to get that tea. We're done here, for now," Corran said. "I'll have a boy go tell the priest we'll need him. The quicklime will keep the rats off the bodies while they wait. Don't take too long—we need to have them buried by curfew."

Rigan grabbed his cloak from a peg near the door and stepped outside, hoping a walk would help to clear his head. He turned down the street to the herbalist's shop and ducked into the store. The air was fragrant with spices, dried flowers and the leaves and nuts of more plants that Rigan could count. Bunches of brittle, desiccated plants hung from the rafters. Two lanterns barely lit the shop, leaving the corners in shadow. Bins and bowls nearly overflowed with powdered and crumbled ingredients for potions, poultices, and elixirs. Rigan had heard whispers that a clever—and desperate—person might even use the plants for small magics: causing a person to fall in love, or warding off evil.

"I wondered when you would come to see me," Mamme Solan rasped. She slipped off a stool and limped around the counter to fetch his order. Silvered hair framed a lined face, her eyes sharp and bright as silver coins. She chuckled. "It was bound to happen. You take after your mother." The herbalist moved around the store, pulling ingredients from shelves and bringing them to her worktable, where she added them to her large stone mortar.

"What do you mean?"

Mamme did not look up from her work, grinding the mixture with a smooth granite pestle. "You've been having headaches lately that don't quite go away," she said, sprinkling a few more powders into the mix. "Your dreams are dark, and you aren't sleeping well. And you're tired. Much more than usual."

Rigan stared at her. He had not mentioned the symptoms to anyone, not even Kell. "Yes, all of that. Am I sick?"

Mamme glanced at him, and her lips twisted in a half smile. "It's not sickness, it's your gift. It takes a while to come to the fore, but it breeds true. Your Mama thought it might be you, of the three brothers. Told me to keep an eye out."

"I'm not sure I know what you mean," Rigan said cautiously, though he was almost certain that he did. His stomach tightened in fear.

Mamme seemed to guess his thoughts. "Don't worry, boy. I'm not going to tell anyone. Didn't betray your mother, now did I? No. We have to stick together," she added, raising an eyebrow conspiratorially.

Perhaps there's more to her potions and poultices than good medicine. But how does she hide her magic from the guards?

"Have you ever put a kettle on the hearth to boil?" Mamme's question seemed to come out of nowhere. Startled, Rigan nodded.

"The steam can lift the lid right off, if you're not careful." Mamme's gnarled hands moved confidently. "That's what happens when power builds and isn't let out. This tea will help. It quenches the fire, so to speak, keeps the 'steam' from building." She looked up and her gaze lingered for a moment on the pendant around his neck. "Still no substitute for taking off the lid from time to time, of course. That's something you'll need to learn, and fast, or it will get worse for you."

"Mama... needed your help for this also?"

"Oh, yes. Of course, she blamed it on her moontimes, but I knew. I suspect your father did, too. She was part Wanderer."

"She didn't teach me much..."

Mamme scooped the mixture into a tin, and added several cheesecloth bags on top. "Of course she didn't. There was plenty of time—she thought." She shook her head. "I'm sure she meant to train you more, when the time was right. But it didn't work out that way."

"You knew, and you protected her."

"I was her friend. Now that she's gone, I'll look after you the same." Mamme leaned closer. "And you'd best be careful. Don't give anyone reason to talk. It's dangerous out there."

"Thank you," Rigan said, digging into his coin purse. "What happens, if the tea doesn't work?"

Mamme's wrinkled face creased in a grin that showed her mottled teeth. "Then you tell me, and I mix you up something special." She looked at him appraisingly. "I have the feeling that you're all your Mama was, and more."

Rigan thanked the herbalist. He was about to head back to the workshop when he decided instead to swing past the dyer's and see Elinor. *I'm too much on edge to face Corran in one of his moods right now.* By the time he reached Parah's shop, his head throbbed.

Rigan ducked inside, glancing around in vain for Elinor. Parah came out of the back room at the sound of the door opening, haggard and red-eyed.

"She's not here," Parah said, answering his unspoken question. Something in her voice frightened Rigan.

"Is she sick?"

Parah looked like she had aged years since his last visit. "No, lad." She swallowed, and blinked back tears. "She's gone."

"Gone?"

Parah nodded, watching the door. "She's very good with the pigments. The ones she makes never turn strange colors, and they don't fade. Her dyes stay in the cloth, and some people said that they felt better when they wore clothing made from cloth she dyed."

A cold knot was forming in Rigan's stomach. *The seamstress near the harbor. The one they burned—*

"You've heard about the fevers?" Parah went on. Rigan heard anger in her tone, and loss. "There's been talk of witches. People making accusations. Names came up. Elinor's name was one of them. She ran away."

Rigan steadied himself against the table; suddenly he did not trust his legs to hold him up. "You're sure she ran? They didn't—"

"I warned her. Helped her."

"Thank you. Do you know—"

Parah shook her head. "No, and I don't want to. Can't tell what I don't know, and neither can you." She dropped her voice. "I know you cared for her, or I wouldn't have told you."

"If you hear—"

"I won't. I told her to run and keep on running. This witch business will die down. It always does—after a few innocents have been killed. But that kind of talk never gets forgotten." She took his hand. "I'm sorry."

By the time Rigan got back to their shop, Kell had dinner ready. Corran said nothing throughout the meal. Rigan was too deep in his own thoughts to care. Kell kept up the conversation single-handedly, filling Rigan and Corran in on the gossip from the marketplace.

Finally, he looked from one of them to the other. "You two are never this quiet. What's going on?"

"We've got bodies still to bury, and the day's mostly gone, that's all." Corran said in a gruff voice. He pushed his chair away from the table, but froze when Rigan spoke.

"Elinor's missing."

"The dyer's apprentice?" Kell asked.

"That talk in the city, about witches? They burned a girl last night. Someone said Elinor might be a witch, too. So she ran." It wasn't the whole truth of why Rigan's stomach was a tight knot, but it was enough to explain away his mood.

"I'm sorry," Kell said.

Corran looked like he was going to say something, but seemed to reconsider. "Come on," he said, putting a hand on Rigan's shoulder. "We've got bodies to bury."

It took Corran and Rigan nearly until curfew to finish the burials. The empty cart clattered behind them as they made their way through the quiet streets. "I have another Guild meeting tonight," Corran said when they reached the workshop. "I'll get cleaned up and go. Maybe it won't run so late this time."

"Be careful."

Corran stopped for a moment, before he thought to manage a smile. "It's just a meeting. What could happen? I might be bored to death?"

He's lying. Rigan's answering smile was just as insincere. "The streets are dangerous. Just... watch yourself."

"Sure," Corran said, looking away. "I'm always careful."

It was quiet after Corran left. Kell was upstairs; Rigan wanted neither silence nor conversation, but of the two, he feared conversation more. *Especially with Kell. He's smart. He's probably already figured out what Corran's been up to. That's dangerous enough. I can't let him catch on about me.*

By eleventh bells, Kell called down that he was going to bed. Corran had not returned and Rigan doubted he would until close to dawn. The solitude gave him the chance to do something he had not wanted to risk with his brothers around.

Rigan moved quickly, gathering the pigments and salt. The past few weeks had been quiet; no one had requested their help with restless ghosts. He worked steadily, adapting the sigils and spreading lines of salt between them. Usually, he drew a banishing circle to rid a home of vengeful spirits. Tonight, using what he had learned from his father's books, he drew a summoning circle.

I'll have to scrub the floor to be rid of the marks before Corran gets back. There's no way I can explain this. He sat in the center of the circle and lit the candles. He grounded his magic as Damian had taught him. Unlike the power he had practiced Below, grave magic was familiar, almost comforting. He could almost hear his mother's voice, encouraging him as she taught him the complicated wardings. The sigils and salt lines took on a warm glow, and Rigan sat back on his haunches.

"I know you're out there," he said quietly, looking out over the empty room. "I know you can show yourselves if you want to. I need to know—is someone controlling the monsters?"

For several minutes, nothing happened. Rigan glanced around the workroom, impatient for an answer. The undertakers' shop was not exactly haunted, but so many corpses came through their door that he took for granted the idea that some of their spirits lingered. Just in case, Rigan and Corran worked a banishment spell at least once a month, when the moon was high.

But Rigan had never tried to call the spirits to him.

The candle flames flickered in a sudden cold draft. Rigan looked up and saw a middle-aged man standing on the other side of the salt line, watching him sadly.

"Tell me what I want to know, and I'll hear your confession," Rigan said.

The man nodded, and Rigan recognised the tailor who'd turned up beaten to death; the one the family swore had been set on by robbers.

'Twas guards, not robbers, that killed me, the ghost said. *The same whore-spawned guards that told my kin I'd been done in by cutpurses, when they'd done all the cutting themselves.*

"I'm sorry."

I heard the guards talking, while I was dying. Talking about the people who disappear. One of them says, 'Not until we hear from the captain. He'll tell us where to grab them from this week, and how many.' And then other one says, 'I wouldn't mind taking a few extra, just to see those blighters run.'

"You're sure he meant the people who go missing?"

The ghost shrugged. *What else could it be? Snatching people off the street when they're going about their business, taking them away to die—that's murder, sure as puttin' a knife in someone's back.*

"What about the monsters?"

Heard one of the guards say, 'Guess the blood hocuses are angry with the potters and the skinners. Sent some ugly-assed sumbitches over there. Figure it's paybacks,' he said.

"Thank you," Rigan told the spirit. "Did you have a confession to make, to help you rest?"

Maybe that was my confession. Won't do you much good, but at least it's been said.

"Then rest," Rigan replied. "And the blessings of the gods go with you." He raised his voice in the ritual song, melodic and deep, and as he sang, the spirit faded until nothing remained.

Chapter Nineteen

In the distance, Corran heard the sound of boots on pavement.

"We've got to get out of here!" Ross yelled.

"Not without all of us," Corran growled.

Calfon grabbed one of Allery's arms and threw him over one shoulder. "Run!"

To Corran's relief, no monsters appeared to slow their retreat. Instead, half a dozen of guards ran toward them, swords drawn. "Halt, in the name of the Lord Mayor!" the leader shouted.

Just another night of hunting monsters, except that this night started to spiral out of control from the beginning.

Allery had alerted Calfon to the new threat, and at first, Corran actually thought it would be easy. Big, black beetles, the size of a man's hand. Compared to the ghouls and the other creatures the hunters had faced down, a few oversized bugs didn't seem like such a terrifying threat.

Then they had found the bodies, dozens of them, all around the old mill where the insects first appeared, though 'erupted' might be a better word for it, as they had burrowed up in waves from the floors. And judging from the corpses, this would be harder than kicking over an anthill or getting rid of a wasps' nest.

Because the insects, the monsters, had burrowed into their flesh. Wide bruises, black with blood, marked the corpses at the old mill. Once inside, the creatures had worked their way into the soft organs; most of their victims had died by their own hand, turning their knives on themselves to find release from the pain.

The hunters struggled to find a way to kill the insects. Blades glanced off the thick, black shells, and the weight of a grown man was not enough to crush the creatures. So in the end, they burned the mill, watched it go up in flames, saw the insects split in the fire, hissing and spitting—

The hunters scattered. Corran shadowed Calfon, knowing that he would not be able to fight his way clear unaided with Allery's dead weight over his shoulder. The rest of the hunters took off down the winding alleys.

Two guards clattered down the alleyway behind Corran and Calfon. Corran heard shouting in the distance as the other guards went after their companions.

"Go!" he yelled to Calfon, leaping up as they ran beneath lines of washing, pulling them down to tangle their pursuers. But the guards kept gaining, and the attempts to stall them had cost Corran precious seconds. Abruptly, he veered onto a narrow causeway crossing one of Wrighton's open sewers. Before the guards could make the corner, he took a breath, held his nose and jumped.

Foul water, dead animals, spoiled produce, and excrement swept by Corran, pushing him down towards the harbor.

This has to be one of the dumbest things I've ever done.

Garbage pummeled him. Broken shards of pottery spun past, scratching his skin like whirling knives. A chunk of wood smacked into the back of Corran's head, making him see stars. He ducked a floating barrel, only to be hit by a dented metal bucket that opened a cut above his eye.

Corran tried desperately to remember the sewer's path as it ran through a steep-sided stone culvert, wondering where he could climb out without too many people seeing him. He strained to hear above the rush of the water and the clatter of the garbage. The street was at least three feet above him.

A woman leaned out of a balcony and dumped a bucket into the canal. Corran managed to dodge the worst of it, as a dead rat floated by. The current accelerated and he looked around wildly, hearing the roar of falling water. There was a large, dark hole beneath the next street, where the sewer plunged below ground.

I'm done for.

He took a deep breath, closed his eyes and said a prayer as the water fell away beneath him, carrying him into darkness.

Corran's lungs were burning when he finally surfaced, stealing a breath just inches from the slime-covered top of the sewer tunnel, gagging in the fetid air. The current swept him on its way and the darkness of the tunnel opened up into the indigo of the starry night sky. Corran dragged himself out as the stream slowed, blocks away from where he'd jumped in, and tried to wring the awful liquid from his clothing.

I hope the others got away. I hope Allery doesn't die. And I hope the gods are listening, because I could sure use a favor to get home in one piece.

Corran crawled to the shadows of the nearest alley, too lightheaded to stand. His eyes and the inside of his nose burned, and his lungs were on fire. Breathing hurt, but he gasped for air and then doubled over, wracked with painful coughing.

I've just swum in the muck of an entire city. That can't have done me any good. Already, his skin felt as if he had sunburn, as if the foul water had burned into his pores. There was water in his ears, making it difficult to hear. He shook his head and nearly fell flat on his face. *I've got to get home. If I'm going to die, I want to die at home.*

He hauled himself to his feet on sheer strength of will, but fell when he tried to walk. He stumbled and hobbled, eventually supporting himself on the walls of the buildings. A half-candlemark's walk took more than twice that.

One block from the shop, he fell to his knees and crawled the rest of the way. Tears blurred his eyes, making it difficult for him to see. Twice, he had to stop to heave up the contents of his stomach. His ears felt as if they had been soundly boxed, aching on the inside all the way to his jaw. Corran's throat could not have hurt worse if he had swallowed broken glass, and his skin itched and burned until he might have considered flaying a mercy.

He dragged himself to the workshop door and pounded with his fist, hoping Rigan and Kell were close enough to hear him. To Corran's relief, the door opened, and he saw Rigan framed in the lantern light.

I think I'm dying. Corran thought, and managed a weak groan before falling flat on his face.

"What in the name of the Eternal Ones have you been doing?" Rigan said, demanded, leaning down to haul Corran inside even as he nearly gagged on the stench. Kell came pounding down the stairs a few steps behind him.

"Just leave me alone," Corran groaned. "It's been a bad night."

"Kell, go upstairs," Rigan ordered. "There's bound to be plague in this filth."

Kell made a rude gesture. "If I haven't died yet from carting corpses around the city, I won't drop over now. Besides, I have as much right to know what he's up to as you do."

"Have you been swimming in the sewer?" Rigan tried to catch his breath through the gagging. Corran attempted to answer, but all he could manage was a harsh, hacking cough that brought up blood.

"Shit. That's not good," Rigan said, looking at the bright red flecks on Corran's lips with alarm. Corran's grip on consciousness was slipping, but he was aware enough to know his brother was close to panic.

"We'll take him out back, sluice him off with water, scrub him down with lye soap," Kell said.

Corran groaned, as close as he could manage to an answer. His vision blurred but he could make out enough to see Rigan run his hands through his hair in desperation.

"This is bad, Kell. Really bad," Rigan said, beginning to pace. "Men die in the sewers. It's why they use convicts to go down to fix things when there's a problem. The water, the air—they're poison. Gods, he's coughing blood."

"We can help him, Rigan," Kell said.

"I can't fix this with some tea and a poultice. The poison's in him. Look at his skin, his eyes. He's already sweating with fever. This is more than we can take care of ourselves."

"Then I'll run for Mamme Solan—"

"No!" Rigan grabbed for Kell's arm, hard enough to leave a bruise. "It's past curfew. You can't go out there. Why in the name of the gods was Corran out this late—and how did he end up in the sewer?"

"Easy, stupid. He's been fighting monsters. Haven't you, Corran?" Kell snapped.

Rigan wheeled on Corran, as fear spiked to anger. "I knew it! There were no Guild meetings, and those men in the gibbets were hunters, just like you."

Corran groaned, but the expression on his face gave Rigan all the answer he needed.

"Damn," Rigan swore. "Did the guards follow you?"

"Only until I jumped into the sewer." It hurt to talk; breathing made his chest ache.

"Go up and make tea," Rigan said to Kell, "and come back with some poultices, too."

"But you said—"

"I know what I said! I'm going to get help. But it will take me a bit to get there and back. At least a candlemark, maybe more."

"No," Corran wheezed. "Dangerous—"

"Screw that. We don't have a choice."

"I'll be all right." Corran knew it for a lie, but sick as he was, he could not allow Rigan to risk himself.

"No, you won't, Corran. You won't be all right. You'll *die* if I don't get you help." He snatched down his cloak from the peg near the door.

"Kell—try not to touch him," Rigan instructed, plunging his own hands into a bucket of water and scrubbing them with the harsh soap. "All the filth and the bad air—it'll make him sick like corpse fever. Gods, his lungs—" He didn't finish his sentence.

"Give him tea," he continued. "Spread the poultices on his skin with a trowel to draw out the poison. Use the leather gloves and cut him out of his clothing. We'll have to burn everything he has on. Put it in the alley for now. If you can drag his sorry ass out of the door, throw water on him, but don't let the filth splash you or you'll be sick, too."

"Where are you going, Rigan?" Kell said, fear in his voice.

Rigan took a breath to calm himself. "I know a man. A friend. He's... good at curing people."

"A witch?"

"Dammit! Why does it matter? If anyone can heal Corran, he can." Rigan grabbed Kell by the shoulders. "If I don't get help, Corran's going to die, Kell. It's in his lungs, down his throat. I'll be right back."

"What if the guards—"

"They won't."

"You don't know that!" Kell sounded terrified.

"Kell, you've got to trust me. Trust me to do this, or we might as well start digging Corran's grave," Rigan said, past the point of being gentle. "I've got to go."

"Damn you, Rigan!" Kell shouted as the door slammed. Kell grabbed the nearest tool at hand and hurled it at the door. The knife stuck fast in the wood.

"He's right," Corran whispered. "I knew... when I jumped in. But I couldn't let the guards—"

"We are not doing this! You are not dying. I forbid you! You can't leave us. You *can't.*" Kell's rage turned into shuddering sobs.

"Kell. Tea. Do what... Rigan said."

Kell dragged his sleeve across his eyes and wiped his nose on his cuff. He looked young and scared. "All right. Just... don't die."

"Not dying... yet." Speaking hurt, but Corran knew Kell needed to hear him.

Kell ran up the steps to get what he needed for the tea and poultice.

Corran hoped he could keep his word. The air in his lungs felt like scalding water. A slow trickle of blood dripped from his nose, which had nearly swollen shut from inside. His throat remained open enough to draw in rasping breaths, but Corran feared it too would close off, irritated by the foul liquid he had swallowed as the sewer's torrent slammed him against walls and debris.

I don't want to leave them. They're not ready to be on their own. Corran clung to consciousness, afraid that if he yielded to sleep he would not wake. Before long, Kell returned, bearing a kettle, a cup, a bowl and bags of herbs.

"I'll mix this up down here," Kell said.

Corran wondered if his younger brother sensed the nearness of death, afraid to leave him on his own too long.

Corran managed a nod and fought to keep his eyes open. The eyelids scraped and burned across his eyes; he wondered whether he would regain his vision if he lived. Another cough doubled him over, and hot blood splattered the floor beneath him.

"Dammit, Rigan! Where are you?" Kell muttered as he mixed up the powders in the bowl and readied the tea. The water on the brazier seemed to take forever to boil.

"You smell worse than a two day-old corpse in the sun," Kell fussed. Corran took it for what it was; a way to keep his mind off other things. "So let's fix that. We'll burn your clothes. I'll get you something to wear, and a bucket of water to scrub up in with some lye soap." He shuddered. "But you're sleeping down here tonight."

With a glare toward the kettle, Kell grabbed a pair of leather gloves and opened the alley door. For good measure, he slipped on a long-sleeved work shirt and wrapped a length of muslin over his nose and mouth. "Come on," he said, gripping Corran under his arms and hauling him to the door. Corran tried to push with his feet, but the fever made him weak.

"You're sweating like a whore," Kell said. "Got to wash you down."

Kell tried to be gentle, but he could barely move Corran. Kell left him sprawled just outside the door and went back for a bucket of water and a sharp knife. The water could not have been colder than room temperature, but it felt icy as it hit Corran with a splash, forcing out his breath in a gasp and making him shudder.

"Sorry," Kell murmured. He disappeared for a moment down the alley to scoop more water from the horse trough, and came back to douse Corran twice more, making certain to get his hair and face. Corran's skin had turned bright red from the poisons in the sewer water, and was exquisitely sensitive: the feel of his shirt and the weight of the water were excruciating.

"Got to get you out of those clothes," Kell said, talking to himself to fill the silence. Corran could only grunt in response, lying flat on his back because he lacked the strength to sit up.

"Modesty be damned," he said with a nervous smile that did not reach his eyes. "Don't move, and I'll try not to cut you." Without being told, Kell seemed to realize that breaks in the skin would make things worse.

Kell slid the knife beneath Corran's sodden shirt and carefully cut the fabric free. Next, Kell cut off his pants and removed his boots. His cloak had been lost in the water.

"Damn," Kell swore under his breath, taking in the mottled bruises where the swift current had pummeled Corran. "Those cuts are going to go sour," he said, eying where sharper trash had slashed or punctured. Corran heard Kell draw in a ragged breath, and knew his little brother had reached his limit. Then Kell lifted his head and squared his shoulders. When he spoke, his voice did not shake.

"All right. More water. Then I'll scrub you. We'll get you back inside once I've rinsed down the floor, so you don't sit back down in your own filth." He spoke with an authoritative tone Corran remembered from his father's voice, and it brought a weak smile to his lips.

"Be right here," Corran whispered, as if he could do otherwise.

Kell doused him again and again with water, until Corran shivered violently enough to give new cause for concern. "Damn," Kell swore under his breath. "Don't you die, Corran! I'm going as fast as I can!"

Kell retuned with a scrub brush and the harsh soap they used to clean up after the dead bodies and lessen the risk of corpse fever. Corran braced himself, but the scratch of the rough bristles and the sting of lye soap on his raw skin made his whole body jerk and tense. He bit back a scream, knowing that too would hurt, given his savaged throat.

"I'm sorry, Corran." Kell's muffled voice and the way he kept his head down, face averted, told Corran that Kell was crying. "I'm so sorry to hurt you."

"Necessary," Corran managed.

Kell murmured apologies as he worked, but despite the guilt he scrubbed his brother thoroughly, even daubing into Corran's ears with a piece of tightly-wrapped gauze to get out the foul water. Corran kept his eyes closed, afraid to look. His skin felt boiled, and he feared that the boar's hair brush might have left him a bloody mess.

"I've been as careful as I can be," Kell whispered. "Scratches would be bad, let the poison in."

The kettle whistled.

"I'm going to roll you onto clean shrouds and pull you inside on them," Kell told him once the scrub down finished. "The water's hot, so I can mix up the tea and poultice. That should help you feel better, make your throat hurt less. Rigan'll be back soon. Hang on."

Kell gentled him onto clean muslin and dragged him back into the workshop as Corran tried not to scream; every jolt was agony. He moved away for a few minutes, and returned with the wide, dull blade they used to mix pigments and a bowl that smelled of herbs.

"If it were normal cuts, I'd clean them with whiskey, but I don't think you'd like that," Kell said, managing a sickly smile. Corran groaned at the thought. "Yeah. So the calendula, sage, and John's wort will help keep the wounds from going bad. There's chamomile, ginger, and licorice in the tea to take down the swelling in your throat. We might put a drop or two up your nose and in your ears, too."

I don't know how much longer I can hold on, Corran thought. *Rigan better get back soon, or I won't get to say goodbye.*

Kell spread the herbal mixture carefully over Corran's shoulders and chest, then used a wad of gauze to daub the mixture onto his face. Even the lightest touch hurt badly enough that he fought to remain conscious, but the poultice slowly started doing its work, deadening the pain, cooling the burn.

Corran managed a nod to encourage Kell to continue. "Better," he croaked.

Kell swallowed hard and kept going until he had coated all of Corran's body with the mixture. Then he crossed to where the tea was steeping and poured a cup. By now, the water had cooled so that Corran could drink without fear of further damaging his swollen throat. He sipped carefully, unwilling to accidently make himself retch. The strange-tasting mixture tingled in his mouth, but felt like balm to the inflamed membranes. "Good," he managed, aware that Kell was teetering on the brink of complete panic.

"You can have more whenever you want. It'll be better cold," Kell offered, as if he were afraid for silence to fall between them. He eyed Corran's hair.

"I'm going to coat your hair with poultice. Maybe we won't have to shave you bald," he said. The leather gloves made touch awkward, but even with that impediment, the healing ointment cooled the skin of his scalp. Kell worked with utmost gentleness, as if afraid Corran would shatter at his touch.

They both flinched as the door swung open. "Corran!" Rigan said, fear lacing his voice. A stranger accompanied him; a man with brown eyes and dark blond hair who stood a little shorter than Rigan.

"Gods. You didn't exaggerate," the stranger said, rushing to Corran's side.

"This is Aiden. He's a friend."

"Is he a witch?" Kell asked bluntly. "Because that's what we need."

Aiden looked up at Kell. "Yes. I am." He turned his attention back to Corran. "Everything you've done is good. It's why he's still alive. But he'll need more to survive."

He looked up at Rigan. "Lay down a line of salt at the doors and windows. Put something made of iron on the sills as well. It'll keep the witch finders from sensing my magic. Go!"

Kell and Rigan hurried to their tasks. "Draw this symbol on the shutters and doors," Aiden said when they had finished, marking a sigil on the floor with water. "It'll strengthen the magic." Kell grabbed chalk and hurried to do as Aiden bid him.

"Do you want to live?" Aiden stared at Corran as if he could see into his soul.

"Yes." *For Rigan and Kell. They need me.*

"Listen closely." Aiden bent close to Corran, showing no fear of contagion. "Don't be afraid. Despite what they say, I'm not going to steal your soul. But I will work magic to heal you, and it will feel... strange."

Corran, his strength waning, nodded his head, just barely, but enough. Aiden smiled. "Good. You'll feel warmth. It might hurt—a lot. The poison is strong and it's gone deep. You're only a few steps from the grave; I think you know that."

Again, a nod in reply.

"Don't fight me. It will take all my power to expel the poison. If you struggle, it weakens me. If you want to live, you must let me do this, despite the pain." Aiden looked at him, and seemed to find the answer he required. "You will feel the poison leaving your body. It will pull at you like a thousand needles. You must let it go. I will cast it out."

He fell silent for a moment. "I can keep you from dying, remove the poison. But I cannot guarantee that this will not leave you changed. It is the best I can offer."

"Do... it."

"Prepare yourself."

For a moment, nothing happened. Then Corran felt a strange warmth envelop him. In the space of a few breaths, the warmth grew hot, pushing through his skin, into muscle and sinew and bone, as if his body burned from the inside, not with fever but with fire. Corran bit back a cry of pain as the burning sensation shattered like embers in the wind, and suddenly he knew what Aiden meant about a thousand needles.

This time, Corran could not stop himself from crying out. Rigan knelt beside him, gripping his left hand through a fresh pair of leather gloves. Kell hung back against the far wall, arms wrapped around himself, watching.

Aiden chanted under his breath. Corran did not recognize the words. As the healer chanted, Corran felt hot needles in his blood, piercing his organs, stabbing his throat, poking through his eardrums. Despite Rigan's hold, his body bucked against the pain.

"Keep him still," Aiden said. "Don't let him fight me. The poison is deep."

Corran was certain the magic would rip him apart from inside. He could feel it perforating his flesh, his eyes, and the fragile membranes inside his nose and mouth, making every breath, every heartbeat agonizing.

In his mind's eye, Corran saw the needles stabbing through his skin, and then from the pin-prick wounds, yellow ichor—the sewer's poison—bubbling up. He envisioned the ichor running down his skin, pooling beneath him like strange blood.

Aiden's voice grew hoarse, but he kept on chanting. Drop after vile drop of the ichor fell, pulled from every fiber of Corran's body by Aiden's forbidden magic. Aiden drew the poison from his muscles and organs, and Corran felt as if he might be turned inside out. Pain drove him from consciousness and forced him awake again. Tremors shook his body, making his teeth clack together. His form went rigid as he tried to keep from bucking and twisting to get away from a pain that came from the core of his being.

Sick as he had been, nothing compared to this new agony. Corran groaned, squeezing Rigan's hand so hard he thought bones might break. He wondered how long it would take for the poison to kill him, and whether the treatment would destroy him first.

"What are you doing to him?" Rigan demanded. "You're killing him!"

Aiden ignored him and continued to chant. Corran's eyes squeezed tightly closed, then he arched and his head fell back. His screams echoed in the workroom, along with Rigan's frightened curses. Aiden's voice grew louder, drowning them out, and the draw of his magic became unbearable. Just when Corran thought it might rip away his soul, Aiden finished with a triumphant shout.

Corran slumped back, completely spent. He felt Aiden press fingers against his throat, feeling for a pulse.

"Is it over? Is he healed?" Rigan sounded as if he had been crying.

"It's done."

"Will he live?" Kell voice betrayed his fear.

"He'll live. The poison's gone."

Corran opened his eyes, pleasantly surprised that they no longer felt like they were filled with sand. He expected to find himself lying in a pool of yellow ichor, but he was completely dry.

"Thank you," he managed, the words barely a whisper.

Aiden nodded. "You were quite a challenge."

"Kell, get Aiden something to eat and some tea," Rigan said. "He needs to replenish his strength." Corran saw the strain in Aiden's face, and his hunched posture spoke of utter weariness.

"You're welcome to stay the night," Rigan offered. "Safer than going out so late."

Aiden shook his head. "Safer for all of you, the sooner I'm gone. The wardings should have kept others from sensing the magic worked here, but just in case, I need to be on my way."

"Pay you..." Corran rasped.

"Rigan already paid my fee," Aiden replied with a glance at Rigan that Corran could not decipher. "It's taken care of."

Once Aiden had left, Rigan and Kell helped Corran onto one of the clean worktables and made him comfortable. "I'll sit with him," Rigan said.

"Nearly morning by now," Kell replied with a yawn. "Don't expect more than bread and jam for breakfast." He laid a hand on Corran's shoulder. "I'm glad you're all right," he said quietly with a tremor in his voice. "You scared me."

"Scared me, too," Corran admitted. Rigan's hand tightened on Corran's wrist, as though to reassure his brother he would not let go.

Tomorrow, Corran would ask how Rigan knew the witch, and what price the healer had demanded. But right now, he could not fight sleep. He drifted off, marveling that he was still alive.

When Corran woke, Rigan had not moved from his chair next to the worktable. "I'm glad you got away," he said, "but you took an awful chance."

"Do you understand why I couldn't tell you and Kell?" Corran asked. He was too tired to argue, but right now, it mattered to him that Rigan understood this was not a game.

"If someone else had fought the monsters, maybe Mama wouldn't be dead." *Or Jora.*

"We fight to keep others' parents, and wives, and children safe," Corran said. "I keep thinking about that when we're fighting." He looked up at Rigan fiercely, challenging him to disagree. "It was worth it."

To his surprise, Rigan did not argue. "Yes, it was. But Kell and I need you alive, here."

"I know."

Rigan wrinkled his nose. "Kell scrubbed you down pretty good, but you still stink. You're my brother, but there are limits, and you're going to need a few more baths before you're allowed upstairs."

"Thanks," Corran said dourly.

"Any time," Rigan returned brightly. He sobered. "Seriously, I'm glad you got away. I've got no desire to send you to the gods."

"I'm not planning to go anytime soon."

Kell squeezed past Rigan, carrying a hot kettle and a cup, along with some cheese, sausage, and bread. Corran felt weary enough to collapse, but he knew the food and drink would do him good.

"You smell really bad," Kell observed, dancing back out of range as quickly as he could. "Burn some candles. People will think we left a body to rot in here."

"We'll figure out a way to get the stink off you," Rigan promised. "Maybe Mamme Solan has special soap."

"Thanks," Corran replied wearily.

Rigan grinned. "Sure. What are brothers for?" Rigan helped him sit up to eat, and Corran noticed that the salt lines and the chalk sigils from the night before were gone.

A knock sounded at the back door. Rigan and Kell exchanged glances, and each of them picked up a knife, keeping the weapons hidden as Rigan went to open the door.

Calfon stood in the doorway, Allery's limp body in his arms. "He's dead."

"Get inside!" Rigan hissed.

Ragged wounds covered Allery's arms and neck where the beetles had burrowed into his flesh. His head lolled, eyes open, blankly staring.

"I couldn't leave him," Calfon said. "He was still alive when the guards came. Those insect things ate him alive, from the inside. I thought I could double back, get him somewhere safe to bind up the wounds, stop the bleeding, until the guards were gone. But when I finally stopped, he was dead." Calfon looked up defiantly. "I didn't know what to do with his body. He fought like a hero. He deserves to have the rites said over him." Only then did Corran's pallor seem to register with the hunter. "What happened to you?"

"He jumped in the sewer to get away," Rigan said. "Nearly killed him."

"Put Allery on one of the tables," Kell said. "The sooner he's painted and shrouded, the better our chances of keeping clear of the hangman's noose."

Pounding on the front door of the shop made them flinch. "I wouldn't bet on it," Corran said. He thought about trying to help, but his body would not cooperate.

"I'll stall them," Kell said. "Shroud the body."

Kell headed for the front of the shop, closing and locking the workshop door behind him.

"We're looking for a fugitive," the guard said when he opened the door.

"I was upstairs sleeping," Kell replied.

"Are you alone?"

"Me and my brothers."

"Where are they?"

"In the back, cutting up the bodies. Been a busy week. Lots of dead people."

"Cutting them up?"

"What did you think happens when you die?" Kell replied, sounding so innocently surprised that Rigan rolled his eyes.

"Take me back there!"

"Do you throw up easily? Because people do, you know. That's why we don't really like to have the families of the dead in the shop. They get queasy when we take off the top of the skull and scoop out the brains, and then by the time we've peeled the face down over the chin, a lot of them have retched."

"Why do you peel off the face?"

"Because we're all faceless when we go to the gods," Kell replied, a complete fabrication. "Of course, that's before we break open the ribs, yank out the organs, and burn the whole body with quicklime. It's really not pretty. Smells awful. You're better off not knowing. But if you insist—"

The door to the street opened and closed. A few minutes later, Kell returned, locking the door behind him. "They're gone," he said, grinning in triumph.

"What were you thinking?" Rigan challenged. "Peel off their faces? Scoop out the brains? What's going to happen when that gets around?"

"We're still the only undertaker in this part of Wrighton," Kell pointed out. "Most people have no idea what happens here. We can always say they misunderstood."

"I think it was bloody brilliant," Calfon replied. "I'm sorry. I didn't think when I came here. I put you in danger. I should have just left Allery. He's past caring now, after all."

"What's done is done," Corran replied with a shrug. "We can't admit to his family that we know what happened to him."

"I understand."

"We'll take care of him," Rigan promised. "We can't give him the full Potters' Guild burial, but we can make sure he has a proper one."

"The gods favored us last night," Calfon said. "But it could have been even worse."

"Yeah. I was thinking the same thing." Corran looked at Allery's corpse. "This is my responsibility."

Rigan walked over and began mixing the pigments "I'll see to him. You're in no shape yourself. We'll get him finished up and out with the new burials tomorrow." He spared a backward glance. "I'm just glad things worked out the way they did," he added.

"So am I."

Chapter Twenty

Four days later, four bodies lay on the worktables: two men, a child, and a woman. Wide tracks, dark with black blood, showed beneath the corpses' pale skin. "Let's get to it," Rigan said. "It's already late, and there's a lot of work to do."

Rigan mixed the pigments, while Corran got the tools. Kell was upstairs, cleaning up after dinner. He had left them two buckets of the specially prepared water used to bathe the bodies, and stoked the fire in the brazier to take the chill off the workroom.

Corran had insisted on returning to work. He felt nearly like himself again, and had to admit that the healer's magic had been powerful enough to bring him back from the brink of death. Every attempt he made to discover how Rigan knew the witch met with vague answers and prevarication. *He's hiding something. I'll figure out what, eventually.*

Corran's knife made a clean incision on the corpse's abdomen. Dark tracks laced from the man's legs to his belly. Bloody trails criss-crossed his back and chest. The second man's body looked much the same. There were fewer tracks on the child, and Corran guessed the insect had burrowed straight into his gut. The woman's body was the worst. The creature had entered through her mouth, ripping out much of her throat as it went, working its way down the chest. Corran swallowed hard and turned back to his work.

The skin of the second man's abdomen opened cleanly beneath the edge of the sharp blade. Black blood oozed from the incision—and beneath the blood, something trembled.

"Rigan!"

Rigan turned, and followed Corran's gaze. "Oh, gods."

Its black chitin glistening, the creature struggled free in a spray of the dead man's blood.

The creature easily measured eight inches long. Front pincers snapped at Rigan and six jointed legs ending in tough, hook-shaped claws cycled wildly, trying to get purchase.

"Burn it!" Corran ordered.

"Watch out!" Rigan yelled. He picked up a pair of long metal tongs, grabbed the insect and turned to shove it into the brazier's hot coals. The monster screeched as its shell blackened and peeled.

"There's a second one!" Corran yelled.

"I see it," Rigan replied, lunging and missing. The beetle moved fast, even bloated as it was with blood.

"What's going on down there?" Kell yelled.

"Stay in the kitchen and close the door," Corran snapped.

The dead woman's belly trembled, and Rigan could see the rounded carapace of a beetle pushing against the skin from inside. Fire might kill the insects, but catching them and getting them to the brazier was another matter.

"Where's the other one?" Corran looked around, worried.

"There!" Rigan smacked the back of a heavy iron shovel onto the insect, then turned the shovel and brought the blade down two-handed, finally breaking its tough shell.

"Oh, no, no, no," Rigan muttered. Another beetle tore through the dead child's belly. The three other corpses trembled as insects dug for the surface.

"Get them to the brazier!" Corran yelled. He scooped his shovel under one of the creatures and lobbed it onto the coals. The fire flared, and the insect sizzled and split.

"You tend to the boy, I'll tend to the woman, and then we'll work on the other man."

Two more beetles climbed out of the child's abdomen and dropped next to the corpse. Rigan swung his shovel, slamming the back of the blade down hard. The monster dodged the blow and Rigan brought the iron blade down again, this time splitting the insect's shell, splattering himself with its stinking black ichor.

Corran dove toward the brazier and laid the flat of the shovel on the coals, heating it for as long as he dared. He then laid the red-hot iron across the belly of the first man's corpse, burning the dead flesh and searing the creatures struggling to emerge. The insects screeched, and the corpse shuddered with their death throes.

Rigan grabbed another wriggling insect with the tongs, hurrying past Corran to get to the brazier.

"Hold steady!"

"You hold steady. I'm keeping this damned thing as far away from us as I can!"

"Drop it in the fire!" Corran yelled.

"I'm trying!"

Getting the blood-slick creature to the fire was easier said than done. Rigan nearly lost his hold on the insect. He sidestepped toward the brazier and dove forward, pushing the creature into the burning coals.

"Oh, gods! The smell!" Rigan moaned. The insect hissed and spit as fire licked around its hard shell. A second later, the carapace split, splattering more black blood across the workshop.

Corran stepped up behind his brother, with another of the things skewered and writhing on a long, sharp knife. Swearing under his breath, he stabbed the knife into the coals, and the creature sizzled.

Cautiously, Rigan returned to the woman's body. "Do you

think they're still alive in there?" The hot iron shovel had burned the corpse's skin black. He grabbed the leather gloves from the worktable and then pulled a shovelful of glowing coals from the brazier.

"Only one way to find out." Corran's knife slit the woman's belly from ribs to crotch, revealing the last two bloody insects. Corran dodged back while Rigan thrust the hot coals into the cavity. The creatures screeched as the fire destroyed them.

"That's all of them," Rigan said. He shook off the thick blood clinging to his clothing, lip curling with distaste. "How many more do you think are out there?" He jerked his head toward the door.

Corran stared at him, equally blood-splattered. "Who knows? It takes maybe two to kill an adult; one for a child. There don't have to be many."

"We'd better get this cleaned up," Rigan said, looking at the mess. "Kell will have our asses if we leave it for him, and I don't even want to *think* about the smell." Black ichor pooled on the floor and splattered the walls. The shovel, dented and bent, leaned against a table.

"Wonderful that we can roast the things to death," Rigan said. "Now—how do we do that without setting the whole damn city on fire?"

"I don't know," Corran admitted. "And there's nothing to say that the next time monsters show up, it'll be these things. Just like the ghouls—we figured out how to fight them, and then we had *azrikk*. Now we get man-eating beetles."

"What are *azrikk*?"

Corran sighed. "Horrible."

Lye soap and the shovel did a good job of cleaning up the workroom, though the smell remained. Corran figured they would need to burn their clothing. Once the fight was over, Rigan grew quiet, deep in thought.

"You all right?"

Rigan shrugged. "How do the monsters just... appear and disappear? Surely *someone* has seen where they come from?"

Corran shrugged. "Ravenwood is full of old tunnels and drains, and plenty of abandoned buildings. I imagine the monsters are at least as good as rats and roaches at figuring out how to disappear. They've plagued Ravenwood for years. Maybe they've been here forever."

"Do you think they're natural?"

"What?"

"Do you think the monsters are occurring naturally? Or they have been summoned to the city somehow?" Rigan asked, thinking of his conversation with the ghost.

Corran regarded the blackened shells in the brazier. "I imagine they come to the city for the same reason rats and stray cats do—lots of food."

"But they aren't here all the time," Rigan pressed. "So why some times and not others? Why some parts of the city, and not others? And if they go away, where do they go, and why do they come back?"

"Why all the questions?" Corran asked, watching his brother closely.

Rigan looked away. "Just thinking about things, that's all."

Just then, three sharp knocks came at the back door. Corran looked up. "I've got to go."

"I'm going with you," Rigan replied.

"No, you're not. You haven't been trained. Stay here and keep Kell safe." Corran grabbed his cloak and sword and headed into the night.

Kell came down the stairs. "He's gone hunting," Rigan said, answering his brother's unspoken question.

"Now what?"

"I'm not going to wait around for the monsters to find us," Rigan said. "What do we have that's really, really sticky?"

Kell grinned and headed over to a corner of the workshop returning with pots of glue and tar.

"We can heat these on the brazier," he said. "The place can't stink any more than it already does."

Kell and Rigan donned leather gloves and heavy work aprons. A strange scratching and scrabbling noise came from outside the shop as they heated the buckets. "Do you think that's them?" Kell asked.

"There's *something* out there, and I'm not about to go look," Rigan replied. "Go stuff rags under the door—just in case."

While Kell hurried to block the opening, Rigan found several long strips of heavy canvas as well as wide leather straps. Kell watched, perplexed, as Rigan began to wind the canvas around himself from ankle to crotch.

"Have you lost your mind?" Kell asked.

"Your turn," Rigan said. "You can use the leather, it's even tougher for them to get through."

"You're serious?"

"Want to end up like them?" Rigan snapped, with a jerk of his head toward the corpses.

Kell shuddered. "I can wrap myself. Go stir the tar."

A few minutes later, Kell was finished. He walked stiff-legged over to where Rigan stood by the brazier. "As armor, this leaves a lot to be desired. I can hardly bend my knees."

"Have you ever seen the Lord Mayor's personal guard?" Rigan asked. "All done up in their tin suits for fancy occasions. I don't imagine they can take a *piss*, let alone bend anything."

More scrabbling, louder and closer than before. Kell glanced toward the door to the front of the shop. "Do you think they got in?"

"No idea. How long does this stuff take to soften?" Rigan said, prodding at the tar. "We don't have all night."

A thud against the alley door made them both jump. "Look!" Kell whispered, pointing.

Black, jointed feet poked beneath the door, shoving the rags aside. "Do you think they can get underneath?"

For all I know they can eat through the door. "I hope not," Rigan answered, not wanting to panic his brother.

New sounds, this time on the porch roof above the back door, then a thump as something hard struck the high window facing the alley. Rigan sprinted across the room and slammed the wooden shutters closed.

"Is the glue ready?"

"Yeah. Now what?"

Rigan grabbed boards from against the wall. "Paint the boards with glue and tar. I'll put them by each of the doors and windows."

"What do we do with the insects, assuming they stick?"

"Burn them."

"Where?" Kell challenged. "Are we just going to walk across to the trash pit with a board covered in monster bugs and throw it on the burn heap?"

"You have a better idea?"

"Yeah. Let's burn them in the fireplace." The large fireplace at the end of the room was rarely used. Heat and corpses did not mix well, and the brazier took enough of the chill off for the brothers to work comfortably without making the bodies rot faster. Kell ran to clear out the odds and ends stored in the fireplace and grabbed a few logs from the pile next to the upstairs hearth. Within minutes, he had a blaze started.

Scrabbling noises echoed from the rafters. Something was definitely moving on the roof. Chittering sounded on the other side of the door separating the workshop from the front of the store. Sharp feet scratched at the wooden door, and pulled away the rest of the rags under the door.

"What did you have in mind?" Rigan asked, licking his lips. "That brazier is too small to handle more than a few of those creatures at a time."

"Bring up the big metal cauldron from the cellar and set in the fireplace," Kell replied. "When enough of those things get stuck, we grab the planks and dump them into the cauldron." It took both of them to lift the heavy cauldron from the cellar and get it into position.

"If they touch you, they can burrow under the skin," Rigan warned. "And you know what happens after that," he added with a glance toward the corpses.

Something hard banged against the door into the front room. "You spread more pitch onto boards," Rigan said. "I've got an idea."

Rigan headed toward the door and took a deep breath, trying to center himself.

Let's see if my magic is worth anything.

He shivered at the sound of the insects on the other side of the door scrabbling across the wooden floor. *How many are out there? Half a dozen? More? More than enough to kill us both.*

Rigan forced down his fear and took a deep breath, trying to block out the sounds. He placed his palms on the door. *I don't dare use fire. Calling on the earth won't help. I don't want to drown us. Air, maybe?*

"Rigan! Whatever you're doing, you'd better hurry. They're squeezing under the door."

Rigan closed his eyes and pushed his power down into the ground to anchor himself. He breathed in deeply and gathered his magic, then thrust it out from him with his breath, envisioning his power moving through the door, sweeping away the insects on the other side.

High-pitched squeals and a rattling, tumbling sound suggested his attempt had been successful. "I think I bought us some time."

Kell stared at him. "Did you just use magic?"

"Now's not the time to discuss it." Rigan hurried back to help Kell tar and position the last of the boards.

"You did, didn't you? That wasn't grave magic. That's how you knew the healer. You're a witch, too!"

Two black, hard-shelled shapes squeezed beneath the alley door.

Great. They're thinner when they haven't gorged themselves on blood, Rigan thought.

"Oh, gods!" Kell exclaimed. More of the insects slipped beneath the door. Their jointed, hairy legs became mired in the tar.

Rigan grabbed a length of wood, wrapped a shroud around the end and dipped it into the tar. He lit the torch and thrust it at the crack beneath the door. The beetles hissed and backed away.

"Are you crazy?" Kell yelped. "You'll set the door on fire."

Four more insects crawled beneath the door. One stuck in the tar, but the others used its body as a bridge. Half a dozen other insects struggled on the sticky board.

Rigan and Kell surged forward with shovels, lifting up the boards as Rigan kicked replacements up against the gap.

"Back up—carefully!" Together, they sent the traps falling into the cauldron. The insects shrieked, exploding with sodden popping noises.

"Rigan—behind you!"

Rigan wheeled and saw one of the giant insects skittering toward him. Kell flipped the creature with his shovel, then brought a length of pipe down onto it, end-first, with all his strength. The shell cracked and the pipe impaled the insect, which screeched and flailed. Kell shook it off into the cauldron, as Rigan held off two more that had skittered under the door to the store front.

"Oh, gods!" Kell said, eyes wide. Four beetles climbed onto a work table and started to savage the corpse lying there.

"Deal with them later," Rigan ordered. "The bodies will keep them busy."

Smoke filled the workroom, making their eyes tear up. The air was foul with the smell of burned blood and charred shells.

"We don't know that we've got them all," Rigan said. "Let's circle the room."

"What about the ones over there?" Kell said, with a jerk of his head toward the creatures still feeding on the corpse.

"Better them than us."

Torch and shovel at the ready, Rigan led the way as they made a check of the perimeter of the workroom, then the front of the shop, but there were no more insects to be found.

"Now, how do we get them off the corpse?" Kell asked.

Rigan grimaced. "If we could just push it—body, bugs and all—onto a pyre and light it, that would take care of the whole problem. We've got to kill the things—otherwise they'll probably dig their way back out of the grave once the food runs out."

Kell looked nauseous. "That's really more than I wanted to picture."

Rigan made another torch from a shroud, watching as the flames rose. "Stay alert—we don't want to find out the hard way we've overlooked one of those sons of bitches." He thrust the torch into the open belly of the corpse. The insects were swollen to three times their normal size, barely able to move. They charred in the flames, popping like ripe melons, spraying Rigan and Kell with blood.

"I am never going to sleep well again," Kell muttered. Rigan moved on to the next body, to make sure they hadn't missed any. By the time they were finished with the corpses both he and Kell were soaked in blood.

"That's all of them," Rigan said, looking around with a sigh of relief. Tar tracked across the floor and blood spattered the walls.

"Corran is going to have a fit when he sees this," Kell replied.

A black shape dropped from the ceiling, landing on Kell's shoulder. "Rigan! Get it off me!"

Kell pulled desperately at the burrowing insect, but the hooked feet and vicious pincers held fast. Rigan acted on instinct, sending his will down to the flames beneath the cauldron, channeling the fire through his hands. He clamped his hands over the insect, careful not to tear it free and hurt his brother further.

"You're burning hot!" Kell shouted. Rigan shoved him against the wall and pinned him there. Sweat dripped from Rigan's brow.

Kell's skin blistered beneath his hands, but he held on, though his brother writhed in pain.

The beetle raised its head from the wound, slick with Kell's blood, and Rigan grabbed it with both hands. Rage and fear coursed through him, hot as the cauldron. The insect squealed and exploded in his grip.

Abruptly, the power left him, and the room spun. Rigan staggered, colliding with a worktable, and nearly fell.

Kell slid down the wall, panting in pain and terror. His torn shirt showed a wicked gash, ringed by a livid bruise, where the insect had begun tunneling. "How... did you do that?" Kell managed between gasps, his eyes wide.

Rigan threw what remained of the insect into the cauldron. Blood covered his hands—Kell's blood—but beneath the gore, blisters rose on his palms as if he had touched a hot stove.

"I just did what I had to do," Rigan said. He sounded a little shocked, even to his own ears.

"That *was* witch magic."

There was no way to deny it, so Rigan nodded. "Yes. And it's worth my life if anyone finds out."

Bloodied, wounded, and exhausted, Kell still managed a broad grin. "That was amazing," he said, awe tingeing his voice. "Corran's not the only one with a secret. Somehow, I didn't think you were sneaking out to see a girl."

"You knew?"

Kell's grin widened. "Yeah. But I never suspected you were doing *magic.*"

"You're not going to tell Corran?"

Kell leaned back against the wall and closed his eyes. "Of course not. What are brothers for?"

Kelly's [illegible] bellowed [illegible] held on, though his another wanted [illegible]

The beast raised [illegible] from the wound. [illegible] Kell's [illegible] and Rigan grabbed [illegible] with both hands. [illegible] through him [illegible] the [illegible]

[illegible]

Through the [illegible] and [illegible] collapsed [illegible]

Kell slid down the wall, [illegible] and [illegible] showed [illegible] Rigan [illegible] began [illegible] Did you [illegible] his eyes wild.

[illegible] clasped his hands [illegible] blood [illegible] on his [illegible]

"[illegible] did what I had to do," [illegible] to his own ears.

"[illegible]"

[illegible] like it anyone [illegible]

[illegible] But [illegible] in a [illegible]

[illegible]

"You're not going to [illegible]"

Kell [illegible] What are the [illegible]

[illegible]

Chapter Twenty-One

Corran was gone, fighting monsters somewhere. He'd refused to answer Rigan's questions, just grabbed his cloak and left. Kell murmured something under his breath about both his stubborn brothers, stomped up the stairs, slammed the door, and went to bed. That left Rigan alone in a workroom full of corpses, several days after the fight with the beetles.

For a moment, he thought about mixing up pigment and getting to work on the bodies. Most nights, he would have done just that. But since the opportunity had been handed to him, he had a theory he wanted to try.

Rigan glanced up the stairs to make sure the door was still closed, then took his cloak and let himself out quietly into the back alley, staying in the shadows in case Kell happened to be watching from the window. It was after curfew, and he knew the danger if he were caught, but that did not slow him down; the need to know was stronger than his fear.

Rigan made his way to the burial ground. Once inside the stone walls, he let out a sigh of relief. The guards almost never came near the cemetery, and after curfew, no one else did, either. Any danger now came from the dead, not the living.

He looked around to assure himself he was alone, then walked to the center of the graveyard, where a shrine to the gods sat in a clearing. He sensed the ghosts gathering like fog, curious to find out why he had come. He and Corran banished troublesome spirits from the cemetery as often as they did the work room, so he was not afraid of the dead. Tonight, he planned to offer them a trade.

Rigan drew the sigils on the paving stones, connecting them with a warded circle drawn in salt, aconite, and amanita. He lit the candles and then looked up. Spirits crowded against the salt line, watching.

"If you can tell me how the monsters come to Ravenwood, and who commands them, I will hear your confessions. Tell me what you can and I'll help you cross over."

Making spirits pay for the release of their soul was blasphemy, or worse, but Rigan was willing to take his chances with the gods. If his suspicions were correct, they had a bigger problem than the monsters, bigger even than the guards.

"Are the guards controlling the monster?"

Yes—and no.

The ghosts parted, and Rigan saw a thin man in his middle years. From his opulent clothing, the gold ring on his left hand, and the wide, ceremonial silver chain across his chest, holding a cape across broad shoulders, Rigan guessed the spirit was the late Guild Master Noran.

"That's not much of an answer." If the Guild Master had still been alive, Rigan might have watched his tone. But dead, and outside the warded circle, with Rigan armed with the banishment ritual, the ghost could cause him little harm. Rigan's growing fear for Corran and Kell's safety pushed him past civility. "Are they, or aren't they?"

Noran glided closer to the salt circle. The ghosts around him pressed closer, as if they were eager to hear. How many of them, he wondered, had ended up in this cemetery because of those damn monsters?

Some of the monsters occur naturally, Noran replied. *Others are created or controlled by blood magic. That sort of dark sorcery comes at a cost, and if it can't be paid in fear and death it will turn on its wielders. It's all about the Balance.*

"I thought the Balance had to do with light and dark—"

A convenient misunderstanding, one that well serves those who control Ravenwood. A willful lie, even, to make the masses more pliant. He shook his head and chuckled. *How would the people feel, knowing their fear, blood, and death feeds the dark magic of powerful mages—the same mages who send the monsters among them to keep from being savaged themselves? It's always about the Balance.*

"You're lying."

Why would I do that? I'm dead. Either you send me on, or I remain here in the mortal realm. You asked a question. I answered. Not my fault you don't like the truth. Now hear my confession and let me go to my rest.

"What about the guards? How are they involved?" Despite the cool evening, a cold sweat rose on Rigan's skin.

The guards' control is limited, the Guild Master continued. *They can summon monsters to certain places at certain times with the use of charms and spells. But the magic controlling the monsters doesn't belong to the guards.*

"So, who's summoning them?"

It takes a powerful blood witch, well versed in the arts of death magic.

Rigan shivered. "That kind of magic is forbidden in Ravenwood."

Noran's ghost laughed. *Dear boy, don't you know by now that laws apply to some people more than others? Magic is forbidden outside of Guild business, but money can buy many privileges.*

"Then who is this blood witch?"

Noran shrugged. *Whoever it is, they won't have come cheaply. You're lucky it's so expensive to hire a blood witch, or you'd have it worse than you do now.*

"Who hires the blood witches, and why?"

Rigan was burning through his limited power quickly. Usually, hearing a spirit's confession was a passive act: the spirit spoke and Rigan listened before murmuring a few words of absolution and illuminating the path to the After. Interrogating a spirit at length was new to him, and it took more out of him than he expected. Rigan's head pounded, and he felt feverish. Bleeding out life force in a cemetery might not be the smartest thing he'd ever done. But he was so close to getting answers, so much was at stake, that he pushed on.

Noran gave an unpleasant smile. *At one time or another, boy, anyone with the means to do so. It's how the game is played.*

"Game?"

I don't expect you to understand. You're an undertaker, he added, disdain thick in his voice. *Pay attention, sonny. I'll only say this once. Men of power are always looking for an advantage over the competition. It's a game with no rules, winner takes all. What damages my enemy benefits me. When goods are scarce, prices rise. And when people are scared, they're so much easier to control. The price of power is keeping the Balance, paying your debts to the darkness. And the blood and death keep the commoners cowed, even as they maintain the Balance. Quite the bargain.*

"So who—"

I've answered enough questions. And I've been dead for years; I don't know or care who's calling the monsters now. I've told you all I'm going to.

"Then let me hear your confession. The night's a-wasting."

Noran's eyes narrowed. *I admit to sending assassins against my enemies. I don't regret it. I paid for spies and I blackmailed other Guild Masters. I would have used a mage myself to control the monsters, but never had quite the gold to spend. I was unfaithful to my wife, if that matters to the gods. I killed my mistress.* He smirked, not a hint of remorse in his eyes.

"Then go to the gods," Rigan said. "And may you receive everything you deserve." Wind gusted through the cemetery. The other spirits fell back from the circle and vanished. As Rigan watched, Noran's spirit faded. Only at the last did his confidence falter, as Doharmu, god of death, opened the gate. Rigan saw the smugness give way to terror, heard Noran scream, and then the cry cut off abruptly, leaving only silence.

Rigan slumped forward, shaking, mouth dry, dangerously spent. Perhaps on another night, he would return to see if any of the other ghosts knew more about how monsters were summoned and controlled. Tired as he was from the summoning, it would take all his remaining energy just to get home. Fever alternated with chills. The ghosts were gone, but he dared not dispel his wardings without making certain that none of the spirits would attack him, or even seek to confess to him. *I'm done for tonight.*

He read the banishing spell, managing the ritual even though his voice trembled with exhaustion. Then Rigan extinguished the candles and smudged away the sigils and salt mixture. He knelt on the wet paving stones, utterly exhausted. Glancing skyward, he reckoned the time from the position of the moon. *Let's hope I make it home before Corran.*

Rigan scanned the cemetery warily, but saw no one, not even the spirits. He gathered his equipment, then crossed the burying ground. At the stone wall, he paused and looked warily up and down the deserted alleys. *The guards don't come near the boneyard. They're afraid of the ghosts.*

The walk home took twice as long as the journey in. Rigan staggered, sweating and shivering. The ache in his head pounded in time with his heartbeat; his vision blurred—which was why he didn't notice the guards come up behind him.

"It's past curfew."

Rigan froze. He had nowhere to run, and he doubted he could outpace the soldiers in his present state. "Pardon, sirs," he said, intentionally slurring his words, trying to sound drunk. "I didn't hear the bells. Just heading home now."

"The curfew bells rang a long time ago. You're breaking the law."

Rigan bowed. "I'm deeply sorry, sirs. I've made a mistake. I won't make it again."

"You know why there's a curfew?" the guard asked, stepping forward. "Because all kinds of bad things come out at night. Thieves. Monsters. Bandits. Which of those are you?"

"None, sir. I'm just trying—"

The guard's fist caught Rigan in the stomach. He doubled over, gasping.

"You were *just* breaking the law," the guard growled. His knee came up, hard, into Rigan's face, breaking his nose. Blood splattered.

"Look at that," the guard said to his companions, who had closed in a circle around Rigan. "He got blood on my uniform. I'm gonna have to buy new pants. Guess who's gonna pay for that?"

"Please," Rigan begged. "I meant no harm." *If they search my bag, will that lead them back to Corran and Kell?*

"Doesn't matter what you *meant*, boy. Rules are rules." Two of the guards grabbed Rigan, pinning his arms, and dragged him into a dilapidated building. Enough moonlight filtered through the single high window that he could see his attackers clearly.

"Now that it's nice and private, we're going to teach you a lesson you won't forget," the lead guard said, baring his teeth. "You'll beg for a hanging by the time we're done with you." He swung a punch, catching Rigan in the jaw so hard he nearly passed out.

The guard on Rigan's right let go of his arm and drove a fist into his side. Rigan arched in pain, then collapsed as another guard brought both fists down into the small of his back. The men rode him down to the shed floor, pummeling him. Rigan could smell alcohol on the guards' breath.

A hand grabbed Rigan by the hair and shoved the side of his face against the floor. He bit back a cry of pain.

"We don't like lawbreakers," one of the guards growled. The hard toe of a boot drove into Rigan's stomach. A second guard kicked from the other side. Rigan felt ribs snap. It was difficult to breathe. One of the guards knelt on his back, with a chokehold on his throat. The world grew red and blood rushed in his ears. *I'm going to die.*

Magic welled up in him, primal and strong. *They're going to kill me. And if they figure out who I am, they'll kill Corran and Kell.*

Rigan reached down into the dirt to anchor his magic and lashed out, fighting for his life, and for his brothers. The man on his back was suddenly gone. Rigan heard a body hit the wall hard enough to break bones. He braced himself for more blows, but with a rush of wind, the other two men were thrown clear. One slammed headfirst into the door, hard enough to split his head like a melon. The other was thrown against an iron pitchfork and choked on blood as the metal tines forced their way through his chest.

Rigan dragged himself to his feet. *I've just killed three guards. With magic.* He shook with exhaustion and pain lanced through his ribs with every movement. His split lip dripped blood, and one eye was swelling shut. Though he had tried to anchor his magic, he knew from his body's reaction that he had pushed beyond his reserves.

Hide. Rigan crawled from the shed. His power rose again, slipping from his control, and the shed came down in a rush, its timbers and walls crushing everything inside. Rigan staggered to his feet and stumbled toward the street. His heart thudded and the heaviness in his chest made it difficult to breathe. Everything around him seemed askew and unreal as fever overtook him, unleashed by the strong magic. The damage the guards had done ached in his bones and Rigan felt certain something inside him had been damaged, perhaps beyond repair.

Rigan looked up and saw a faintly glowing figure approaching—*Mama.*

The spirit beckoned and Rigan had no will to refuse, more terrified of what was behind him than what lay ahead. He tried to speak her name, but only a croak came from his swollen lips. Rigan limped toward the apparition, loss and longing overcoming terror. *Mama, is that you? We've missed you so much. Mama, wait! I'm coming!*

He moved as fast as his injured body would allow, but the figure always remained out of reach. *Mama, help me get home.*

Alaine Valmonde appeared as Rigan remembered her from his childhood, more than a decade younger than when she died. She motioned for him to hurry and he managed to hobble on. *Not much farther.*

The back door to the undertaker's shop was in sight. Alaine's ghost stopped in the shadows on the far side of the doorway, just beyond where the light shone from the upper windows.

"Mama," Rigan croaked. He had so many questions, so much he wanted to ask her—about the magic, the Wanderers—but he did not have the breath to say the words.

Alaine pointed to the doorway, shaking her head as Rigan tried to move toward her. She looked at him wistfully, a sad smile on her lips, and made the sign of blessing before vanishing.

Rigan's remaining strength failed him. He collapsed against the door, and slid to the ground. The door opened inward and he fell flat on his back, looking up at his brothers, who both had weapons readied.

Corran's eyes widened in shock. "Get him inside!" Corran and Kell grabbed Rigan's arms and dragged him into the workshop, slamming and bolting the door behind him.

Rigan groaned in pain as the movement strained his broken ribs.

"Get water," Corran ordered. "And prepare a poultice." Kell ran to do his bidding.

"Who did this to you?" Corran demanded.

"Guards," he managed, though his swollen mouth muffled the word.

"Why were you out? What were you thinking?"

Rigan tried to shake his head, but it hurt too much. Corran bent down and lifted him in his arms, wincing as his brother cried out in pain. He laid him on a worktable and turned away for a moment, hiding his face as he tried to regain control. Corran rarely let on that anything was more than he could handle; his reaction added to Rigan's terror.

"How could you be so careless? Was this about a girl?" Corran stripped away Rigan's torn and bloody clothing and flinched when he saw the bruises underneath. Rigan's labored breath struggled against the pain from his broken ribs and smashed nose. Blood trickled from the corner of his mouth.

"I have a mind to thrash you myself for being so stupid," Corran growled.

"Shut up, Corran." Kell's voice was flat and hard. "It wasn't about a girl. He's a witch, with a lot more power than simple grave magic, and he's been going Below to learn how to use it." For the first time, Rigan realized how deep Kell's voice had become. He was no longer a child.

More astonishing, however, was that Corran did what he was told.

"Someone made your face more of a mess than it usually is," Kell joked as he dipped a cloth in the icy water and gently daubed at Rigan's injuries, grimacing as his brother winced. "Sorry, Rigan. I know I said I wouldn't tell."

"You knew and didn't let me know?" Corran sounded stunned.

Kell did not look up from his work as he carefully cleaned the blood from Rigan's wounds. "About you joining the hunters or Rigan being a witch? The answer to both is: yes."

"How long?"

"Around the time you started practicing with the hunters. That's when you both started sneaking out, when you thought I was asleep." He chuckled. "I made bets with myself on which of you would get back first, and how close you would come to running into each other in the alley."

"If anyone finds out..."

Kell looked up. "Yeah, I know. If either of you gets caught, we all die horribly. Trying not to think about that, since I'm just the cook. Not even a true apprentice yet."

For a while, Kell and Corran worked in silence. Rigan fought not to lose consciousness, though he wished for a respite from the pain. "How did you find out he could do more than grave magic?" Corran asked.

"The night the insect-monsters came," Kell replied. "Rigan blasted them back from the shop door. And then one of them fell on me and started to burrow. He was scared for me. His hands grew hot like coals. He made the monster fall away, and then burned it to death with his bare hands."

"That burn on your arm—"

"Rigan did that. He saved my life."

"I swore on Mama and Papa's graves I would protect the two of you. Damn fine job I'm doing," Corran said bitterly.

"Actually, you *do* do a damn fine job. You can't control everything."

Corran felt down Rigan's chest, noting where his brother flinched at his touch. "We need to bind his ribs. Whoever beat him did a proper job on him. Let's just hope nothing's broken inside."

Undertakers had a better idea of how the body was put together than anyone but chirurgeons. Preparing a corpse for burial provided a lesson in anatomy, and handling the remains of those who died from various ailments was a primer in medicine. Corran's hands moved swiftly and surely, taping up Rigan's broken ribs before gently feeling his abdomen for signs of deeper injury. Finally, he let out a breath and stood back.

"From what I can tell, I don't think they damaged his innards. We don't dare take him to a doctor."

"The Lord Mayor's Guards did this," Kell replied, contempt clear in his voice.

"Yes. But what I want to know is, why was Rigan out there?"

"I think you'll have to wait for an answer," Kell said. He added an herb mixture to the pot of hot water they kept simmering on the brazier. Some he used for a cup of tea, cooling it with water from the cistern. The rest he used to prepare a poultice, which he spread on strips of cloth Corran had ripped from a new shroud.

"I'll dribble tea into his mouth; you start wrapping up the worst injuries," Kell said.

Corran complied without a retort.

A GREY FOG enveloped Rigan and he could hear voices murmuring in the distance. The figure appeared before him and he recognized her immediately.

Mama. Is it really you?

She smiled. *You've done well. You were very brave. Your gift is powerful.*

There's so much I want to ask you.

You have to go back. There is work to do.

Everything hurts.

You must return. I can't explain. It will be worse if you aren't there.

Don't go, Rigan begged, as Alaine began to fade.

Learn to control the magic, Rigan. Don't fear it. Use it to shift the Balance.

Alaine was gone.

A knock at the door silenced the voices and he woke.

"AIDEN. THANK THE gods," Kell said.

"Why does he look familiar?" Corran sounded uneasy and suspicious.

"I'm Aiden. A friend. I sometimes glimpse something that is about to happen. That's how I knew to come. With luck, I can save Rigan."

"He's the reason you're alive," Kell snapped with a glare at Corran. "Rigan fetched him that night you came out of the sewer, or you would have died."

Kell turned his attention back to Rigan. "We thought we'd bound up his wounds. Is he bleeding internally?"

"It's not his body," Aiden explained. "Magic has a price. Your brother's power triggers when he's in danger. He's been learning to control it so he doesn't hurt himself, but whatever he did has taken its toll."

Rigan tried to say something, but his body would not respond. His breath came in shallow gasps, and his heart beat rapidly, pain taking him in and out of consciousness.

"You have soot and chalk?" Aiden's tone was curt.

"We're undertakers. Of course—"

"Give them to me." A pause. "You want him to live or not? Do it!"

Footsteps sounded, and Aiden grunted as if acknowledging being handed the materials.

"What are you doing?" Kell asked.

"Marking the sigils. They'll help me with the working. He must have drawn on a lot of power to do this to himself. Thank the gods for my foresight, or I might not have been here in time."

Foresight? Rigan thought. *Aiden never mentioned that. Does Damian know?*

"If I felt his power, someone else might have, too," Aiden continued. "Let's just hope they didn't have time to trace it." He paused. "Boy!"

"My name is Kell."

"I want you to lay a line of salt by the doors and windows, and place iron across the thresholds, like before. You remember this mark? When you're done with the salt and iron, take the chalk and make it on the doors and shutters. And pray the gods are with us."

Rigan slipped back into the shadows, catching only fragments of the conversation.

"—thought he was just sleeping."

"—worse than before."

"—Corran wouldn't have gone if he knew."

"—not much left."

The next time Rigan came around, he could hear Aiden's chants and Kell's muffled sobs. Aiden's voice rose and fell, and gradually the pain receded. *Either I'm getting better, or slipping over to the other side.* Finally, the chant stopped.

"Will he be all right?" Kell's voice trembled.

"If he wakes."

Rigan wanted to comfort Kell, but he could not make his body respond. Shadows folded around him and he gave in, too tired to struggle.

Thick fog enveloped him Rigan and he felt cold, and utterly alone. Voices sounded from the darkness. Some cried out for loved ones, others denounced those they blamed for their deaths. The stronger ghosts pushed forward, forcing themselves on his consciousness.

Share your warmth. I left gold in the wall of my shop. No one knows it's there. I'll tell you where it is if you give me a little of your heat.

I know secrets worth a king's ransom. Give me what I ask, and you can bargain for a fortune with what I'll tell you.

Bring a message to my wife, and she'll reward you handsomely. She's desperate for word from me. I promise she'll believe you.

A streak of white fire cracked like lightning through the fog. Alaine was back, limned in golden light, and she was angry. She interposed itself between the grasping spirits and Rigan.

Leave him alone!

She turned to her son. *Run.*

In the next heartbeat, Rigan was back in his body, thrashing hard enough that he nearly toppled to the floor. Alaine's voice rang in his ears. He shivered with cold and alternated between numbness and excruciating pain.

"Easy," Kell said, pressing his shoulders down, his touch firm but careful. "You've done enough fighting for one day."

"Mama—"

Kell's expression grew concerned. "Mama's dead, Rigan."

"I saw her."

"That's not good," Kell replied, staring at him with red, puffy eyes.

"She led me home."

Kell laid the back of his hand against Rigan's forehead, the way Alaine had when they were small. "You're running a fever. I'm not surprised, with what you've been through."

"Corran?"

"He stayed with you as long as he could, until he thought you were going to be all right, and then left on the hunt," Kell said. "Damn fool."

"I heard another voice." *I must have been hallucinating.*

"Aiden came to the door not long after you came home. He said something about someone 'hunting' you." A steely note had come into Kell's voice.

"Did you forget what they do to witches?"

"Oh, gods," Kell murmured. He helped Rigan lift his head enough to drink more tea. "Looks like you get to sleep down here for a while. Don't mind the company—they don't snore. Neither of us wanted to try to haul your sorry ass up the stairs."

"Sorry." Rigan's jaw was stiff and sore from the beating he had taken. A couple of teeth felt loose. Split, swollen lips made talking hurt. *I'm glad I can't see a mirror.*

Kell sighed. "I'd ask you what you thought you were doing, being out that late, but you need your rest, so I'll leave you to it." He grimaced. "Congratulations on making Corran madder than I've seen him in ages. He was so scared you were going to die, he was ready to kill you himself."

"Thanks."

Kell wrung out a cloth and pressed the cool compress against Rigan's forehead. "Did the guards recognize you? Should I be packing to run away?"

"The guards are dead."

Kell froze. "You killed the guards?"

Rigan grunted in acknowledgement.

"With magic?"

Another grunt.

"Maybe I really *should* go pack," Kell said. He shook his head. "Damn, Rigan. Like living here wasn't dangerous enough. Between you and Corran, this hero stuff is going to get someone killed."

Two nights later, Corran headed back to the shop after a late night with the hunters. Ghouls had slaughtered two entire families, a dozen people, and Corran was certain he would see the bloody remains in his dreams forever. The fight had been short and brutal, and the bodies of the ghouls were still ablaze on the garbage heap as he limped home. Corran didn't let down his guard until he had the door to the workshop locked behind him. Rigan looked up from where he was sitting by the fire.

"You didn't need to wait up," Corran said, taking off his cloak.

"We need to talk."

Rigan's tone made Corran stop. The room was not brightly lit enough to work on the corpses. *Why was he waiting here in the dark?* Three bodies had already been prepared, ready for the cart in the morning. Corran frowned. The fourth table held a fresh shroud and a few sharp knives.

"Rigan?"

Rigan turned away, toward the shadows. "My magic is a danger to you and Kell, Corran."

Rigan's tone sent a chill down Corran's spine. "Aiden said control would come with time. You're learning. You'll get better."

"I've killed six men, Corran." Rigan's back was to his brother, and Corran could see how tense Rigan's shoulders were. His brother clenched and unclenched his right fist.

"Rigan—"

"I made one man's heart stop, burned two men alive. Another three got thrown against a wall so hard it split their skulls. Then I brought a building down on them."

"You were protecting yourself," Corran countered. "You would be dead if you hadn't fought back. There's no shame in that; they got what they deserved."

"But why should *I* have the power of life and death?" Sorrow and guilt colored Rigan's voice. "How many more will I kill?"

"Come on, Rigan. Let's have a drink. You're still alive. I don't care how many guards or robbers you have to kill to keep it that way. No one will miss them."

"Do you know what they call something that can't control the urge to kill? A monster. And you hunt monsters."

All of a sudden Corran realized the reason for the knives and the shroud. His eyes widened, and he took a step forward. "Rigan—"

"I'm dangerous, Corran. I've thought about running away, going Below to stay with Damian and the witches, but what if I never learn to completely control… *this*?"

"Stop it." Corran snapped. "You haven't hurt anyone who wasn't trying to kill you."

"What happens if I get sick and a fever puts me out of my head? I could kill someone. Maybe you or Kell. You need to make sure that doesn't happen. The knives are sharp. I won't fight."

Corran swept the knives and the shroud off the table. "Dammit, Rigan. No!"

"Corran—"

"Have you *lost your mind?*" Corran roared. "You aren't a monster. I'm not going to kill you. Whatever happens, we'll deal with it."

Rigan's shoulders relaxed, just a little. "I need to go Below again.

There's no guarantee how fast I'll learn, or whether I *can* learn to fully control the power."

"Then we do what we've been doing, only we quit lying about it," Corran said, sitting on the edge of the table. "Apparently, we weren't fooling Kell. I continue hunting and you continue training with your teachers, and every day we see to the dead."

Slowly, Rigan turned around. Even in the shadows, Corran could see the bruises and half-healed gashes from the beating he had taken. He fought down fury. *If you hadn't killed the guards who did that to you, I would have. Dammit, Rigan, that was too close a call.*

"Corran?" Rigan sounded lost.

Did he really think I'd kill *him? That I could think he was a monster?* Corran ran a hand back through his hair. *I've been so obsessed with fighting the monsters, I wasn't paying enough attention here at home. Gods, Rigan's had to fight for his life. I could have lost him.*

I wasn't there to help.

"Rigan, nothing's changed." Corran's voice was tight. "I don't pretend to understand your power, but you're still my brother, and we'll get through this. You'll learn to control it. I'll get better at fighting. We'll be all right." He stepped forward and before Rigan realized what he meant to do, Corran threw his arms around his brother's shoulders, pulling him into a desperate, bone-jarring hug.

Gods! He looks like a beaten dog, Corran thought as he released him, stepping back to look at him appraisingly. *He's got the power to kill someone with a touch, and he's worried about my approval?*

"You've got another hunt coming?" Rigan's hands had unclenched, but they were shaking.

"Yeah," Corran replied.

He poured whiskey and handed a glass to his brother. He leaned against the table, and after a moment's hesitation, Rigan joined him. Rigan knocked the whiskey back in one, his hand still shaking.

"The less you know, the less trouble I can get you in," Corran replied. "Come on. Let's have another drink. The dead can wait."

Chapter Twenty-Two

MACHISON FLED, KNOWING, without needing to look over his shoulder, that his enemy was nearly upon him. The corridors of the Lord Mayor's palace were strangely empty, unusually silent, except for the sound of his heaving breath and running footsteps. His pulse pounded in his ears, and the muscles in his side twinged painfully. He had not run so far, so fast, since his army days, many years ago. The benefits of his position had made him soft, vulnerable.

He stole a glance behind him. The old woman kept a steady pace, closing the distance. Wiry and gaunt, all bones and sinew, her unkempt gray hair fell in straggles around a lined face. She shouldn't be able to catch him, shouldn't be able to even get close, but her steps sounded just behind him, and her outstretched hands clawed at his robe.

"You're not real," Machison puffed, but he lacked conviction, and did not stop running. "I'm dreaming. You're not real."

"What makes you think dreams aren't real?" Her voice sounded like shifting gravel; it reminded him of the Oracle. "Dreams are real. So are curses. All those curses called down by the ones who've lost their loved ones to your guards and monsters—oh, they're real enough. You'll see."

"I'm not here. You're not here. None of this is happening."

A mirthless laugh answered him. "You're certain that you control the living. It's the dead you'd best be fearing."

Machison found himself in the dark, no longer running. He could not see the old woman, and in the silence his heartbeat hammered in his ears. "The dead bear witness," the old woman said. "The dead remember. They will have their justice. They will be avenged."

MACHISON SAT BOLT upright in his bed. Sweat-soaked sheets clung to his body, blankets twisted around him as if he had fought a battle in his sleep. He felt for the amulet around his neck, but it brought him no comfort.

And it obviously didn't keep the dreams at bay.

He made himself breathe slowly, calming himself. A quick pat down of his arms and chest reassured him that no damage had been done. He could feel the anger building in his gut. *Was the dream a warning? What of the old woman? How do I destroy her? If she comes at me with a knife in my dreams, will it actually hurt me?*

Machison glanced down at the unbroken circle around his bed. He remembered checking the lines of salt on all of the doors and windows before getting in his bed. Enough evidence had proven the blood witch's power was real; he did not doubt that the wardings were genuine and had been performed correctly.

So she's not a spirit, he concluded. *Not a ghost or a wraith. A vision? Or, perhaps, a witch with enough power to get inside my head, twist my own mind against me? Could Blackholt be doing this, or is it someone else entirely, someone unknown to me?*

That last thought chilled him with its possibilities. *Whoever it is, I think, she can't actually be in my head. Else why not kill me when she had the chance? No, a vision of some sort.*

Another possibility presented itself. *The Wanderers. They're witches, beholden to no one. People shun them, but even so, they know to fear the wise women and show them respect. Jorgeson advised waiting to get rid of them, using them in our plans. That was a mistake. They have to know we intend to drive them out; maybe they've decided to strike first. I'll have Jorgeson take care of them. No mercy.*

Machison swung his legs off the bed, knowing sleep would elude him. He stepped carefully over the salt circle so as not to break it. No sense in making it any easier for his enemies. The banked embers in the fireplace glowed hotter as he poked them back to life, and he settled into a chair facing the fire. The remains of his unfinished glass of whiskey still sat on the side table, and he picked it up, toying with it as his thoughts raced.

We push the Wanderers away, they come right back. It's true in every corner of the League. Why do they come? Why return? We run them to ground, kill them; they turn up a season later to repeat the dance again. The Wanderers traveled these parts when the Elder Gods reigned, so the legends say. Is that where they get their magic?

He snorted at the thought. *The Elder Gods might as well still reign. The commoners believe in them yet. Oh, the Guild Masters love their new gods, and they get what they pray for—and pay for. The Elder Gods were never usurped; they stepped aside. Maybe they got bored, they certainly haven't done much in recent memory.*

Gods and monsters. The monsters he could control, but gods were something else entirely. Machison had his hands quite full already with Merchant Princes and Guild Masters, and keeping Crown Prince Aliyev happy.

Machison's instincts had served him well. He'd always been able to balance a betrayal with a favor, an enemy with a patron, with the deftness of a master juggler. Now, when the stakes were highest, he worried that he was off his game.

He didn't trust Blackholt, though the man was useful. Valdis was at least Machison's man, his loyalty bought and paid for.

Trust no one. Not that Machison ever really had. He knew what he wanted, and it was more than just keeping his comfortable position and generous stipend. Aliyev considered him his lapdog and he hated the role, but he would play along with the charade for now to better his station and increase his power. Gorog at least approached things straightforwardly, laying out the rewards Machison would gain for pressing to keep—or improve—the Merchant Prince's advantage.

Means to an end. Playing a long game. Checkmate in five moves.

Machison took another sip of his drink. *Patience. I knew when I started that this would take years to accomplish. And now, the Garenoth agreement brings the next prize in sight. I won't let anyone take that from me—certainly not those damn filthy Wanderers.*

Machison had spent more than a decade building connections, currying favor, making sure people in positions of power owed him. Blackmail, curses, hostages, and threats had accomplished his agenda when honeyed words and dubiously ethical deals had not. His ruthlessness and gamesmanship had served him well, and as Aliyev's power and Gorog's fortunes rose, so did Machison's hold over Ravenwood.

Ravenwood isn't enough. It never was; not for Gorog, and not for me. The Garenoth deal will ensure our ascension as power brokers in the League itself, maybe even win Aliyev and me favor from King Rellan himself. Wealth and power, and the security that comes with them; maybe even a hand in the King's court. We're at a crucial moment, and I can't afford to be merciful. Not when we're so close.

The knock at the door came as expected.

"Come in."

Valdis slipped into the room, in a sinuous, fluid move. "You've had a problem with the wardings?"

"They aren't working."

Valdis raised an eyebrow. "You've been attacked?"

"Not physically."

"Dark magic, then?"

"Nightmares. More vivid than they should be. Almost real. I don't want to find out whether or not they really are."

"It's possible," Valdis said after a moment's consideration. "If the dreams are being sent by a powerful enough witch, injury in the dream can cause injury in the waking world."

Machison remembered the old woman in the dream. "I'd just like to get a good night's sleep."

"I'll have to do some research into the nature of the problem, but I can arrange for a good night's sleep in the meantime," Valdis replied. "Anything else?"

"I want a sanctuary," Machison said. "I want a place inside my room where I can retreat and be untouchable by magic."

The blood witch frowned. "That will be more difficult."

Machison glared at him. "If you can't do it—"

Valdis raised a hand in appeasement. "I didn't say I couldn't do it, just that what you're asking is not a simple task. It requires strong magic, and to provide the level of protection you seek, against the sort of powers you fear? It will require a spell many might consider to be... damning."

"If it keeps me alive, I won't have to worry about being damned. What do you need?"

Valdis considered for a moment. "I'll need to consult my grimoires, it's not a common working. There is risk involved—both for you and for me."

"What kind of risk?"

"You have to understand," he said, licking his lips nervously, "I haven't read this spell in quite a while. But the items required are of dubious legality and morality—"

"And?"

"These items are difficult to obtain, and while a blood witch must cast the actual spell, the *objects* have to be acquired by the one who will benefit from the spell, to seal intention."

"Intention," Machison repeated.

"It is very dark magic, dark enough to stain the soul. Both our souls," Valdis replied, meeting Machison's gaze intently, as if challenging the Lord Mayor to back away from such a dangerous path. When Machison did not, Valdis blinked and went on. "That's why the recipient of the spell must be complicit in gathering the items. There's blood involved—yours and mine, and that of other people. Magic that taints the soul requires a contract of sorts with the Dark Ones. Protection like that comes at a high price." He paused. "On the plus side, it will strengthen our bond and make it more difficult for Blackholt to harm either of us. I believe it might even weaken him in the process."

"What about the Wanderer witches? Will it protect against them?"

"To an extent. But we know very little about their magic. The Wanderers we've captured with any real power killed themselves before we could learn anything about how their magic works."

"Make it happen, and make sure the protections hold—even against Wanderers," Machison snapped.

A look crossed Valdis's face, like a soldier given a suicide mission, but it vanished as the witch pressed his lips together. "As you wish, m'lord."

"Will Blackholt know? When you work the spell, will he feel it?"

"It's likely, given the power of the invocation."

"Can we hide it?"

"From Blackholt? I'm not sure."

"Blackholt's still useful to me. I need to keep him on my side, preferably on a short leash." *I need to teach that arrogant bastard who's boss.*

"I think that will be possible," the witch replied. "Those without magic will sense nothing, although your servants may talk when they see the markings on the floor."

"Leave that to me."

Valdis nodded. "Once the working is complete, I can place a distraction spell around your private rooms. Unless another, fairly powerful witch is looking for magic, it won't be obvious."

"And Blackholt?"

"We'll be most at risk of him noticing during the working itself," he said, glancing toward the door as if he expected the senior witch to come barging into the room. "When the power is called forth."

"Then I'll arrange for him to be occupied at the time. How soon can you be ready?"

"I will confirm what you need to collect. And then I'll need to prepare myself for the working."

"Make it quick," Machison growled. "I'm not a patient man."

THE LORD MAYOR'S mood soured after Valdis left. He needed the blood witch's cooperation, and with witches, it was best not to earn their ire. The working would increase his own protections and help rein in Blackholt, and he already had precautions in place to keep Valdis beholden to him, solidly under his control. Still, the blood witch had seemed truly disquieted by Machison's request, and the Lord Mayor found his hesitation disturbing. *I stopped worrying about my soul long ago.*

He recognized Jorgeson's knock, though he wasn't expecting him at this hour. "Enter."

"Sorry for disturbing you, but you need to hear this."

"Trouble?"

"Word from my spies."

"What happened?"

"An attempt was made on Ambassador Jothran's life," Jorgeson replied.

"By whom?" Machison snapped.

"The evidence points to the Itaran ambassador, Kirill, but it's all circumstantial and likely to have been planted. As you can imagine, Ambassador Halloran is extremely concerned."

Of course Halloran is concerned. He's got to take Ravenwood's role in the negotiations, and someone is trying to kill his counterpart.

"You don't think it's Kirill?"

Jorgeson shook his head. "Doubtful. Itara might benefit from disrupting the negotiations between Ravenwood and Garenoth, but not significantly."

"Look harder. It could have been a proxy strike. Maybe an Itaran Merchant Prince has a score to settle with one of Garenoth's Merchant Princes—or perhaps one of the other ambassadors wants to make sure everyone's going into the negotiations mistrustful and looking for treachery."

Jorgeson's expression suggested the ambassadors would be fools if they *weren't* looking for treachery, but he kept his peace. "I've got my best men taking a close look at the movements of the ambassadors—discreetly, of course. I have spies among the servants in the ambassadorial suites."

"And Jothran survived?" Machison rubbed a hand on the back of his neck, easing the tension that threatened a headache.

"Yes. He wasn't even actually hurt, which makes me more suspicious that the strike was meant as a distraction."

"How have the other ambassadors reacted?"

Jorgeson raised an eyebrow. "Predictably. Ambassador Arlan requested enough additional bodyguards to fight a small war. Vittir's assistant, Belson, was already feeling vulnerable since his master's murder; I can't say much about his current state, since he's barricaded himself in his rooms and won't come out. The other ambassadors have managed to retain their dignity, though it doesn't require a mind reader to know that they're all waiting to see what happens next, and to whom."

He hesitated, then added, "I'm looking into whether or not Kadar had a hand in the matter," in a tone that brought Machison up short.

"You think that's likely?"

"It's a strong possibility. Kadar wants better terms for himself, at Gorog's expense. Surely he at least suspects that Gorog won't give ground without a fight. He might believe he benefits by seeing Gorog—and you—discredited with Garenoth."

"Aliyev and Gorog will be livid," Machison replied. "They'll want answers. If it is Kadar behind it, there will be repercussions. Gorog will retaliate. No telling what Tamas will do."

"Hardly something we can ask," Jorgeson pointed out.

Machison scowled. "I wasn't suggesting we *ask*. Gods above and below! I hate having to find things out the hard way." He sighed. "Double the guards watching the ambassadors. Tighten your hold on the servants. Make it clear to your spies that they'd best have their ears firmly to the walls. If Kadar wants to meddle with the negotiations, we'll make him work for it."

"As you wish, m'lord. I'll bring you my next report in the morning."

With that, Jorgeson gave a perfunctory bow and let himself out of the room.

Machison sat staring at the closed door for several minutes after Jorgeson left. Understanding the nuances of League politics was like puzzling out the workings of a lockbox; the interlocking mesh of gears and levers that, when pushed and pulled, moved everything around them.

Kadar doesn't even have to scuttle the negotiations to score a win. All he has to do is bring a shadow over how they were handled, while protecting his own interests. Then he can whisper into Aliyev's ear that Gorog and I are to blame.

"Two can play that game," he murmured. "Kadar needs to be sent a warning."

Chapter Twenty-Three

Kell maneuvered through the Market, dodging oncoming carts and stepping around fresh puddles of horse piss. Fear hung heavy in the air. He could feel it in the furtive glances and hear it in the murmurs of the crowd, in the unnatural hush of the vendors, in the way people held themselves, as though ready to flee at any moment.

The Lord Mayor's guards did not take the deaths of three of their own lightly; they were far more motivated to find the killers—they seemed to believe a group of hunters had lured them into the old house and collapsed the roof—than they had ever been to fight monsters. Guards went door to door, making enquiries, and frightened merchants, eager to deflect attention from themselves, told lies. Rumors flew from one end of Wrighton to the other, faster than the crow can fly.

To the brothers' great relief, nothing had yet led the guards to the Valmonde's shop. When the accusations and wild tales had finally quieted, the guards determined that a tremor had brought down the building and chalked it up to an act of the gods.

The prophet hawked his visions of doom near the League monument, attracting a crowd. Some of the onlookers jeered and heckled at his claim that the monsters afflicting the city were the judgment of the gods, but a few looked stricken with conscience. Kell repressed a shudder at the memory of the large beetles, and felt his temper rising at the thought of people feeling guilty about their own murders. Afraid he might say something he would regret if he listened longer, Kell took up his cart and resolutely walked away.

He parked the cart and made his way into the first shop. "I need some more pigments," Kell said, when his turn came at the counter. "Business has been brisk."

"In any other trade but yours, that'd be a good thing," Parah said. "But then we've all had a run of hard luck lately."

Kell nodded, commiserating. "Too bad the monsters couldn't have come last week, when we had guards on every corner. Give them something useful to do." He left it up to interpretation whether 'useful' referred to the guards fighting the monsters, or the monsters killing the guards.

Parah winked. "I hear you. Truer words were never spoken."

Kell paid for the pigments and thanked her. If she'd noticed that he had bought more than usual, and a bag of salt as well, she did not say anything. Some of the pigments were to hide Rigan's still-healing bruises. It would not do to have people wondering about his injuries.

That meant Rigan was house-bound until he healed. He could not go with Corran to the cemetery, so his duties fell to Kell, on top of fixing meals and trading with the merchants, though Rigan helped as much as he was able. The beating and the toll the magic had taken slowed Rigan's recovery, and impatience made him snappish. Kell had already let the others know not to expect anything more creative than stew or cheese and dried meat until his brother was back on the job and out of his hair.

"Treating yourself, Master Kell?" Ebby, the tea vendor chuckled as Kell spared a coin for a cup of her specially-blended brew.

"I deserve it," Kell declared, adding sugar to the drink and pausing to enjoy the aroma. "I'm highly unappreciated."

"You might be the only business that didn't lose coin the last few weeks. We all come your way, sooner or later. But when folks are afraid to come to the market, the rest of us go home with light purses." She paused. "Got any more of those charms? Good luck's been scarce lately."

Kell produced his last three amulets. "They've been in demand, what with all that's been going on. What's your fancy?"

Ebby chose a talisman and paid, and Kell slipped the other two charms into a pocket.

"Got any tips for me?" Kell asked, holding up an extra bronze and twirling it between his fingers. Ebby's tea was popular, and most people who shopped in the market stopped at her stand. That meant Ebby heard much of the neighborhood gossip, including who might be sick and not expected to recover. The Valmondes might be the only officially-appointed Guild undertakers in this part of Wrighton, but some of the other undertaking families were known to poach along the edges of others' territories, an infraction which the Guild did not police as diligently as they could. Kell jealously guarded 'his' streets, doing his best to curry goodwill to head off competitors.

Ebby put another pot on her little brazier to boil. "I heard the cobbler's son has a fever. The silversmith's old grandmam looks peaky. One of the wagon men had his leg crushed day before last when two rigs collided; that kind of thing can go bad fast."

"Much obliged. I'll keep an eye out." Kell had long ago gotten over the ghoulishness of inquiring about the neighbors. He finished his tea and gave back the cup. "Let me know if you hear anything else," he added as he headed back to his cart. Ebby assured him that she would.

"Bring me your dead!" Kell shouted as the cart rattled on the cobblestones. "Valmonde Brothers Undertakers. We'll send you out in style!"

Some chuckled at Kell's cries, others admonished him, but no one ignored him. Tom the silversmith flagged Kell down as he passed by the shop. "My grandmam passed over last night," he said. "I want you to send her off and do it right."

Kell never let on that Ebby had told him. "I'm sorry for your loss," he said in an appropriately solemn tone.

Tom and Kell carried the dead woman down the stairs together. Tom's wife made a sign of blessing as they passed out of the shop, and together, Kell and Tom laid the old lady's body in the cart. "She'll be buried in the Smiths' Guild's lot in the cemetery?"

Kell quoted him a price. "That gets you the full Guild honors, a Guild place in the yard, additional prayers from the priest, and our best preparation."

Tom dug out his money from a leather purse beneath his tunic and handed over the fee. "See that she's sent off well."

Kell assured him that he would.

As he passed a stable, a man came out to meet him. "Got one for you," he said, motioning for Kell to come closer. "One of our wagon drivers lost a leg in an accident. Surgeons couldn't help him. The blood went bad."

The man's body lay on a bed of straw. His stump was bandaged and bloody. The corpse looked fresh. "How long ago did he die?" Kell asked.

"Just a candlemark or so. We haven't gotten rid of the leg, if you want to bury them together."

"Sure," Kell said. "Give me both. But who's paying for the burial?"

The stablehands had gathered around, and they looked at each other. "I guess we are," the man who had hailed Kell said. "He wasn't from around here. How much will it cost?"

Kell quoted them a third of what the silversmith had paid, knowing the stablehands had little coin to part with. "It's not going to be fancy," he warned as the men dug for their coins. "But it'll get the body marked, a decent shroud, and a place in holy ground."

"Done," the stable hand said, handing the money over to Kell. "Thank you. We weren't sure whether we could do right by him or not."

Kell pocketed the money and smiled. "Valmonde Brothers takes good care of you. Tell your neighbors."

So far, Ebby's tips had been spot on, and as Kell continued his rounds, he worried about the cobbler's boy. He slowed as he passed the shop, looking for signs of mourning. No ash mark over the doorframe, no black cloth in the window. Kell murmured a prayer under his breath, and went on his way. *Not today, thank the gods.*

One of Kell's informants was waiting for him when he came around the corner by the weaver's shop. Kell pulled out a couple of bits of dried licorice from his pocket and handed them over to Tek, who accepted them happily.

"What do you hear?" Kell asked.

"There's a dead man at the whorehouse. Stabbed. I heard Mistress Rose is in a hurry for you to come by and take him."

"Done," Kell said, walking on as Tek jogged alongside.

"The midwife has two for you," Tek added. "The knife-maker's daughter had a rough time with the birth. Neither made it."

"I'm sorry to hear that. Are they with the midwife, or the knife-maker?"

Tek gave him the directions. "No one's seen the potter's son, Allery, in days," he went on. "He hasn't shown up at your place, has he?"

Kell looked away. "We'd have said something to the potter if he had. Someone has to pay for the burial."

"That's what I figured." Tek followed him to the end of the block, and Kell paid him a bronze for the information.

"Did the Lord Mayor pay you to bury those guards that got squashed when the quake came?" Tek asked.

Kell forced himself to keep a neutral expression. "The Lord Mayor has his own men for that, up in Vista."

"Thought maybe he'd use someone local. Especially if there wasn't much left to bury. Been talk that it might have been a witch what killed those guards." He pointed toward several odd markings chalked on a nearby wall. "Of course, with those Wanderers scribbling their spells on the walls, there's no telling *who's* behind it all."

"Loose talk like that'll get someone killed," Kell warned. He glanced at the chalk marks, remembered his conversation with the old Wanderer woman, and shivered.

Tek shrugged. "Just telling you what I hear so you keep paying me. Wouldn't do to have nothing to say."

Kell headed to the midwife's first. The dead woman looked no older than Rigan, and her baby lay swaddled on her chest, as if he were only napping.

"The family gave me money for the burial and asked me to arrange it," the midwife said. "Her father wants Guild honors and the Guild lot." Her voice caught. "He asked me to deal with you because he didn't think he could." She gave him the full Guild fee twice over. "That's for her, and for the babe as well."

Kell swallowed hard and looked away. "We'll take care of it."

She thanked him and he moved on, but despite the sunlight and the day's mild breeze, Kell's mood darkened.

It's all part of the job, he told himself. *Easier on the families for us to handle things than have them do it all themselves.* He didn't usually mind taking in corpses of adults. Children—especially babies—were the worst.

Kell pushed his mood away and forced himself to sing out his call loud and clear. The next stop was Mistress Rose's whorehouse. The madam was waiting in the doorway, and she signaled for him to come around to the back. Kell was used to it; having the undertaker's cart out front could be bad for business.

"I wouldn't pay for the son of a bitch's burial at all if there was a trench I could throw him in and be done with it," Rose said as she led Kell up the back stairs. "Even better if it was a latrine." A few of Rose's ladies smiled at him as he passed, and one threw a kiss. Kell blushed and kept his gaze on Rose's back.

"The guy took a swing at one of my girls," Rose said, escorting Kell into a well-appointed bedroom. "Tried to rough her up. We don't stand for that around here. She defended herself." Rose paused. "Of course, the guards might not see things that way."

"You need him to disappear?"

"I'll pay for extra of that quicklime you use so no one will recognize him if someone gets it in his head to dig him up."

"All right. What else?"

"Put him in the pauper's corner," Rose said, with a malicious smile. "You know any tricks about burying someone so the gods won't take them? Like upside down or with the wrong markings? I'll give you an extra coin if you make sure his trip to the After won't be easy."

"Believe it or not, you're not the only person who's ever asked that."

Rose chuckled. Her voice had been coarsened over the years by whisky and pipe smoke. She had likely been beautiful when she was younger. Now, she looked shrewd and hard, but rumor had it she treated the girls in her house well. Kell looked at the dead man. It wouldn't take many such incidents for Rose's visitors to understand the need for 'manners.'

"You have two older brothers, don't you?"

Kell nodded, pulling the dead man and the bed sheet onto the floor. It was going to fall to him to get the corpse downstairs, and the ride would not be gentle. He would have to drag the body by its feet. *He can't get any deader. And I imagine it will amuse Rose's girls.*

"Tell your brothers to stop by sometime. I'm grateful for your help. First visit is on the house." She gave Kell an appraising look. "I'm sure I could find a girl who'd be willing to make a man of you."

His cheeks burned. "Thanks for the offer," Kell managed. "But I've got to get back with the bodies."

"The dead aren't in any hurry."

Half certain Rose was teasing, and half terrified she wasn't, Kell ducked his head to avoid eye contact. "Maybe another time," he said, hoping desperately it would be a year or two before anyone else died at the brothel.

Rose chuckled as Kell headed down the steps, pulling the dead man behind him with a disconcerting string of *thuds* as the corpse's head hit each step. By the time he reached the bottom, all of Rose's girls who weren't occupied had come to watch.

"This isn't our normal way of handling a body, in case anyone asks," Kell felt obliged to point out.

"It's better than he deserves," said a dark-haired girl who might have been a year Kell's senior. A bruise around her throat suggested she was the one who had killed the client. "I wouldn't have minded if you'd have just rolled him down the steps."

"Can you drag the son of a bitch behind your wagon? Carrying him's too good for him," a redhead asked. She stood beside the girl with the bruised throat with her arm protectively around her shoulders and a fierce look on her face.

"People would talk," Kell replied. He hauled the sheet-wrapped body out the door and manhandled the corpse onto the wagon.

"Have a care no one sees him," Rose said quietly, as she paid Kell his usual fee and a tidy sum extra. "It's the Chancellor of the Exchequer."

As if we didn't have enough trouble already. "You're kidding."

Rose shook her head. "We get all kinds here. Long as they pay and mind their manners, everyone's welcome." She looked toward the brunette. "Tell him what you heard from that blighter, Doria," Rose urged. "Kell's doing you a big favor."

Doria eyed Kell with suspicion. "We were talking a bit, before we got to business. I asked him about the building that collapsed on the other side of Wrighton. He said the Lord Mayor's men hadn't ruled out magic. They think a witch might be loose somewhere in the city. Best you be careful."

"Thanks for the warning," Kell replied, just about managing to keep his voice level. "I'll keep my eyes open." He dug out the charms from his pocket. "If you're worried, I've got a few charms left. Just the thing to give you some peace of mind."

Doria pulled out several warm coins from a small bag hidden in her bosom and took one of the charms. "I'll take all the luck I can get," she muttered.

"You won't be sorry," Kell promised.

"Come back and see us sometime," Rose urged with a winsome smile.

"When you're older!" the redhead added. The other girls laughed, and Kell resisted the urge to bolt, forcing himself to keep his head up as he walked to the wagon.

What a day. I've got a corpse in the back the guards could hang me for—probably blame me for stabbing him, too, if they catch me. Everyone's talking about the quake, and the Lord Mayor is looking for Rigan, even if he doesn't realize that's who his witch is. Just lovely.

Kell dumped some quicklime on the dead chancellor's face before he left the alley behind the brothel, and pulled the tarpaulin tight around the bodies. The next stop was The Lame Dragon, to see if Prendicott had any trade for him.

Before he went to the back door of the inn, Kell ran a hand through his hair, hoping Polly would be there to greet him. He rapped at the kitchen door, but it was the stern cook who answered his knock. "Nothing today," she said.

Kell shifted, trying to see past her.

"She's gone, boy." The cook's expression softened. "Took off before dawn."

Kell looked at her, stunned. "Why?" He remembered the man they had buried, the one Polly had knifed, and felt fear curdle in his stomach.

"Don't know for sure, lad," the cook said, dropping her voice. "She didn't confide in me. Something scared her, and she ran. Don't think she'll be back."

"Do you know where she went?"

The cook shook her head. "No, and I don't want to know. What I don't know, I can't tell."

Kell managed to nod, and remembered the other reason he had come to the door, besides checking for bodies and hoping to see Polly. "Can I give you coin for a pot of stew?" Kell asked, digging out the money as the cook gave him a skeptical look.

"Hungry?" she said in a voice raw from kitchen smoke.

"It's for the knife-maker. His daughter died giving birth and he lost both her and his grandchild. Here," he said, pressing the coins into her hand. "That should pay for the stew and a boy to run it over to him. Tell him it's from a friend."

The cook frowned. "Is this a joke?"

"No joke. It's just... the decent thing to do." After the day Kell had, it felt good to do something nice for someone.

"All right," the cook said slowly. "You could take the man in the small guest room upstairs, save yourself a trip."

"Is he dead?" Kell raised an eyebrow.

"Not yet. But the way he's been coughing, he can't last much longer. Keeping everyone up, way he hacks and croaks. I'm surprised one of the other lodgers hasn't put him out of his misery. Don't imagine anyone got much sleep."

"It's against Guild rules to take people before they're dead," Kell replied pleasantly. "You wouldn't believe how often I get asked."

The cook sighed. "Ah, well. Worth a try. Come back tomorrow. He'll probably be dead then." With that, she shut the door.

Kell squeezed his eyes shut and took a deep breath. *Polly's gone. Did someone suspect what she'd done to that bastard that tried to hurt her? Was she afraid of the guards?* His chest hurt at the thought of Polly being arrested. Much as he hated to have her gone, it would be worse if she had been taken to the dungeons. *I want her to be safe. But I also wanted her to be here, with me.* With a heavy sigh, he headed off to continue his rounds.

Kell had a few more stops to make, which included going to see Widgem at The Muddy Goat. He considered not going, since it wouldn't do for someone to get curious about the bodies in the cart and have a look. Before he left the relative safety of the Dragon's rear yard, Kell snuck a peek at the contraband corpse from the brothel. The quicklime had begun to eat through his face, and the body's unfortunate journey down the brothel steps had been partially facedown. It would take a lot of imagination to recognize the Chancellor in his present state.

Satisfied, Kell headed off. The spate of recent deaths had provided a bumper crop; with luck—and if Widgem was in a good mood—the amulets he would buy from him to sell on would more than make up for the few coins he had spent.

He turned the corner toward the Goat and saw guards on either side of the street, stopping everyone, questioning them before they were allowed to move on. For a moment, Kell froze. *If I turn around, I'll draw attention. There's nothing to do but go on.*

He raised his head and joined the queue. *Really glad I didn't wait to use the quicklime until I got home.*

"What's in the cart?" the guard barked as Kell came up for inspection.

"Bodies," Kell replied. "I'm an undertaker." The guard walked around to the back and moved to lift the tarp. "You might not want to do that. The one on top died of fever." He shook his head. "Horrible, it was. Bleedin' from the nose and ears, eyes turned yellow and popping out, near ready to explode." He dropped his voice. "I had to handle him extra careful, 'cause it's very catching."

The guard drew back as if the cart were on fire. "What's your business here?"

"Making my rounds," Kell said jovially. "People die every day, and we give them their last ride." He glanced up at the tavern's sign, then gave the guard a conspiratorial look. "If I were you, I'd avoid the mushroom soup. Last time it was on the menu, we had three new 'customers'—not saying that the soup was to blame, you understand."

The guard looked stricken. "I ate the mushroom soup for lunch."

Kell gave him a patently fake smile. "Oh, then. Not to worry. That was a few candlemarks ago, right?" He peered at the guard, who had gone a bit green around the gills. "If you're still standing, it must have been one of their good batches."

"How do I know?" The guard's gruffness was gone, and he sounded worried.

"Bad mushrooms are trouble," Kell sighed. "Starts with farting, then the shits. Next you puke fit to bring your innards up. And when there's naught left to puke, the blood comes." He offered the guard a half-hearted reassuring look. "I'm sure you have nothing to worry about."

The guard waved Kell on, no longer worried about anything in the back of his wagon.

It was the clear that the guard had told his companions about the corpses and the mushrooms, because they all gave Kell's cart plenty of room when he parked behind The Muddy Goat. Kell forced down his turmoil over Polly's disappearance and headed inside. He bellied up to the bar and ordered a tankard of ale, scanning the room.

"If you're wantin' Widgem, he's in the back," the barkeeper said. "Been busy. Everyone who isn't staying the night wants to get home early. Folks are nervous."

Kell took a sip of the ale. "Yeah, so I've seen. What news have you heard?" The barkeeper gave him a look, and Kell shrugged. "It's not like my customers keep me up on the gossip."

The barkeeper poured drinks for several of the other patrons and handed over a bowl of watery soup to one of the men. "News? Monsters, fever, the usual," he finally said. "Oh, and a couple of guards were too dumb to stay out of a ramshackle house and got squashed when the roof fell in, so you've got some saying it must be witches." He snorted and shook his head. "Things aren't built right, they fall down when they shake. Ain't no magic involved."

"Anything else?"

"I hear the hunters have been out in force."

"Oh?"

"About a week ago, there was a big commotion a few blocks from here. 'Course, everyone does the sensible thing and pulls the shutters and stays inside. But I heard tell that there were men, dressed all in black, out battling these creatures, right?" He leaned closer. "Hunters. Now I didn't see it, I wasn't there. But some who were say that when they looked out a second time, all the monsters were dead and the men in black were nowhere to be seen."

Kell took another sip and raised an eyebrow. "Makes a good story. And what about the guards?"

The barkeeper muttered an oath. "Can't leave well enough alone, the guards can't. Instead of being happy someone else did their job for them, they've been asking lots of questions."

"Are they getting any answers?"

"Not that I've heard. The only thing folks like less than the monsters are the guards."

Kell left an extra coin for the information, and headed for the back. Widgem was holding court, perched on the battered chair like a corpulent, threadbare prince. He looked up, saw Kell and dismissed his hangers-on.

"Master Kell!" Widgem's features were florid, and he mopped his brow with a stained kerchief.

"What did you bring me?" Kell asked, settling into a chair across from him.

Widgem withdrew his pouch of treasures. "I think you'll like what I've got today." He spilled the pouch out onto the table and watched as Kell picked over the contents.

"Very nice," Kell muttered. "Working with a better sort of witch, are you?"

"Keep your voice down!" Widgem looked over his shoulder nervously. "It's not wise to say some things aloud."

Kell picked out half a dozen amulets and set them aside from the rest. "What do you want for these?"

Widgem named a figure, and Kell rolled his eyes and halved it. Widgem countered, and Kell settled in the middle.

"All right!" Widgem grunted. "Highway robbery, that's what it is! You'll have me in the poorhouse at this rate."

"Ravenwood doesn't have a poorhouse," Kell replied, leaning back in his chair.

Kell counted out the coins as Widgem watched to ensure none were counterfeit. Kell held one or two of the charms up to the light, looking them over closely.

"I'm wounded you think I would cheat you," Widgem said, putting a hand to his heart.

Kell gave him a sideways look. "You would if you thought you could get away with it."

Widgem chuckled, baring worn, tobacco-stained teeth. "Yer too smart, Kell Valmonde. I can't get nothing over on you."

"Humph. The moment I start believing that is the moment you strip me naked and sell me for labor to a cargo ship," Kell replied, only half in jest.

Widgem gathered the coins into his voluminous, ragged velvet bag with fingers the size of sausages. "Have to say, I'm a bit disappointed, lad. Thought by now someone in these parts would have tried to pawn a Potters' Guild ring. You haven't seen one around, have you?"

Kell went cold, but he kept his face neutral. "Why would I?"

"Didn't you hear? The potter's son went missing about a week ago. No one's seen or heard from his since. Figured he's dead—and the dead in these parts all come to you."

"Only if someone pays their way," Kell replied.

Widgem slapped his hand against the table and roared with laughter, ending in a wheeze. "You're a businessman, Kell Valmonde, sure as I am. I like that about you. Always about the silver."

"If we stay as busy as we have been, I'll need more amulets from you in a week. People like having a bit of luck in their pocket," Kell said, standing. "Good doing business with you."

"Come back anytime. Always in the mood to do a deal," Widgem promised. Kell grimaced. Trading with Widgem left him feeling in need of a bath.

Good thing we tossed that ring of Allery's in the sewer, Kell thought. *Widgem could probably get more by turning me in to the guards than he'll make off what I buy from him in a year.*

He returned to the cart. A glance told him no one had disturbed the contents. With a sigh, he grabbed the poles and headed out.

The late afternoon shadows grew long. Although he refused to think about Polly running away, her absence—and the possibility that she was in danger—darkened his mood. Kell's stomach rumbled, but he had one more stop to make. He turned off his normal route, heading toward the large white turrets and spires of the Avenue of Temples.

The temples were old, each one a work of art, and the avenue was arranged from the greatest to the least, with the minor deities and half-forgotten godlings at the very end. White paving stones covered the street itself, so that at midday the glare made a person avert his gaze. Most of the temples were roofed and walled in the same stone, creating a tableau of dazzling, other-worldly beauty.

At the head of the street was the biggest temple of all, to Oj and Ren, the Forever Father and the Eternal Mother, the creators of everything and the most powerful gods of the pantheon. Dozens of temples lined the Avenue, and shrines to lesser deities dotted the sacred groves on the hills beyond the wall.

A large marble spindle marked the temple of Vashte, the god of weavers. The temple of Bon, god of blacksmiths, had a huge granite anvil in its outer court. Kell dragged the wagon past the enormous stone potter's wheel outside the temple of Qel, and the larger-than-life terra cotta horses standing eternal watch outside the sacred courts of Jorr, god of farriers.

Every Guild was represented, and the opulence of the carvings on each edifice testified to the Guild Masters' wealth and pride, sparing no expense to woo the gods' favor, and to outshine the other Guilds. Kell maintained the small household shrine to the Valmonde family spirits, since neither Corran nor Rigan were especially devout. It was he who noted the feasts and fasts, the vigils and prayers, and made sure that, if the gods were real, the Valmondes did not run afoul of them. *We have enough trouble as it is.*

The temples at the far end of the Avenue were worn with age, their marble stained with time. These were the oldest gods, the fearsome spirits, and the entities long-worshipped and greatly dreaded. They were the stuff of myth and legend, the horrors that came in dreams, ethereal beauty with a bloody edge. Ancient names: Ardevan, Eshtamon, Balledec, Coldurran.

The Guilds demanded tribute for the new gods, the patron deities of the trades; upstarts, all of them. The people of Ravenwood did as their masters bid them, taking their offerings on the feast days to the Guild gods' temples, making their prayers when custom demanded. But late at night, when illness struck or misfortune overtook them, those worshippers brought their true prayers and gifts to the Elder Gods, and it was these ancient beings that they honored in the shrines in their homes and the desperate petitions in their hearts.

Halfway down the Avenue, Kell saw his destination. Doharmu, god of the Undertakers' Guild, Lord of the Golden Shores, welcomed his worshipers to a temple made of black basalt. Of all the Guild gods, only Doharmu, god of Death, was also one of the Elder Gods. His temple stood out like a thundercloud among the blindingly white structures surrounding it. Here at least, Kell knew no one would object to his cart of corpses, nor was there any danger of the bodies being interfered with. It had been a while since he had visited the temple, and the sight of the huge, black edifice sent a chill down his spine. Unlike the other temples, which often boasted elaborately carved and gold-inlaid doors, Doharmu's home had no doors at all, just a shadowed portal like the mouth of the grave.

Kell forced himself to climb the steps. The other temples were covered with bas relief murals praising their gods and depicting their triumphs. The outer walls of the Doharmuran were smooth and plain. A vast obsidian skull, tall as a man, sat in the wide outer court. Its empty gaze followed Kell as he reached the top of the stairs and readied himself to enter.

Doharmu required no sacrifice, because everyone came to him in the end. He asked for no pageants, because the dead have no rank. The god of undertakers had need of few priests, because all those born into his Guild and its magic were his priests and priestesses, in the course of their work.

Kell steeled himself to walk into the gloom. Torches in sconces lit the way, though they did little to dispel the shadows. Inside, a parade of carved skeletons adorned each wall. All walks of life, from king to beggar, had their place, as did all of the Guild trades and the professions. Kell could pick out the chandler and cobbler, fishmonger and boatwright, tailor and cooper, and many more. Some of the skeletons were stooped with age, and some were crawling infants—all came to Doharmu.

Kell swallowed hard, shivering in the temple's chill. *Cold as the grave.* He clasped his hands to keep them from shaking, and made his way through the empty chamber. If the god's acolytes were present, they did not make themselves known. Banks of candles glowed along the walls, yet the ceiling vaults and side chapels seemed to swallow their light. Doharmu's temple was a very pretty crypt.

Two rows of columns made from artfully stacked human bones

flanked him as he proceeded. Atop each sat a carving of a skull, each turned slightly away from the others.

A large onyx statue of a hooded figure stood by the altar. Beneath the statue's carved robes, Kell could make out the strong muscles of a warrior in his prime, a huntsman victorious. Death could be a cheat and a thief, but he was never a weakling.

Kell trembled as he reached the statue. A small tray filled with gravel sat on the dais at its feet, ready to accept the only offering of interest to the temple's god. Kell knelt before the tray and pulled a knife from a sheath on his belt. With one swift cut, he drew the blade shallowly across his wrist.

"Dark Father," Kell said. "I ask nothing for myself. But please, in your mercy—and you can be merciful, Lord of Death and God of Rebirth—please protect my brothers—and Polly." He paused. This was completely out of his experience, and he made it up as he went, flourishes and all. He hoped Doharmu liked flowery language. Priests seemed to. *Maybe he prefers things plain-spoken. After all, he's Death.*

Kell cleared his throat. "Polly ran away, and I'm afraid someone wanted to hurt her. And my brothers are in danger. I don't know what to do. Please. I will pay any price. Just keep Polly safe, and protect Corran and Rigan. They're all I've got."

Warm blood dripped onto the gravel. He opened his eyes, and watched the drops fall. The blood vanished into the stones, like rain on thirsty ground. A wind stirred past him, making the candles flicker wildly, howling through the skulls atop each column.

Your prayer has been heard. The voice sounded in Kell's mind, making him jump. He looked down at his arm. The wound was healed.

I will grant your petition. Count the cost.

Chapter Twenty-Four

WITH KELL'S HELP, Corran and Rigan prepared the day's dead with just enough time to call on the priests of the relevant Guilds, finishing the job by suppertime.

Darkness had fallen by the time they reached the cemetery. Corran and Rigan lit torches, casting the graveyard in eerie shadows.

"Five dead. If we get them all done and down before curfew, it'll be some kind of personal record," Corran grumbled.

Rigan looked toward the priest blessing the last body. "Digging five graves in the time we've got left is going to hurt come tomorrow, that's all I've got to say."

"How did we end up with an extra priest?" Corran asked. The steady rhythm of their shovels striking ground, dirt filling the blades and sliding free, was a familiar, comforting cadence.

"The suicide's mother paid extra for him," Rigan replied, wiping his forearm across his face to clear the sweat from his eyes. "The woman who killed herself when her husband drowned their baby. Her mother wanted vengeance. I guess the Old Ones are better at that than the Guild gods."

"That's because the Elder Gods just might be real," Corran said, continuing to dig. "The new gods are just stories the Guilds made up to make themselves feel important. No one actually believes in the Guild gods, except the Guild Masters." He paused. "Except for Doharmu, of course, but then he's an Elder God too."

Rigan shrugged. "I guess if you're desperate for help, you call in the gods that might be on your side—which wouldn't be the Guild gods. You want revenge, you go to Eshtamon."

Eshtamon's priest wore a simple gray robe. He laid the dead woman's body in the open grave and circled the hole twice, once in each direction. A candle in a bowl burned at the head of the grave, and at the foot lay a tray of tarnished valuables, paid in tribute to the god.

"Eshtamon, lord of the crossroad and the gallows, hear me!" The priest slowly circled the grave and stopped by the candle. "God of the lost and the wronged, attend my prayer."

He dropped powdered incense onto the candle, changing the color of the flame. The sharp scent of myrrh wafted on the breeze. "Bring vengeance on the one who caused this woman's death. Punish him, lord of thorns, with your iron teeth and sharp claws. Rend his flesh and break his bones. Heap lamentations on his head until he can bear no more, and destroy his soul."

The priest raised his left arm and let the long sleeve of his robe fall back. In one smooth slice, he brought a sharp knife down along the flesh, opening a bloody wound. The priest held his arm over the candle, allowing the blood to drop into the bowl.

"Once, for the asking. Twice, for the hearing," he said as the drops fell. "Thrice—let it be so."

Corran's eyes widened and he stopped digging. "Rigan," he hissed, with a nod toward where the priest leaned over the bloody bowl.

Something stood at the end of the suicide's grave, a silhouette that wavered in the torchlight. The priest fell to his knees as the dark figure gestured over the grave and spoke words Corran did not catch. For a few seconds, Corran felt trapped by the shadowy figure's gaze. Then the image winked out, taking with it the bloody candle and bowl, leaving the trinkets for the priest.

"Shit," Rigan muttered. "I've never seen that before."

"Seems that Eshtamon was listening," Corran said, before returning to his digging, unwilling to let his brother see how much the vision had shaken him.

"Can't say any of the Guild gods have ever shown up for a burial," Rigan said as he filled and emptied his shovel.

"I'd say that's probably a good thing."

The priest pocketed the offerings from the foot of the grave. He said something under his breath, and the gash in his forearm healed as if it had never been. Then he turned to where the brothers stood, chest deep in a newly dug grave.

"Tell the woman's mother that her daughter will be avenged." With that, he shouldered the small pack he had brought with him and walked into the night.

Rigan looked as spooked as Corran felt. "Keep digging," Corran said, with an eye toward the woman's grave. "We've got two more to bury, and hers to fill in. I don't want to push our luck tonight."

A candlemark later, they were shoveling dirt into the next-to-last grave when Rigan straightened. "Did you hear something?"

Corran slapped the mound of dirt with the back of his shovel, and paused to listen. "Like what?" The wind clattered through the high branches, and swept across the grass. Overhead, clouds slipped across a nearly-full moon. In the distance, an owl hooted and the tower bells rang.

Then he heard it: the sound of digging, coming from a back corner of the graveyard. Half a dozen gray figures closed in on them. *Shit. Those look like* hancha.

The creatures had the shapes of men, but their skin was obsidian, like a long-dead corpse. Feral, yellow eyes gleamed from sunken sockets over hollow cheeks. *Hancha* were vengeful spirits that possessed the dead, animating them with unnatural strength, fuelling their hold on their host bodies by consuming freshly-killed human flesh.

"Watch out!" Corran reached for his knife and wielded the shovel like a staff in his other hand. "Behind you!"

Rigan ducked, swinging his shovel, and the iron blade sank into the monster's abdomen just beneath the ribs. Even so, it kept moving. Clawed hands ripped at Rigan's sleeve as the animated corpse lurched forward. Corran thrust his shovel forward, knocking the creature backward and driving the point of the blade through its open belly, severing the spine and cutting the monster in two.

The *hancha*'s legs kicked out at Rigan, knocking him backward, while its hands dug into the dirt, pulling its upper body toward fresh meat.

"Two more behind you!" Corran warned.

"I see three coming from the back." Rigan scrambled to grab the nearest torch, and brandished it at the advancing corpses.

"We just buried those bodies last week," Corran said. "I recognize some of them."

"Well, they're back," Rigan snapped. "And if we're lucky, we'll get to bury them again."

Corran and Rigan lunged in opposite directions, taking the offensive. *Hancha* were tough to destroy and would put up a good fight, but they had all the swiftness of a drunkard.

The spirits that possessed them transformed the corpses, elongating the arms, stretching bony fingers into calcified talons, sharpening and lengthening the teeth. The creatures could not talk, but they shrieked like the damned to distract their prey.

Corran swung his shovel with his full might, slamming one of the *hancha* in the head so hard that the bones in the corpse's face shattered. Still, it continued to shamble towards him.

Rigan thrust his torch at the closest creature, lighting its moldering clothing on fire. The monster never slowed, even as its hair singed and the dead skin charred. Thick smoke rose from the burning *hancha*, and Rigan struggled not to gag from the stench.

Fire might not stop the *hancha*, but as the flames consumed them, their movements became erratic. "Hit them harder!" Corran yelled. "But watch out for their blood. It burns!" He swung his knife, tearing into the creature's neck, sawing at bone until he could send its head flying. The body continued to writhe, even as Corran drove the heavy iron shovel blade down again and again, chopping the rotting corpse to pieces. The limbs thrashed, heaving across the ground. Where the blood splattered Corran's bare flesh it raised welts.

"Heads up! We've got more coming!" Rigan yelped as four more *hancha* closed on them, two from each side.

Rigan moved into position, so that he and Corran were fighting back to back. "Why are they here?" Corran's voice was hoarse with the smoke. "What called them?"

"No idea," Rigan countered. "But we've got to stop them from leaving the cemetery."

Corran sliced with the blade of his shovel, bringing the solid wooden handle down across one creature's head with enough force to split bone. He barely danced out of the way of a second *hancha* as it grabbed for his face with one clawed hand and snatched at his shirt with the other. His knife sliced through the stiff, dead flesh to the ribs, but the monster kept coming. Rigan fended off two more creatures, thrusting his torch at their ragged clothing, sending them up in flames. Corran thrust with his shovel's handle, breaking ribs and shattering bones, then slammed the solid iron blade into knees and arms with a crunch.

Rigan and Corran were exhausted but the *hancha* were relentless. They would remain animated with ancient, foul energies until the sun rose. "They'll outlast us," Corran said, breathing hard.

"We've just got to be smarter than them. Their brains are rotting, after all."

Four tireless *hancha* might as well have been an army. Burning the creatures slowed but did not stop them, and the dead bodies took a beating no living man could have survived. Cutting the monsters to pieces was effective, but dangerous and difficult. Their torches guttered, nearly spent.

Corran and Rigan bled from fresh wounds and burns from the monsters' blood. Corran gathered his strength and bellowed as he ran at the two closest *hancha* with a fresh burst of energy. That drew them away from Rigan, who fought two more opponents of his own. Corran swung his shovel at the creatures's kneecaps, crippling them as the bones broke beneath the iron blade.

Two of the torches flickered out, leaving the brothers in a shrinking pool of light. Clouds hid the moon overhead. Corran summoned up all his rage for another salvo, using his shovel to keep one *hancha* at bay while he closed on the other. He dared not take his eyes from the advancing monsters. Despite their grievous injuries, the *hancha* were undeterred. Corran dove forward, thrusting his long knife through the chest of the nearest creature and heaving the blade upward, slicing through rotted flesh and organs. He pushed the creature backward, kicking its feet out from under it, grabbed a torch and stabbed it into the *hancha*'s open belly. The monster jerked and writhed as the fire consumed it.

The other *hancha* launched itself at Corran, knocking him to the ground and slamming his left arm against a grave marker, hard enough to dash the knife from his grip. His shovel was useless at this range, and it took all his waning strength to keep the *hancha* from clawing him open. The *hancha* brought its bony fists down with more power than Corran thought possible, snapping his head to the side and making his vision swim.

He cried out as the creature dragged its sharp fingers across his chest. Blood soaked his shirt. He tried to get his legs up, but the monster pinned him. One skeletal hand closed around Corran's throat, choking off his breath. He beat at the thing with both fists, but the cold, stiff body did not yield.

"Stay down!" Rigan yelled. A wave of blue-white fire swept across the burying yard, turning night to day. Corran felt the flames sizzle just a few feet from his face.

The fire cut through the *hancha*, blowing apart rotten bodies and shattering decomposing heads. Heat scorched Corran, and a bloody rain covered him in gobbets of dead flesh, burning everywhere it touched. The *hancha* that had knocked him to the ground careened to one side, missing its head and shoulders. The strange fire took only seconds to spread across the graveyard before it vanished, but in that moment, nothing stood in its way.

Corran managed to roll over and rise onto his forearms as Rigan dropped to his knees, spent.

"You... did that?"

Rigan nodded, not looking up. "The *hancha* was killing you."

"Damn."

"We've got to get out of here." Rigan warned, his voice frayed. "That had to reek of magic."

"The bodies," Corran grunted, dragging himself to all fours.

Body parts were scattered across the cemetery—decomposing, badly burned and hacked to pieces. "The guards will haul us out of our beds and hang us for murder," Rigan groaned.

"Good thing I'm here." Kell emerged from the shadows. "You two look like something the cat puked up."

"What in the name of the gods—" Rigan was pale and shaking, but he managed to get to his feet.

"Sit down before you fall down," Kell ordered as Corran staggered. "I'll get the bits into the grave and cover them over. I have some green vitriol with me for the remains. We'll see to you once we get home."

"I'll help," Rigan said. He raised an eyebrow at Kell's incredulous glance. "I'm in better shape than I look. Most of the blood on me isn't actually mine."

"Corran's going to give you an earful once he stops bleeding,"

Rigan said under his breath as he shoveled the corpse limbs into the open grave. Finding and burying the pieces went quickly, though there was no hiding the gobbets of dead flesh and congealed blood splattered across the grass.

"Lucky for all of us I don't listen well," Kell replied. He did more than his share filling in the grave, then wiped his brow and leaned against his shovel. "Here's hoping the crows and vultures will take care of the rest."

CORRAN SAGGED BETWEEN Rigan and Kell as they made their way back to the workshop, struggling to remain conscious. Blood plastered the shreds of Corran's shirt to his skin, and he winced with every movement that jostled his damaged chest and bruised ribs. Weeping burns peppered his face, arms and shoulders. The bells in the city tolled, announcing the start of curfew.

"Just a little further," Rigan murmured. He held a knife ready in case the guards discovered them but they reached the alleyway behind their workshop without incident.

"You two are going through our supplies a little too quickly for my liking," Kell grumbled as he pulled a kettle of hot water off the brazier. Rigan eased Corran onto one of the tables, and gently stripped away what remained of his shirt.

"I thought you weren't going to use magic." Corran managed, barely above a whisper.

Rigan lowered his eyes. "I tried not to. I didn't want to bring the guards down on us, on top of the *hancha*. But then that thing tackled you, and I knew I couldn't fight my way out alone. It was the only way I could think of to get it off you."

"Thanks."

Kell steeped medicinal herbs in hot water and looked at Corran's injuries. "What a mess," he said. He looked at Rigan. "You don't look much better."

"What were you doing in the cemetery, anyway?" Rigan asked.

Kell glared at him. "It turned out to be handy, wouldn't you say?"

"I wasn't criticizing. But it was almost curfew, and it's not safe—"

"You were late," Kell said, preparing a poultice. "I was worried. Figured at worst you'd need a hand digging the graves, since you had more bodies than usual. So I headed over."

"You're just lucky those creatures didn't get you," Corran said.

"I stayed out of the graveyard, once I saw what was going on," Kell replied. "Give me credit; I'm not stupid. I knew there wasn't much I could do to help with the fight, but I stuck around in case you needed me." He looked up with a grin. "And you did."

Rigan put a hand on his brother's shoulder. "Kell, thanks. I'm pretty sure I couldn't have buried the remains and gotten us both out of there by myself."

"You're welcome," Kell said with a satisfied smile. He turned his attention back to Corran. "I'll let you off with a warning, since you look like death warmed over; don't scare me like that again."

He turned to Rigan. "How about sitting down? You don't look much better than Corran."

Rigan sank into a chair and rested his head in his hands. "I just need to rest," he said. "I grounded my power better this time, so I didn't get knocked flat on my ass."

Corran groaned, too miserable to reply. Four deep gashes on his chest bled heavily. Cuts and punctures from the *hancha*'s sharp fingers showed on his arms and belly.

"Let's hope I can get those clean," Kell fussed, daubing at the wounds with a mixture of alcohol and witchhazel. Corran bit his lip at the sting. "No idea what's on those things's claws," Kell continued. "And we don't need the burns going bad."

He barely spared a glance in Rigan's direction. "Take a table. We've got room."

Rigan did not argue. "I tried to stay out of their way, but the *hancha* got in a few good hits," he said ruefully, looking at the bloody slashes on his arms. "Make sure you do a good job cleaning cuts," he added, exhaustion heavy in his voice. "Mine are already starting to go sour."

"You'll have to wait your turn," Kell replied primly. "I'll get to you."

Rigan hauled himself up onto a table, and felt the fight in every aching muscle. "I'm amazed no one noticed the magic," he said. "I thought for sure the guards would storm in once the *hancha* were dead."

"The guards don't notice anything they're not paid to notice," Kell grumbled. "Doesn't mean no one paid attention."

Corran felt a chill. "What do you mean?"

Kell finished cleaning his wounds and returned with a bowl of herbal paste and a shroud torn into strips for bandages. "What made the *hancha* rise?"

"I wondered that myself," Rigan replied, "but I was too damn busy fighting them off to wonder for long."

"Did someone call the *hancha* to attack you and Corran because they knew you'd be in the cemetery? Or did some dark magic just happen to make them rise tonight, the way the monsters seem to, coming and going without any rhyme or reason?"

"I don't know," Rigan answered. "But if someone meant them to attack us, then they intended for us to die. They wouldn't have known about my magic—although they might, now."

"There are a lot easier ways to kill us," Corran grumbled. "Seems a bit extreme."

Kell shrugged. "It would look like a monster kill," he said. "Everyone would have thought you were just in the wrong place at the wrong time."

"Ravenwood is a big enough shithole without imagining monster-assassins," Rigan replied. "I mean, we're nobodies. Even the Guild barely knows who we are."

"Speaking of which, Guild fees will be due again soon," Kell said.

Rigan sighed. "Yeah. Sad to say it, but it's a damn good thing there've been so many deaths, or we wouldn't be able to pay the fees and the taxes too—and still pay off the guards."

"How far do you think those bribes go?" Kell was nearly done patching up Corran, and he stirred up more of his foul-smelling mixture to clean up Rigan's injuries.

"Not far enough to keep me out of the noose for magic, or get Corran off for being a hunter," Rigan warned. "All they do is keep the guards from breaking our windows or stealing our tools. It's protection money, pure and simple—protection from the guards, not the monsters."

"That's what I figured," Kell replied.

Corran saw the flicker of something dark in Kell's eyes as his brother looked away. "Kell, did something happen when you were out on your rounds?"

Kell let out a deep breath. "It's nothing."

"Bullshit," Rigan said. "What's the matter?"

Kell slumped. "Polly—the serving girl at The Lame Dragon—she's gone. Ran away."

Rigan frowned. "Was she in trouble?"

"Maybe she thought she was."

"Just like Elinor," Rigan said. Corran and Kell both looked up at that. "She was too good at mixing pigments. Someone started talk that she might have magic. So she ran before they could take her."

"I'm sorry," Corran said, seeing the hurt on his brothers' faces. "Looks like none of us are very lucky in love."

"Doesn't bode well for carrying on the family name," Rigan said with a sigh. He looked at Kell, who was staring at the floor, and placed a hand on his shoulder. "I'm trying to tell myself that it's better for Elinor to have run and maybe gotten to safety than to be taken by the guards, or by a mob," he said quietly. "I know it's cold comfort, but it's true for Polly, too."

Kell swallowed hard. "I just hope she's safe. But I won't ever know whether she made it or not."

"Then until we have proof of the worst, let yourself believe the best," Corran advised, feeling his heart clench as Jora's loss ached afresh. He let it go unsaid that the finality of knowing might be worse than the scant hope of wondering.

Kell gave a curt nod and turned back to the business at hand, dipping a cloth in the healing elixir and gently daubing at Rigan's injuries; his brother tried not to wince at the burn of the antiseptic or the sting of the herbs. "You're not as banged up on the outside as he is," Kell added, nodding at Corran. "But you'd better eat something if you pulled that much magic out of thin air. You look like you're going to pass out."

"I started to ground myself when I saw Corran go down, and after that, I just reacted."

"Is that bad?" Kell wound the gauze around Rigan's arm and ribs.

"Only if I want to keep living," Rigan replied. "I did better this time, but that's why I still need training. The magic pulls too much from me, instead of drawing energy from around me. It's like pumping a well dry."

"I am not going to be the last Valmonde standing," Kell said, staring them both down, hands on hips. "So the two of you had better figure out how to do what you do and stay alive—you hear me?"

Corran chuckled. "Yes, sir. We'll do our best."

"I can't promise we'll stay safe," Rigan said tiredly. "But I can tell you we'll be as careful as possible."

Kell poured medicinal tea for Corran and Rigan and brought it to them, helping Corran sit up so he could sip the healing brew. "Not what I want to hear, but I guess it'll have to do."

Chapter Twenty-Five

"WHAT'LL YOU GIVE me?" Widgem thumped down his bag of treasures in front of Kell, spreading out his latest consignment of charms.

"Not bad. Not bad at all," Kell said, picking one up and examining it. "I figure you keep the strongest ones for yourself?"

Widgem grinned. "Perk of doing business. But I save the best of the rest for you." He pulled out a basket of odds and ends. "And I've got some bargains here, if you care to have a look. The shell comb is nice. Only one tooth broken. Couple of small charms. A pottery chit good for a free ale over at Sailors' Watch Inn."

Kell looked up. "Have you ever had their ale? Tastes like donkey piss." He chuckled and went back to sorting through the motley treasures. "You wouldn't happen to know what the brass key opens, would you?"

"Old Ban Donolan's widow tossed it out with the trash," Widgem replied. "But the brass ought to be worth something."

"If old man Donolan had a treasure hidden somewhere, it would be a shock to everyone in Wrighton."

"Couple of nice beads there, and a pair of ivory dice that should be worth something," Widgem said.

"The dice aren't too bad," Kell allowed, holding them up to the light. "I've got no use for any of the rest of it." He sat back and dug out his purse, then slapped the coins down on the table.

"I think you'll find it a fair price, considering what I've already paid for the amulets."

Widgem rolled his eyes. "Fairer than picking my pocket, but not by much," he retorted, though Kell could tell he was satisfied. Haggling was a game both enjoyed. "I guess it'll do." He gathered the coins and swept them into his coin pouch. "I'll see you in a couple of days." As Kell began to rise from his seat, Widgem grabbed his arm.

"Watch yourself. Something's brewing. Been more people gone missing lately."

Kell sat back down and leaned forward. "What do you know?"

Widgem looked around before replying. "You don't last as long as I have without keeping your nose to the wind," he said in a low voice. "People are nervous, and the guards are wound tighter than usual. Haven't you noticed the way men've been disappearing? No good reason, just gone all of a sudden. And how whenever the milk goes sour or the babies get colic, everyone's sure it's 'cause a witch or a Wanderer's been meddling? More monsters lately, too. Don't know why; don't need to know. But a word to the wise: keep your head down and stay out of people's way, if you know what I mean."

Kell nodded. "Sure. Thanks."

He pushed through the unwashed crowd in the tavern's common room, and sucked in a deep breath of fresh air once he was outside.

Two more stops, and then it's home for supper. He felt jumpy, but he could not fault Widgem's warning; the sense of something in the offing had already set his nerves on edge.

"I've got news if you've got a bronze to spare." Tek sidled up to Kell, appearing out of the shadows of a nearby alley. Kell jumped at the sound of the voice. The boy's soot-smudged face sported a bruise on the temple, and fresh blood oozed from one corner of his lip.

Kell dug out a bronze and flicked it to the boy. "What do you hear?"

"There was a brawl down on the docks. Seems that the Mayor's guards cleared most everyone away from Wharf Street. Some of the Wanderer merchants didn't take kindly to getting pushed out of their usual places. They did some pushing in return."

Kell frowned. "What happened?"

"Near as I can make out, there were a couple of Wanderers selling from their carts down on the wharf. The guards tried to arrest them. Most of the time, they'd have just scattered, or taken their carts and run. But today, it turned into a fight."

"And?"

The next thing I knew, people were yelling at the guards. The merchants were mad about the guards closing off their traffic, and the dockhands were mad that they wouldn't get paid because the guards had the wharves closed down. There was a brawl and—"

"Then what?"

"I got clobbered," Tek replied, displaying his bloodied lip like a badge of honor. "It was my own fault. I kicked one of the guards in the shins. He tried to grab me, and he cuffed me a good one, but I got away."

"And the Wanderers?" Kell asked, wishing he had a better view of the waterfront. He could hear a commotion in the distance.

"Oh, you know them. They're slippery sons of bitches," Tek said. "Good at starting things, and leaving someone else holding the bag. I imagine they'll be gone by sundown, on to somewhere else. But I've never seen the likes of it, that fight. Like a match to tinder. Everyone's been angry at the Mayor's guards, what with monsters and talk of witches."

"They're still fighting? Has the Mayor sent reinforcements?"

Tek shrugged. "Not yet. He's got the streets all blocked off this way. You still going to pick up that body I told you about?"

"We're the only undertakers in this part of Wrighton. Someone needs burying, we go get them."

Tek raised an eyebrow. "That's going to take you awful close to the docks."

"The chandler's house is still in our territory, and the wharf is several blocks beyond it. Can't leave the family with a body going sour on them, now can I?" *Not to mention that it's the chandler's aunt, so it'll be a full Guild burial.*

"Watch your back," the boy said. "Tempers were getting pretty nasty."

"I'll be in and gone before the guards ever notice," Kell assured him. "And I'm the undertaker. No one ever cares about what we do."

"Yeah, well. It'll get ugly if the guards get reinforcements."

"Thanks for the heads up." Kell tossed Tek another coin. "Good information. Keep it up."

Tek tugged his forelock and hurried away. "Gods bless you. I know what I'm going to spend this on!" The boy ran off with this windfall, while Kell pondered his next move.

If Tek's right, heading towards the docks could be a dangerous move. But if I go home without a Guild burial, Corran will have my head. And the Guild Master might make trouble about it. He sighed. *I'm not actually going to the docks. I'll still be several blocks away. And I've got a cart full of bodies—hardly anything anybody else wants. It's pretty easy to tell my business. If it looks too dangerous, I'll turn around and go home, Corran be damned. Tek loves a good story. What if he made the whole thing up, and then I don't pick up the body? There'll be the dark gods to pay then, that's for certain.*

Forcing down his nervousness, Kell turned the cart toward the chandler's house. It was downhill from The Muddy Goat, meaning the return trip would be all the harder, laden with yet another body. *Someday, I'll make Corran buy me a donkey. Until then, I guess I get to be the ass.*

As he approached the docks, Kell could hear raised voices and smell smoke. His route had taken longer than usual and sunset had begun to color the sky. Kell hesitated, but forged ahead. *I'm not going to be the reason we can't put meat on the table for dinner*, he thought, setting his jaw.

Sosten, the chandler, lived three blocks back from the waterfront, at the edge of the Valmonde's territory. He did well for himself, as the neatly painted sign and storefront attested.

"You're late." Sosten glared at Kell, but his eyes darted toward the disturbance at the waterfront.

"Been a busy day," Kell replied.

"Started to wonder whether you were coming," Sosten replied, as he watched Kell struggle to carry the dead weight of the old lady to the cart. He didn't offer to help. "Sounds like things have gotten out of hand down by the docks."

"You know anything about that?" Kell asked, huffing as he wrestled the corpse into place, doing his best not to handle the body too indelicately while the next of kin was watching.

"People been talking about it all afternoon. Damn Wanderers, starting trouble again."

"Sounds like an awful lot of people to just be Wanderers."

"You know how it goes. Someone gets a fight going, and everyone else piles on. You're not going on that way, are you? Wouldn't advise it." Sosten dug for his coin purse. "Mind you settle her with full Guild honors. Here's an extra silver for making the trip, even though you were late."

He handed over a small bundle of candles. "And these are for your brothers, with my regards. Now don't dally. If I hadn't been waiting on you, I would have closed up the shutters for the night a candlemark ago. Don't want any trouble." With that, Sosten disappeared inside.

Kell threw a sheet over the bodies and walked around to the front of the cart, picking up the long shafts and leaning into his task. Thanks to the fight, the lamplighters had not yet made their rounds, and the streets were darker than usual. Sounds of the disturbance carried, echoing from the buildings, closer than before.

It can't hurt to have a look. Corran and Rigan will want to know what's going on, and if I have a good tale, I might not get quite such a dressing down for being late with supper.

He pulled the cart into an alley two blocks away from Sosten's shop and parked it in the shadows. Kell made his way carefully to the far end of the street, being sure to hug the walls and stay in the shadows. He could still see little of what was going on, so he crept down a second block, to where the alley opened onto a view of the wharfs.

A mob of men and women armed with torches shouted obscenities at the Mayor's guardsmen, who answered their taunts with threats. The guards were armed with swords, but the mob had taken up whatever tools were handy, brandishing kitchen knives, fireplace pokers and fishing spars, among other implements. From what Kell could see, there were several hundred residents, facing down a few dozen of the Mayor's men.

Sweet Doharmu—this won't end well, Kell thought, scrambling back into the darkness. He moved quickly down the alley, anxious to be well away from the noise and fighting.

He ran the last half block and tugged the wagon into motion.

I need to get out of here. The cart was heavy and the road steep. Much as Kell wished he could sprint for home, he dared not abandon the bodies. *Sosten would string me up by my thumbs if I left his old auntie by the side of the road. He'd have the Guild after our hides.*

Cursing under his breath, Kell tugged the cart with all his might, wishing he had someone behind to push.

"You there! Stop!"

Kell leaned forward, struggling for one step and then another, wanting to be away from whatever was going on behind him.

"Wanderer! You with the cart! Stop in the name of the Lord Mayor!"

Boots clattered on the cobblestones as guards ran toward him. Kell's heart pounded as the soldiers surrounded him. He lowered the cart slowly, trying to make sure it did not roll down the hill. "I'm the undertaker! Not a Wanderer."

"You've got a cart, don't ya?" one of the guards retorted.

"And it's full of dead bodies. I'm the undertaker."

"Put your hands up, or you'll *need* a gravedigger." One of the guards brought his sword point up to Kell's chin, nicking the skin. "No more of your lip."

"Please. You're making a mistake—"

The guard's sword flicked and opened a cut on Kell's cheek. "Shut your mouth."

"Bunch of dead bodies in the back, like he said," one of the other guards reported, pulling the sheet away.

"All I care is that he's got a cart," the head guard replied. "Our orders were to round up the damn Wanderers, and get them off the streets. Take him."

Terror flooded through Kell. He jerked away as a guard grabbed for his arm, and dodged between the soldiers.

"Get him!"

Kell tripped over garbage and flailed, keeping his balance and charging down the alley. He hoped the soldiers would relent after a few minutes' chase, but as he plunged on into the night, his pursuers gave no sign of giving up.

Panic surged through him. It was one thing to outrun the market guards—they were hardly the Mayor's best and brightest—but the wharf guards were hardened soldiers. He slipped and careened into the gutter, but kept his feet under him.

He ran for his life.

Kell plowed forward, steering by instinct, his only goal to get as far away from the harbor as possible. He vaulted over broken crates and shattered barrels, doing his best not to notice the large rats that squealed and ran across his path. He was totally lost, utterly terrified, and a long way from home.

"Gotcha." Two guards stepped into the mouth of the alley, as a third closed behind him. Kell leaped for a low balcony, hoping to pull himself up.

Strong hands grabbed his legs and yanked him to the ground. Kell hit hard, the impact knocking the breath from him. One of the guards straddled him and hit him across the face with his fist. Kell struggled against the man's weight.

"I'm the undertaker!" he yelled. In the struggle, a pouch fell from Kell's jacket. The guard held it up, dangling the lucky amulets by their cords.

"Undertaker, huh? These are charms. What are you—witch or Wanderer?"

"I told you—"

"Bloody Wanderer." The fist struck again, knocking Kell's head to the side. Another blow snapped his head back, splitting his lip and loosening a few teeth. Blood filled Kell's mouth. His ears rang and one eye was swelling shut.

"Please. I'm the—"

The next punch brought darkness.

KELL WOKE SLOWLY. It was dark, even when he opened his eyes, but gradually his vision adjusted. As consciousness returned, so did pain. He groaned and tried to sit up. Rough rope bound his wrists and ankles.

"It's no use," a nearby voice said. "They tied us tight."

Kell managed to raise himself onto his elbows. "Where are we?"

"An old barn. Maybe a warehouse." The man's deep voice was heavily accented, and Kell strained to understand him.

Kell could make out the man's silhouette in the moonlight that filtered through the holes in the building's walls. "What are they going to do with us?"

"Nothing good."

Kell's head pounded and he could not see out of one eye. His ears buzzed, and he ached in so many places that he wondered whether the guards had continued beating him even after he passed out. His ribs burned as he took a deep breath. “How long have I been here?”

“It was dark when you came and it’s still dark. It’s been a couple of bells at least.”

Kell gingerly lay back down. The floor beneath him was hard packed dirt, and the building smelled of hay and dust. *There are dozens of old barns and warehouses around the city. We could be in any of them.*

Corran and Rigan won’t have any idea what’s become of me, or where to look. Gods help me.

He heard others talking in low tones close by. Kell could not understand their words; eventually, he realized they were speaking the odd dialect the Wanderers used among themselves. “Are you all Wanderers?”

“Probably,” the man replied. “I don’t know you. But your blood calls to me. I thought I knew all of our people.”

“I’m not a Wanderer, but my mama had Wanderer blood. I’m an undertaker.”

“Well, we’re all likely to need your services very soon. I don’t believe the guards mean to let us leave. My name is Zahm. What is yours?”

“Kell.”

“I am sorry to meet you like this, Kell. If we’re going to die together, it’s best someone knows your name.”

Kell slipped in and out of consciousness. He thought he heard the bells peal nine times, but he was no longer sure what was real and what was a product of his unquiet dreams. *If it’s past tenth bells, Corran and Rigan already know something’s wrong. Maybe Corran and the hunters will find us. Maybe Rigan can track me with his magic. But they’d better hurry.*

The next time he came around, he heard the stranger near him calling out to the others. Voices replied in the same dialect, perhaps a dozen speakers. "Little brother," Zahm said, to Kell. "Are you awake?"

"Yes."

"Ah. Maybe good, maybe bad. Good that I can talk to you. Bad, because it might be better not to know what's coming."

Kell felt a cold chill at the man's words. "What did you find out?"

Zahm was quiet for a few moments. "How old are you, little brother?"

"Fourteen."

"A man, in the ways of my people. Old enough to hear truth."

"Tell me."

"Sohar and Dojne say they heard the guards talking. The Lord Mayor sent the guards to rid the city of Wanderers."

"Why?"

"What does today's reason matter? There is always an excuse. The guards have been telling people we are to blame for the monsters. That we are witches."

"Are you?"

Zahm gave a low, bitter chuckle. "Not in the way they mean it. But such lies are convenient."

"These men aren't the only Wanderers." Kell had often seen the nomadic merchants with their pushcarts and wagons, in the streets near the docks and the byways where traffic was heaviest with shoppers. He remembered the old woman he had met in the alley and the strange sigils chalked on dirty walls. He'd never seen many of the Wanderers together, but he felt certain that there must be more than a dozen.

"No. But the others will hear, and flee if they can. And the Mayor will have what he wants."

Kell's heart sank. "They won't try to rescue you?"

Zahm barked a laugh, and repeated Kell's question for the others, who gave the same gallows chuckle. "No, little brother. We fight only if cornered, or when the odds favor us. There are already too few of our people, and so many who would kill us. They will mourn us, and perhaps avenge us, but they will not save us."

Kell struggled against the ropes that bound his wrists. "Then we have to save ourselves. If I roll closer, can you loosen these knots?"

"All the while you slept, I have tried to untie myself and others," Zahm said. "My fingers are bloody, and we are still bound." Inch by painful inch, Kell shifted closer, until he felt the man's hands against his wrists. Zahm struggled with the ropes, but after a long while, he sat back with a curse.

"There has to be a way out." *Corran and Rigan will be searching for me. I've just got to stay alive long enough to be found.*

"There is a way out," Zahm said. "But I fear it leads only to the Golden Shores."

For a while, the barn was quiet. Then one of the men began to sing. The others gradually joined in. The tune was mournful and the words were strange, but Kell did not need a translator. *It's a death song. A prayer. They don't think we're going to make it out.*

"You have family, little brother? Someone to remember you?"

Kell forced back a sudden tightness in his throat. "Yes. My brothers." *And Polly.*

"We believe that so long as one person remembers you, you are not fully dead." The singing continued, sad and haunting in the darkness. "I will sing your name and ask the gods to grant your soul mercy. Make your peace, little brother. I fear we don't have much longer."

Kell strained against the rough rope until it cut bloody gashes in his wrists and ankles. He ignored the pain of his damaged ribs, trying to roll across the floor, searching for a nail or a bit of metal, anything that might help him cut his bonds. His energy was quickly spent, his head spun from the effort and he found nothing.

If I die here, what if Corran and Rigan don't find me? What if there's no one to say the chant and prepare my body to meet the gods? No one will paint my face or mark my shroud. Cold fear gripped him.

Not all the dead are sung for or marked, or even buried. What of sailors lost at sea and soldiers in battle? Or the ones who have no one to pay for their burial? Those questions had never bothered him before. Now, they seemed urgent.

It hurt to move his mouth, and his swollen lip muddled his words, but Kell closed his eyes, and began to recite the chant he had heard Corran sing over so many of Ravenwood's dead. In his mind, he heard his brothers' voices—and the voice of his father—rise and fall. His chest burned and his throat was raw, but Kell finished the chant. Only then did he realize that the Wanderers had fallen silent as he sang. When he finished, they murmured a single word in unison.

"*Senton.*"

"It means, 'let it be so,'" Zahm said. "You sang well. And now, we are ready. We face what comes."

Outside, the bell tolled ten times.

A lantern flamed, and Kell squinted at the light. His eyes adjusted, and he saw that their prison was a rundown warehouse. Eight of the Mayor's guards filed in, armed and grim-faced.

"Been a busy night." It was the guard who had captured Kell: a man early in his third decade, with a muscular build and a square-jawed face. "I don't imagine you mind too much that we were busy. Gave you a few more candlemarks to say your prayers." The other guards chuckled.

A bitter thought occurred to Kell. *I guess the lucky amulets were a fraud. Figures Widgem would get the last laugh at my expense.*

"The wharf riots got out of hand," the guard said, as he and the others walked among the prisoners. "People got killed. Couple of buildings went up in flames. Monsters got loose. Good thing we all know who to blame."

Kell remembered Tek's warning about the guards, and Sosten's casual acceptance of the idea that the Wanderers must be at fault. *The guards set the whole thing up. The Mayor wants a crackdown, and the guards managed to find a way to pin all the trouble on the Wanderers. And with us dead, no one will know the truth.*

"Seems your people deserted you. I considered hanging the lot of you," the guard taunted. He glanced up at the high beams overhead. "But it seemed like too much work. A couple of the men wanted to torch the building, but that might attract attention."

He drew his sword. The sound of steel against leather sent a shiver through Kell. "So we'll just deal with you the way we handle all the other vermin. Hold still, and we might make it quick." Something in the guard's eyes told Kell not to expect even that much mercy.

"A curse on you," Zahm said, his voice quiet and steady. In the lantern light, Kell got his first good look at the Wanderer. He had brown hair and fair skin, with high cheekbones, and Kell guessed him to be in his thirties. "May your bones break and your blood boil. May your children hunger and your women lament. And may you exist in misery without end, now and beyond the grave."

"*Senton.*" Kell joined in as the others spoke their agreement.

The guard rushed forward and grabbed Zahm by the throat, dragging him up from where he lay. "You've got a big mouth for a dead man."

"I go to my gods," Zahm replied, his voice choked by the pressure of the guard's grip. "They welcome us. They will avenge us."

"You sound certain of that," the guard spat. "Maybe they will. But they're sure not here to help you now, are they?"

Eight guards. At least twelve of us. We're bound, but there's got to be something we can do. Kell glanced around, looking for any sign of resistance in the Wanderers. Most looked spent. Some had been roughed up even more than Kell, and appeared to be barely conscious. But he caught a glimmer of defiance in their eyes that gave him courage.

If we're going to die, let's go out fighting.

The guards moved toward the prisoners, swords in hand. Zahm brought his knees up fast and kicked out with his bound feet, connecting hard with the lead guard's groin.

"Son of a bitch," the guard groaned as his knees buckled. He dropped Zahm, and the Wanderer landed another kick to the guard's knee, which gave with a crunch. The guard howled and fell to the floor.

Kell had been waiting for his chance. As the other guards surged forward, he brought his feet up, bending his knees, coiled to strike. His kick sent the soldier closest to him sprawling on his ass.

All around him, the prisoners fought for their lives, marshaling their strength for one final struggle. One of Zahm's people bucked to his feet with an acrobat's grace, startling a guard, and head-butted the soldier with enough force to drop the man like a stone. The rest swept their legs or kicked to keep the guards at a distance, sending a few unwary soldiers into the dirt.

"Hanging's too good for you," one of the guards growled. He lunged forward, running a Wanderer through. Blood burst from the prisoner's lips and sprayed from the wound in his chest. The guard withdrew his blade, then thrust again and again until the man fell back and lay still.

A young Wanderer, who looked to be Rigan's age, twisted his feet through his bound arms, bringing his hands to the front of his body. He brought both fists up in a powerful punch that sent a guard reeling, blood streaming down his face from a broken nose.

"You'll pay for that!" the soldier bellowed, charging the Wanderer. His blade gleamed in the lantern light, and the young nomad's head toppled from his shoulders, rolling to one side as his corpse fell to the other.

It was a futile, doomed rebellion, but Kell gave it his all. They had made peace with their gods, and resigned themselves to death, but that did not mean they would go willingly to the After. He cheered silently at the surprise in the guards' faces as their prisoners refused to die without a fight. Zahm downed the first guard permanently, but the next guard came at him from the side, staying out of range of the Wanderer's powerful kick.

"You bastard," the guard snarled, plunging his sword into Zahm's belly.

Kell pushed off with his feet and managed to angle himself to kick the guard in the ass with all his might, sending him sprawling over Zahm's blood-soaked body. The guard hauled himself to his feet and wheeled on Kell. His blade moved in a blur, slashing across Kell's chest.

Kell tried to roll out of the way, though his ribs protested every movement. The sword came down again, slicing across his back. A boot caught Kell in the side with enough force to pick him up and turn him over. Kell bit back a cry as he landed. Blood soaked his shirt. If his ribs were not broken before, the savage kick had surely snapped them. Breathing hurt.

"I'm not done with you," the guard growled.

Kell's strength was fading, but he mustered enough for one last kick, striking the guard hard enough in the shins to earn a howl of pain. Anger beyond reason blazed in the guard's eyes as he lifted his blade. "Go to the Dark Ones."

The blade glinted in the light; it slashed across Kell's belly, biting deep. Kell struggled for breath, choking on his own blood.

"It wouldn't do for people to find your bodies with sword wounds," the guard said. "People might talk. So we've got a surprise for you. That's why we left you alive. He likes the hunt."

A door slammed open, and the lantern went out. Kell could see nothing in the darkness. He heard the rattle of a metal cage, the crack of a whip. Something growled.

"Should we light the lantern and let them see what's coming for them, or leave them in the dark?" a man's voice said from near the door.

"Leave it dark."

The door closed. Kell heard a low growl and the scratch of claws against dirt. The thing the guards released smelled of musk and blood. It sniffed the air, and growled again.

Oh, gods. The guards sent in a monster to finish us.

Kell held absolutely still, barely breathing. For a few minutes the barn was silent, except for the snuffling of the creature. A low cry sounded from the far side of the room, and the thing shifted, orienting on the sound. Kell heard the sound of digging and the patter of dirt falling like rain as the monster clawed into the earthen floor. It roared as it closed on its prey. The terrified Wanderer screamed, kept on screaming as the thing bit down with the snick of teeth and the crunch of bone. Bile rose in Kell's throat as he heard a thrashing sound, like a dog worrying a rabbit, shaking it back and forth to snap the spine. The screams suddenly stopped.

Kell's heart hammered. His mouth was dry, and he doubted he could draw a full breath even if he dared. He heard the creature moving in the dark, claws clicking against the hard-packed dirt. The monster snuffled and padded closer. A stiff-bristled muzzle nudged Kell's shoulder. He bit his lip to keep from crying out, but he could not stop his body from trembling.

The creature nudged him again, sniffing the blood on his clothing. Then it turned, and Kell swallowed, hoping against hope it had moved on.

The creature roared. Four sharp claws slashed across Kell's throat. Darkness took him and the pain ended.

Chapter Twenty-Six

"We want protection!"

"What is the Guild *doing* for all the money we pay you?"

"If the Lord Mayor can't keep us safe, maybe we stop burying the dead!"

Angry voices rose from the floor of the Guild Hall as Guild Master Orlo gestured for calm. "I know you're upset—"

"Upset?" Tolen Erstine, an undertaker from Skinton, rose to his feet. He was a big man, strong from years of digging graves, and this lifetime of hard work showed in every craggy line of his weathered face. "We're *angry*. Why don't you and the rest of your fancy Guild Masters come down from your villas and live with us for a while? See what it's like to be hunted by monsters? Maybe then you'd use some of the hard-earned money we pay you to *do* something about the problem!"

The mood of the crowd was ugly. Even by the sober standards of undertakers, Erstine was known as a serious, reasonable man, but tonight even he looked like he had been pushed past his limits.

"It's not about the money. You don't see what those... things... do to the bodies." Georg Russe, an undertaker from the harbor area, added, standing to join Erstine. "It's not like a knife fight, or a beating. These creatures, these monsters, they *eat* people. Rip them apart. Gnaw on their bones."

"It ain't right." Widow Sulla, who buried the dead from the tenements and hovels north of the harbor, spoke up. She was spare and tall, with broad hands and ropy muscles, and the flinty look in her eyes made it clear she was not easily spooked.

"It just ain't right," she went on. "Decent people can't go abroad without fear for their lives. I keep burying this many children, there ain't gonna *be* people in Ravenwood in a few years. Women dead, too. Just tryin' to go about their business, and they get chewed up and left by these monsters." She stamped her foot. "High time the Guild did something to stop it!"

The crowd rumbled assent.

"We just need a little more time." Orlo raised his hands to urge for calm.

"Time? How many more people gotta die while you get *time* to think about this?" Russe shot back.

Corran and Rigan, standing in the back of the room, exchanged a glance. "I've never seen Old Man Erstine give a shit about much of anything," Rigan said under his breath.

"Never thought I'd hear Georg Russe say it wasn't about the money," Corran murmured. "We've buried enough folks from his territory when he held out for more than the family could pay."

In theory, the Guild was supposed to unite tradespeople for mutual support. In reality, it worked like most families Corran knew—messy, flawed, and weighed down with old hurts and resentments.

"We can't let panic make us lose our heads," Guild Master Orlo protested. "We must stay calm."

"You can stay plenty calm up in your villas. That's where all the guards are, keeping the monsters off your streets. We don't ever bury one of the Guild Masters' children, or anyone from the Merchant Princes' families or the nobles," Sulla countered. "I'm as happy as any of you to bury someone whose time has come, but not like this. Not ripped apart by monsters and sent too soon to the After. It ain't right. What are you doing about it?"

"Damn hard to do business when they keep making curfew earlier and earlier," Russe added, his face reddening.

"And if it weren't the curfew, we'd be fearin' the monsters," Sulla agreed. "Can't do our work out at the cemetery without worrying *we'll* be next if those things show up."

"The guards only care about running down curfew-breakers," Russe said. "Not hunting the godsdamned monsters."

"We are fortunate to have the Lord Mayor's guards to help us," Orlo said. "They're doing all they can."

"If the guards won't hunt the monsters, then make them stop hunting the hunters!"

The hall erupted in agreement and Orlo began to pound on the podium with his gavel. "Order! Silence!"

"Or what?" Sulla yelled. "You gonna set the guards on us?"

"Do something about the monsters, or get out of our people's way for doing it themselves—and stop taking our fees for nothing!" Erstine added.

Corran and Rigan kept to the shadows along the back wall, unwilling to be drawn into the conversation. *We don't dare join in,* Corran thought. *Not with what Rigan and I are doing. We've pushed our luck to get away with it this far. But if we stand out and say something, someone might start to wonder.*

"That's enough!" Orlo roared.

A handful of men and women started to their feet in support of the Guild Master. Erstine, Sulla, and Russe remained standing, defiant. Their supporters also rose, and the groups faced off against each other.

"You're all crazy," a man yelled from Orlo's side of the room. "You're going to bring the Mayor's guards down on all of us."

"We can handle the guards," one of Russe's supporters shot back. "Shit, the guards can't even fight monsters."

"The Lord Mayor won't let the hunters keep getting away with breaking the law," another man shouted. "And the guards can make our lives miserable if they come searching for lawbreakers. No one will be safe!"

Orlo had reached his breaking point. "*Quiet!*" he bellowed. At his shout, guards burst from the rear doors, and formed a cordon across the back of the room.

Corran grabbed Rigan and pulled him further into the shadows, stepping into an alcove off the main hall. At the sight of the guards, the crowd quieted, but the mood grew darker.

"Is this what we get for our money, Guild Master Orlo?" Erstine's voice was thick with contempt. Sulla fixed Orlo with a murderous glare, and Russe looked angry enough to take a swing at someone.

"Everyone, sit down," Orlo ordered.

"You didn't answer us," Erstine pressed. "What are you going to do about the problem?"

"I'm not going to stand by and watch agitators ruin what it has taken this Guild generations to build," Orlo shot back. "I'm not going to go to war against our own Lord Mayor, who has sent all the troops we can afford to protect us. I'm not going to support lawbreakers taking the law into their own hands. That's what I'm *not* going to do." He had clearly had enough.

"These hunters—how do we know what they're really up to? Oh, they'll kill a few monsters to get you on their side. Who watches them to see what they do *after* that? Once they've killed off the creatures, why should they go away? They'll get rid of the monsters, and the next thing you know, they'll be the ones killing your women and children, and threatening your businesses unless you pay them to go away."

Orlo was warming to his theme. "And they *won't* go away—they'll know suckers when they see them. You'll have traded one set of monsters for another. Human monsters with weapons, coming back again and again to bleed you dry."

The Guild Master drew himself up. "That's why we can't sanction the hunters. Because they're just another type of monster. We have to trust the Lord Mayor. We have to trust the guards to protect us—and Ravenwood. I know you're scared. And we'll do something about the monsters," Orlo promised. "Just don't take the law into your own hands. That will only make the problem worse."

Corran and Rigan slipped out before the Guild meeting ended, unwilling to be drawn into the argument. They walked in silence for several blocks before either dared speak.

"He's lying," Rigan said. "I don't think he means to do anything."

"Not a thing. Erstine and his crowd, though... They're probably already taking action on their own."

"You think they're going to get in trouble with the guards?" Rigan asked.

Corran shot him a look. "You mean, will the guards assume they're hunters, since they spoke out in favor of action?"

Rigan nodded.

Corran sighed. "Maybe."

"That's why I wanted to stay in the back, out of sight," Rigan said. "I didn't want either side pulling us in. The less anyone thinks of us, the better."

"It can't go on like this, you know," Corran replied. "The monsters, the killing. Couple of times now, when we've gone out, we've found signs that there are other groups, other hunters. And there'll be more yet, unless the guards step up."

Rigan shrugged. "I don't know. Some people can put up with a lot of shit to ignore a problem. You heard the Guild Master, talking about how lucky we are to have such a great Lord Mayor who does so much for us, and how the Guild protects us. Did you see the folks eating that up? How fast he turned them on the hunters?"

"You still think there's magic involved? That someone's summoning the monsters?"

"I'm certain of it—but I don't know *who* or *how*—or why. And I sure as the Dark Ones don't know how to stop it. I'm hoping I can get some answers when I go Below."

"If your… friends have any real power, why aren't they doing something to stop whoever is controlling the monsters?"

Rigan glanced behind them before he replied. "I have a suspicion about that. The guards don't go Below often, and neither do the monsters. What if someone made a deal? The witches get to live in exile without being hunted by the guards, and in return, they don't interfere Above."

Corran caught his breath. "Like the protection money we pay the guards so they don't wreck our shops."

"Yeah. And maybe the witches Below don't have the kind of power it would take to fight someone strong enough to conjure and control the monsters. Maybe they're hiding because they couldn't fight and win. But still, it all seems a little… cozy."

"I thought you trusted Damian and the others."

Rigan shifted uncomfortably. "Damian saved my life. He offered to train me. Aiden has healed both of us. What choice did I have except to trust them… at least that far? But there've been too many questions I've asked that don't get answered. And there've been times when I've wondered, while I'm training, whether Damian's really pushing me to improve my skill, or just to test what I'm capable of."

"You mean, seeing whether you're a threat?"

"Maybe."

"Shit." Corran ran a hand back through his hair. "Isn't there anyone else who can train you?" The memory of Rigan waiting in a darkened workshop for a knife in the back, afraid of what he might become, was still too raw to forget.

"Aiden."

Corran glanced at Rigan. "The healer?"

Rigan nodded. "I trust him. My gut says he's all right."

"If you could learn how to do that kind of magic, having a healer in the family might come in handy," Corran replied.

He could still feel the bruises from the last hunt, and the gashes that Rigan had stitched, which had still not quite healed.

"I'm not sure I'd be able to learn healing magic," Rigan replied. "But control, focus, grounding—I'm betting he could teach me those. The question is, how do I ask, without letting Damian know I don't trust him, and without putting Aiden in a tight spot?"

Corran did not have a good answer for that. By now they were back at the workshop. "If Orlo has his way, they'll end up blaming everything on the hunters," Corran said.

"He has to oppose the hunters," Rigan agreed. "Because right now, the hunters are heroes, and I'm sure the Lord Mayor won't let that stand."

"That puts us in a bind," Corran replied. "Because we really can't stay out of the fight when the monsters come, but I'm afraid the guards—or the Guilds—are going to lay a trap for us."

"Do nothing, and people turn on you for letting them down," Rigan said. "Show up to the fight, and get caught."

"Yeah. That's exactly what I mean."

TWO CANDLEMARKS HAD passed, and Corran was pacing the workroom. "Something's wrong. Kell should have been back long ago."

"Maybe he stopped off to have a drink with friends at The Lame Dragon," Rigan replied, worry clear in his voice.

Corran frowned. "I doubt it. Not after what happened with Wil. And Kell wouldn't be late. Not past curfew."

"He could be anywhere in Wrighton," Rigan drummed his fingers, revealing his own anxiety. "Maybe there were more bodies to pick up than usual."

"He's been doing the rounds for years now, and he's never been late. Not even with that fever last winter, when he brought so many bodies we had to work through the night to keep up."

"I remember." Rigan mused, fingers tapping. "Maybe he got

hailed for a few more bodies than usual," he suggested. "Or he could have gotten delayed if the guards cordoned off streets, what with the riot on the wharves." They could see the glow of burning buildings along the docks from their upstairs window, and more than one neighbor had dropped in to catch them up on the gossip.

"Maybe," Corran allowed. "But it doesn't make much sense for the guards to force people to break curfew."

Rigan raised an eyebrow. "It does if the guards want a few more fines to collect. Sounds *exactly* like the kind of thing they'd do."

Corran's thoughts churned. *What can we do? How do we find him? Where do we even start? Even if we try to retrace his steps, it's after curfew. We're just as likely to land ourselves in the Mayor's prison—or worse—as we are to help him. But Kell's depending on me, dammit. If he's in trouble, he's expecting us to help. He knows about the hunters, and Rigan's magic. And right now, I'm damned if I have a clue what to do.*

"Can you find him with magic?" he asked, turning to Rigan.

"Don't you think I've tried?" Rigan buried his hands in his hair. "I tried to think about Kell and focus on him. I went upstairs and picked up his shirt, thinking that might help my magic pick up his 'scent' or something." He shook his head, despair clear in his eyes. "But I haven't felt anything that might be a clue—and I'm afraid to push too hard, or we'll bring the Mayor's mages down on us."

"We can't just sit here!" Corran's fear and frustration spilled over and he lashed out. "He could be hurt. He could be in danger. And I don't know what to do." He wondered for a moment if Rigan fully understood just how much that admission cost him, but saw from the look in his brother's eyes that he did.

"We'll get him back," Rigan assured him.

Corran turned away. "How do you know? How can you *say* that? We don't even know where to start."

A rap at the back alley door startled them. Rigan went to answer the door, while Corran stepped back and took up a large knife, holding out of sight. A young boy stood in the doorway, eyes terrified but resolute.

"Are you Kell's brothers?"

"Yes. Who are you?" Rigan asked, motioning for the boy to step inside. He glanced both directions in the alley before he closed the door, but saw no one else.

"I'm Tek. I give Kell tips on who's died, and he pays me." The boy had a street-wise look to him that made Corran wonder just what he had seen to make him so obviously afraid.

"You've taken a chance coming here after curfew," Corran said, putting the knife away as Rigan went to fetch something for Tek to eat. "Do you know where Kell is?"

"I told him not to go."

"Go where?" Rigan asked, setting down the food and a cup of tea. Tek gobbled the bread, meat and cheese hungrily and washed it down with tea before he answered. Corran fidgeted impatiently.

"I warned him about the riot," Tek said with the last mouthful still swelling his cheeks. "Told him the guards were looking for trouble, and that it was getting bad down there."

"Why did you think he would go near the riot?" Rigan pressed, refilling Tek's cup, which the boy guzzled gratefully.

"He said he had to pick up a body from the chandler. That's down toward the docks. I told him not to go, but he said he'd be all right."

Rigan and Corran exchanged a glance. "When was that?"

"It was starting to get dark," Tek replied. "He said his rounds were taking longer than usual. So maybe eight bells?" He leaned forward. "I went down there later. I worried about him, you know? And I saw the cart—but not Kell."

"He wouldn't abandon the cart," Rigan said, looking stricken.

"The guards were rounding up Wanderers on the harbor," Tek said. "It turned into a big fight. So I kept my eyes open. I saw the guards go into an old warehouse. It looked like they had prisoners."

Tek wiped his mouth with the back of his hand. "I couldn't get near the place—and I'm pretty good at giving guards the slip," he added with pride. "There were a *lot* of guards around it."

"When was that?" Corran asked.

"About a candlemark ago. I had to lie low because the streets are lousy with the Mayor's men. And it took me a while to find your place. Ain't never needed to go lookin' for an undertaker before."

Corran swallowed hard. "Can you tell us where the warehouse is?"

Tek gave them directions, and Rigan looked up. "I know that block. It's not far from the dyer."

"Thank you for coming to tell us, Tek," Corran said, digging in his pocket for a silver coin. He handed it over to Tek, whose eyes widened as if he'd never seen such a thing in his life.

Tek hesitated before taking the coin. "I like Kell," he said. "He's nice to me and brings me food sometimes. I don't want him to be hurt."

"Do you need to sleep here?" Rigan asked. "It's after curfew. Risky to be out."

Tek looked around the workroom and made a sign of blessing. "In here with dead people?" He caught himself. "I mean, thanks, but I need to be going."

Rigan handed Tek an apple and a chunk of bread. "For the road," he said with a lopsided smile. Tek gave him a cockeyed salute, and headed for the door. Just before he reached for the knob, he turned. "I hope you find him. I hope he's all right."

He let himself out into the alley and vanished into the shadows.

As soon as the door closed, Corran began gathering weapons, deciding on his sword, a staff and a long knife. He looked up and found Rigan already wearing his cloak. "Where do you think you're going?"

"With you. To get our brother."

Corran shook off his hand. "You can't. I'm going to round up the hunters. You can't let them know about your magic."

"And you can't call the hunters into this," Rigan argued. "It could be a trap. Maybe Tek wasn't telling the truth. Maybe someone suspects you're a hunter, and they sent the boy to lead you all into an ambush."

"Did you see him? He looked scared to death."

Rigan's gaze locked with Corran's. "He could have been scared of a lot of things. Maybe he was telling the truth, but maybe someone else made him come here. Or maybe he's just a kid who's in over his head. But if you lead a team of hunters down there, you'll all end up in gibbets, just like the others."

"So what's your plan? Sit here and wait for Kell to come back?"

"This is a family matter," Rigan said, voice quiet but steady. "I can navigate Below and get us to the harbor out of sight of the guards—which is another reason to leave the hunters behind. We go in, we get him, we bring him home."

"What good can your magic do?"

Rigan did not look away. "It can kill—just as well as your staff and knife. And maybe that's all it needs to do."

With a growl, Corran pushed past his brother and opened the door. "Come on, then. We've got a long way to go."

It was strange to put Rigan in the lead, Corran thought, as he followed his brother down alleys nearly too close for his shoulders to fit. Rigan moved with the confidence and dangerous stealth of a predator. *How have I not noticed the way his magic changed him? Has being a hunter done the same to me?*

Rigan led them to an old building and down a flight of rickety steps to a cellar. To Corran's astonishment, his brother held out a hand and spoke a word. A tongue of blue flame flickered in Rigan's palm, lighting their way. "Follow me."

They crossed several dank, debris-filled rooms before Rigan opened a hidden door and they descended old stone steps.

"Are you taking me to the witches?" Corran asked as they navigated a dark tunnel.

"No. We don't dare bring them in, for the same reason we can't bring in the hunters. If this is a trap, or if it goes wrong, we don't want to get anyone else killed or captured," Rigan replied in a tight voice.

Corran was used to taking the lead and making the decisions. It chafed to be the follower, though he was completely out of his element here, even more so when it came to magic. *I've seen what Rigan can do with my own eyes, and I've heard him tell of what else he's done. I've got to trust him.*

Despite the tales he had heard from Rigan, Corran was astonished by his first glimpse of Below. "It's true," he murmured, trying not to gawk.

"Yes, it's true," Rigan replied with a hint of dry amusement. "Did you think I made the whole thing up?"

"Sometimes, I wondered."

Bells chimed the hour, reverberating in the vast cavern.

"Here we are." Rigan's voice jarred Corran from his thoughts; they had been walking for a long while. They stood in front of a battered wooden door. "We'll come up between the chandler's shop and the harbor front," Rigan warned. "It's as close as I can get us. We'll have a block or so to go, and there might still be guards around."

Why have the guards become so focused on the Wanderers? Corran wondered. *Sure, they push them to be on their way from time to time, but the Wanderers never really leave. They just change location. Or is this some scheme of the Mayor's because of all the fancy outsiders in town, and Kell just was in the wrong place at the wrong time?* He hated to admit it, but Rigan's suggestion was equally possible. *Is it a trap, trying to draw out anyone with enough backbone to fight? Maybe the Mayor just wants to tighten his grip, get rid of the 'troublemakers.'*

A jerk of Rigan's head indicated they had reached their destination, a dilapidated warehouse with a sagging roof and cracked, weather-beaten siding. Corran and Rigan waited and watched from the shadows, but they saw neither light nor movement.

Corran gave his brother a questioning glance. Rigan shook his head, then shrugged. They circled the building once, checking that no guards were watching from hidden vantage points. Silent, abandoned buildings hunkered over dark, deserted streets. *Why would the guards capture Wanderers and bring them here? If they want rid of them, why not just chuck them out of the city gates and be done with it?*

Corran and Rigan approached the door cautiously, weapons ready. To Corran's surprise, the door swung open when they pushed it. The unmistakable smell of blood filled the air. No movement came from inside. Rigan lit a lantern.

Bodies littered the floor of the warehouse, lying in dark pools.

"Kell?" Corran called softly. In the flickering light of the lantern, they could see the extent of the carnage. Corran took a step, and his boot struck a severed head, which rolled to one side, revealing the face.

"Something's been gnawing at them, tearing them up," Rigan said. His voice sounded tight as a cord about to snap. "Monsters."

Corran looked down at the headless body. "A monster didn't do that. Too clean. Had to be a sword." He looked around the warehouse, as panic rose in his chest. "Kell!"

"Over here." Rigan dropped to his knees beside one of the still, blood-soaked forms. Cold settled into the pit of Corran's stomach as he went to stand beside his brother.

Kell lay still and pale, eyes staring. The gash across his throat exposed his spine, and blood soaked his shirt. His arms were marked with deep bites, and sharp claws had sliced through his shirt and pants, ripping deep into his flesh.

"Do something!" Corran begged, turning to Rigan.

Rigan's face twisted with grief. "I can't raise the dead."

"Then *what damn good is your magic?*" Corran roared. His

outburst ended in a sob. "He fought them," he said, noting the bruises on Kell's face and the cuts on his hands. "The bastards tied him up, and he still fought them."

A growl sounded behind them. Corran and Rigan climbed to their feet, weapons ready. Grief would have to wait.

They smelled the creature before they saw it. Corran gasped in recognition at the squashed, bat-like face, with its wrinkled snout and wide, toothy maw. It was the stuff of nightmares. This creature must have weighed more than most men, larger than the beast Corran had faced before, and its four powerful legs ended in sharp claws. Red, angry eyes fixed on them. It shrieked with rage, and charged.

Corran went right; Rigan went left. They had never fought a beast like this together, but years of working side by side allowed them to anticipate each other's moves. Corran's staff landed on the creature's thick skull with an audible crack. The beast howled, but kept on coming. Corran leaped out of the way a heartbeat before sharp teeth *snicked* on the air where his leg had been.

"Hey, ugly!" Rigan was no swordsman, but he had carved up enough corpses in the mortuary to know how to use a knife. He jabbed the beast as it charged, managing to throw himself out of the way before it could trample him.

Corran was back on his feet, staff twirling. This time, he caught the creature under the chin with full force, stunning it enough for him to thrust his sword hilt-deep into the monster's side. The creature bellowed, but showed no sign of flagging.

The brothers slowly circled the monster as it eyed them, deciding which looked like weaker prey. It leaped toward Rigan much faster than something its size should have been able to move, and he stumbled back, trying to stay out of the way of its jaws. Sharp claws raked across his left shoulder, opening four bloody gashes.

"Rigan!" Corran was already moving. *Use your magic!* He urged silently.

Rigan jabbed the knife in his right hand into the monster's neck, hard enough to go all the way through and out the other side. The creature took another swipe at him, but Rigan rolled clear. Corran barreled toward the beast, landing with his full weight on its back and bringing his staff down across the creature's spine just behind the skull. With a wheeze, the monster collapsed, Corran riding it as his staff cracked down again, with bone-splitting force. He raised his sword and sank it hilt-deep into the creature's flesh. *That's for Kell.*

Corran did not rise until he had yanked his sword from the monster's side and brought it back down with deadly finality, cutting off the head. He got to his feet, staring at the creature's body and the spreading pool of black blood. "I don't think it got here by accident."

"Maybe we interrupted something," Rigan said, getting to his feet. He looked around warily, and Corran wondered if he, too, had the sense that they were not alone.

"Or maybe we ruined the chance to pin the blame on someone or something else." Corran's voice was dangerously cold. A hunger for vengeance filled him, a need that went down to his bones. Monsters had taken his mother and killed his lover. Now, Kell was dead. Rage boiled Corran's blood, bordering on madness.

If it helps me get the job done and avenge Kell, then madness is welcome.

Three guards emerged from the shadows on the other side of the warehouse. "Well, look at what we've got here," one of the guards said, his voice slurred by drunkenness. "New recruits."

"Was that your pet monster?" Corran demanded.

The men laughed. "Wasn't nobody's pet, but it was damn useful, 'til you killed it," the guard said. He nudged the body closest to him with his boot. "Actually, I'm glad you're here. The fun was over way too soon."

Fury replaced grief as Corran and Rigan launched themselves at the drunken guards. The men drew their swords, only to find that their attackers were past the point of fear. Corran's staff moved in a blur, disarming one guard with a bone-crunching smack to the wrist and then slamming the weapon into his forehead hard enough to crack his skull.

Rigan fought with two long knives, the worn, familiar grips comfortable in his hands. As Corran went after the second guard, Rigan stalked the third.

"You'll hang for killing a guard," the soldier blurted once he realized that their 'easy prey' intended to fight to the death.

"There won't be any witnesses," Rigan grated.

Corran wondered if his brother's magic could kill all of the soldiers at once, and remembered that the last time he lashed out, it had brought the roof down as well. Magic might be his last resort, but right now, Rigan's rage and grief demanded a physical outlet.

The guard snarled and came at Rigan in a drunken fury, and Rigan's knife laid the man's left arm open down to the bone. The sword opened a gash on Rigan's shoulder, but he was too focused on vengeance to feel the pain.

"You're going to bleed like Kell did," Rigan promised in a low, cold voice.

A few feet away, Corran eyed his new opponent with the emotionless practicality he had learned fighting monsters. The soldier was skilled with his sword, despite being drunk, but Corran blocked him with his staff at every move. As he watched, fear gradually dawned in the man's eyes.

Finally, Corran rushed the man with a succession of jabs and swings that sent the guard stumbling backward. He knocked over the lantern, and the oil spread. Flames licked at the debris scattered across the floor. The guard's boots lodged on the body of one of the dead Wanderers and he tripped.

"Damn you!" The soldier yelled as he landed flat on his back in the dark, pooled blood. The fire behind Corran lit the warehouse in flickering light and shadow.

Corran's staff swept the sword from the soldier's hand, breaking his fingers and knocking the weapon out of reach. The next blow to the stomach made the guard spit up blood. Corran fell on top of the man, pinning the guard's wrists with his knees. He clasped his hands together and slammed them across the man's face with all his might.

"You killed my brother."

A whimper was all the guard could manage with a broken jaw. Corran's next blow snapped the man's head to the other side. "You made him suffer."

The guard gave a guttural bleat. Corran's bloody fists beat against his face once more. "You did it for sport." Corran leaned in closer. "I'm an undertaker. I know how to take a body apart. I could do it while you're still alive—and make it last a while." He saw terror and pain in the guard's eyes. "Did you make him beg for his life? Did you enjoy it?"

"Mercy!" the guard managed, blood bubbling with each breath.

Corran swung his fists again with his full might, feeling the man's neck snap with the force of his blow. "That's as merciful as I get tonight."

Only then did Corran register that Rigan was not with him. He looked up, and saw that his brother had the last guard up against the warehouse wall, pinned a foot off the floor. Rigan's hand was in the center of the man's chest, limned with a faint yellow light.

"I'm sorry I killed your brother!" the guard babbled, terrified.

The look in Rigan's eyes bordered on madness. "Kell. His name was Kell." Rigan did not move, but a thin trickle of blood started from the guard's mouth.

"*What are you doing?*" the guard shrieked. More blood leaked from his nose, then the corners of his eyes. Rivulets of blood ran from both ears.

Rigan tightened his hand over the guard's chest. Corran watched in horrified fascination as droplets of blood-sweat formed on the soldier's forehead. The guard gave an incoherent cry, twisting against the power that held him, but Rigan's stony expression never wavered.

"I said you would bleed like he did." The knife in Rigan's left hand moved too fast to follow, opening a thin, sanguine line across the soldier's throat. He clenched his right hand, as if to stop the guard's beating heart, and in the next instant, the man's corpse slumped to the floor and the golden light winked out.

Corran rose to his feet, still staring. Rigan closed his eyes and swallowed hard. He staggered, and looked like he might collapse. His face was pale, and his hands shook. He took a shuddering breath and collected himself. Then he bent and retrieved his second knife, and turned toward Corran. Both of them were covered in blood. Corran tore off a piece of his shirt to bind the gashes on Rigan's leg.

"We've got to get out of here," Corran said. Smoke filled the warehouse; the fire had spread too far to extinguish.

"Get Kell," Rigan replied. "I'll cover us."

Now that the fight was over and vengeance won, Corran's whole body trembled with the aftershock, as grief and pain surged through him. He bent to pick up Kell's body, cradling him in his arms, and headed for the door at the rear of the barn.

"They'll know someone killed the guards," Corran said. "The others will come looking."

"Not for a while. Not until they can sort out the bodies from the fire—if there's anything left," Rigan replied. "Come on. We need to take Kell home. We have work to do." As they slipped down the dark alley, the warehouse behind them burst into flames.

Chapter Twenty-Seven

"TRY HARDER." MACHISON'S words came out as a snarl.

"You'd do best to remember your place," Blackholt replied. The temperature in the room dropped as blood witch's magic rose. The Lord Mayor felt gooseflesh rise on his arms, and a real and terrifying chill in his veins.

"*You* work for *me*."

"And we both serve Crown Prince Aliyev, for as long as it pleases him," Blackholt replied. "He gave you use of my services because he knew you needed my help to keep the city under control. To maintain the Balance."

Machison reined in his temper. If Blackholt realized he and Valdis had conspired against him, he did nothing to show it, or to suggest that anything had weakened his power. "Could you read anything from the filthy Wanderer I brought you?"

Blackholt turned part way to look at Machison, his expression a mixture of amusement and disgust. "Wanderer blood is rich with power. But I learned nothing."

"Nothing?" Machison nearly roared in frustration.

"Did you expect a manifesto?" Blackholt mocked. "Some kind of itinerant peddler conspiracy?" He did not bother hiding his contempt. "The Wanderers are a threat because they exist. Magic is in their blood, passed on to their children and bastards. They don't *do* magic, they *are* magic. They've had generations to perfect it."

"And you don't see that as a threat?"

Blackholt chuckled. "Why do you think the Wanderers… wander? Why they're reviled wherever they go? Oh, there are the rumors about stolen children and thieved chickens, but those things happen regardless. It's because they're the last of an old race, and old magic protects them and curses them; legend has it, Eshtamon's magic. They may even affect the Balance. The Wanderers can't be eliminated, but they are condemned to never find home."

"I don't give a rat's ass about legends and dead gods," Machison railed. "If they're a threat, then they can *wander* elsewhere."

Blackholt shrugged. "And you have set your guards on them, have you not?"

"Yes. You know that."

"Did you count the cost?"

Machison's eyes narrowed. "Meaning?"

"In the legends about the dead gods, Ardevan cursed them to be hunted and reviled with no place to lay their heads. Eshtamon couldn't break the curse, but he gave them cunning and the magic to outwit their enemies and avenge their losses."

"You didn't bother mentioning this before."

"You didn't ask. And after all, it's only legend." The blood witch's back was to Machison now, but the Lord Mayor could hear the smirk in his voice. They both knew the commoners still revered the Elder Gods, even while they made token offerings to the Guild deities.

"So do they pose a danger?"

Blackholt gave him a bemused look. "If they didn't before you sent the guards to purge them, they surely do now."

"And the marks they scrawl on the walls? What of those?"

"A secret language, steeped in old magic," Blackholt replied. "A code, to warn and direct one another. Sometimes a curse on their enemies. Maybe more. They haven't exactly been... cooperative about explaining it."

"Then I'll have the guards paint them over, or scrub them off."

"Magic is not so easily dispelled. Once marked, such sigils cannot be easily expunged."

"What of the hunters' blood? They're not Wanderers. Mere rabble. What did you read in them?"

Blackholt rounded on him, eyes cold. "Do you think blood is like a parchment, that can be unscrolled and read at will?"

"I suspected you were a fraud." Machison took a risk goading the witch, but anger drove him on.

"You want to know what I read from the hunters' blood?" Blackholt countered, lifting an orb streaked with brown, dried blood and holding it out toward the Lord Mayor. "I read defiance. Anger. Fear for their families, and an abiding hatred for the monsters... and the one who sent them."

Machison's head came up sharply. "They know the monsters are sent?"

Blackholt fixed him with a stare. "They suspect. And when they learn the truth... it will go badly for you."

"And it won't for you?"

"My patron won't allow it. Nor will my magic."

"Don't flatter yourself. Your fate is linked with mine." Machison watched as Blackholt turned away, and wondered anew whether the blood witch felt the tendrils of control that Valdis assured Machison now existed. *Perhaps so. He's surly, but a little less full of himself than usual.*

"What of the other rogue witches?" Machison pressed.

"I am watching them."

"*Watching* them! Why do they still exist?"

"Because they respect the truce," Blackholt replied. "*Your* truce, or have you forgotten?"

"Times change."

"The witches Below have little power, barely hedge witches," Blackholt said. "A few healers, a seer or two, and the rest can conjure fire or read omens. Nothing that poses a threat. Only four have any true ability, and two of them are my men." He paused. "But there is a newcomer… someone who bears watching."

"Who?"

Blackholt shrugged. "That remains to be seen. It may be nothing. His power may not develop, or it may kill him. Or he might become an asset."

"You're playing with fire. Have him killed and be done with it."

Blackholt chuckled. "Now if I made a habit of that, where would the princes of Darkhurst find witches for their employ? My men are watching the newcomer. If he shows promise, they'll subdue him, remove him to where he can be controlled. Tutored. And the healer is gifted, though certainly not a threat. He could be useful."

Machison heard what wasn't spoken. *Broken. Bound.* It made him look at the blood witch in a new light. *Do you serve willingly, or does Aliyev hold your leash even more tightly than I do?*

"Making assumptions is dangerous." Blackholt's voice was cold and sharp, like the edge of an icy knife. Whether the witch could read Machison's thoughts or was just a good guesser, he got his point across.

"See that they don't cause problems," Machison ordered. "And if this 'newcomer' of yours proves useful, tell Aliyev—or Gorog—that I expect a bounty for providing him."

"Keep your part of the bargain and Aliyev will give you his gratitude, which is worth even more. Fail, and it really won't matter."

Machison bit back a retort, refusing to rise to the bait. He turned and stormed up the steps, though the blood witch gave no indication that he noticed the Lord Mayor was gone.

* * *

"We've made a sweep of the wharfs." Jorgeson's voice was level, all business; that cool, emotionless tone he took when he wanted Machison to remain calm. Machison hated it, even though he also respected Jorgeson's control.

"How many?"

"A dozen, give or take a few. The guards were careful to let the monster finish the prisoners off, to cover the disappearances. We lost eight guards in the process."

"If the guards were 'careful,' they would still be alive." Machison's voice was a low growl.

"The danger with snatching men from the street is that someone might notice and go looking for them," Jorgeson answered. "Especially in a city like Ravenwood."

"Hunters or Wanderers?"

"Could have been either. Wanderers might have traced their kin's magic, although they don't usually fight unless cornered."

"Taking that many should have let them know we wanted all of them."

Jorgeson nodded. "Still. They've survived because they run more than they fight. For the good of the group, even if they lose individuals. Prudent."

"Hunters?"

Jorgeson frowned. "Unclear. Two of the guards who weren't killed in the fire died from sword strokes. But one had his heart crushed from within."

"How is that possible?" Machison asked, feeling tendrils of cold fear wrap around his own heart. "Magic? Are the witches helping the hunters?"

Jorgeson paused. "If magic killed the guards, then it's got to be Wanderers or witches, and both have reason to hate the guards."

"There must be retribution."

"What do you suggest?"

"Set the witch-finders on their trail. Pull in your informants. If you've got a suspicion about someone being a hunter, seize them and burn out their home. Blame it on the witches. It could be Wanderers, but why take a chance?"

"Blackholt might not take kindly to that."

Machison glowered at him. "Leave him to me."

"This will cause… unrest. You're in the middle of trade negotiations," Jorgeson cautioned.

"So would an uprising. Better that our trade partners see we can maintain control. Secure the harbor, assure that trade will not be interrupted."

"The hunters we arrested may be Guild members," Jorgeson said. "Go after too many of their members, and they'll protest—take their cases to the Merchant Princes, maybe even the Crown Prince."

"And risk the trade agreement that will put gold in their pockets? Not likely, no matter how many of their members they have to sacrifice. The Guilds profit by scarcity. Wipe out one Guild family, and another moves in to fill the void. So long as we don't damage their ability to meet their trade obligations, and the treaty preserves their quota of exports, they might see it as an ill wind that blows good." Machison gave a feral smile. "And as for the Merchant Princes, so long as they don't miss a payment from the Guilds or their trading partners, a little blood won't bother them."

And if the Merchant Princes don't complain, the Crown Prince won't give a damn what we do. All we have to do is keep the money flowing. That's why I had Jorgeson take the hostages from the Guild Masters. They'll have a reason to pressure the Merchant Princes to get the best agreement, which means keeping the status quo that favors Gorog. Between the hostages and their own self-interest, they won't make trouble, at least, not until the negotiations are over.

"Any more from your spies about Kadar, or the ambassadors?" Machison asked.

"The Itaran ambassador received a letter from home with ill

tidings," Jorgeson replied. "A death in the family, under suspicious circumstances."

"An assassination?"

Jorgeson shrugged. "The letter the spy read was careful to say nothing too clearly, but that was the impression."

"Given the time it takes to get a letter to Ravenwood from Itara, the strike would have to have been planned more than a week ago. Delicate timing, if the intent was to affect the negotiations," Machison mused.

"The same occurred to me," Jorgeson replied. "Not too difficult for anyone in the right circles; these negotiations have been publicly planned for some time."

We've planned deaths under far more complicated circumstances, Machison thought. "Any idea who was behind it?"

"Hard to say. It's not impossible for Kadar to meddle beyond Ravenwood's boundaries, but it's a bit more ambition than he's shown so far, and a big risk if the deed was ever traced back to him."

Machison guessed that his chief of security had dispatched riders to Itara as soon as he heard the news. "If not Kadar, then who?"

Jorgeson grimaced. "This is Itara we're talking about. They make Ravenwood's politics look like child's play. Bloodthirsty sons of bitches, all of them. The killing might have been sanctioned by the ambassador's own Merchant Princes, a reminder to keep them on their toes—or else."

"What more have you learned? What of the strike against the ambassador from Garenoth? Have you found out who was behind it?" Despite his efforts, Jorgeson's scheming and Blackholt's magic, the Lord Mayor's instincts warned him the negotiation process remained fragile.

"We think it may have been Solencia," Jorgeson replied. "But I don't have hard evidence. Not enough to sway the Merchant Princes."

"Then work behind the scenes. Dispatch an assassin to Solencia on a fast horse. Have him kill someone close to the Solencian ambassador, as a warning."

"As you wish. And to your earlier question, the Wanderers we haven't killed or captured have disappeared, but not in the same manner as before. We're finding sigils here and there throughout the neighborhoods, especially down near the wharfs."

"You think the Wanderers left them as a curse?"

"That's exactly what I think. I don't believe Blackholt's explanation. Even if none of our witches understand the nature of the symbols, I believe they have been placed with ill intent. We tortured one of the Wanderers we caught, trying to reveal the truth about sigils. All we got were obscenities and creative language damning us to painful deaths."

Machison snorted. "Ever think maybe that *was* the translation?"

Jorgeson's lips twitched upward in a cynical smile. "Yes, actually. Or close to the mark in intent, if not exactly word-for-word. I had the men scrub the marks with salt and lye, carve them out of the wood, paint them over with pitch blessed by the priests. Blackholt bled the Wanderer dry and made a potion from his blood that he said would weaken the curses, if it didn't break them entirely."

The Lord Mayor's fist came down hard on the table. "I will *not* have those godsdamned Wanderers interfering in the trade talks, not with their filthy presence *or* their dirty magic!"

Jorgeson weathered the storm of his master's ire without reaction. "We've taken a Wanderer and his family," he replied. "Given them to Blackholt to break. Before this, we just had the men. But with a wife and two children, maybe the prisoner will tell us what we need to know." He paused. "Blackholt can be quite creative."

"Tell me at once if you learn anything," Machison ordered. From the way Jorgeson's jaw tightened whenever Blackholt's name came up, he suspected his security chief shared his own misgivings.

"Of course, m'lord."

Machison was quiet for a moment. "Do you think the Wanderers have fled Below? And if they have, can your men follow them?"

Jorgeson hesitated, choosing his words with care. "It's possible that a few individual Wanderers may have taken temporary shelter Below. But they prize their independence, and they have always been more likely to flee beyond the city walls. They won't abandon their carts, and they stick with their clans."

Thick as thieves.

"You've only answered half my question."

"I would not advise sending guards Below. Especially now, during the negotiations."

"Why?"

"Below is as large as Ravenwood, maybe even larger," Jorgeson replied. "It would require a force as large as the one that patrols Above—and they would be at a disadvantage from the start, on unfamiliar territory." He let that sink in for a moment. "Personally, I think it would be a slaughter. People go Below to disappear. And so long as they don't come back to trouble us, why do we care? Our men would be outnumbered against residents with nothing to lose, and the repercussions could spill over into Ravenwood."

Machison's scowled. "Then make damn sure your soldiers keep those bastards bottled up."

"That's the plan," Jorgeson said with a smile. "While I wouldn't advise sending in a regiment, a few assassins should be able to maneuver quite well Below."

Machison echoed the smile. "I like that. Simple, swift, focused. But be sure to consult me once a target is identified."

"I've already got informers in place," Jorgeson assured him. "Some well-situated people who pay attention to who comes and goes. If a suitable target turns up, we'll take care of it."

"Consult me first," Machison snapped. "I'll decide whether it's kill or capture."

"As you wish, m'lord." Jorgeson paused. "There is... one more thing."

"Oh?"

"I've got a man at The Muddy Goat, Widgem. A real rotter, but he's well positioned to hear gossip. After one of the last fights, one of the hunters was mortally wounded. A guard recognized him as Allery, the potter's son. He's surely dead, given his wounds, but there's been no burial in the Potters' Guild's lot at the cemetery, and Widgem's checked the dodgers and pawn shops for Allery's Guild ring, without success."

Machison shrugged ill-humoredly. "So? Either this potter of yours wasn't as badly injured as your guard thought, or his friends dumped his body, along with the ring. Did you go to the potter's house to arrest him?"

Jorgeson nodded. "Aye. And his family swore up and down that he was missing, but they claimed to know nothing else."

"Interesting," Machison mused. "Keep an eye on the potter and his kin. And tell your Widgem fellow to stay sharp. If that ring surfaces, I want to know who brings it to him."

"Yes, m'lord."

Sleep came quickly after a few glasses of whiskey, though his dreams were far from quiet. Machison tossed in his bed, too warm and then too cold, his nightclothes sticking to his sweaty skin. He panted for breath, heart racing, tongue flicking to wet dry lips.

He was alone. That was strange enough, for him to be anywhere without his guards. To find himself standing in a darkened alley in a seedy part of Ravenwood alone was impossible. He had not traveled outside the Lord Mayor's palace without bodyguards since he had risen to the position years ago. And given the current state of events, to even consider going abroad without backup was suicidal.

Yet there he stood, alone, unarmed. Waiting.

Then he saw her, standing silhouetted in the torchlight. The old Wanderer woman stared at him with scorn.

"A curse on you! Death to you! You're nothing but a painted

tomb, full of rot. You will pay for what you've done." The hag stared straight into his eyes, and he could not will himself to look away. He felt each word like a lash, felt the chill of her magic settle around him, tightening as the curse took hold, weaving its way into soul and skin and bone. The Wanderer's eyes blazed with clear purpose and cold malice.

Machison turned, fleeing down the dark alley. It twisted and turned, but never opened onto a street. Her laughter followed him, drove him on, and sent him careening in panic as his feet slipped on the cobblestones.

He fell, opening bloody cuts on his knees and palms, then pushed up again, running though the air burned in his lungs.

It had been years, decades, since he had pushed his body like this, and from the way his heart raced, his death might come any moment. He heard her laughter again, and found in terror the energy he needed to keep running.

The narrow confines of the alley fell away suddenly, and he stood before the temple of Toloth. He clambered up the steps, threw himself into the shadowed interior like a fugitive seeking sanctuary. His foot caught, and he sprawled, facedown on the cold stone floor. Torchlight, smoke and the blow to his head made his vision swim, and he tried to raise himself to his knees.

The old Wanderer woman stood in the candlelight before the altar, but when Machison blinked, it was the oracle he saw, hunched and hidden in her hooded robe. "I warned you." Her voice rasped like a rusted iron hinge.

"I tried—"

"Too late. The current is already too strong."

"Surely there's something—"

The oracle laughed, a cold, joyless sound. "Death is close. The dead condemn you. Beware the—"

Machison lurched up in his bed, gasping for breath. Cold sweat streaked his face, and his heart felt as if it might rip out of his chest with its frantic pounding. He closed his fists on the damp sheets and blinked, trying to calm his panic.

Nothing new. Just nightmares. He could not remember how long it had been since he'd had a peaceful night's sleep. Memories of the dreams haunted his waking hours, while the portents and omens stalked him while he slept. The night terrors were slowly robbing him of his sanity. He dared not allow a woman to share his bed all night, for fear that he would wake, weak and shaking. Once had been bad enough, and it still annoyed him that he had been forced to kill one of his favorite whores sooner than usual because she had witnessed something he could not allow to embarrass him.

Machison passed a trembling hand over his face and drew in a deep breath. *Damn the Wanderers, and damn the oracle. This isn't over yet. I'm still breathing.*

And I won't go down without a fight.

A candlemark later, Machison lay in bed, staring at the ceiling, unable to go back to sleep. He heard a rustling in the outer room of his suite, and sat up silently, reaching for the sword beneath his bed. For a moment, he considered calling out to his guards, but they would be in the hallway beyond the parlor, and he did not want to give an intruder the advantage of even a few seconds' head start.

Machison rose to his feet, sword in hand. He had grown plump and comfortable on the fruits of his appointment as Lord Mayor, but once, years ago, he had served the Crown Prince as an officer in the army of Darkhurst. Leaving a soldier's life behind was easy, but many memories would be with him for the rest of his days—like how to fight with a sword. How to kill.

Given how many enemies he had made, it was wise not to be completely dependent on bodyguards. As he stalked toward the connecting door in his bare feet, Machison wondered whether the intruder had bribed his guards, knifed them, or merely entered by another means.

He slammed the door open and got his answer immediately,

as he spotted draperies rippling in the breeze from an opened window. It had been tightly closed and latched when he went to bed candlemarks before. *The wardings hadn't worked. Either Valdis is useless, or there's stronger magic afoot here than we reckoned.*

"Come out!" He took another step into the room. He scanned the small sitting room and saw no one. Frowning, he started to lower his sword when a dark-clad figure dodged from beneath the heavy draperies, knocking him over and striking his sword hand against the floor, hard enough to loosen his grip and send the weapon skittering out of reach.

A scarf covered the attacker's face. His muscular body pressed the Lord Mayor against the floor, pinning him down in spite of Machison's kicking and struggling. His left hand grabbed his attacker's right wrist, holding a wicked looking blade at bay.

They tumbled over each other, and in the next moment, Machison was on top, though his victory was short-lived before the man bucked, using his legs for leverage, this time knocking Machison onto his back and pinning him with his knees. The knife wobbled, inching closer to the Lord Mayor's throat, and he felt sweat trickling down his face at the struggle.

Too late, the Lord Mayor saw a glint of silver in the man's left hand, and hissed in pain as a knife slashed across his chest, through his nightshirt and into his skin. In the next moment, the attacker wrested loose of Machison's grip and crossed the room in a few strides, leaping onto the windowsill with the grace of an acrobat. But before he vanished into the night, the assassin hunkered on the sill and dropped a coin onto the floor.

Blood dripped from the wound on his chest and Machison closed his eyes, willing himself not to pass out from the pain. It hurt to breathe, hurt to move, but he forced himself up and staggered toward the open window, leaving a trail of crimson drops.

Despite the torches that lit the grounds outside his manor, Machison saw no one. He closed the window, grimacing at the sharp pain the movement caused, then bent to pick up the coin the assassin had left behind.

The face stamped on the coin was that of Merchant Prince Kadar.

Machison pressed the tattered remnant of his nightshirt against his ribs, staunching the flow of blood, and stumbled to a chair.

He turned the coin in his bloody fingers, thinking. *Did Kadar send the assassin? If so, then is this to put me on notice not to favor only Gorog in the negotiations? Perhaps he's worried that he won't get the extra percentages he wanted?* Accepting Gorog's bribes positioned him as one of the Merchant Prince's proxies, fair game for whatever private pissing matches he might have with his peers.

Assuming it's not someone framing Kadar, since that's just as likely, he thought. He and Jorgeson had done exactly that to cover for Vrioni's murder. *Or Kadar's letting me know that he knows what we did to Vrioni and Vittir and Throck.*

Still, that did not ring true. If Kadar sought vengeance for being blamed for Vrioni's death, he could have had the assassin strike a killing blow. Machison had no doubt that had the struggle continued, the assassin would have bested him. *He would have overpowered me, unless I was extraordinarily lucky.* He had no difficulty imagining his body lying in the parlor with a knife in its chest, and pushed the thought away with revulsion.

Since I'm not dead, it must be a warning, either to me or to Gorog. And while I'll pay Doharmu for my own sins, I'll be damned if I want to be Gorog's whipping boy. So whose game is it, and what's at stake? And more to the point, who'll be coming for my head next?

Chapter Twenty-Eight

THE RETURN TRIP through Below was much more difficult, since they dared not be seen.

"Can't you make us invisible?" Corran asked. Kell lay against him like a sleeping child.

Rigan gave Corran a sour look. "No. Right now, my magic's like a club. I can hit people with it. Nothing fancy. And I don't want to attract the witches."

"Would they give us up to the guards?"

"I don't think so, but I don't want to drag them into it. This is our problem."

The bell pealed twelve times, ringing out over the deserted streets. Rigan led the way and Corran followed, with his cloak thrown over Kell's body to hide it from view. It might fool a passing glance, but it would hardly survive careful scrutiny. *If we get caught, there'll be no way to convince them that we didn't kill Kell. What a choice! Tell the truth and hang for killing the guards, or lie and hang for killing our brother.*

Corran felt numb, too spent even for rage. He retreated into a cold, dark place inside himself so that he could function, at least for long enough to do what must be done. He met his brother's gaze, and saw such pain that he averted his eyes, wondering if Rigan had seen the same in him.

A man appeared, blocking their way. Rigan tensed, reaching for his knives. Corran had no easy way to draw a weapon with Kell's body in his arms.

"You were reckless."

Rigan relaxed, recognizing Damian's voice, and lowered his swords. "They took my brother."

Damian regarded him for a moment, then stared into the shadows where Corran stood. "You need to get home quickly. I'll shield you. Come."

Damian strode off, and Rigan beckoned for Corran to follow. He felt an odd prickle on his skin. *Magic?* Corran stayed close behind his brother and Damian, clutching a dagger in one hand despite the burden of Kell's body. *If we're discovered, I'll be damned if I'm going down without a fight.*

Damian took them a different way than they had come, through older, disused areas of Below. Corran realized that the air around them shimmered slightly, distorting everything they passed. *He said he'd shield us. Is this his magic?*

Finally, they reached steps leading up. "Once you're out, I'll create a diversion to distract any nearby guards." Rigan made to argue and Damian cut him off. "Not enough to get myself caught. Just something to make them look the other way."

"Thank you," Rigan replied, his voice raw.

"You've gotten better at drawing on power from outside yourself, but you're still spent. You need to rest. Return to us as soon as you can; there's much to discuss."

Rigan made his way carefully up the steps and signaled for his brother to follow. Corran's arms burned with Kell's weight, and he had to turn sideways up the narrow stairs to navigate the passageway. They emerged into the cool night and deserted streets.

Smoke hung in the air. As soon as they stepped outside, the prickle of Damian's magic vanished and the shimmer in the air cleared. Corran felt exposed.

"Let's keep moving," Rigan said. "I don't want Damian to put himself at risk needlessly."

To Corran's relief, they reached the alley behind the workshop without incident. As they crossed the threshold, he found himself listening for Kell's footsteps upstairs, and bit back a sob as the reality of their loss sank in. Rigan moved quickly around the room, closing shutters and lighting lanterns.

Corran drew his cloak back and laid his brother's body on a worktable. In the lamplight, Kell looked younger, despite the gray pallor of his skin and the blood streaking his face. Corran's hands shook as he cut the rough ropes that bound Kell's wrists and ankles. He felt his anger flare when he saw the true extent of the damage. "We were too easy on them." His voice was harsh with unshed tears, tight with rage.

Rigan came to stand beside him. He did not speak, and his uneven breathing told Corran that his brother was fighting back sobs; his face was so utterly wracked with pain that Corran had to look away. "We need to bury him tonight," Corran said.

"I know." He reached out and took Kell's hand. "I'll draw a fresh bucket of water."

Corran laid a hand on his brother's shoulder. "First, we bind up that leg of yours."

Rigan moved to protest, but Corran's expression stopped him.

"Sit," Corran ordered. Rigan winced as he eased onto one of the worktables.

Corran brought a bucket of fresh water and a clean cloth, along with soap, vinegar, and willow balm. Monster claws often carried taint or poison; the wound could go bad quickly. Corran handed Rigan the whiskey, and he took a swig from the bottle without hesitating.

"You've lost a lot of blood."

"Didn't feel it."

Corran kept his head down, focusing on the task to maintain his fragile control. He was close to breaking point, and he was sure Rigan was on edge, too. His brother stifled a cry of pain as Corran cleaned the wound. He used the willow balm last, to ward against infection, trying not to think about the fact that it had always been Kell who had mixed their salves and elixirs. He bound the gash with clean gauze.

"Can you put weight on the leg?" Corran asked. He avoided looking at Rigan's face. They might just get through the next few candlemarks if they didn't look at each other, didn't acknowledge the loss. *Not yet. Not until we finish what has to be done.*

"I think so," Rigan replied. He tried to take a step and his leg gave out, but he caught himself on the table and straightened. He took another step without falling, and then another. A sheen of sweat on his face testified to the exercise of will required.

"Damian said you needed to rest."

"I'm all right for now."

"I am not losing both of you," Corran growled.

"I'll take care of it—later. We have work to do," Rigan said, pain evident beneath his steel resolve. "It won't get any easier."

Corran found solace in the comforting familiarity of mixing the pigments. The smell of the ingredients and the motion of grinding and stirring anchored his shattered concentration. His thoughts were jumbled, his mind hazy with grief. Periodically, he listened for the creak of a riser or the sound of Kell's voice, and every disappointment plunged him further into darkness.

Rigan worked without speaking, crying silently, shoulders shaking. His hair fell to cover his face as he bent over his work.

The tears Corran did not shed made his throat burn and his eyes sting. Memories returned, of the night he and Rigan had prepared the materials when their mother readied their father's body for burial.

Of another night, when the three brothers had worked together to bury their mother. *It wasn't supposed to be like this,* he thought, blinking until his vision cleared. But Corran knew the truth of it. *It was going to be one of us, sooner or later, with me fighting for the hunters and Rigan with his magic. I just never thought it would be Kell.*

Rigan brought him the wash, redolent with hyssop, asphodel, and cypress, a mixture said to ease a spirit's transition to the After. Candles added the scent of myrrh and rosemary. Usually, Corran found the blend of fragrances comforting, but tonight, comfort was nowhere to be found.

Corran cursed under his breath as they stripped away Kell's blood-soaked clothing, exposing livid bruises and deep gashes. It was a last favor to the dead to purify the body, to send them to the After ready to meet the gods, a sacramental dignity. Tonight, it just reminded Corran of how young Kell was, and how much life had been forfeited. The water washed away the blood and covered the smell of death. Corran moved through the process slowly, feeling like he had aged decades in the last candlemarks. *Or maybe I'm just dreading what comes next.*

Corran turned to stare at the wall of undertaker's tools for removing the organs of the deceased. He could not find the will to take them up. "I can't," he said raggedly. "Not after all they did to him. I just can't."

Many of the dead go to the Gods without that done. I don't want to remember him like that. Their mother had spared the three of them seeing the final step in preparing their father's body, and Corran kept Rigan and Kell from that view as a last memory when she died. Now, just the thought pushed him beyond the limits of his strength.

"They broke his ribs," Rigan said in a flat, cold voice. Corran needed a moment before he could speak.

"Hand me the cloth strips. We'll bind them," Corran said.

"It's too late for that."

Corran's rage flared. "Do it!" Rigan stared at him for a moment and then complied. He lifted Kell's slim shoulders as Corran passed the linen around and around the body. Corran's hands shook, and his stomach tightened with pain and anger. Pale, silent, eyes hooded, Rigan looked like it took all his will to remain standing. *Whatever he did back at the warehouse took a toll. He needs to heal, more than he's letting on. When this is over, we need to talk. I don't want to lose him to his magic.*

"Hand me the pigments," Corran said. His voice sounded strange and distant. Rigan brought the bowls of red, blue, white, and black paste and set them next to Kell's body. "Sing with me. I can't do it alone. Not tonight."

Corran swallowed hard and dipped his thumb into the white pigment. His first attempt to sing the sacred chant was a dry croak. He took a deep breath and this time, Rigan's quiet tenor joined him.

The words of the death song had always given Corran peace, even when he had buried his parents. No solace was to be found tonight.

Open the gate, for the fallen
Make clear the path.
Accept this soul, we beseech you.
Lead this spirit in the paths of light
To the Golden Shores.
Protect it from the darkness
And keep it from straying into the
House of the Destroyer.
For this soul has been blessed.
This spirit seeks your protection.
Hear me, gods and spirits, for I am he who digs the grave.
All is ready. Gifts and offerings have been made
And now deliver this soul
To safe and final rest.

Doharmu, attend!
Oj and Ren, Eternal Mother and Forever Father, hear me!
Open your arms, and accept this soul
Safe and peacefully into the sanctuary of your Golden Shores.
Let it be so. Let it be so.

Corran and Rigan made their way through the death chant, and though their voices wavered and caught, they managed to complete the litany. Only when they were finished did Corran dare look at his brother, and saw that Rigan's face was as tear-stained as his own.

Rigan marked a sigil in ochre on Kell's abdomen, a dark orange slash against his pale skin, the mark for 'life.' He drew another complicated marking with white chalk on the chest, just above the linen strips that bound Kell's ribs, this time for 'breath.' Blue woad sealed Kell's lips with another sigil, the sign for 'spirit.' The final rune was drawn in soot on Kell's forehead, for 'soul.'

"It's done," Corran said, his voice tight. "I just wish we could say goodbye."

A strange look crossed Rigan's face. "Maybe we can."

"What are you talking about?" Corran said, uneasy at the look in Rigan's eyes.

Rigan stretched out his hand, palm down, over the first sigil. His eyes closed, his tear-streaked face tight with concentration. After a few seconds, the ochre sigil began to glow.

"What are you doing?" Corran stared at the glowing rune.

Rigan's hand hovered above the second marking, and the white sigil glowed almost too bright for Corran to look at. Next, the blue mark that sealed Kell's lips burned like the summer sky. Finally, Rigan held his hand steady above the soot mark on Kell's forehead, and pinpricks of light shone from the darkness like stars.

I'm sorry.

The voice startled both of them. Kell's apparition stood at the head of the table that bore his body. Corran stepped back, heart pounding.

Rigan opened his eyes, his expression a mix of amazement and satisfaction.

"Is it really you?" Corran managed to ask, though his mouth was dry.

Kell's ghost nodded. *I can't stay. But I wanted to say goodbye. And I'm sorry that I got caught. Thanks for—* he gestured toward the preparations they had made for his corpse.

Corran's knees felt weak and his chest ached. "It's too soon. This wasn't supposed to happen."

Kell's expression was somber. *I don't want to leave. The guards loosed the monster to cover up the killings. They're using the creatures. Stop them.*

"Go in peace," Corran said in a strangled voice. "We won't ever forget you, Kell."

Kell smiled sadly and the look in his eyes told Corran that everything he wanted to say and couldn't was already understood. Love, forgiveness, grief—acknowledged and shared. Kell looked as if he were about to answer, but the image began to waver, fading. Corran could not make out the words Kell's lips formed. The image winked out, just as quickly as it had appeared.

Rigan slumped to the floor.

"Oh, gods! What did you do?" Corran dropped to his knees beside his brother, realizing that throughout the exchange with Kell's ghost, Rigan had said nothing. "Come on!" Corran urged with a note of desperation in his voice. Rigan lay still, deathly pale and unresponsive, breath slow and shallow.

"Dammit! I'm not losing both of you! Come on, Rigan! Stay with me." He felt for a pulse, and found one, though his brother's erratic heartbeat and clammy skin fueled his panic.

Corran grabbed a bucket of cold water and a bottle of whiskey. He doused Rigan with the frigid water. To his relief, his brother sputtered and roused, blinking through the icy rivulets that ran down his face. Corran knelt and forced Rigan's mouth open, trickling the strong whiskey between his lips. Rigan gasped, turning his head, and motioned for Corran to stop.

"What did you do?" Corran demanded.

"I learned how to summon spirits as well as banish them," Rigan replied in a hoarse whisper. "It's like confessing the dead, only a bit different. I've been using it to find out more about how magic is being used to conjure the monsters. The spell works, but there's a cost."

"What kind of cost?"

"A thread of my soul."

Corran stared at Rigan, speechless and stunned. Finally, he found his voice. "Why didn't you tell me? Why did you risk yourself?" *How many threads are in a soul?*

Rigan's gaze held the same pain Corran felt. "Because we all needed one last moment together." He broke down, sobbing. Corran folded him against his shoulder, holding him close as he had not done since Rigan was a small boy, letting him cry, as Corran's own tears ran hot down his cheeks. Finally, his brother pushed away, and dragged his sleeve across his eyes.

"Come on," he said, not daring to look at Corran. "We've got to finish this."

CORRAN AND RIGAN took turns carrying Kell's shrouded body and their shovels to the cemetery. The body cart was still missing.

Just in case, they'd brought weapons. *We're in so deep at this point, there's no turning back. If the guards catch us with Kell's body, we'll hang. Might as well hang for being armed, too.*

Behind them, the horizon glowed. The fire in the warehouse had spread, and in the distance, Corran could hear shouts as Wrighton mustered to fight the blaze. Add that to what was still aflame from the riot near the harbor, and it would be a wonder if half of Ravenwood was not in cinders by morning.

Just a day before, that possibility would have terrified Corran.

Funny how loss changes your perspective. "At least the guards have something better to do than search the graveyard," he muttered, grateful for the distraction.

Moonlight lit their way. Once they were within the cemetery, Rigan lit a lantern, shuttering it to dim the glow. The cemetery was empty, even of the restless spirits and bobbing orbs that sometimes watched their work.

"If we bury him with the Undertakers' Guild, someone will notice," Rigan warned.

"I know. We'll have to put him in the back."

Even in the dim light, Corran could see the anger in Rigan's face at this final indignity, burying their brother in a pauper's grave.

"What if we put him with Mama and Papa?" Rigan asked. "If we're careful removing the sod, it might not be noticed."

Corran nodded. "All right. Let's get it done."

Corran laid Kell's body gently on the grass, then closed his eyes and swallowed. As long as he did not think of the shrouded body being Kell, he could function. Picking up a shovel, he began to dig.

Rigan stayed above on watch. Corran was surprised Rigan could walk, let alone consider digging the grave. *I've got to get him to rest—to do whatever he needs to heal—or I'll have lost them both.*

When the grave was ready, Rigan handed Kell's body down to Corran, who laid their brother out on the cold dirt before saying a final farewell. Together, he and Rigan filled the grave, and the slip and crunch of the shovels in dirt was the only awful sound in the still night air.

They finished, and Corran moved to pick up his cloak. Rigan hung back. "What are you doing?" Corran asked.

Rigan set a bowl at the head of the grave with a candle in it. "How much do you want vengeance?"

"With every fiber in my body."

"What about your soul?" Rigan asked. Corran met his gaze.

"If that's what it takes. Yes."

"Then there's one place we can turn. Because we won't find justice from anyone else."

The thought of praying to Eshtamon, the ancient god of vengeance, had occurred to Corran, but he had pushed it aside, unwilling to drag Rigan into more danger. Now, he saw calm acceptance in his brother's gaze, the same cold practicality he felt inside, the knowledge that there was nothing left to lose.

"All right," Corran replied. "But we don't have a priest."

Rigan produced a small tray for the offerings, and a few stoppered bottles of incense from a pouch beneath his cloak. "I grabbed a few things while you were getting ready," he said. "I remember what the priest said when he made the vow over the suicide's grave. Even if I get a few of the words wrong, I think the Old Ones care more about intent than form."

There's no going back from this, Corran thought. *But what do we have to lose? The guards will figure out Kell was among the dead when they find the cart. They might be after us already. And if they don't hang us for trying to save Kell, it will be for Rigan's magic or me being a hunter. At least, this way, our deaths have purpose.*

"What now?" Corran asked, coming to stand at the head of the grave.

Rigan set the tray at the foot of the grave, and dug into his pouch for a few silver coins and a ring that had been their father's—offerings to the Old Ones. He walked widdershins around the grave, then reversed his course. Rigan lit the candle in the bowl and stood, raising his face to the sky.

"Eshtamon, lord of the crossroad and the gallows, hear me!" he shouted. "God of the lost and the wronged, hear my prayer. The blood of your children, the Wanderers—our mother's people—runs in our veins." Rigan reached into one of the pouches of incense and sprinkled some of the powder into the candle flame; it sizzled with a reddish glow, and spread the unmistakable smell of myrrh onto the wind.

"Bring vengeance on the ones who took our brother from us, and who caused the deaths of your Wanderers. Punish them, lord of thorns, with your iron teeth and sharp claws. Make us the instrument of your vengeance, and let us rend their flesh and break their bones. Use us to heap lamentations on their heads and destroy their souls."

Corran felt a chill that had nothing to do with the night wind as his brother raised the silver blade in his right hand. A swift cut, and blood ran from the wound he made in his left forearm. He held his arm over the candle, face expressionless, and let the blood drip.

"Once, for the asking. Twice, for the hearing. Thrice—let it be so."

A gust of wind blasted through the cemetery, swaying the trees, nearly taking Corran and Rigan off their feet. They blinked, and a figure stood at the foot of the grave, the silhouette of a man, with a presence that Corran knew in his gut was not mortal.

Corran and Rigan sank to their knees. Corran kept his hand close to his knife, alert to a trick, and noticed that Rigan did the same.

"*Speak.*" The bass rumble of the Elder God's voice echoed from everywhere all at once.

"M'lord," Corran replied. "We ask to be the instruments of vengeance on those who took our family from us."

"*You are a hunter, and the one who called me is a witch. You already fight for vengeance. Why do you trouble me?*"

"There is no justice," Rigan answered, daring to raise his head. "So many dead, and no power cares to stand against the monsters. Give us justice—for our brother, our mother, our father, and for your Wanderers—and we will be your weapons."

"*Has your brother not already paid a high enough price for his bargain?*" Eshtamon's voice rumbled through the night like thunder.

"What do you mean?" Corran asked, stunned.

"*He begged Doharmu for his brothers' safety. His willingness to sacrifice himself if necessary was clear.*"

"Gods, no!" Rigan murmured. "Oh, Kell, what did you do?"

Corran's jaw set, and he glared at the Elder God. "What of our offer?" He would deal with the rest later, if they survived.

"*An interesting bargain.*" Flickering candlelight hid the newcomer's features, but the voice made Corran imagine a gaunt old man with a wily gaze.

The figure appeared to come to a decision. "*I accept your plea, and promise you vengeance. In exchange, I become the guardian of your souls.*" The words felt like ice in Corran's blood. "*You will be my champions, and I your patron.*"

Eshtamon moved closer, but although he passed by the candle, it did not illuminate his face. The old god laid a hand on Corran's head. Corran gasped as power flowed through him, setting every cell on fire.

"*You are my warrior. I cannot make you immortal, but I can bolster you against death. I give you great strength and unflagging stamina. But heed me well, Corran Valmonde. I cannot keep your soul. Eventually, all souls move on. What you do with the gifts I give to you may well cost your soul its final rest and redemption.*"

Eshtamon lifted his hand from Corran's head, and he fell forward onto his hands and knees, trembling as if touched by lightning. He turned to see Eshtamon stepping to Rigan, who faced the dark god, looking pale but resolute.

"*Rigan Valmonde,*" Eshtamon said as he laid his hand on Rigan's head. "*You are my champion mage. I will add to your own power, that you might grow in your magic and become a mighty sorcerer. But beware. Magic always has a price, and even with my gift, it is possible for you to draw too deeply and destroy yourself. If that should happen, your soul will not find its way to the Golden Shores, but will wander the shadowed places for eternity.*"

Eshtamon stepped back from them, onto the freshly turned grave dirt. "*I will come to you again, my champions. I cannot assure victory, but with my gifts, I give you the means to win your vengeance. You have paid a dear price. Use your gifts with care.*" With that, the Elder God vanished, and the candle in the bowl flickered out, leaving them alone in the night.

Chapter Twenty-Nine

CORRAN HALF-DRAGGED, HALF-CARRIED Rigan to their workshop. His brother was barely conscious, murmuring in his delirium, his skin cold and his breathing shallow. Corran focused on putting one foot ahead of the other, all the way back. *Back. Not 'home.' It can never be home without Kell.*

A haze of smoke hung in the air. It was past curfew, but Corran could hear shouts in the distance as Wrighton turned out to fight the blaze. He knew that should have mattered more to him. *But right now, all I care about is getting Rigan back safely.*

With a sigh of relief, Corran turned the key in the door. The shutters were still closed tightly, but he moved with long practice in the dark, guiding Rigan to one of the empty tables.

Normally, the tables would have been full. But Kell's last cartload of bodies was still lost somewhere in Wrighton, and so the workshop was empty. It scared Corran that Rigan said nothing on the long walk back from the cemetery, and that he had allowed Corran to heft him onto the table like a sack of grain. 'Scared' wasn't the right word; 'panicked' was closer to the truth.

This will have all been for nothing if I lose both of them on the same night, Corran thought, too terrified to feel his own exhaustion. He lit a lantern, and brought out the bottle of whiskey. After a moment's hesitation, he went upstairs.

The last time I came up here, Kell was still alive. He pushed the thought out of his mind and found dried meat and cheese for both of them. The embers in the fireplace had grown cold.

At the back of the hearth, an iron cauldron of vegetable stew was still warm. *Kell made that for dinner, before he left to do his rounds. Gods! Was it just a few candlemarks ago? It feels like another lifetime.*

Corran blinked to clear his vision and swallowed hard, then grabbed some bread to go with the meal. He returned to the workroom and found himself at a loss.

"I don't know what to do." Healing a soul-damaged witch had not been covered in his apprenticeship.

"Food might help," Rigan replied. His voice was too quiet. "Rest. Not having to kill anyone for a while, or summon the dead, or sell our souls to an Elder God."

Corran poured him a glass of water and another of whiskey. Rigan reached for the whiskey first, and knocked it back as his brother helped him sit, then lowered him back down.

"Eat." Corran pulled off bite-sized pieces of bread and gave them to Rigan so that he did not have to sit up again. He broke off bits of cheese and meat as well. Rigan ate, then asked for water. His gaze slid toward the whiskey bottle, but he didn't ask.

"You're still pale, and you're too cold."

"I just need to rest."

Maybe in the morning, I can get Parah to come. Her plant medicine can cure a lot. And I think she knows something of magic. Morning can't be too far away by now. Gods! It feels as if we've lived days since sundown.

Corran watched his brother drift into an uneasy sleep. He ate his portion of the cheese and meat, and choked down the bread although his stomach was too tight with grief and worry to feel hunger. Even the slug of whiskey barely helped.

I'm exhausted, and Rigan looks worse. Is there a limit on how much magic someone can do in one day? He's used a lot in just a few candlemarks. How do I fix it? And if I can't fix it, how do I find Aiden before it's too late?

Urgent knocking rattled the back door. Rigan tried to sit up, but Corran pushed him back. "I'll get it." He reached for a knife and kept it hidden behind his back as he went to the door.

"Corran! It's Mir. Let me in."

Corran opened the door and the blacksmith slipped inside. "There's trouble, Corran."

"Not tonight, Mir. I can't." Corran was blocking Mir's view of the workshop and Rigan lying on the table. The questions Mir might ask were too dangerous and the answers too painful.

"Corran, the guards are blaming the fires and the deaths on the hunters. You've got to find Rigan and Kell and get out before we all hang."

Corran stared at him. "Kell's dead. The guards—"

"Oh, gods." Mir looked stricken. "When?"

"Tonight. We just buried him."

"I'm so sorry, Corran. But the guards are coming. You've got to get out of here."

"And go where?"

"Below." Corran and Mir turned to look at Rigan, who was rising to a sitting position by sheer strength of will. He looked awful, but a resolute gleam burned in his eyes and the set of his lips warned Corran not to challenge him. "I can get you to sanctuary."

Mir looked from Rigan to Corran. "All right. Grab what you can carry and let's move. The guards are likely headed here right now."

Corran dashed up the stairs. He grabbed two rucksacks and stuffed them with clothes. On impulse, he reached for the dice and cards the three brothers had often played with in the evening, and a small carved wooden bird their father had made for Kell. He snatched the last of the dried meat, cheese, and bread, along with a full wineskin. Finally, he dug in a drawer for candles, and took two small lanterns from hooks on the wall. Flint and steel were always in his pocket. Noises below told him Rigan and Mir were gathering essential tools to carry on their trade.

Corran looked around at the only home he and Rigan had ever known. *It's just a house now, without Mama and Papa and Kell. Just a shell.*

Pounding at the door to the front of the shop roused him.

"Corran, hurry!" Mir hissed.

Corran shouldered the packs and took the steps two at a time. Rigan was on his feet, and a slight shake of his head told Corran not to try to offer assistance, though he saw that Rigan had grabbed his staff as a walking stick. Mir carried a bag with the undertakers' tools. Corran swirled his cloak around his shoulders and tossed Rigan's cloak to him, grabbing his own staff and sword. Rigan had two long knives thrust through his belt.

"Let's go!" Mir stood at the alley door. The guards were still pounding at the front, but it wouldn't take them long to think to check the back.

"Someone's betrayed us," Corran said. *Are they here to capture me, for being a hunter? Or to take Rigan as a witch? How were we found out? Were we sloppy in hiding ourselves, or is there a traitor among us?*

"Follow me," Rigan said, leading the way. They hurried as fast as they dared, and Rigan set the pace, moving far more quickly than Corran expected. Shouting carried on the night air as the guards finally broke down the shop door.

Corran heard a crash, then a short while later, an explosion. He glanced behind and saw the shop—their home—go up in flames. *That was too close.*

"Thanks," Corran murmured to Mir.

"The others are at the new training site. How do we get them Below?"

Rigan veered into an alley, then down a ginnel so narrow he had to turn sideways and suck in his stomach to fit. He opened a grate at ground level just wide enough for them to wiggle through, and they came out in a musty cellar.

"Where's this sparring room of yours?" Rigan might be going on nothing but willpower, but the set to his jaw told Corran that his brother had resolved to see this through.

"In the basement of the old bakery, up from the butcher shop. It's only a few blocks away.

"There's a way up from Below near there." Rigan saw the hunter's dubious expression and shrugged. "There are connections to Below just about everywhere in Wrighton, if you know where to look."

"Hurry," Corran urged. Mir had a shuttered lantern, and now he opened it enough for them to see. Corran let out a breath of relief, glad that Rigan did not have to summon the hand-fire he had used before, or that they did not have to reveal his brother's secret just yet. *I trust the hunters with my life. But can I trust them with Rigan's life?*

Rigan wound his way through a maze of cellars, passageways, and tunnels. *How did he have time to explore all of this? Or is it the magic guiding him?* Corran glanced at his brother, worried that any new expenditure of power would come at a dear cost.

"We're here."

Corran and Mir looked at Rigan.

"The old bakery should be just a short distance past that door." Rigan leaned heavily on the staff, his eyes fever-bright. Corran knew better than to say anything. *It's been a long night, for both of us. And likely to get longer.*

"I'd rather not get jumped by a bunch of nervous hunters," Corran said to Mir. "I'm not up to another fight. You want to go first?" He could hear familiar voices talking in low tones. Mir gave the knock that was the hunters' signal and the voices fell silent.

"It's me, Mir," he called quietly through the old door. "I've got Corran and his brother with me. For the gods' sake, don't attack."

Despite the warning, Mir opened the door carefully, and held his lantern high so that there could be no mistaking his identity. When none of the hunters moved, Mir stepped through the doorway, followed by Corran and Rigan.

"What's going on outside?" Calfon moved forward to shake Corran's hand. He took in his injuries at a glance, and then frowned as he looked at Rigan.

"Nothing good," Corran replied. "This is Rigan, my brother."

Calfon, Trent, and Ross nodded in acknowledgement. "We can use reinforcements," Calfon said to Rigan, who gave a weary nod. "Glad you made it," he added, turning to Mir and Corran. "But you might have just come to the slaughter pen. We've been debating whether to wait and see what happens, or find a way out, beyond the city walls. The Mayor's guards have less authority out there. They might not be able to track us."

"I can hide you Below."

They turned to look at Rigan.

"Going Below is as dangerous as walking into a guardhouse," Calfon replied.

"Not if you know what you're doing. Not if you have friends."

Calfon regarded Rigan as if retaking his measure. "And you have friends Below?"

"Teachers. They can shelter us, or get us out," Rigan replied.

Calfon's gaze flicked to Corran, who nodded.

"He's telling the truth."

Calfon looked to Ross, Trent, and the others. "Anybody got a better idea?"

They shook their heads.

"All right," Calfon replied, looking at Rigan. "Below it is. How do we get there?"

* * *

THEY TOOK ALL the weapons they could carry. Rigan was the only one not burdened with gear. Corran guessed that the others saw the same brittle resolve as he did and realized that Rigan already had all he could handle just staying on his feet.

Rigan led them through rat-infested basements, along reeking drains, and long-buried streets that had not seen the light of day in generations. How he knew where he was going, Corran hadn't a clue, but his brother moved with the certainty of a dog on a hunt. The group moved through the ruins in silence, speaking only when necessary. In the stillness, the reality of their situation finally caught up with Corran.

Kell's dead. The shop, the house—gone. The guards have to know I'm a hunter, or they wouldn't have set the shop on fire. I'm a wanted criminal. And Rigan—he'll burn if they find out what he is.

We indebted ourselves to an Elder God for vengeance; and Eshtamon's gifts came with dark warnings. What have we gotten ourselves into?

More to the point, can we get ourselves out?

"We've been walking a long time." Calfon stopped and wiped his sleeve across his brow. "Do you really know where you're going?"

"We've been in Below this whole time. It's big. As big underneath as all the neighborhoods are above," Rigan said.

"If this is Below, there's no one home," Ross ventured.

"We're taking the back way," Rigan replied. "Some of the people who live Below go Above as well. If the Mayor's put a bounty on us, there's no sense tempting fate."

Corran hadn't thought about that. The implication made him catch his breath. *It's never going to be the way it was. No matter how tonight ends, everything we knew is gone forever.*

Rigan led them a bit farther, then stopped. "I need you to wait here."

Calfon looked skeptical. "Why?"

"Because I want to make sure my teachers are all right with guests," Rigan replied.

"And if they're not?" There was a growl beneath Calfon's tone; the hunter was clearly close to the breaking point.

"Then we go now. Take the passage beneath the walls and out of the city, tonight," Rigan answered.

Rigan opened a door and moved forward, and Corran grabbed his arm. "Not alone." Rigan was barely staying on his feet. He nodded, relenting.

"We'll be back," Corran told the others, though he could see clearly that being left behind did not sit well with Calfon.

Rigan's lantern lit the way as they moved into the next room. "Something's wrong." He looked around at the too-quiet house. "Damian or Alton—one of the other witches—should have met us at the outer door."

Corran doubted his gut could tighten further, as cold dread knotted in the pit of his stomach. He drew his sword, unsure what good it would be if magic had not sufficed to protect the witches.

Rigan moved from room to room with a familiarity that confirmed Corran's suspicions as to his secret trips Below. One room, a small bedroom, bore evidence of a fight, with an overturned bed and a chest tipped on its side, contents strewn across the floor. Rigan turned a corner, and froze. Corran came up to stand next to him, and saw the bloody handprint on the whitewashed wall. Rigan leaned his staff against the wall and drew his long knife, holding it in his left hand, leaving his right hand free for magic.

He's not up to another fight, certainly not one involving magic. And what can I *do, if the enemy is a witch?*

Rigan moved forward cautiously, with his brother right behind him as they entered a large open room littered with bodies.

"Gods!" Rigan swore in a choked voice. The lantern's light caught the red glint of blood on the floor. He rushed forward, while Corran remained a few steps behind, sword raised, watching Rigan's back and keeping his eye on the door.

"What happened?" Rigan moaned as he moved from body to

body. Corran dared to glance in his brother's direction. He saw no movement from any of the downed witches, and the blood that pooled near his feet was dark and thick, a few candlemarks old.

Rigan looked up at Corran, his expression bereft. "They're all dead."

"Guards?"

Rigan closed his eyes, struggling to push his feelings aside. "I don't think so. The wounds aren't from swords. There are all kinds of injuries. Someone had to have pretty strong magic to do this, and to get inside the wards and this far into the house—it had to be someone they trusted."

Corran watched his brother stagger to his feet and make a slow circle of the room, looking down at the faces of the dead. "People are missing," Rigan said, more to himself than to Corran. "Damian. Alton. Aiden."

"Elsewhere?" Corran asked, worried that any moment Rigan's strength would fade and he would collapse.

"Not many places left to look," Rigan replied, sounding heartsick. Together, he and Corran searched the back rooms, and found no one. They were heading toward the front when a sound made them both go still.

"This way," Rigan whispered, leading them back to the bedroom with the overturned furniture. Swords raised, the brothers came around the upended bed from different sides, and found two people huddled behind it.

Aiden was sheltering a woman beneath his body, and he came up fast, blue light crackling around his hands, ready for a fight. Rigan remained motionless, giving his friend a chance to react.

"You're all right," Rigan said, slowly lowering his sword. Corran did the same, holding his hands out to the side to signal that he posed no threat.

"Rigan?" Aiden slumped, and the blue light faded. "Thank the gods." A bloody gash marred his face above his left eye.

"Glad you're both safe," he said. "Kell?"

Rigan shook his head miserably. "He didn't make it."

"I'm sorry."

At that moment, the woman stirred, and when she sat up, Rigan felt his breath catch in his throat.

"Elinor?"

She startled at his voice, blinked as if she could not be sure of what she saw, and then sagged against Aiden with a relieved smile on her face. "Rigan. You're safe."

"I'm *alive*. I'm not at all sure any of us are safe. We need to get out of here, and then you can tell me what happened. Are you hurt? Can you move?"

"Yeah. The distraction spell kept us from being noticed, but it messes with your head, makes it harder to tell how much time has passed. I think we were under longer than I intended—long enough that it started to wear off, if you saw us."

Corran gave Aiden a hand up, while Rigan helped Elinor to her feet. Aiden glanced at the fresh blood and bruises marring the brothers' faces. "You both look like shit."

"Like Rigan said, let's get out of here, and then we can trade stories," Corran replied.

"And go where?" Rigan asked. "I don't know anywhere else to find shelter Below."

"I do."

They turned to Elinor.

"I wasn't staying with the witches," she said. "I just came here to train. I've got a place we can go."

"We've got others with us," Corran warned. "Hunters." He could see the questions in Elinor's eyes, and expected to have the invitation withdrawn. But to his surprise, she just shrugged.

"Then it'll be a tight fit. Come on."

Elinor led the way.

They found the rest of the hunters waiting in the entry hall, and a whispered, heated argument died at the sound of their approaching footsteps. Calfon was angry, and both Mir and Trent looked like they were moments from taking a swing at him. The others watched in silence.

"We can't stay here," Corran said, cutting off their questions. "But Elinor's got somewhere safe we can go."

"Safe? *This* was supposed to be safe," Calfon challenged. "And when were you going to tell us that your brother's a witch?"

Corran stepped forward, putting himself between Calfon and Rigan. Behind him, Aiden stepped up to stand shoulder to shoulder with Rigan, as did Elinor. "It wasn't hunter business," Corran replied, his voice a low growl. "Now we're getting to safety, with or without you. Either head for the door, or get out of the way."

For a moment, Calfon and Corran stood toe to toe, and Corran braced to defend himself. Finally, Calfon stepped back with a muttered curse. "You'd better be right about this, Valmonde."

Elinor led them through the quiet streets with Aiden beside her. They stayed in the shadows, mindful that whoever had attacked the witches was still at large. Corran remained beside his brother, ready to support him if his strength finally gave out. Rigan kept going, tight-lipped and grim-faced. The hunters surrounded them, half in front, half following behind, weapons hidden but at the ready.

Twists and turns took them through the narrow passages. By now, they were far from the witches' house and the main market, in a less inhabited part of Below. They followed Elinor to an apartment a few steps below the street. A lantern glowed behind the shutters. Elinor motioned for them to stay back as she approached the door and rapped out a pattern on the wood.

"You'll be the death of me, Elinor!" Polly said, opening the door. "Where in the name of the gods have you been?"

Elinor managed a wan smile. "It's a long story. And I brought friends."

Polly looked up, frowning as she recognized faces from Above, her gaze coming to rest on Corran and Rigan. "Well, don't just stand there," she said, hands on her hips. "Come in. But you'd best plan to find your own food, because I'm not cooking for the lot of you."

Rigan collapsed just inside the doorway, and Corran caught him, breaking his fall. Aiden pushed forward, helping him ease his brother to the floor.

"Get him into the back room," Elinor said, motioning for them to follow her. Corran and Aiden carried Rigan into the back.

The dim lantern light revealed two cots and the meager personal items Elinor and Polly managed to bring with them when they fled. Corran and Aiden settled Rigan onto one of the cots. Voices sounded in the other room; Polly sounded like she was giving the hunters a stern warning about minding their manners.

"What do you need?" Elinor asked.

Aiden rattled off a list of herbs. "I'll also need hot water to make tea and mix a poultice."

"Can you help him?" Corran asked.

Aiden frowned, skimming a hand above Rigan's body. "I'll do what I can. I've used a lot of power just keeping Elinor and me alive."

"I'll be back in a moment to help," Elinor promised, then fled to gather the items Aiden had requested. Aiden turned his attention back to Rigan. Corran slid down the wall in the corner to sit on the floor, out of the way, feeling utterly helpless.

Aiden took a deep breath and let it out. "You don't really know me. You don't completely trust me. But I am trying to do the best I can for your brother, and I need to know what magic he's done in the last day."

"We found our brother, Kell. He'd been mauled by a monster. We killed the monster."

"With magic?"

Corran shook his head. "No. The old fashioned way. I'm a hunter. Rigan's good with a blade; comes with the business."

"And then?"

Corran ran a hand across his eyes. He could do with another shot of whiskey, or even a cup of coffee, anything to keep him on his feet. "There were guards hiding in the back of the warehouse. They were drunk and they came after us. They taunted us about the way they killed the prisoners and used the monster to cover it up. I killed two of them. Rigan... killed the third."

"Magic?"

"Yeah. There was this glow, the soldier started bleeding, and then he died."

Aiden cursed under his breath. "Anything else?"

"Rigan called a flame to his palm, so we didn't have to use a lantern."

"Minor magic, not too much of a drain. There had to be more."

Corran swallowed. "We got Kell back to the shop. Rigan and I prepared the... prepared Kell for burial." His voice broke, and he looked up at Aiden defiantly. "We were both took it pretty hard. I said that I was sorry we hadn't had the chance to say goodbye, and Rigan did something with his grave magic, and the next moment Kell's ghost was standing by the table. It was really him." Tears streaked down Corran's cheeks, and he brushed them away with the back of his hand.

"How in the name of the gods did Rigan know how to call to the dead?"

"We banish restless spirits. It's part of what undertakers do. But Rigan found out how to summon the ghosts. He's been able to hear their confessions for months now, ever since our mother died."

Aiden cursed again. "And?"

Retelling what happened made Corran realize just how much magic Rigan had used. A cold fear started in the pit of his stomach. "We went to the cemetery. We were both pretty broken up, and we were talking about making someone pay. We'd seen a priest perform a ritual a few weeks ago—"

"You didn't—"

"We prayed to Eshtamon, and sold him our souls."

Aiden went utterly still, and Corran knew a storm was brewing. A faint, blue glow limned the man's outline, then winked away. *Do witches glow when they're angry? Rigan glowed when he killed that guard.*

I have the feeling we're in deep shit.

"And then what?" The healer's voice sounded tight.

"We barely got back to the shop for me to patch Rigan up, when Mir—one of the hunters—came to warn us. So Rigan brought us Below." Corran paused. "We didn't have a choice. If we had stayed, we'd be dead by now. How bad—"

"He's not already dead, so there's a chance he'll pull through," Aiden replied.

"Dead?"

"He hasn't told you much about his magic, has he?"

Corran shook his head, still numb. *Dead. No, not dead. Please, no.*

Aiden turned back to the cot, and his hands moved over Rigan's body, glowing with faint blue light. "Magic done properly draws from the power of the universe around us," Aiden said. "Done wrong, it burns you up from inside. Rigan has the potential to become a powerful witch, but that takes years of training. Native talent alone will get you killed." He shook his head. "The last time Rigan channeled so much power, it almost killed him. What you're telling me—I don't understand how he made it here."

"Eshtamon."

"What?"

"When we made the bargain, Eshtamon called us his champions. He said I'd be hard to kill. And he promised to add to Rigan's magic."

Aiden turned to stare at him. "You didn't just do a ritual or see a figure. An Elder God actually *talked* to you?"

Given the way the night had gone, Corran hadn't considered that remarkable until right now. "I just thought we did the working right."

Aiden cursed. "Well, that explains why he's not dead. It doesn't guarantee that there was no harm done."

Elinor returned with a tray holding all of the items Aiden requested. She knelt on the other side of Rigan's cot. Aiden gave quiet commands and Elinor did what he requested. Rigan lay quiet and still. Corran watched them work, his chest tight with fear. *I'm absolutely useless. My brother is dying, and I'm useless.* Elinor responded efficiently to everything the healer requested, but Corran could see her biting her lip hard enough that it bled. *She's the one Rigan was courting. She really is a witch. If he had any doubts about whether or not she cares for him, I think the answer is right there.*

Corran looked up as someone sat down beside him. Polly had been feisty and sure of herself when they got to the house; now, she looked older and worn. Her eyes were red with tears she was too stubborn to shed, at least, not in public. "Mir told me about Kell," she said. "I'm sorry."

"He liked you a lot," Corran said, hearing his voice hitch and looking away as he squeezed his eyes shut.

"I liked him, too." Pain made her voice raw. "How's Rigan?"

Corran shrugged. "Not good."

"I figured." She was sitting close enough that their shoulders touched, but she made no move to comfort him; just being there was enough. After what seemed like forever, Aiden turned to them.

"Elinor and I have done everything we can," the healer said. "He's a little stronger, but he's been badly drained. Let him sleep. In the morning, once I've rested, I'll do more."

Corran nodded. "Thank you. I'll sit with him."

Aidan barked a laugh. "Beggin' your pardon, but you don't look much better."

"Take my cot," Polly offered. "I'd better go check on the others before they cause a mess. Don't think I'll be sleeping much tonight."

With that, she climbed to her feet, brushed off her skirt, and headed into the next room.

Aiden stood, and Corran realized how wan and pale the healer looked, as if tending to his brother had sapped all of his remaining strength. "I need to find a quiet corner and get some sleep. You could use some, too." He followed Polly into the front room, where Corran could hear the hunters conversing in low voices.

Elinor still knelt beside Rigan, holding his hand. She smoothed a lock of hair out of his face before she realized that Corran was watching her.

"It's all right," Corran said. "He'd like that."

Elinor blushed and looked away. "I'm glad you got out, and I'm sorry about Kell. Was it the monsters?"

Corran shook his head. "Monsters and guards." He swallowed hard. "Thanks for letting us stay." Belatedly, he realized he was covered in blood and grave dirt. *I look like a brigand, or worse.*

Elinor shook her head. "Nice to see faces from home. I don't know what happened, but if you're down here, it must be bad."

"It was."

"You know, there's no one living in the back rooms. They'll need some tidying up, but we're away from any of the main thoroughfares. No one bothers us here. You could do worse for a hideout."

Hideout. Not far from the truth. The hunters were wanted criminals; the Valmonde brothers had attracted the wrong kind of attention. "I'll tell the others," Corran said.

"Polly can get you something to eat."

Corran shook his head. "I don't think I could keep anything down—not with everything that's happened."

"Then get some sleep. I'll sit with Rigan. If anything changes, I'll wake you right away."

Corran wanted to argue, but his body gave him little choice. He stretched out on the cot and fell asleep, too exhausted to dream.

* * *

Being underground and in perpetual night took some getting used to. Corran woke with a start, fighting down panic in the unfamiliar room. A half-shuttered lantern kept them from complete darkness. A moment later, his memories caught up to him, and he looked over to where his brother lay. "Rigan?" he asked quietly, crossing to kneel beside his cot.

Color had returned to Rigan's face, and his chest rose and fell steadily. Lank hair, damp with sweat, fell across his gaunt face; shadows darkened his eyes. Corran felt for a pulse, and closed his eyes, thanking the gods, as he felt a steady beat beneath his fingertips. *That was close. Too close.*

Aiden and Elinor were gone, leaving Corran alone with his brother. He placed one hand around Rigan's, and gently pushed the hair back from his face with the other. "Please don't leave," Corran begged quietly. "I can't lose both of you. Aiden's done all he can. It's up to you now. I know you're tired"—his voice broke and he blinked back tears—"but I can't do this without you. Please, fight the darkness. It's too soon for you to go to the After. Too soon for you to leave. Please, Rigan. I need you. I can't do this alone."

Corran slumped down next to the bed, resting his forehead on the mattress, fingers still twined with Rigan's. He must have fallen asleep, because he did not hear Aiden's approach.

"He's looking better." The healer's voice startled Corran awake. "I'll work on him some more. He'll be all right."

"Thank you."

"Glad I could help. There were so many I couldn't save."

Corran remembered the bodies at the witches' house, and Rigan's conviction that someone had betrayed them. "What happ—?"

Aiden shook his head. "If you don't mind, I'd rather wait until Rigan can join the conversation. I'm not sure, right now, I could get through it myself, and I'd rather not do it twice."

"Fair enough."

"I'll stay with him," Aiden offered. "Go get something to eat. Your hunter friends have been asking for you."

Corran rose and moved stiffly toward the adjacent room. Mir, Calfon, and the others looked up as he entered.

"Is Rigan all right?" Trent asked.

"Aiden says so. He looks better." He sat between Trent and Mir. Polly brought through a tray of bread and honey; adequate provisions given that they had not been expected.

Beyond the light, the darkness seemed thicker than before. The circle of lantern light barely reached all of the hunters. "How did you know to warn us?" Corran asked Mir.

Illir, Ross, Ellis, and Tomor sat in silence, still stunned at their sudden change in fortunes. Dilin, Calfon, and Trent stood near the windows and faced the door to the street, on watch.

"Calfon warned me," Mir replied. "He was just getting home when he saw guards heading to the lamp shop."

"If I had been a few minutes later, I'd probably be dead. I saw the guards heading up the street, so I hung back. They were arguing with my father. I heard my name and I ran," Calfon said.

"Did they—" Corran started, and had to stop to steady his voice. "Did they burn the shop?"

"Is that what happened to you?" Calfon asked, staring at Corran in horror. "Gods, no! At least, not that I saw." He looked stricken. "Do you think they will?"

Corran shrugged. "I don't know. Didn't expect them to burn our place, but they did."

"The Guild is going to have a fit," Ross said.

"They'll disavow us," Trent replied. "Like they did Bant and Pav and Jott. And if our families are smart, they'll go along with it. No reason for them to pay for our mistakes."

"They never brought Pav and the others for burial." The hunters all turned to look at Corran. "I had hoped that, them being Guild, the Mayor would make an exception. But he didn't. And Rigan and I couldn't retrieve the bodies, not without questions being asked on why we were coming to bury three 'traitors.'"

"You did the right thing," Trent said, clapping a hand on Corran's shoulder.

Then why doesn't it feel that way?

"I don't like this, staying Below..." Calfon looked worried, and Corran saw his hand resting on his knife.

"Do you have a better idea?" Corran met his gaze. "Elinor said there are enough empty rooms. We could move in, have a place to stay while we figure out what to do next." He forced himself to drink some of the tea Polly had set out for them, and to choke down a piece of bread, though he was still too worried and grief-stricken to be hungry.

"How's Rigan?" Mir asked.

"He pushed himself too hard. I just came through to make sure you were all right. I'll go back to him in a moment."

"We're on the run, there are probably bounties on our heads, we're hiding Below," Mir replied. "I'm not sure any of that counts as 'all right.'"

"It's got to be better than where we were," Trent said.

"If Rigan's a witch, he could have fought beside us," Calfon said.

"And brought the guards down on our heads," Corran said, his voice strained by tiredness. "He's new to magic. He hasn't yet learned to control his powers. That's what made him sick."

"Back off, Calfon," Trent said. "We can talk about this later. Corran's had a bad night. We could all use some rest. It's thanks to Rigan we're safe."

"We need a plan," Calfon replied.

"Yep," Corran agreed. "And you're welcome to stay up talking about it. But I'm going to go sit in Rigan's room until he wakes. I'll see you in the morning—or whatever counts for it down here."

He walked back to the small bedroom, and found Aiden next to Rigan's bed.

"He's doing better," Aiden assured him. "He'll wake soon, once he's ready."

"How many threads are in a soul?" Corran blurted out the question that had been worrying him since his brother's collapse in the workshop.

"No one knows. Maybe it's different for everyone. Souls can't really be unwoven; it's just a phrase, a way to picture something that can't be seen."

"So there's a limited number of times he can do a working like the one he did last night, but no way to know how many?" *If that's how magic actually works, it's a fool's bargain.*

"No set number, not that I've ever read."

"I don't mean to sound ungrateful. I'm glad we could tell Kell goodbye. But not if it costs me Rigan, too."

"Your brother has talent, and the bargain you made enhanced that. Right now, we won't know his limits until he hits them." Aiden held out his hand a few inches above Rigan's chest. "He's regaining his strength."

"What, exactly, is happening in this trance he's in?"

"Elinor and I are sustaining him," Aiden replied, as if it was the most obvious thing in the world. "We're contributing a little of our own energy and magic to bring him back, give him strength."

"Bring him back? From where?"

"The edge. A witch can spend so much of his own life energy that he runs out. The body remains, might even function, but the witch's essence is gone. Rigan was close to that edge."

Corran watched his brother's chest rise and fall, and felt for a pulse, reassuring himself. He sat on the floor next to the cot, wondering how long it had been since they left the workshop. *Several candlemarks, at least. Maybe half a day. Probably light outside by now. How much of Wrighton is burning? And did the guards burn the shop because of Kell, or Rigan, or me? Gods, we've made a mess of things.*

Chapter Thirty

Rigan woke slowly. Pain came first—a dull, bone-deep ache. Still, less pain than before, and breathing came easier, too. He heard a hum of voices in the distance. Their presence comforted him, letting him know he was not alone in the dark. The darkness rolled in and out like the tide, pulling him under and lifting him back up. Rigan did not fight it.

Gradually, the black waves subsided, and as they drew back, he came to himself. He opened his eyes and stared at the ceiling. Guttering candles in the lanterns cast wildly flickering shadows across the walls.

"Rigan?" Corran's voice cut through the last of the fog.

"How... long?" The words felt like ash in his dry mouth.

Corran lifted him up and pressed a cup against his lips. "Seems like forever. Can't tell time in this damned place. Probably overnight. How do you feel?"

It all came crashing back—Kell's savaged body; the fight in the warehouse; the cemetery and the oath to Eshtamon; fleeing the guards with the city burning behind them. He swallowed hard. "Tired. But I don't think I'm dying anymore."

Corran's hand tightened on his arm. "Aiden says it was too damn close."

"I remember getting to the witches' house, finding the bodies—with Aiden and Elinor alive—then nothing after that," Rigan said.

Corran filled him in on what had happened. "Aiden said he'd tell us about what happened with the witches once you were awake," he concluded.

Rigan was quiet for a few moments. "I'm not sure how long we can stay here."

"Calfon had some opinions on that last night. I put him off until I knew you were going to be all right."

Rigan wondered if he looked as spent as he felt, and from the worry he saw in his brother's expression, gathered that was the case. They both looked up as Aiden entered.

"Good to see you awake," he said, with a nod to Rigan. "Feeling better?"

"Yeah. Thanks for fixing me up."

"Thank Elinor and Polly—they took the lot of us in," Aiden replied. He knelt beside Rigan's cot and passed a hand over his body, eyes closed. Finally, he opened his eyes. "Better."

"There wasn't much room for 'worse,'" Rigan said.

"Aiden, you said you'd tell us what happened," Corran prompted. "If there's someone out there after Rigan—besides the guards and the witch finders—we need to know about it."

Aiden swallowed hard and sat down on the floor. "Damian and Alton," he said in a tight voice. Rigan stared at Aiden in disappointment, if not quite shock.

"Damian?"

Aiden had a sick look on his face. "I didn't want to believe it, either. Maybe if I'd let myself put the pieces together sooner, I could have stopped it then, but I just didn't think... I have a touch of foresight, but it's not consistent. It doesn't always come to me when I need it to, but sometimes it does." He glanced at Rigan. "It's how

I knew to come to your workshop the night you almost died. How I was able to meet you halfway when you needed me to save Corran. It's a skill that I never revealed to Damian, or any of the others. I'm not sure when I stopped trusting Damian," Aiden admitted. "I never really liked Alton. He was a sanctimonious prick."

He sighed and looked down. "Maybe it was because Damian always seemed to have a reason to be going Above. None of the rest of us went more than we had to. After all, we'd gone to live Below for a reason."

"Do you know where Damian and Alton went after they killed the others?" Rigan asked. Corran glanced at his brother, hearing an edge in his voice he had only heard once before—in the barn where Rigan had killed Kell's tormentor. A whisper of cold slithered down Corran's back at the hard glint in his brother's eyes.

"No. I don't think they stayed Below," Aiden replied. "But I'd better not see them again."

"Why did they do it?" Corran asked. "I don't know anything about magic, but why would they turn on their own?"

"I don't know. I've been asking myself that, and I just don't know. But I did find out something else that I didn't have time to tell anyone before... everything happened."

"What's that?" Corran asked.

"I'm certain that magic is behind at least some of the monster attacks," Rigan said. "I've been gathering evidence for a while now, and there's no doubt in my mind—someone very powerful is summoning the monsters, and using them to keep the rest of us under control."

"How do you know this?" the healer asked.

"I can hear the confessions of the dead," Rigan replied. "And sometimes, the dead understand things after they've crossed over that they didn't realize before. Perspective, I guess. Things the ghosts said to me started to add up, made me wonder whether the monsters weren't being controlled somehow."

"You think magic is involved?" Aiden said.

"Oh, I think monsters have always been present. Every old book I could get my hands on in the sanctuary's library talks about them. But there were hints, things said in riddles and ideas in between the lines that made me suspect that sometimes, witches with the right kind of power can summon such creatures and make them do their bidding. And I think it's got something to do with the Balance."

Corran looked up sharply and frowned. "Why?"

"Something a Wanderer woman said to me made me wonder, and one of the ghosts told me more," Rigan replied. "What everyone we know talks about—the idea of good balancing out bad—I don't think that's it at all. If I've put the pieces together right, someone powerful, important—the Lord Mayor, someone like that—is using blood magic, and all the death and pain caused by the monsters and guards feeds his power. And that… that blood magic has to be accounted for—*balanced*. I think that's what *the Balance* really is. But I think they've stepped over a line, tipped the Balance somehow, and that led to problems, like more vengeful ghosts. I suspect whoever it is—and his blood witch—are drawing more out than they can put in themselves, and if it weren't for the killing and the fear, they'd lose control over the magic. Hence the monsters."

"Sweet Eshtamon," Corran murmured.

"Did Damian know what you were researching?" Aiden asked.

Guilt glinted in Rigan's eyes. "I asked Baker about the monsters, and she told me what she knew. Later on, I brought it up with Damian, but something about his reaction made me drop it. I didn't completely trust him, so I never brought it up again."

"How long ago was this?"

Rigan shrugged. "Maybe a few weeks. No more than that."

"That's when some of the old books went missing. I didn't think anything of it at the time, but I went looking for some rituals and healing lore, and several of the manuscripts were gone. I just thought one of the others had borrowed them for a working. Now I'm wondering if your questions made Damian nervous and he didn't want you to find what you were looking for."

"Is it true?" Rigan turned to meet Aiden's gaze. "Can witches summon and bind monsters?"

"I don't know." Aiden's voice was raw and honest. "I'm just a healer, with a little foresight that's none too reliable. I can't do the big magic. None of the witches Below are true mages. More than a hedge witch, less than a wizard—a lot less. Still enough to be worth a noose Above."

"Was there a bargain, that no monsters would come Below if the witches didn't go Above?" Corran asked, remembering something Rigan had said.

"I've always suspected it," Aiden replied. "It was too clean a coincidence without some kind of deal. We stayed Below, didn't meddle, didn't get the in the way, and in exchange, the guards left Below alone."

"And so do the monsters. Which suggests they go where they're told," Rigan said.

"Yeah. I never thought about it, but that would make sense."

"So why break the deal now?" Corran mused. "If the witches of Below weren't powerful enough to pose a threat, why murder them?"

"Maybe whoever is summoning the monsters didn't want to take a chance," Rigan said. "Maybe the stakes have changed, and the mage didn't want to risk having his plans upended. Maybe we became a threat to the Balance."

Rigan looked from Aiden to Corran. "If that's true, staying Below isn't safe for us—any of us. If the deal is broken, then we're not safe from guards *or* monsters—and Damian might come back to finish what he started."

"We're safer here than Above, at least for a while," Corran countered. "If the monsters come, let them. We'll hunt them, make ourselves useful. And if you're right," he added, looking from Rigan to Aiden, "then we need to find the sons of bitches who are summoning the monsters and make them pay. Make it end."

"That kind of magic is rare—and expensive," Aiden said. "If your guess is right, Rigan, we could be going up against the Lord Mayor—and powerful witches."

"That might explain why the Lord Mayor is so against witches that don't work for him—or Wanderers," Corran mused. "He's not going to want to risk any sort of opposition."

Rigan looked to Aiden. "We need to know more about what kind of magic it takes to summon the monsters. If the books here are missing, can we find more outside the city walls?"

Aiden considered for a moment, frowning. "Maybe," he said. "There are monasteries with libraries. We might be able to find something there."

"Are you crazy?" Corran challenged. "Leaving Ravenwood is far too dangerous."

"What if we could end this?" Rigan said, meeting Corran's gaze. "We sold our souls to the god of vengeance. He made us his champions."

"I figured that was more of an honorary title."

"Don't think so—I'm still alive."

Corran flinched. "All right," he said, lifting his hands in a placating gesture. "Let's just say that we didn't imagine the whole thing, that Eshtamon really came, really gave us a... calling." He passed a hand over his face. "Gods, I can't believe I'm saying this."

"You can't doubt it, Corran," Rigan said. "We want to avenge Kell, and we promised vengeance for the Wanderers, too. If we can stop whoever's controlling the monsters, we'll have what we asked for."

"Big task for two people, don't you think?"

"No one said you had to do it on your own." They turned to look at Aiden, and then Corran's gaze traveled beyond the healer to see

Elinor and Trent standing in the doorway. He wondered how much they had heard, until he saw the look of quiet determination in their eyes.

"We're in this to the hilt now," Trent said. "We've been talking, and we've agreed: we're staying. We'll clean out the back rooms, hunker down until we can figure out a plan. And in the meantime, if the monsters start coming Below now that the witches are gone, we'll do what we've been doing—kill the miserable bastards."

"I can live with that," Corran said. He glanced at Rigan. "We both can."

"I'm not a fighter, but it sounds like you could use a healer," Aiden volunteered. "If we can find enough old books and manuscripts, we stand a good chance of figuring out how to fight Damian and Alton when they show up again, and take down whoever's behind this."

"Where are you going to find books like that?" Trent asked.

"Those monasteries I mentioned? They were abandoned after the League seized them. They belonged to the Elder Gods, and the League wanted allegiance given to the Guild gods," Aiden said. "They left the temples here in the city—must have feared a revolt if they tore them down—but regular people didn't care as much about the monasteries. Some of them are in the city, but most are outside the wall. I'm guessing the monks who lived there fled or were killed. The League left them to rot. The monasteries outside the wall are our best bet. Once you're feeling better, I say we go do some looting for the cause."

"I know a place you can start."

Polly had joined them. She looked uncomfortable, and covered her discomfort with defiance. *Oh, yeah, she and Kell would have made a good pair,* Corran thought, his heart clenching. "What kind of place?"

Polly managed a smug grin. "I've been mapping the ruined parts of Below. Something to do, you know? There are whole areas where no one goes, no one lives. It's not real... safe. The buildings are in bad shape. Roofs caved in, floors rotted. I was exploring one day and I found a library in what's left of one of the buildings. Most of the shelves were empty, but one whole section was blocked with wood and rubble, so there might be something that got left behind. I left everything where I found it, but I can take you back there."

"As soon as I'm back on my feet," Rigan promised.

"I'll go with you," Aiden replied. "And in the meantime, I want to go back to the witch house and take any books Damian left behind. He might have missed something."

"Count me in," Elinor added. "Don't know that I'd be much good in a fight, but there's strength in numbers."

"It's a start," Corran said, meeting Trent's gaze. "More than we'd have Above."

And maybe, just maybe, a chance.

Chapter Thirty-One

A WEEK LATER, monsters came Below.

"They're *lida*," Calfon reported to the group gathered in the bare living space they had cleared for themselves behind Elinor and Polly's rooms.

They were sheltered and relatively safe. Aiden, Polly, and Elinor taught them the basics on how to survive Below, and so far, the Lord Mayor's guards had been mercifully absent, as had Damian and Alton. Corran was happy for any break they got.

"They're coming in through the sewers," Trent added. "Below connects through drains, sewers, even some chimneys. That's how we get enough fresh air down here to keep from suffocating. But if the air can get out—"

"Other things can get in," Corran supplied.

Trent nodded. "The best way I can describe *lida* is maggots the size of a man's arm. They ooze a poison that breaks down skin, and they swarm, eating their prey in layers as the poison dissolves muscle until there's nothing left but bone. Oh, and they move fast and attack in groups—hundreds at a time."

Illir looked queasy. "That's just wonderful."

Calfon grimaced. "If you go down under a dozen of them, they can strip skin from bone in minutes."

Corran shuddered, and he saw the same reaction from the others. "What kills them?"

"Fire, for certain," Calfon replied.

"They don't like salt, but it won't kill them," Ross added. "Burning and crushing are our best bets. Hacking them up is tricky—do it wrong and you just make more of them."

"Illir and Dilin scouted the area where the *lida* were sighted," Calfon continued. "We're pretty sure they're coming in through the drains, up from the harbor. There are catch basins beneath the grates in the streets Above. They empty into deeper drains that run down to the harbor. That's where the *lida* are."

"What weapons do we use?" Trent asked.

Calfon gave a wicked grin and held up a pottery oil lantern, about the size of an apple. "Got us plenty of these and a good bit of oil. We pair up, go into the drains, and when we find the *lida*, lay down a wide patch of oil. Lure the *lida* into the oil, then light the lamps and hurl them, to set the oil on fire. Poof!" he said, clapping his hands. "Cooked *lida*."

"It could work." Corran liked the idea of fire traps in the drains much better than trying to hack their way through a pile of giant flesh-eating maggots.

"You think your brother and Aiden would help us?" Trent asked.

Corran shook his head. "Sorry, but they just left with Polly to go scout the ruins for more books. The sooner they can figure out the magic behind the monsters, the sooner we can stop whoever's summoning the creatures. Elinor's agreed to stay here so we have someone watching out for both groups."

"Same fight, different battle. All right, then. It's daylight Above. We don't want to attract attention, and sending smoke up out of the drains will definitely do that. So we wait until after curfew, and go out when there are fewer people to see the smoke," Trent said.

"And hope that the guards figure they don't get paid enough to check out the drains, if they do see something," Tomor added, raising an eyebrow.

"Beautiful thing about that is, any guards we kill in the drains get blamed on the *lida*," Illir replied. "That's a bonus, if you ask me."

The hunters chuckled.

"Get some food and sleep," Calfon said. "We'll let you know when it's time to go."

That evening, when the night was darkest, Corran and Dilin slipped into the drain. Corran paused, listening. The street overhead was silent, as was the tunnel before them. Corran nodded to Dilin and they moved forward, sticking to where the shadows were deepest.

The entrance from Below opened into one of the catch basins underneath the street. A grate in the roadway above him gave Corran the first glimpse of stars he had seen since the night of Kell's death. Another grate on the floor of the catch basin led into the storm drains.

Corran paused over the grate to examine the handholds carved into the stone wall. There was a landing about six feet below him, past which the drain dropped off into darkness. He hoped with all his heart that Trent's information was correct about the lower drains being large enough for a man to walk through. *I've got no desire to get wedged down there, with or without* lida.

"Let's go."

Corran and Dilin bent and lifted the iron grate. It was heavy, even with both of them to bear the load. Getting it back into place once they were inside was going to be a challenge.

Corran went first. He set a small, tightly-shuttered lantern inside a pot to hide its light, and let it down with a rope until it settled on the landing. Dilin handed him their rucksacks, and Corran lowered those as well. The lantern gave just enough of a glow for Corran to see the handholds as he climbed. Dilin eased himself into the hole after him, and they leaned against each other, one foot splayed against the opposing wall of the pipe, as they drew the grate back into place over their heads.

Inside the rucksacks were several torches made of wood and rags, extra candles, and the small oil pots Calfon had given them. They each carried wineskins of lamp oil as well as flint and steel, in case the lantern went out. They had staves and long knives, and both of them carried coils of rope.

"Down," Corran said. He handed Dilin the rope for the lantern pot and gently lifted the pot over the edge of the landing to light his way. Dilin let out the cord so that the pot hung a few feet below Corran, letting him see a little of the pipe ahead of him. More handholds were carved into the stone walls, and Corran wondered how far down they would have to go before the drains leveled out.

The bottom was closer than he expected, a little more than six feet below the platform. As he felt his boots touch solid ground, Corran took the pot and gave the rope a tug, signaling for Dilin to begin his climb. The pipe they'd just come down looked to be twice as wide as Corran's shoulders, and the tunnel was about half a foot higher than his head. *Trent was right so far. Let's hope the rest of the drain looks like this.*

Within a few minutes, Dilin landed beside him. Corran wound up the rope they used to let down the pot and slung it over his shoulder. The pot they would leave behind, in the hope that they might use it when they returned—if they exited the same way they entered. Corran withdrew the lantern, and opened the shutters.

"Bigger down here than I expected," Dilin murmured. "I never even knew these drains existed before the other night."

"Ravenwood is full of surprises," Corran replied. The lantern gave them their first good look at the drain tunnels. They were wide enough for two men to walk abreast with their arms outstretched, and at least six and a half feet high. Walls made of old brick, with barrel vault ceilings, stretched as far as they could see, dry except for a trickle of water down the center. The drain smelled musty, but much better than the sewers.

"Plenty of food for the *lida*," Dilin said. They picked their way around rat skeletons stripped clean. Occasionally they passed larger prey, an unfortunate cat or dog that had wandered in or whose body had washed down with the rains.

Corran spotted a human skeleton, picked bare. "Wonder if that poor bastard was dead before they found him?"

"Listen," Dilin whispered. Corran froze, focusing on the darkness beyond the lantern's light. He heard a faint scuffling sound, then nothing.

They lit torches, and Corran set the lantern on a brick outcropping to light the way back. He and Dilin slung their rucksacks over their shoulders and followed the tunnel as it sloped downward.

The smell of spoiled food and rancid ale hung in the air. Corran guessed that some of the buildings above them dumped their refuse into the drains instead of the sewer. He strained to listen for the creatures.

A few feet before the tunnel branched, Corran raised an arm for Dilin to stop, and pointed into the darkness. An odd rustling noise sounded ahead of them, growing louder. Brandishing their torches, Corran and Dilin moved forward, shoulder to shoulder, staves at the ready as they turned a corner.

"Shit!" Corran yelped. Black slime coated the wall and floor. *Lida* feasted on the slime, their corpse-white segmented bodies pulsing. Each *lida* stretched at least two feet long, as thick around as a man's arm. The creatures swarmed over one another, forming a writhing mass. Corran forced back the urge to retch. Whether the *lida* heard them, smelled them or felt the vibration of their approach, Corran did not know; but all at once, the tide of creatures surged forward.

"Gods above and below!" Corran thundered, his shout echoing in the drain. "Use your torch!" he ordered, lowering his own brand to keep the creatures at bay.

Dilin held his ground, alternately thrusting his torch at the *lida* and pushing them back with his staff. Corran held his staff under one arm as he grabbed an oil pot from his pack and lit it. "Fire!"

The pot smashed on the brick floor just ahead of the tide of *lida* and burst into flames. The creatures reared back with eerie squeals. Dilin held his ground, still ready with torch and staff in case the *lida* were bold enough to brave the flame.

To Corran's horror, the wave of creatures parted around the flame and slithered up the walls. They stank of rot, their toxic mucus glistening in the torchlight.

"Fall back!" Corran yelled, laying a wide line of oil across the floor and up the walls. Dilin swept his staff across the walls, knocking the creatures from the walls and ceiling to fall into the fire. Corran lobbed one pot after another, striking the floor, walls, and ceiling, before igniting the oil. Flames roared, incinerating the front line of monsters and forcing the others back.

One of the huge maggots dropped onto Dilin's shoulder and he screamed as its acid burned into his skin. He tore at it, blistering his hands, and managed to tear it free. He hurled it into the flames. It hit the floor with a wet smack, writhing amid the flames. It hissed and sizzled until it popped like an overstuffed sausage, spewing blood and a thick pus that stank like a corpse left to ripen in the sun.

"Are you all right?" Corran shouted. He struggled not to retch at the smell.

"I can move my arm, but *damn*, it hurts like it's on fire," Dilin said. The rustling noise came again, seconds before more *lida* swarmed into view from a nearby passageway.

"Fall back behind the oil line!" Corran ordered.

Dilin and Corran dipped their torches to the oil, and a fiery ring blazed up, nearly blinding them. The *lida* roiled, hissing angrily. Corran lit more pots and threw them against the ceiling and walls to cut off pursuit. As the two men retreated, Dilin splashed the floor and walls with oil from his wineskin. "That's all I've got—it had better work." He favored his damaged arm. The acid had eaten through the cloth of his shirt and the first layer of skin, leaving a swath of bloodied tissue over most of one shoulder.

Corran's torch set the oil ablaze. Corran threw more and more pots past the flames, aiming for the rear of the mass of creatures, leaving them no quarter. It was growing hot in the tunnel, and he hoped they didn't end up roasting themselves alive with the monsters.

"Is it working?" Sweat beaded on Dilin's face, and his hair hung limp across his forehead. His eyes looked glassy from pain.

"Well, they aren't advancing. That's something."

"Fire's dying down," Dilin replied. Their torches guttered; the replacements in Corran's bag would have to do them to get out. He had no desire to be trapped here in the dark with the monsters. Seeing Dilin's wound painted a vivid picture of what it would be like to die beneath the squirming mass of those creatures: dissolving slowly, awake to know it.

"I think we got them all," Corran said. The floor of the tunnel was covered with the blackened bodies of the *lida*, charred and split open.

"Let's get out of here," Dilin said in a tight voice. "My arm's useless. And I don't feel too good." They retreated, with Dilin watching the rear, while Corran led the way back to the grate where they entered.

"Wait!" Corran stopped so abruptly that Dilin bumped into him. "Do you hear that?"

Rustling sounded ahead of them. *More* lida, *between us and the way home. And we're nearly out of oil.*

"I'm not going to be much good if it comes to another fight," Dilin said. "I'm going to be lucky if I can haul myself back out of the pipe."

The strange shuffling noise echoed from the old brick walls. Corran's heart sank. There must be huge numbers of them.

"We're going to make it. Stay back-to-back and we'll keep them at bay with our torches."

More rustling, closer now. Corran's torch guttered. "We're almost to the grate."

"We're not going to get out," Dilin said bleakly.

A wave of corpse-pale *lida* flowed down the tunnel toward them, cutting them off.

Corran grabbed the remaining torches from his pack, lit them and threw them to the ground. They blazed, halting the creatures.

"I've got a few oil pots left," Corran said. "I'll use them to drive the creatures back. Once it's clear, you run for it."

"What about you?"

"Just go!" Corran ordered.

"But—"

"Go!" Corran roared, and threw a lit pot. The bomb exploded and the creatures shrieked. Dilin dropped his spent torch and picked up a fresh replacement, running for his life toward the entrance.

He's not going to make it. Lida filled the tunnel, heaving and shuddering across the floor. They surged forward, cutting Dilin off from the pipe and forcing him against the wall, climbing over each other to get to him. Dilin screamed.

Corran flung his torch into the midst of the huge maggots. The monsters drew back, and Dilin collapsed, sliding down the wall of the tunnel, bleeding. Corran grabbed the other torch and charged forward with a reckless battle cry. *I am not going to die cowering before a bunch of slugs.*

A wave of flames blasted out of nowhere, and the creatures shrieked. The fire swept in a sheet from side to side, hot as a forge, scattering the monsters. Corran pushed Dilin down and shielded him with his body.

The corridor in front of them became a tunnel of flames as the entire stretch of floor, ceiling, and walls blazed so brilliantly that the brick glowed red. Corran threw one arm over his nose and mouth as his lungs protested and his eyes teared.

As quickly as the fire came, it vanished.

Corran blinked, trying to readjust to the dark after the blinding flames, and glanced down at Dilin, who lay pale and unconscious, breathing shallowly, blood seeping from burns deep enough to reveal muscle. Corran dropped his staff and unsheathed his knife.

Footsteps sounded ahead, and Corran drew back into the shadows.

The tunnels offered no good hiding places. *I might not win, but I can make it expensive.*

A dark form appeared in the torchlight, kicking its way through the charred corpses of the *lida*. The newcomer stopped several paces away, within the glow of Corran's nearly spent torch, and lowered his hood.

"Let's go home," Rigan said.

CORRAN HELD HIS questions until they were back at the building they'd claimed as their home and he had handed Dilin off to Aiden for healing. "I thought you weren't going to be back until you'd gotten into the old monastery," he said. "Not that I'm complaining."

Rigan snorted. "Polly got us to the building, but we realized we'd need different tools to get in. Looks like more of the walls collapsed since the last time she was there. Lucky for you, we came back and Elinor told us where you'd gone."

"What made you decide to come after us?"

Rigan raised an eyebrow. "Besides the fact that your plan was breathtakingly risky?" He shrugged. "Since we were back, it seemed like a good idea to see if you needed some backup. Aiden went to check on two groups, and I took the other two. Mir and Tomor were already heading back when I got to their drain, so I kept going until I found you and Dilin."

"You've got good timing," Corran replied. "I didn't think we were going to get out of there on our own. I'm not sure how badly Dilin's hurt, but it looked awful."

"Well, you're out. And I'm still in pretty good shape; I think I'm getting the hang of grounding my magic."

"Do you think the magic was enough to call attention to us?"

Rigan shrugged. "No way to tell. I guess we'll know soon enough."

The [illegible] off [illegible] Dungannon? [illegible]

A [illegible] the charred [illegible] within the glow of Cormac's [illegible] torch, and lowered his head.

"Let's go home," Ragan said.

[illegible]

[illegible] back at the building [illegible] Hanrahan [illegible] "I thought you [illegible] going to be back [illegible]" [illegible] "Not that I'm complaining [illegible] we [illegible] once the women [illegible] we came back and [illegible]

[illegible] "Hamon?" [illegible]

Ragan [illegible] "Besides the fact that your plan was [illegible] we went back, it seemed [illegible] and Farour were [illegible]

[illegible] "I didn't think we [illegible]

"Well [illegible]

"Did you [illegible]" Ragan [illegible]

Chapter Thirty-Two

"AT LEAST IT'S not *hancha*," Rigan muttered. Decaying flesh littered the ground, letting them know they were on the right trail.

"Looks like they were dragging someone," Trent said, bending to examine the marks. "And we seem to be heading in the same direction."

Only two days had passed since Corran and the hunters had gone after the *lida*. Rigan and Aiden had postponed returning to the old monastery to help with the aftermath of the fight, and stayed close just in case the monsters returned. Dilin would not be fit to travel for a while, Aiden cautioned. The *lida*'s acid would leave ugly scars, and he'd find moving painful.

By the time they were ready to go back to the monastery, Polly returned from the market with the rumor that ghouls were slinking around the more deserted stretches of Below, including the area near the house they had claimed for their own.

"It's too dangerous, going into the ruins," Trent protested, when Rigan and Aiden raised the suggestion.

"You're going to go after the ghouls anyway," Rigan countered. "So while you're there fighting them off, Aiden and Polly and I will see if we can find anything. Elinor will be ready to patch us up when we get back."

"I don't like it." Corran glared at Rigan. "What if you run into ghouls inside the monastery? We won't be able to help you."

"Unlikely," Rigan argued. "Ghouls need to eat. They're not going to find any fresh bodies in a half-buried library."

"Except yours."

"Aiden and I can hold them off with our magic, and Polly's good with a knife. You'll see—we'll be in and out before you're even done fighting."

Rigan watched Corran struggle with his thoughts. Going into the ruins would have been dangerous enough *without* the ghouls. But the ghouls had to be stopped, and if Rigan and the others stood any chance of bringing the monster-summoning witch and their sponsor to account, they needed all the arcane knowledge they could get.

"I'm in," Corran said eventually. "But I don't like it."

THE OLD MONASTERY was a long way from the busy marketplace, and a half-candlemark's walk from the house they shared with Polly and Elinor. The once-handsome building was the best preserved of the dozen near it, which were little more than heaps of stone. Parts of the old façade still stood. None of the walls looked sturdy, and three had partially collapsed. Polly scouted a way through the rubble to get to a stairway and into the lower chambers, where the old building was better preserved. It was a fine plan, until the ghouls showed up.

Aiden's limited foresight provided a good idea of where the monsters nested in the nearby ruins, but he could make out nothing farther below. Corran and the hunters spread out across the handful of blocks where the ghouls had been sighted, after a careful sweep around the old monastery to ensure that none of the monsters were in the upper floors of the ruin. Despite the careful preparation, Rigan's stomach knotted. Hancha *were bad enough. Ghouls are worse.*

Hancha might not have enough awareness to notice approaching footsteps, but ghouls were far more clever and significantly more dangerous.

Aiden carried two knives and a staff. Rigan brought along two long knives, saving his magic for when it would be most effective. Polly gripped a wide, wicked-looking knife, and a hardness in her eyes assured Rigan that she knew how to wield it.

A recent memory flashed in Rigan's mind. *Kell, returning with a corpse that had a single knife wound through the ribs. His brother had insisted the man be cursed, buried where the soul would never rest. And the corpse was clutching strands of hair in one hand, hair the color of Polly's.* Rigan eyed the girl with new respect. *Damn, you picked yourself a spitfire, Kell.* He felt a stab of loss that made him look away. Aiden glanced at him, worried, but Rigan shrugged and moved a step ahead so the healer could not read his expression.

They descended the stairs into the cellars of the monastery. Rigan forged ahead, acutely aware that the lantern's glow illuminated only a small area, leaving the rest of the cellars in darkness.

"This way," Polly said, tugging at Rigan's sleeve to steer him toward the left.

As they walked, they heard the sharp squeals and guttural barks the ghouls used to communicate. Aiden and Rigan exchanged a silent glance. *If the ghouls are arguing among themselves, all the better for us.* They shuttered their lanterns and turned to Polly.

"Guard the lanterns and watch your back. Yell if you see any coming, and stay out of the way," Rigan whispered.

Polly glared at him. "I can take care of myself."

"I know you can. But not here and not now." Rigan met Polly's gaze and saw fire and steel.

"All right," she hissed. "But only because you need someone to watch your back."

Rigan and Aiden slipped along the wall, blue handfire lighting their way, closing in on the room where the ghouls had gathered.

Eight ghouls clustered around the savaged remains of a rotting corpse. They jabbered among themselves, elbowing each other out of the way as they plucked gobs of flesh from the body, twisting off fingers and toes like choice morsels. One whiff told Rigan it was not a recent kill.

Rigan eased a rucksack off one shoulder. He and Aiden carried a bag of the same kind of small clay pots that had proven so effective against the *lida*. Burning the ghouls was the easy part; getting out alive—with the manuscripts—was going to be more difficult.

A movement to the side caught Rigan's eye, and he felt as much as saw Aiden move into position beside him. *I'm not happy with those odds. We're not likely to get reinforcements, but the ghouls might.*

Rigan swore under his breath as the ghouls froze, turning toward the doorway. In the next moment, all eight of the creatures were moving toward them, fast.

Rigan unsheathed one of his knives, a long, wicked blade, good for hunting and razor sharp. "What are you doing?" Aiden demanded. "You can't get close enough with that. They'll tear you apart."

"Maybe not." Rigan balanced the flat of the blade on one finger and a touch sent it spinning. He pushed with his magic, and the blade whirled faster, airborne. It picked up speed as it scythed through the air, heading for the advancing ghouls.

The silver blur sent black ichor flying as it sliced through a ghoul's throat, cut another's chest open and decapitated a third, finally sticking with a dull thud, embedded in the forehead of the tallest of the monsters. Three ghouls fell and did not get back up.

"Better odds. Nice trick," Aiden said, as he and Rigan fell back, weapons in hand. Undeterred, the remaining ghouls trampled the bodies of their comrades, their focus fixed only on the two men.

"Let me." Aiden thrust out his right hand, closed his eyes and jerked back his fist. The crunch of bone snapping filled the chamber, and two ghouls collapsed, legs shattered. Magic evened the odds, but they would weaken quickly relying only on their power. Aiden and

Rigan surged forward. Rigan slashed down with his long knife, and the blade bit into the arm of the closest ghoul, taking the limb off at the elbow. Foul blackness poured from the wound, and the creature shrieked but kept on coming, as its companion tried unsuccessfully to get behind Aiden. A scuffling noise in the corridor outside caught Rigan's attention briefly, but the ghouls came at him too fast for him to be distracted, and he could only hope that Polly could hold her own.

Rigan brought his knife down with his full strength, two-handed, and cleaved one of the ghouls from shoulder to hip. The monster shuddered and fell to its knees, awash in stinking humours, then dropped backward to the floor and lay still.

Aiden's blade slashed across the throat of his nearest attacker, deep enough to sever its head. Skull and torso fell in separate directions with a dull thud, staining the stone floor black. Aiden and Rigan circled their opponent. A shared glance signaled the attack, and they lunged forward at the same instant, running their blades through the ghoul's chest, skewering it.

The ghoul's body trembled violently, nearly ripping the sword from Aiden's hand. Rigan gripped his weapon two-handed, forcing his blade deeper. With an ear-splitting scream, the ghoul went still.

Rigan and Aiden froze, waiting. Rigan assessed the dismembered ghouls on the floor, relieved to see that none of them had risen again. He stepped back, pulling his sword free, as Aiden did the same. The ghoul fell to the ground.

"Not exactly what I had in mind," Rigan said, keeping his eyes on the dead ghouls. He kicked the bodies, sword ready to strike, but nothing happened. Just for good measure, he sent the heads of the nearest ghouls rolling, and Aiden walked among the other bodies, making sure each was stabbed through the heart and decapitated. Rigan retrieved the knife still stuck in the skull of one of the ghouls. He wiped it clean and returned it to its sheath, keeping the second knife in his hand.

Polly. Rigan ran for the doorway. He nearly fell over the body of a dead ghoul. In the darkness, Polly's outline was barely visible, except for the glint of her steel knife. Ichor the color of shadows dripped from the blade.

"Got him." Polly said in a flat tone, her eyes hard. Rigan wondered whether this dark strength was new, Polly's way of dealing with the grief of Kell's death and of losing everything Above, or whether experience had honed a hardness she'd always had. *Maybe some of both.*

"Nice work," Rigan said, as Aiden joined him. He caught the healer's wordless glance between the body of the dead ghoul and the blade in Polly's hand. Rigan wished he dared destroy the bodies with green vitriol, but the air was close in the ruins and he had no desire to smother them. He made do with salt and aconite from a container in his sack.

After a moment, Rigan looked up. "I still want to look for that manuscript."

Aiden wiped his blade clean against the leg of the dead ghoul. "I'd be happier if we got out of here, the sooner the better."

"I've got to look. You can go help Corran—"

"And leave you wandering around to find a few more ghouls in here?" Aiden shook his head. "No. I'm coming with you. Let's go."

"Stay close," Polly said, leading the way.

Rigan and Aiden followed, alert for threats. The vaults beneath the north wing were still in passable condition considering the building's long abandonment. Rigan and Polly carried lanterns, while Aiden held a torch, creating light sufficient to help them navigate the stairs and corridors, but not nearly enough to suit Rigan, who watched the shadows for attackers.

"Why would the priests leave anything valuable behind?" Rigan asked, liking the expedition less the longer they remained in the building. "And if they did, why hasn't anyone stolen it yet?"

"I don't think they intended to leave permanently," Polly replied.

"They abandoned the building in a rush, probably when the walls collapsed. The priests either scattered or died."

"So there was no one left to come back for it—or no one who knew if there was anything important," Aiden filled in.

"We don't know that they didn't take everything they could reach," Polly added. "The shelves I could see looked bare. But if the rubble buried some of the shelves, and the priests were in a hurry, they might not have taken the time to dig out the rest, and looters might not have thought to look."

"Or, of course, we could find a whole lot of nothing," Aiden pointed out.

"We could," Polly admitted. "But I'm betting that after the collapse, they probably couldn't get down to the cellars. It's been years since then—people have salvaged some of the cut stone for other uses. They weren't trying to dig it out, but they've opened enough of a hole for us to get in. So if there were texts that got left behind, that people forgot about or they thought they were destroyed—"

"They may still be here."

Aiden slowed as they came to the end of the hallway. "Looks like we'll know one way or the other in a moment. We've arrived."

Rigan opened an old oak door, his torch aloft, and caught his breath, staring at walls covered nearly floor to ceiling with empty shelves. He sighed as he imagined them filled with leather-bound manuscripts and yellowed scrolls. The damage from the collapse was clear in the cracks splitting the stone walls and the rubble from the ceiling. He could see where they'd covered over the holes in the ceiling, laying foundations for Above.

Rubble appeared to have sealed off another section of the room, and Rigan hoped Polly was right about what lay beneath the wreckage.

Aiden frowned, then turned to the empty shelves, running his hands over them.

"Aiden?"

"Give me a minute. In the witch's house, the library had secret compartments, for texts that were potentially dangerous."

He paused, still feeling his way along the back of the shelves. A quiet *click* answered his efforts, and he smiled.

"Oh, yes," he murmured, reaching in and withdrawing a handful of papers and old scrolls. "If these were important enough to hide, they might be just what we need."

He and Rigan stuffed the books and parchments into their rucksacks. When they were finished, the healer looked at the tumble of rock that hid the rest of the room.

"Let's start digging," Aiden said. "And try not to bring any more of the roof down on us."

The work went slowly. They proceeded carefully, worried about triggering more damage. After a candlemark, they cleared a hole through to the other side, but only large enough for Polly to fit through.

"I don't think we can make that any larger without having it collapse," Rigan said, sitting back on his haunches.

"Tell me what to look for, and I can bring it back for you," Polly offered.

Rigan frowned at her. "It's not safe. We have no idea what's in there."

She glared back. "*Now* you worry about that? Come on, we spent all this time digging. We've at least got to find out what's in there."

"Rigan and I can't fit through the hole," Aiden said.

"So... tell me what to look for," Polly repeated. "I can read Common, but if it's in an old language, I might need to hand things through for you to see."

Rigan handed her one of the lanterns. "Push this through first, and make sure it's safe to go in."

Polly swallowed hard. "Right. Give me a bit." She belly crawled through the small hole, pushing the lantern ahead of her, and vanished beyond the cave-in.

"Polly?" Rigan called.

"I'm fine," she replied. "I was right—there's an alcove here, and it's still got old books. Maybe a couple of dozen." They heard a muffled exclamation, then a curse, and some stomping.

"Polly!"

"Damn spiders. Look, I don't want to poke around in here any longer than I have to, so I'm just going to hand stuff out and you can figure out what's important."

"That will work," Aiden replied. "Ready when you are."

Half a candlemark later, Polly slithered back through the hole. She was covered with dust and cobwebs, but she flashed Rigan and Aiden a triumphant grin.

Aiden sat on the floor examining the parchments and books that Polly had retrieved. "Seeing what's here makes me want to know what's missing," he said with a wistful tone. "Most of the books are histories. They were likely shelved together. We might be able to find some reference to past monster attacks. I won't know until I've had time to study them. But..."

"What?" Rigan pressed.

"There are plenty of mentions of other libraries at monasteries outside the wall. I think we've got to figure out a way to get to them and see what resources might have been left behind."

"If Damian or the people he's working for thought something would give away their secrets, they wouldn't leave the evidence for someone to find," Rigan said.

"No—if they knew the books existed. With luck, they haven't thought about the monasteries."

Rigan glanced at the lantern and realized it was beginning to sputter. "We've been gone too long. Corran's going to be frantic—when he finds out I'm not dead, he'll kill me for worrying him. We need to get back."

"Grab what you need, then," Polly said. "I really want to get out of here too. Move your asses. We don't have all day."

Rigan's heart sank as he heard stumbling footsteps from the far end of the dark corridor. "Someone's coming."

More ghouls headed toward them from the southern corridor.

"Go!" Polly ordered. She took off, with Aiden and Rigan close behind her, heading back the way they came. The ghouls closed the distance with surprising speed, reaching the top of the stone steps just as Rigan and the others thundered their way toward the door to the outside.

"Wait!" Rigan said as the ghouls started up the stairs.

Aiden stopped a few feet inside the doorway and turned. "Are you crazy?"

"They'll kill again if we don't stop them. And if we want to come back and search for more hidden books, we might as well fight them now as later."

"Bad odds, Rigan. Not a fight we can win."

"We can if we cheat." Fire lanced from Rigan's hand. Aiden gripped his shoulder, amplifying his power and grounding them both. A wall of flames rose, cutting off the ghouls from their prey. The blast of magic knocked the creatures back and the ghouls shrieked, angry at being denied fresh meat, flailing and scrabbling. The fire spread rapidly, charring their filthy bodies and corpse-pale skin. Then, to Rigan's horror, the ghouls dragged themselves to their feet, staggering forward.

"Shit! That's not supposed to happen!" Aiden cried. He kept one hand firm on Rigan's shoulder, and drew his sword with the other as the ghouls walked toward them, bodies aflame, arms outstretched, hands grasping.

Rigan sent a blast of power that threw the ghouls back against the far wall with a bone-shattering crunch. Fire burned away the creatures' clothing and hair, searing what remained soot-black. The ghouls dropped and lay still. Then, as Rigan stared in amazement, the monsters regained their feet and started toward them again.

"I thought fire killed those things!" Polly yelped.

"So did I." Rigan's voice was taut with concentration. Aiden glanced at him, and Rigan caught the unspoken warning. Rigan was pulling hard on the magic, draining both of them. They could not keep up the fight for long.

"Got any more ideas? Because I don't want to fight them all by ourselves." Aiden glanced behind them, but Corran and the other hunters were nowhere in sight. *This was supposed to be simple. By the time Corran and the others realize something's wrong, we're going to be up to our asses in ghouls.*

"Hacking them apart works, right?" Rigan licked his lips nervously as the ghouls lumbered closer.

"It did the last time. But fire was *supposed* to kill them, too. And that obviously isn't working now."

Rigan glanced at Polly, a desperate plan forming in his mind. "Is there more than one way in and out?"

"Yeah," Polly said. "The other way is harder, but we came in from the east side—"

"That's all I need to know." Rigan licked his lips. The plan was reckless, maybe suicidal; but it was the best he had, and if they were going to get out alive, they needed a way out *now*. "Can you take us out the long way? Maybe through a corridor that wouldn't hurt anything if it... wasn't there anymore?"

Polly and Aiden exchanged a glance. Aiden gave a curt nod, silently throwing his support behind Rigan. Polly rolled her eyes and muttered a vulgar curse. "Follow me, and spare me the details. But if you get me killed, I'm going to haunt your ass."

Rigan hung back as Polly took the lead, and Aiden stayed close, unwilling to let him take all the risk. Rigan used himself as bait, making sure the ghouls saw them head into the corridor, lagging behind enough to tempt the creatures with the promise of an easy kill.

"You're cutting it fine," Aiden grumbled.

"We've got one shot." Rigan's voice was low and hard, his concentration focused on the ghouls. Polly led them through a long hallway, and Rigan stayed just out of reach of the ghouls, ensuring the monsters followed him, holding off until they were in sight of the night sky.

"Get out of here!" Rigan growled, turning to face Polly and Aiden.

"Together, or not at all." Aiden's jaw was set, and Polly looked furious and determined.

Rigan thrust out his right hand, took a deep breath, remembering his training with earth magic, and yanked his closed fist back. The vaulted brick ceiling shuddered and gave way in a roar and a cloud of dust, collapsing in an avalanche of stone and brick. Rigan thrust out his torch like a lance, and a gust of power extended the flames, igniting the rubble.

Burning figures struggled to rise from the pyre. Rigan raised his hand and the rest of the ceiling and supporting walls gave way with a crack like thunder.

"Run!" he yelled, coughing on the dust. He tripped and nearly went sprawling, but Aiden's hand closed around his wrist, hauling him forward, dragging him out of the passageway. Rigan stumbled down the steps behind Aiden, gasping for breath and choking. With a roar, the corridor behind them collapsed as they cleared the ruins and burst into the tunnels of Below.

"That was too damn close," Aiden panted, trying to catch his breath. "What were you thinking?"

"I was thinking about grounding my power so I didn't end up flat on my ass," Rigan replied. He was covered with dust, sweat, and ghoul's ichor. A trickle of blood ran from his hairline down one cheek from a gash on his temple. His hands trembled, but he did not appear to be on the verge of collapse.

"What in the name of the Dark Ones did you do?" Corran, Trent, and Mir appeared on the edge of the wreckage, looking bloodied and worse for the wear. Relief flooded over Rigan, and he found himself unable to stop laughing with the sheer, blessed knowledge that they weren't all dead.

"Rigan?" Corran still sounded angry, but worry won out.

"I'm all right," Rigan said, finally regaining control. "The training's paying off. And whatever Eshtamon did to me, it seems to keep me from frying myself with magic. Really, I'm all right."

"Then if you're *quite* finished," Corran said, hiding his relief, "we need to get out of here. Someone might just notice part of the street collapsing into Below."

"AFTER ALL THAT, let's see if what we hauled out of there was worth the excitement," Rigan said when they finally made their way back. "We didn't have much chance to look at the books before we had to grab and run."

Aiden turned up the lantern and, together, they carefully unpacked the books, manuscripts, and scrolls from the rucksacks.

Rigan looked at a roll of parchment and tugged gently on the thin string holding it closed. Carefully, he placed the fragile old paper on the desk and smoothed it flat. The faded ink was legible, and carefully scribed lines of text covered the pages, interrupted in places by diagrams and drawings.

"Can you read it?" Rigan asked, bending closer and squinting. The lettering was neat but cramped, and he blinked, trying to make out the words.

"Looks like an account of the last days before they abandoned the monastery," said Aiden. "From what I can make out."

Rigan frowned. "Why hide something like that?"

Aiden shrugged. "Won't know until we read it."

"So was it worth it?" Corran asked after Rigan and Aiden had spent a few more candlemarks reading the manuscripts and arguing about their meaning. "Did you get something worth running into all those ghouls?"

"It's another piece of the puzzle," Rigan replied, sitting back in his chair. He ran a hand through his hair. "According to what we found, in the final days before the priests abandoned the monastery, there was a big surge in monster attacks. The attacks convinced the priests that the warlords were controlling the monsters, sending them in as advance troops, maybe even summoning them from the Dark Places."

Corran grimaced. "So you were right," he said. "The attacks back in Wrighton weren't accidents."

"No, they weren't." Rigan's voice was just as cold, and Corran heard the same longing for vengeance. "My bet would be the Lord Mayor's behind them. Nothing happens in Ravenwood without him knowing about it. I just can't prove it yet."

Corran closed his eyes and let out a long breath. "It would make sense," he said after a moment. "Why the guards don't seem to do anything effective against the monsters. They wouldn't, if their boss was sending the creatures in the first place."

Rigan nodded. "I don't think the Guild Masters are in on it. We've lost too many Guild members to the monsters. And I doubt if the higher-ups above the Lord Mayor can find the city on a map, for all they care. Can't imagine them bothering with something so day-to-day. Or if they knew about it, they'd hand it off to someone else to do their dirty work. Which brings us back to the Lord Mayor."

"If Machison is behind this, I want to kill the bastard," Corran said, his voice deadly quiet.

"So do I," Rigan replied. "But we've got to be sure."

Chapter Thirty-Three

"We're getting closer." Rigan bent to examine a dark pool of old blood. For the first time in his life, he was outside the walls of Ravenwood, trying to liberate another abandoned monastery from a monster to retrieve more precious lore books.

"It's a real shame these buildings have been left to rot," Corran said. "They must have been impressive in their day."

Rigan shrugged. "From what we've learned, once the League got more powerful, the Crown Princes didn't want anyone challenging their power, and they feared the monks serving the old gods as much as they did the witches they couldn't control. They were a threat, so they had to be eliminated."

"So why did they leave the temples in the city, if they were afraid of people worshipping the Old Gods?"

"Politics," Rigan said. "Regular people don't care about a bunch of monks cloistered away in the country somewhere, but they would have put up a hue and cry if the temples at their doorstop were knocked down. The League left the temples intact, with a few minor oracles, and then pushed the Guild gods on the people, to give themselves money and influence." He shrugged. "At least, that's my theory."

"So the Crown Princes got the King's backing, and laid siege to the monasteries," Aiden finished. "Captured the monks and scholars, stole everything valuable that the monks didn't hide, and that was that."

"Nice history lesson, but before we can go after more scrolls, we've got a monster to evict." Rigan bent down to examine a dark stain on the ground. "Looks like blood."

"So she's wounded?" Corran said.

"According to the lore," Rigan said, "this is part of what a strix does. It feeds on the blood of children, and then regurgitates it to mark its territory." He dropped six silver coins into the goo and turned them with a stick, staining them reddish-black.

"And you're doing that why?" Ross asked, looking as if he might be sick.

"Protective charm," Rigan said. He set his jaw and teased the coins out of the blood, laying them out on strips of cloth. Then he added a sprinkle of salt and made a mark with soot on each cloth before rolling them up and twisting them into long strands. Rigan handed one to each of the others, and took the sixth for himself. "Tie it on your right forearm," he instructed.

"We're going to kill a vampire witch with a bloody coin?" Corran asked incredulously.

Rigan shook his head. "We're going to kill her with our blades and an iron stake, and then set her body on fire. Then we bury what's left with salt, aconite, and amanita powder, and seal the cairn with charms. The coins are extra protection."

"Can I just mention that I liked the kinds of monsters we fought back in Wrighton a whole lot better?" Ross replied, tying the rag around his arm.

"You don't hear any of us disagreeing," Corran said. "But Aiden and Rigan need information, and we can't get to the library without going through the strix."

"Do you think the strix is controlled by this blood witch we're after?" Ross asked.

Rigan shook his head. "Doubtful. Most of the monsters you fought inside the city were beast-like. Vicious, but dumb. The ghouls aren't smart, just good at hiding and tracking prey. Even the *hancha* aren't clever—they're relentless. A strix is more powerful. They've got their own type of magic, and all the old books say they're wily. Pretty sure it's operating independently—which makes it even more dangerous."

Aiden had uncovered references to the old monastery in the books he and Rigan had liberated Below. His foresight warned them about the monster, and the healer and Rigan had spent days poring over their growing library of forbidden lore and old grimoires, trying to figure out the nature of the creature; everything had matched the description of a strix.

"This one is double trouble," Rigan reminded them. "Vampire and witch—and nasty as the Dark Ones."

"I found something," Trent said, and Rigan looked down at the body of a girl, perhaps about twelve years old, her throat a bloody, open wound. The ground beneath her was dry.

"She's been drained," Corran noted quietly.

Rigan sighed. "Come on. We want to be done and gone by sunset."

Tall trees towered above them. Even at midday, their sprawling canopies blocked out much of the sunlight. Rigan and Corran led the way, with Aiden, Mir, Trent, and Ross behind them.

"I don't like this," Trent groused. They were a candlemark's walk into the forest, and the sunlit fields were far behind them. With every step, the woods grew darker and colder. "Too quiet."

"Yeah. I noticed that, too," Ross replied A few minutes before, the woods had bustled with life. Leaves rustled overhead, small animals skittered out of their way, and birds twittered in the branches. They they'd forded a small stream, and the woodland sounds had stopped altogether. Even the breeze stilled, no longer swaying the canopy overhead. "Darker here, too," he added, glancing to either side, gripping his weapon.

"Means we're getting closer," Aiden replied. "Can't be far now."

"Your foresight show you anything else?" Corran asked.

The healer shook his head. "The only thing I'm reading now is danger, and I don't really need magic for that."

Moss and bare dirt gave way to a rocky, narrow pass between huge boulders. As they pressed forward, thorn bushes snarled the trail, close enough to snag clothing and skin. *We're being herded. The strix doesn't want to be surprised.*

Rigan took reassurance from the weight of the iron blade in his right hand, and the rucksack on his shoulder filled with the essentials to lay the strix to rest. Until now, he had used his magic against beasts or brigands, but never against another witch, except in his practice sessions with Aiden or Damian.

He glanced at Aiden. After all their studying, he and the healer had found hints that the authoritative texts on the kind of magic they needed—summoning, banishing, and creature control—were kept at the chapterhouse at Bordwin, now abandoned.

"I think we've found it." Corran nudged Rigan and pointed toward the ruins ahead. The main section, made of carved stone, listed to one side, fire-scarred, windowless and partially collapsed. The outbuildings looked worse, including a wooden barn—the thatch roof sagged, and its weathered wood walls seemed barely capable of sustaining their own weight. Shutters hung akimbo, and the door stood ajar.

A warning prickled at the back of Rigan's neck. Every instinct screamed for him to turn back, and a glance at Aiden confirmed that the other witch felt the same. Rigan set his jaw. "We know the plan. Let's get to it."

Corran and Trent led the way, and Rigan and Aiden followed with Mir and Ross, all of them holding their blades at the ready. Rigan and Aiden lit torches. Rigan rehearsed the banishing spells he and Aiden had memorized to keep the strix at bay until they could rid the ruins of the monster. Both Rigan and Aiden carried empty rucksacks for the manuscripts they planned to retrieve, and another bag with the salt-aconite mixture, protective powders, and the items needed to work the banishing. Rigan hoped their preparations would be sufficient.

Rigan's breath misted in the cold air. His skin rose in gooseflesh, and he was certain they were being watched. *She knows we're here.*

Rigan glanced at Trent and Ross. The rucksacks slung over their shoulders were filled with bags of salt, sage, and hyssop to make a warding circle, along with pentacle amulets made from the bones of pigs and chickens to seal the protective ring. All part of the banishing he and Aiden had prepared—but first they needed to find the strix.

"Can you sense her?" he asked in a low voice.

Aiden closed his eyes, drew in a deep breath, and stood completely still for a moment. "She's not in the stone tower. She's in the barn. That's where she stores her kills."

Rigan moved to tell Corran and the hunters, who eyed the barn warily. "Do it," Rigan ordered in a low voice. Trent and Ross nodded in acknowledgement. They pulled what they needed from their sacks and walked away from each other, spilling a line of the warding mixture behind them as they traced the circle around the barn. Just in case, Corran traced a thick line of salt across the wide porch around the stone building, enough to keep anything inside from venturing out.

A shutter thumped against the warped wall, though the air was still. "She's waiting for us," Rigan murmured. He glanced at Corran, who stared at the half-open door, lips pressed together in a tight line. Rigan's amulet could not shield him from the strix's notice, nor could Aiden's deflection spell, and the bloody coins offered scant protection. Not this close, not on the threshold to her lair. His heart thudded, and his stomach twisted into a tight knot.

Aiden began drawing the binding sigils in the dirt around the barn, and then moved to set the candles and wards. Rigan and Corran made ready to go inside, while Mir, Trent, and Ross stationed themselves around the barn.

"Time to move," Corran said. He carried an iron sword as well as a staff made of rowan wood, which Rigan had painted with sigils for greater protection. A stolen crossbow hung on a strap across his back, along with the quarrels that Aiden had made especially for this hunt, marked with pigment and carved with runes.

"Done," Aiden said behind them, closing the salt circle and starting to chant. Ross moved to hang the bone-stars on the thorn bushes, making a second ring around the salt. If their research was right, the circles of salt and bone would trap the vampire inside.

Trapped animals fight the fiercest, Rigan thought.

He stepped through the doorway into the dark interior. The single room smelled of blood and dirt, with the sickly sweet undertones of rotting flesh. Light filtered in through gaps in the boards and holes in the battered shutters. Old blood stained the floorboards and the walls. Dirty, guttering candles flickered beside a large, gleaming knife and a filthy mortar and pestle on a wooden table scarred with cuts and burns. A rusty chain and manacles hung from a beam overhead. The barn's huge single room stretched out before them, empty.

Rigan brought the heel of his boot down hard on the wooden boards and listened to the hollow echo. "There's a room beneath us," he said quietly. "It's probably got a dirt floor." That was why the strix had chosen the barn over the tower: proximity to fresh dirt to anchor her magic.

An unseen force threw Rigan against the wall so hard that he expected to crash through the warped old boards. A moment later, Corran went flying in the opposite direction, slamming hard against a beam. Rigan expected Trent, Mir, and Ross to come running, alerted by the noise. When they didn't, it occurred to him that a witch who could remain invisible could likely silence sound as well.

Rigan staggered away from the wall, raising his blade, eyeing the empty room. He caught a glimpse of gnarled hands and long, sharp nails, there and gone in the blink of an eye, but not before five bloody gouges ripped down his left shoulder. He swung, aiming more from instinct than magic, and heard a shriek as his blade bit into something substantial.

"Corran, watch out!"

Corran had his feet under him, but he looked dazed. Again Rigan caught a glimpse of their attacker as bony fingers scratched long, deep slashes across Corran's back. Corran swung his staff and nearly lost his footing when he hit nothing but air.

Rigan sent tendrils of his magic down, grounding himself. The earth beneath the barn was foul, polluted by the strix's lair, and he recoiled at the touch. He was already moving forward as Corran swung again, looking for a chance to block her next strike.

There. The strix's form shimmered for a second as she lifted her arm to strike at Corran; a wrinkled old woman in filthy rags. Rigan swung his blade two-handed, aiming for the witch's midsection, feeling the tip of his knife find purchase. The strix screamed, and his blade came away wet with old blood.

"Can you see her?" Corran asked, ready with his staff and sword but unable to get a fix on the enemy.

"Glimpses," Rigan replied, scanning the room. "How in the name of the gods can something hide in a room this empty?"

The air shimmered to Rigan's left and he dove toward it, knife leveled to slide through ribs and take the strix through the heart. He stumbled and fell as his blade met no resistance, wheeling just in time to see Corran thrown against the wall, hard enough to shake dust from the old thatch.

"Come and get me!" Rigan roared, trying to draw the strix away from his brother. Crazed laughter filled the room.

Corran lashed out with his sword, and the cackle faded to a hiss as his point drew blood. The witch's fist appeared and disappeared just long enough for a vicious backhand strike across his face, snapping his head to one side and making him stagger. He reeled, but his body reacted from long practice, catching his balance and letting him pivot to bring his staff around with his full strength. This time, it connected with a bone-snapping crack.

Rigan ran for the spot where the witch had to be, only to feel strong, bony hands shoving him, sending him stumbling in the other direction. He turned in time to get a glimpse of the strix's full form just as one hand clawed down his brother's arm, tearing away the protective charm and slashing through the strap that held his crossbow and quarrels. In the next instant, the witch's sharp nails dug into Corran's shoulder, fixing him in place, while her head ducked and her mouth opened wider than jaws should stretch, sinking sharp, stained teeth into Corran's throat.

"Corran!"

The strix raised her head, mouth covered with Corran's blood, and grinned at Rigan, using his brother's body as a shield. Her claws sank inches deep into Corran's shoulder, while blood flowed down his chest from the gaping wound in his neck. The strix shook Corran like a rag doll, sending his weapons flying.

Rigan started forward, but the strix tightened her grip and Corran's eyes flashed as he bit back a cry of pain, struggling against the witch's grasp. "Run the bitch through," he ordered.

The strix laughed. "Go ahead, Rigan. Put that blade right through your brother and into me, and I'll have all the blood I need."

"Leave him out of this," Rigan replied, advancing slowly toward the strix, trying not to look at the blood staining Corran's tunic. "Fight me and settle this, but leave him out of this."

"Rigan, don't—"

The strix laughed and dug her nails in tighter, making Corran wince. "As you wish."

Reality twisted. Everything changed.

Between one heartbeat and the next, the ramshackle barn vanished, and with it, Corran and the strix. Rigan stood alone in the front hall of a grand manor house. Doors opened on both sides of a corridor, and a sweeping stairway led to more floors above. Gray light filtered through dirty windows, providing just enough illumination for Rigan to get his bearings. Dust covered the parquet floor, and cobwebs hung from the huge candelabra. Rigan's eyes fixed on the spot where the strix had held Corran captive. A fresh pool of blood marked the floor. Next to it lay Corran's staff, crossbow, and sword.

"*All right, hunter,*" the strix mocked, her voice coming from everywhere and nowhere. "*I will fight you. Show me your magic. Amuse me.*" Her laugh echoed through the hall.

"Where's Corran?"

"*Every fight should have a prize. If I win, I keep all that lovely blood. If you win, you get him back, a little worse for wear. But you're going to have to settle this quickly, because he's bleeding steadily. Every drop makes me a little stronger, and him a little weaker.*"

"Show yourself!"

"*Find me.*"

Rigan thrust Corran's sword through his belt. He still had his pack, with the materials he would need to end the strix. He gripped his iron blade white-knuckled, then stared down the row of doors.

Are we still in the barn, or somewhere else? If we're somehow still in the barn, then the strix can't get past the circles outside. We're trapped. I can't help Corran until I kill the strix. How do I kill what I can't see?

He forced himself to take a deep breath. Drawing on the earth to power his magic had not worked, so this time, he called to the air. It was stale and sluggish, but not as tainted as the blood-soaked ground.

"Come and get me," Rigan muttered. He raised his left arm, palm toward the sky. He let the power flow through him, bursting from his open hand in a torrent of fire that hit the ceiling and fanned out, flames licking every corner and catching in the dry wood. As the flames caught, the fire fed back into Rigan's power, grounding him.

The strix screamed, and in the next heartbeat she stood before him. Madness flashed in her white-blue eyes, and lips stained red with blood parted over viciously sharp teeth. She hurled herself at Rigan, hands raised in claws.

The torrent of flames ended abruptly, and Rigan leveled a horizontal blast of fire at the strix, who vanished, appearing behind and to the side, raking sharp nails down his sword arm. He wheeled, slashing with the knife, opening a deep gash on her shoulder with the point of the blade.

Burning wood fell all around them as smoke filled the room. Sweat ran down Rigan's face as he and the strix circled. "Fire or sword. One way or the other, you lose," he grated, trying to ignore the pain from his wounds, pushing his fear for Corran from his mind.

"I've still got blood to feed me," the strix replied, her voice harsh. "You're nearly spent. And when you fall, I'll have your blood as well."

Rigan felt drained by his magic, despite his attempts to ground his power. The wounds were likely poisoned, and his head pounded. Blood soaked his shirt. The strix sprang at him again and Rigan dodged aside, barely evading her sharp nails. His sword bit deep, ripping her right arm open to the bone from wrist to elbow, a lethal strike if she were mortal.

"Stand still, boy. Don't fight. I'll be quick."

Rigan dove toward the strix, dropping and rolling to come up behind her, where Corran's crossbow lay. She charged toward him and he pushed her away with a blast of fire as he scrabbled for the bow. Enraged, she fell back, then came at him again. Rigan pulled the trigger and let the spelled quarrel fly.

The arrow took the strix square in the heart. "You can't kill me with an arrow," she mocked.

"An iron tip will work just fine."

As Rigan spoke, black veins branched and spread across the strix's body from the quarrel protruding from her chest. He seized his chance as the witch hesitated, and brought the iron sword around with his full strength, slicing through her neck and sending her head rolling.

The walls of the great hall shimmered, twisting and folding. Rigan stood in a burning barn as flaming thatch fell around him, blistering his arms and shoulders, singeing his hair. The strix's body lay a few feet away, her severed head a short distance beyond it. *This whole place is going to fall in on itself any moment, and I've still got to find Corran*, he thought, forcing himself to move.

Rigan pushed the witch's body against one of the burning beams, smiling grimly as the flames caught in her rags. From the bag on his back, he pulled a pouch of salt, amanita, and aconite. He shook the bags over the crone's corpse and sent a short blast of fire to incinerate her, kicking the head onto the pyre and taking a sliver of satisfaction from watching her burn.

Overhead, a beam groaned and more embers fell. *Running out of time.* When Rigan's magic touched the ground beneath the barn, he'd known where the witch had bled her victims. *Corran's down there,* he realized, *but how do I get to him?*

His gaze fell on a pattern of lines on the filthy floorboards. Rigan dropped to his knees, searching for a trapdoor, heedless of the blazing thatch that peppered his back and arms with burns. Blood and sweat soaked his shirt and his hair hung against his forehead. *We can't last long in this.* He found what he was looking for and heaved the trapdoor open. The stench of old blood hit him like a blow. "Corran!"

Rigan dropped into the darkness, and crouched until his eyes adjusted. Conjured handfire gave him enough light to see. The ground made a wet sucking sound with each step; the smell was overpowering, making him swallow hard to keep from retching. Overhead, he heard the flames roaring and felt the scorching heat through the floor. Odds were good the roof would come down, trapping them both. Rigan pushed those worries to the back of his mind as he made his way toward the crumpled figure lying on the blood-soaked ground.

"Gods, Corran." Rigan did not pause to feel for a pulse or check for breath. *I'm not leaving him here, no matter what.*

He rolled his brother onto his back, and tried not to notice his silence. Rigan grabbed Corran beneath the arms and pulled him toward the trapdoor when a crash sounded overhead. Sparks flew through the gaps in the floorboards, burning his face. A wave of heat washed over them, taking his breath away. The temperature climbed rapidly. *Can't get out that way. Trent and Ross won't be able to get in until after we're cooked—not that it'll take long.*

With the fire blazing over their heads, Rigan no longer needed his magic to see. One side of the rough cellar sloped down. He dragged Corran a few feet, breathing a sigh of relief when they were no longer directly under the burning structure. Rigan stared up at the ceiling and stood, extending his arms. Rough wood met his touch. He forced the power up and out, smashing through the boards and opening up a vision of the night sky.

Rigan panted with the heat and the exertion of magic. Sweat and blood ran in rivulets down his back and arms as he bent to get a good grip on Corran. Drawing again on his power, he managed to hoist his brother up and roll him onto the ground.

A crash behind him warned Rigan they were out of time, as the burning barn collapsed. He jumped, feeling flames on the back of his legs and his boots. He caught the edge of the opening with his arms, and tried to get a toe-hold to push himself up.

"We've got you." Trent and Ross grabbed Rigan's arms, hauling him up and out. Rigan lay face down on the cool ground, heaving for breath, heart crashing. He tried to push himself onto his knees, and succeeded on the second try.

"Corran—"

"He's breathing," Trent said.

Rigan shifted to get a better look at his brother. Blood ran from deep gashes carved across Corran's arm and chest, and from the raw bite in his throat. He lay pale and still, and Rigan felt his own heart skip a beat. *I've barely survived losing Kell. I can't lose Corran, too.* Despite Trent's reassurances, Rigan reached out to grasp Corran's wrist, pressing his fingertips into the flesh, waiting to feel the thready beat of a pulse. *Alive—barely. Eshtamon said he'd be hard to kill. Please, please let that be true.*

In the distance, Rigan could hear Aiden chanting, making sure that the strix's spirit would not return. Mir and Trent faced away from the burning barn, watching the rest of the ruins.

Rigan lay waiting for his heart to quiet. His skin was peppered with burns, his lungs ached and his eyes stung. But he was alive, and so was Corran—and the strix was gone.

"Let's bind up the worst of your wounds and get the two of you out of here." Aiden knelt beside Corran, making a careful examination. He reached into his pack and pulled out a flask of water infused with cleansing herbs and washed Corran's wounds, then dressed them with a poultice and fresh bandages. Aiden laid a hand over the most serious wounds, and began to chant quietly.

Rigan watched the healer with worry and admiration. Aiden looked pale and haggard, and Rigan knew his friend's magic had helped to defeat the strix, kept her contained within the wardings placed around the creature's lair. His foresight had helped them track the strix's movements, so that they didn't go in completely unprepared. But witches had their limits, and Aiden looked like he was nearing his.

After a few moments, the healer was finished. He turned to Rigan. "Before we go after those books, I need to treat the wounds she gave you, else they'll go bad."

"I've had worse. Save your magic."

"Can't have you bleeding all over the manuscripts," Aiden replied, raising an eyebrow. "Shut up and let me see to your injuries."

As Aiden got to work, Rigan glanced at his brother. Corran looked far too pale, even given the moonlight. His shallow breathing hitched with pain, and blood stained his clothes black. "We're going to have to carry him out," Rigan said.

Trent gave him a sidelong glance. "You're going to have your hands full just walking out."

Ross returned just then with four sturdy, newly-cut saplings. He fished in his pack for rope. "I'll rig a travois." In a few minutes, Ross had tied the four poles in a rectangle, then secured his cloak over them.

"Load him on." Ross and Trent grabbed Corran by his shoulders and feet and fastened him with the rest of the rope.

"Go," Trent said. "We need to get Below."

Aiden helped Rigan to his feet, and together they headed for the tower. They paused at the doorway, and Aiden called on his foresight, checking for danger. "She's gone," Aiden said after a moment. "And there's nothing else in there. The strix kept people away from the site, but I don't think she ever cared for the tower. Too far away from fresh dirt. Strixes need the dirt to anchor their power and regenerate."

"Let's go see what remains of the library," Rigan said, dusting himself off. "We've still got a long ride ahead of us."

It did not take long for them to find the library. "Empty," Aiden sighed.

Rigan stood staring in silence. He'd known it was unlikely the Crown Prince's soldiers had left anything of value behind, but he still felt his heart sink when they found the room filled floor to ceiling with bare shelves.

Aiden gave him an encouraging slap on the shoulder. "Come on. Soldiers cleared it, but monks and scholars built it. You think they left the good stuff out in the open?"

Together, they began to examine the back of the bookshelves and the shelves themselves, tapping gently, running their fingers lightly over surfaces, looking for hidden catches, eying spaces to see if dimensions added up.

"Got something," Aiden said after several minutes. Rigan heard the *snick* of a latch opening, and a hidden drawer slid out of the center bookshelf. "Never mind, it's empty."

"I found something," Rigan said a moment later when a section on the back of the bookcase he was examining swung open, revealing a hidden cache of books. They searched the rest of the room, but discovered no other hiding places.

"Let's load up what we've got, and get out of here," Aiden said.

Trent and the hunters greeted them with relief. "It's about time," Mir muttered. "Going to be a long walk back to the horses." They had borrowed horses from a stable not far from the city wall. Aiden made sure no one would remember them. *Bad enough to hang as a hunter, let alone a horse thief,* Rigan thought.

Ross maneuvered until the ends of the travois poles were on his shoulders, then rose from a squat. "Let's go."

Rigan focused his attention on putting one foot in front of the other, trying to ignore the pounding headache. He had remembered to ground himself, had tried to anchor his power as best he could, but it had still taken a toll, despite his gift from Eshtamon. Losing blood hadn't helped; his wounds sapped his strength.

When they reached the horses, Trent and Ross lifted Corran off the travois and laid him across his saddle, securing him with rope. It took Rigan two tries to get onto his horse, before he held out his hand for the reins to guide Corran's mount. "Give him to me," he said, hoping they could not see how hard he squeezed his knees against his horse to keep his seat. Trent met Rigan's gaze, and handed over the reins.

"We'll get both of you back Below," Trent said, guessing Rigan's thoughts as he stared at his brother's still form. "I promise."

"That's all I can do." Aiden sat back. His hands were covered in Corran's blood, and he looked like he might pass out from exhaustion.

"Will he live?" Rigan sat on the other side of the bed, where he had kept vigil for the last three candlemarks. He had helped Aiden remove Corran's blood-soaked clothing and wash his wounds, grimacing at the deep slashes and the bruises that purpled his brother's back and shoulders. Rigan's hand gripped Corran's wrist, reassuring himself that the pulse beneath his fingers was steady.

Aiden blew out a long breath. "I don't know. He's still with us, so that's something." He shook his head. "Rigan—I don't know why he didn't die candlemarks ago. How could he lose this much blood and still be alive?"

Rigan wrestled with that question through the long night as they stitched up Corran's wounds and salved the burns that blistered his arms and face. He had waved away Aiden's concerns about his own injuries.

"Eshtamon said he'd be a lot harder to kill," Rigan said quietly. "Not entirely immortal, but… protected."

Aiden looked up as he washed his hands in a bowl of water. "I'd say Eshtamon kept his part of the bargain tonight. But I'm not entirely sure whether it's a blessing or a curse."

"The bite—"

"You were with him when it happened. You didn't see her feed him her blood, so he's not going to turn. And she didn't drain him, although any normal person would have bled out from those wounds." He managed a tired smile. "Good thing you have an Elder God on your side."

Rigan was still watching the rise and fall of Corran's chest. "I'm not counting on Eshtamon showing up to save us beyond what he's already done. I don't imagine he helped us out of the goodness of his heart. Pretty sure there's something in it for him. But we were out of other options, and it was the best deal we were going to get."

Aiden dried his hands and turned to Rigan. "No more excuses. You need healing, too."

Rigan knew arguing was pointless. His arm and back ached. Blood made his shirt black and stiff, and a scattershot of blisters throbbed across his arms, shoulders and back. He drew a deep breath, still tasting the smoke that made his throat and chest burn. He'd been drawing on his magic to stay upright since before they got back to the house.

"You can't keep doing that." Aiden raised an eyebrow. "You think I don't know why you're not passed out on the other bed? I know you said you grounded your magic before you burned the barn down around your ears, but I also know you're not anchored now, and I doubt you bothered on the ride back."

"I'm functioning."

Elinor brought up food and whiskey for Rigan and Aiden while the hunters stayed downstairs, keeping watch. She laid a comforting hand on Rigan's shoulder and he reached up, twining his fingers with hers. Only then did he realize how filthy his hands were, streaked with blood, soot, and dirt. Elinor tightened her grip, reassuring him with her presence. She came and went from the room more times than Rigan could count, fetching whatever Aiden needed, helping him prepare water and poultices. Polly stayed with the others, putting food on the table and tending their less serious wounds.

"You killed the strix, stayed alive, and got Corran out," Aiden said, moving around Corran's bed. "Now it's time to let me fix you up." He poured a couple of fingers of whiskey into a cup and pressed it into Rigan's hand. "Drink that. Then we're going to get you out of your bloody clothes and wash out those gashes before they get infected. I wasn't kidding about the taint on those claws."

Rigan knocked back the whiskey, flinching as it burned his raw throat. Moving gingerly, he peeled his shirt off, closing his eyes as the fabric stuck to partly-scabbed gashes. Blisters dotted his hands and forearms. Now that he actually looked at his shirt, he saw dozens of charred holes where embers had fallen on him. The tight skin across his shoulders let him know there were more burns than he could see.

"She got you good."

"I did her one better," Rigan replied, but there was no triumph in his voice.

Aiden poured whiskey into another cup, then walked back to Rigan. "We'll clean it out with whiskey, then cleanse with magic. I'm not taking any chances. Brace yourself."

Rigan clenched his teeth as Aiden dribbled the whiskey across his open wounds, biting back a cry of pain. His hands gripped the sides of the chair, arms tensing, and his back arched. When it was over, his forehead beaded with sweat and his breath came fast and shallow.

"The cuts are already going bad," Aiden said without looking up. "Worse than Corran's. Makes me think the taint festers in magic."

Rigan swallowed hard, trying to stay upright. He knew he could not hide his fever from the healer, and he flinched at Aiden's touch.

"I added more sage to the water, and some agrimony," Aiden continued through Rigan's silence. "Along with what Elinor put in there—and her own magic—it should knock out anything witchy."

Rigan stiffened as the water stung against raw flesh, and hissed through his teeth.

"From that reaction, I'd say the medicine's overdue," Aiden observed.

Rigan focused on his breathing to distract him as Aiden stitched the deepest gashes closed, covered them with salve, and bandaged the wounds. When he finished, he handed Rigan another whiskey.

"Drink that. You need to sleep. I'll sit up with both of you. Elinor can change off with me toward morning. Corran's not going anywhere. Trent and Ross have the first watch." He gave a tired smile and patted the scabbard on his belt. "And just in case, I've got a spelled blade. You're safe."

"Wake me if anything changes." Rigan glanced at Corran's sleeping form.

"I will. Now—you can best help Corran by getting some sleep and letting the poultices do their job. I've got your back."

Chapter Thirty-Four

"I EXPECTED A better showing." Crown Prince Aliyev's disapproval was clear both in his tone and the cold appraisal in his eyes.

"Our spies have kept us informed," Machison replied. "Sarolinia and Kasten have the most to gain by interfering in the negotiations. Jorgeson's confirmed that Kadar or his representatives have been in touch through intermediaries. We're certain Sarolinia was behind the attack on the ambassador from Garenoth, and that Kasten had something to do with the recall of the Itaran ambassador. We've countered their efforts, and the negotiations are moving forward."

"Whispers are reaching King Rellan that the agreement is in danger," Aliyev said, as if he had not heard Machison. "He has no personal leaning toward either Kadar or Gorog—and less toward Tamas—so long as money flows into Ravenwood. It's of no interest to him which of the Merchant Princes prospers more, and I thought I made it clear to you that I was not willing to endanger the agreement for the benefit of any one party."

He turned to look at Machison with a cold stare. "The King is likely to see any threat to the League's stability—or its prosperity—

to be an attack on his person. I have been warned that Rellan is... concerned, and watching the situation very closely."

"The situation is under control." Machison met Aliyev's gaze, matching his unyielding stare.

"That's not what I hear."

"From Blackholt?" Machison gave a snort. "The man is insane, drunk on his own importance."

"Have a care. His power is real."

"And he dribbles out its benefits to make his patrons beg for his support," Machison grated. "The king's addiction to using high-powered blood mages is what's causing the real problem."

"A matter of opinion, and beside the point," Aliyev snapped. "Ravenwood needs to maintain its ranking. This agreement must be completed successfully. I will not permit squabbling over a few percentages of profit to undo the fortunes of the entire city-state. I thought I was putting my best man and my most powerful blood witch on this issue." His voice was low and cold. "Was I mistaken?"

"I won't fail you, m'lord. But I am not sure of Blackholt's loyalties—to you or to me."

"What makes you doubt them?"

"Blackholt's choice of monsters, and his timing and location of the strikes, have not followed my direction as they should," Machison replied. "I believe he's actively working against me. He's arrogant and sloppy, and it's given the hunters and witches an opening they were all too happy to exploit."

"That's your problem, not mine. And not Blackholt's."

Machison seethed. "Perhaps Blackholt sees no reason to avoid mistakes if he pays no consequence when they're made. He fears no one—not even you."

Aliyev fixed him with a glare. "Then he is a fool." He turned away. "I will consider what you've said. But have a care: your performance has not inspired confidence."

"The trade talks with Garenoth continue without interruption, still moving in your favor despite the efforts of our enemies," Machison promised. *All Aliyev and the King really care about is gold in their pockets. They'll have that—and Gorog will keep his edge, which means gold for me as well.*

"The meetings have continued, but hardly without interruption," Aliyev corrected. "And while the monsters and the guards have been active, the Balance is askew. You are behind on the Cull."

"We've done everything we promised, kept our part of the bargain," Machison shot back. "Kept the commoners in line and frightened."

Anger flashed in Aliyev's eyes. "It's not enough. If we fail to keep the Balance, earning the ire of a few Guild Masters or Merchant Princes will be nothing in comparison to the consequences."

"The Cull is Blackholt's job. My guards have done their part. Seeing these negotiations succeed is my priority," Machison countered. "They're going well—why else would Kadar send an assassin after me?"

"I don't know what you're talking about."

"Just a few days ago, an assassin attacked me in my rooms. He got close enough to cut me with his knife. I fought him and he fled, but he left behind this." Machison withdrew the coin with Kadar's face on it and held it up. Traces of his blood still darkened the stamped metal.

"This... is none of your concern," Aliyev said finally. Machison could practically see the wheels turning in the Crown Prince's mind as he assessed the possible reasons for the attack.

"Really? Because it felt like my concern, my lord, when the knife nearly opened up my ribs," Machison snapped. Aliyev's reaction told him that the Crown Prince suspected a proxy attack, perhaps related to other affairs.

"Despite our differences of opinion, I have no desire to lose a valuable asset."

"Should I expect future visits?" Machison ground out, teeth

clenched. *I do not want to be a bone pulled between two hungry dogs.* "If so, I'll alert my guards."

"Leave Kadar to me." Aliyev sounded weary. "I led him to believe he stood to gain ground in this negotiation. Obviously, he doubts that, and is trying to remind me of what he sees as our agreement. You were... a convenient way to leave a message."

"Perhaps in the future, a letter might be preferred?" Machison's tone barely hid his fury. "Because if a brigand appears in my rooms again, I'll make sure his head is on a pike by the city gates come morning, no matter who he's beholden to."

"Point taken. I'll see that you're not inconvenienced again." Aliyev poured himself a drink. "And since I'm safeguarding your life, use the time wisely. The Guilds are restless."

"They're always restless."

"The Guilds are tired of petitioning the Merchant Princes, and have started sending their representatives to me. I turn them away, of course, and send them back to yammer at Gorog or the others, but it's an almost daily complaint from one Guild or another, about losing their members to the monsters, or seeing the city go up in flames."

"You heard 'almost daily' from the Guilds before Blackholt began manipulating the monsters," Machison said. "Some of those Guilds are seeing retribution for shielding hunters among their own. A word from you to your witch might make him less sloppy with his magic."

Aliyev shrugged. "You wanted Blackholt; you control him."

For just an instant, Machison saw a glint of fear in the man's eyes. *Perhaps you can't completely control him, either. I took the gift of Blackholt's abilities as a gesture of support. Did Aliyev set up both Blackholt and me to fail so that he could eliminate two 'liabilities' without repercussion, and draw Gorog out into a vulnerable position at the same time?*

"You—and Blackholt—serve at my pleasure," Aliyev said. "Get

the city, the witch, and the negotiations under control and don't embarrass me, or I will be forced to take measures. Am I making myself clear?"

"Yes, my lord. Completely." Long experience kept Machison's tone neutral, but he was certain Aliyev had read the full extent of his resentment.

BACK AT THE Lord Mayor's palace, Machison restrained himself from pacing only by remembering how much the wound from the assassin's blade still ached. Every time he winced, it stoked his anger at being Aliyev's proxy.

"What of the men you sent after the hunters?" he snapped at Jorgeson, not bothering to hide his surly mood.

"They were only partially successful."

"Explain."

"I sent the guards after the men we were able to identify as hunters—the undertaker, the lamp merchant's son, and several others. Their orders were to capture the witch and the hunters and burn their shops."

"And?"

Jorgeson's lips pressed tightly together. "The men set the fires. A few of the shops were saved, but still badly damaged. The warning was quite clear."

"But the men—"

"Escaped," Jorgeson replied curtly, eyes straight ahead, standing rigidly at attention. "We traced their movements and concluded they'd taken shelter Below."

"Then get them! Damn the agreement, I want those hunters!"

Jorgeson waited out Machison's temper, remaining silent until the Lord Mayor had time to rein in his anger. "Our... arrangement with Below is based on practicality," he said with deference. "As we've discussed, we don't have the strength in numbers. Send a few, they're unlikely to come back out. Send in a regiment, and they're likely to start a war, one we're ill-prepared to win at this moment. They're already on edge after the attack on the witches."

Machison clenched and unclenched his fist. "Are you saying we just *let them go?*"

Jorgeson shook his head. "You misunderstand me, m'lord. We don't send guards. We send assassins. We hunt the hunters."

A smile quirked at the corner of Machison's lips. "Go on."

"I've contacted my spies in the Guilds. The hunters that fled were among the most skilled of their kind."

"You almost sound like you're praising them."

Jorgeson shrugged. "It's a mistake to underestimate an enemy. I'm merely stating a fact, m'lord."

Machison grunted, and gestured for Jorgeson to continue.

"We have names, thanks to our spies and what the witch-traitors from Below have told us. Corran Valmonde, the undertaker. Most likely also his brother, Rigan. Mir, the blacksmith's son. Calfon, the son of the lamp merchant. Trent the butcher, Dilin from the shipwrights, Tomor the cobbler, Ross the farrier and two others, Ellis and Illir, from the Coopers' Guild. All tradesmen from Wrighton, all hunters. It would be imprudent to assume, just because the Guilds have officially disavowed the hunters, that there might not be a... reaction to retaliations against their own. The men were all well-regarded before they took to hunting. Their friends might have ideas that don't line up with the Guild Masters'. For that matter, who knows how the Guild Masters really feel about them? And remember—the commoners consider the hunters to be heroes, not brigands."

Aliyev's warnings still rang in Machison's ears. *Can't allow this to get out of hand. Daren't allow it to affect the negotiations. Can't have the Guilds missing shipments—or withholding their goods. Can't have the rabble rioting in the streets, either. Damn. This is beginning to feel like a cage.*

"Are there any hunters left Above?"

"Fewer each day. We'll flush out any hold-outs, or drive them so deep that they won't dare return."

"Well done. We've got to keep the Guilds working against each other, competing for advantage. Keep the residents frightened of their shadows, keep the Balance. Make sure that when you capture any hunters, you leave evidence that they were betrayed by rival Guilds. That should give the Guilds something to argue about."

"It should indeed, m'lord."

"And what do your spies hear of Kadar?"

"Nothing new. There's bad blood between Kadar and Gorog, going back a decade," Jorgeson said. "I've heard several versions of why that is, but it all comes down to money and pride. With the current negotiations, their resentments have gotten worse. I suspect Kadar was warning you—or the Crown Prince—that if he doesn't get more of the spoils in the new agreement, he will cause problems."

It may be nothing personal, but it could still get me killed, or beggar Ravenwood if their sniping manages to foul the agreement with Garenoth. I have no problem about rising with Gorog's fortunes, but I'll be damned if I fall with him. We've got to be careful.

"And the Wanderers?"

"Gone, for now. That's the best we can hope for."

He remembered the old woman from his nightmares, and suppressed a shiver. "Let's keep it that way." He thought for a moment. "What about their sigils? Did the prisoners reveal what they were meant to do?"

Jorgeson shook his head. "No, m'lord. Blackholt was inventive with his methods, murdered the man's wife and children slowly and painfully in front of him, before turning his knives and magic on the man himself, but he gave us nothing."

"So we have no idea whether or not the sigils are still active?"

"Not for certain, no."

"Do better," Machison snapped. "We've on dangerous ground between Gorog and Kadar. We can't afford to slip up." He didn't need to say *we won't survive any more mistakes.*

Machison's stomach churned as he descended to Blackholt's dungeon. He swallowed hard, breathing through his mouth to avoid the worst of the stench.

"Back so soon?"

Machison could not mistake the mockery in Blackholt's tone. *Maybe the very act of employing his services taints the soul. Perhaps it's like the Dark Ones, whose promises are lies and whose gifts are always traps.* "What of the witches Below?"

"An interesting outcome. The safe house was destroyed, and the witches are dead."

"All of them?"

"All of those I wanted dead. Two were my men carrying out my orders, and the other two might be of use, once we break them."

"Have you captured them?"

"We're tracking them. They're the two I already told you about—a gifted healer and an undertaker with uncommon magic for his trade. They would be useful to Aliyev… or others."

"Undertaker? One of the Valmonde brothers?" Machison remembered Jorgeson's report a few candlemarks earlier. "Our spies believe the Valmondes are hunters."

"The witch's brother is a hunter. But he was not—until circumstances forced his hand. Now that he knows the guards are looking for him, that may change."

"How difficult can it be to find and capture two 'middling' witches?" Machison demanded. His head throbbed.

"Not difficult at all, if they *were* middling witches," Blackholt replied. "As it turns out both are more than we initially thought them to be."

"A danger to us?"

"A minor obstacle," Blackholt said with a dismissive wave of his hand. "The healer's power is not offensive. Neither, for the most part, is the undertaker's. And yet, that's where the surprise lies. According to my man, the undertaker has used his magic to kill on several occasions. Interesting."

"Interesting? If he's a danger, put an end to him."

Blackholt smiled. "He could be a valuable asset. Magic of that strength is rare. It's a shame to waste it. We will capture him and make a prize of him for the Crown Prince, take his brother as a surety, make use of his magic."

"An unwilling witch? Sounds more likely to kill us than to be of any use."

"One could say the same thing about an unwilling woman, yet you've taken enough of those to your bed, haven't you?"

Machison glared at him. "If the Crown Prince wants new pets, let him take the risk himself. Too much is at stake right now. Get these missing witches out of our way before they can cause problems. I want the witches captured and the hunters dead." *If these witches actually do have potential, I'll keep them myself, as a surety against Blackholt and Gorog.*

Blackholt had the ill grace to look amused. "As you wish, m'lord. But you ought not be in such a hurry to hear the voices of the dead."

Machison froze, recalling the words of the oracle at the temple, words he had shared with no one, words that echoed in his nightmare. "What did you say?"

"The Valmondes are undertakers. They have grave magic. Not true necromancy, but something that enables them to banish the restless dead. I have it on good authority the younger Valmonde's magic goes beyond the usual. He can summon spirits as well as banish them, burn a man to death with fire, and hear the confessions of the dead."

The last words sent a chill through Machison no fire could warm. "Confess the dead?"

Blackholt's smile was triumphant, catching the Lord Mayor by surprise. "It's a rare skill, being able to hear the secrets the dead confide. Dirty secrets, old sins, broken confidences, the kinds of things that should never come to light. The things men take to their grave."

Machison did not need much imagination to see the danger in such power, especially if it were to be seized by the Merchant Princes, used against their enemies. "It's too dangerous," he said. "He can't be permitted to remain free."

"He's proving to be a hard man to capture."

"We can't let Kadar—or anyone else—get their hands on him,"

"I'll see to it, immediately."

Valmonde would be the greatest threat to Blackholt, not to me or to the Guild Masters or the Merchant Princes. He'd be the best weapon against the blood witch. The oracle was right. The tide is turning, and I need to rein in Blackholt, regain control of the situation. Perhaps Valmonde is just the tool needed to make that possible.

Chapter Thirty-Five

DILIN NEVER SAW the arrow that killed him.

"Down!" Mir yelled, too late.

The crossbow quarrel tore through Dilin's chest with enough force to knock him back against the stone wall of an old house. Dilin stared uncomprehendingly, eyes wide with pain and shock. Then he slid down the wall, leaving a bloody trail.

Another quarrel ripped through Corran's shirt, skimming his shoulder, and he belly-crawled beneath a wagon. Mir cursed as a third bolt hit the wall an inch behind where he had just been.

Panting, Corran looked at Mir. "You hit?"

"No, but it was bloody close."

"Dilin—"

"Can't go back for him now. He's gone." Mir shifted to get a better view of the location of the sniper—the upper level of a building across the street.

"We can't stay here," Corran said.

Another quarrel flew, hitting the wagon above their heads. This time, they smelled alcohol and burning cloth, and saw bright tongues of fire where the flaming arrow blazed against the dry wood of the wagon.

"Shit," Mir breathed. Corran followed his gaze. The street was largely deserted, lit only by a few widely spaced torches. They were in one the quieter sections of Below, but that just meant fewer witnesses. The block ahead of them afforded little protection, and they did not want to lead the archer back to their house.

"Come on!" Corran rolled beneath the wagon and came up on the other side, careful to stay low and keep the wagon between him and the archer.

"Think we can move this thing?" Corran asked, setting a hand on the wagon and rocking it back and forth. The cart's broken wheel turned stiffly, and he guessed the wreck had sat abandoned for quite some time. But with both of them putting muscle into the effort, they got the wagon rolling slowly down the street.

"Now what?" Mir asked. Another quarrel sailed past his head.

"Haven't figured that part out yet," Corran grunted as he heaved the wagon on, inch by inch.

"Makes you wonder why here and why now, doesn't it?" Mir reached for the quarrel that had nearly taken him in the head. "Army issue," he said, turning it in the faint torchlight. "Whoever he is, he's not an amateur."

Corran, Dilin, and Mir had gone to the marketplace for supplies, a week after the fight with the strix. Just a normal errand, something someone in the household did every day or two, and that made Corran wonder: who had been watching them, to know their routine?

"I wish we could warn the others," Corran said. "Whoever's up there didn't just happen upon us." An archer with a military-issue crossbow, hiding in an abandoned building on a desolate street in a forgotten undercity? Nothing coincidental about it.

"Assassin?"

"That's my bet." There were no more shots, and that worried Corran. A steady barrage would have assured them of the archer's location. Odds were good that the assassin was shifting position while they were pinned down. They had not worn their swords to the market, but each man had a long knife and a selection of daggers. Still, a crossbow could pick them off from a distance, long before they could reach their attacker with a blade.

"If you've got any great ideas, now would be a good time to mention them," Corran growled.

A *twang-thud* sounded from the other side of the street, and both Corran and Mir dropped to the ground as a quarrel hit their side of the wagon.

"Run!" Mir yelled. The two men ran for the shelter of the nearest alley, as two more bolts shot after them. One sliced into Corran's hip, slashing his skin but glancing off the bone. The other caught Mir in the shoulder. He stumbled, gasping in pain. Corran grabbed him by the arm and nearly dragged him around the corner.

"Damn. We've got to bind that." Corran ripped a strip of cloth from his shirt and tied it around the hunter's shoulder. Blood soaked through almost immediately, but it was better than nothing.

Corran heard footsteps, and froze. Mir's eyes widened as he heard the same thing. The archers were on the move, heading down to the street. The hunters had become the prey.

"Inside." Corran pushed open the nearest door, pulling Mir with him into the dark interior. The long-abandoned house smelled of rats and dust, and the dim torchlight outside didn't penetrate the gloom. Corran and Mir staggered into the room, and Corran's boot kicked at debris. *Hide. We've got to find a place to hide.*

He would have given anything for Rigan's handfire, though Corran was grateful his brother wasn't in danger with them. The assassins weren't stupid; they would figure out that their quarry had gone to ground in one of the old buildings along the alley. But perhaps in the darkness, Corran might be able to level the battlefield.

"Can you use your arm?" Corran whispered beside Mir's ear, not wanting to give away their position. Mir nodded.

"Get around the door. And hope for the best." Corran went left as Mir went right, both drawing their long knives and waiting.

Crossbows were distance weapons, and the archers gave up their advantage the moment they came down to ground level.

The door to the street opened and their pursuer thrust a torch into the darkness. Corran lunged. He swung his blade high, going for the throat, but the assassin blocked him with a blade of his own. Mir attacked from the other side, and his blade sliced across the man's belly. The assassin jabbed his torch toward Mir, forcing him back, then pivoted as Corran pressed forward again, scoring a deep cut on the assassin's shoulder and narrowly evading a strike aimed for his own throat. Even so, the killer's knife scored a gash in Corran's bicep that made him bite back a curse.

Corran backed up a step and Mir pushed forward, between the doorway and the assassin. The hired killer angled himself so that he could keep both men in view, showing neither of them his back. Corran glanced at Mir, who blinked in agreement.

In the next breath, Corran dove forward, angling his knife for the assassin's face, forcing him to block the blow. Mir lunged, sinking his knife deep into the hired killer's side with one hand and dashing the torch from his grip with the other. Corran dove to grab the torch before it could set the building on fire, and came up in one smooth movement, slashing his blade across the assassin's throat. The man fell to his knees, struggling for breath as blood soaked his clothing. Corran threw the torch out of the door into the street.

"Move!" Corran hissed. He and Mir left the body where it lay and retreated further into the darkness of the house, trying not to stumble over the refuse littering the sagging floor. They had bested one attacker, and both been injured in the process. Mir stumbled, and Corran got under one shoulder to help him keep moving. From what Corran had seen in the torchlight, Mir looked spent; he would not be up to another fight. Given Mir's injuries, there was no chance of outrunning the second assassin out in the alley; at any rate, the moment they stepped through the doorway, they'd be framed like targets for the kill. The best they could do would be to use the slim advantage of the darkened building, and hope that they could elude their pursuer.

If we die here, would Rigan and Aiden even find our bodies? Corran fought back despair, stoking his anger to keep on going. They would not have long to wait for the next attack.

Corran shifted his weight and felt the old floorboards give. He bit back a yelp as his foot sank through the rotted wood, and he stumbled, pitching forward. More of the floor fell away, and Corran went with it. Mir grabbed him by the arm, choking back a groan as he strained his damaged shoulder, but it was enough to yank Corran back from the edge of the abyss and send the two men tumbling over gods knew what in the darkness.

A moment later, the second assassin stepped up to the doorway. He had a crossbow in one hand and a candle in the other.

"You've put up a worthy fight," the assassin said, his lips twitching into a cold smile. "But it ends now."

"Who sent you?" Corran knew the man could see them, and before he took a quarrel to the chest, he at least wanted to know the name of whoever had paid for his murder.

"Does it matter? You won't be telling anyone."

Corran and Mir scuttled back, trying to put as much distance as they could between them and their attacker, futile as it was at this range. The assassin moved forward, his candle illuminating a dim circle in the darkness.

"Humor me. The dead can't talk." Corran tried to keep the man talking, to forestall the inevitable. And as he stared at the candle and gauged how much light it shed, a desperate hope flared.

Corran dragged himself backward again, and Mir pushed back with his feet, sliding across the filthy floor. If they stayed here much longer, Mir would bleed out.

The attacker took another step. "I was hired by the head of the Lord Mayor's guards," he replied, a note of pride in his voice. "Though sending assassins is too good for street ruffians."

So there's a hierarchy for who gets to kill you? I guess I should feel honored, Corran thought. "How did you find us?"

The assassin's laugh was cold. "It's what we do. I'm very good at my job," he said as he aimed his crossbow. At this distance, he couldn't miss Corran's heart.

"Time to go," the assassin said softly. He took one more step… and pitched headlong through the crumbling floor as the weakened boards gave way beneath his weight.

"Go!" Corran rasped, hauling Mir to his feet. They kept to the wall, shuffling carefully to keep the floor from collapsing completely beneath their weight, making their way toward the door. Far below them, they heard a body hit hard dirt.

We could step outside and find out the hard way that there was a third archer. We could get back to the house and find everyone else dead. Corran pushed down those thoughts, intent on getting to the doorway. They'd retrieve Dilin's body later, give him a proper burial. But right now, staying alive and keeping his brother and his friends safe was uppermost in Corran's mind, all else be damned.

THEY HAD ONLY gone a block when a voice sounded behind them. "What's your hurry?"

Corran and Mir froze.

"Hello, Corran."

"Who in the Abyss are you?"

"Someone who's been looking for your brother."

Corran felt himself go cold. "Damian."

"I wasn't sure you'd know my name. Turn around. We'll go into that building over there. Try to run and I'll make you beg for permission to breathe."

Corran turned, and saw the tall witch silhouetted against the dim glow of torches. "This makes it easier than I dared hope," Damian said.

"Makes what easier?" Corran challenged, though he had a good idea of what Damian's answer would be.

"Finishing the job. Both of you, open that door and go inside." He gestured toward the entrance to another dilapidated, abandoned structure.

Corran weighed his chances. He glanced at Mir, and then both men bolted.

Corran hadn't gone five steps before he crashed into an invisible wall, as solid and unyielding as stone.

"You're not going anywhere except into the building," Damian said. "Move, or I'll burn you where you stand."

"We're moving." Corran made no attempt to hide the anger in his voice. Damian's handfire lit the way, illuminating the shabby room.

"Sit," Damian ordered, gesturing toward the wall. He tossed a length of rope to Corran. "Tie his hands."

"He doesn't pose you any threat."

"Tie. His. Hands."

Corran scowled, but did as he was ordered.

"Now remove your knives—all of them—and slide them away from you. Try anything, and I'll burn your friend before you can draw another breath."

Corran felt a killing rage building inside, but he said nothing, sure that Damian could read his thoughts from the look on his face.

Damian tossed a set of manacles to Corran.

"Put them on."

He glowered as he closed the heavy cuffs around his wrists. "You betrayed the witches."

"Necessary losses," Damian said with a shrug. "They were becoming... inconvenient."

"For whom? You, or the Lord Mayor?"

Damian ignored him. "They were content staying Below, wasting their magic on hedgewitch work. Then your brother showed up, with promising power. He made progress quickly enough to make him a threat—or an asset, to the right people. He started to ask questions. The others were listening, and bringing up things better left alone. I had to stop them before they became a problem. And I knew he'd be valuable."

"So you and Alton killed the other witches—and for what?"

Damian shrugged. "I don't expect you to understand. The game is a lot bigger than fighting ghouls or burning *lida*."

"Did you come back to finish Aiden and my brother?"

"Is that what you think?" Damian sounded genuinely amused. "That I overlooked them? They were the only two of real value."

"Value?"

Damian chuckled. "A witch of Rigan's potential? Powerful men will pay good money for a tool like that, properly broken and trained."

Corran's fists tightened. "Stay away from my brother."

"Actually, you're going to bring him to me."

"Are you the one summoning the monsters?" Corran's gaze locked with Damian's gray eyes. He took cold satisfaction in the witch's surprise.

"Me? No. But thanks to Rigan, I realized that magic presents many more possibilities than I had ever considered. In fact, that little... incident with the witches? In a way, I've Rigan to thank for my change of heart."

"Rigan?"

"He got me thinking. I had never wondered about the why and wherefore of monsters before. Then I realized that Rigan was on to something, and when I went Above, I learned just how limited my thinking had been."

Damian sneered. "Those stupid witches Below could only worry about not getting caught, healing a few fevers, warding off monsters and guards. But Above..." He waved his hand toward the ceiling. "Magic is done on a whole different level. I could feel it as soon as I stepped into the street. And I wanted to be part of that."

"So tell me, did you kill the witches to curry favor? Was that your first assignment?"

The witch chuckled. "It proved I was sincere. Bringing in you, Rigan, and Aiden will earn me a place at the table."

Corran glanced to where Mir sat slumped against the wall, blood staining his shirt, soaking through his bandage. His friend was dying, and Corran's odds didn't look much better. But maybe, with luck, he could keep Rigan and Aiden safe.

"Whose table?"

"My patron's."

"I'm surprised you're sharing the spoils with Alton. Where is he, anyway?"

Damian's lips twitched. "Delivering a message."

"So you've come back for Rigan—and we're the bait."

"Very good. You worked it out for yourself. No need to take on the rest of the hunters. Just bring Rigan and Aiden to us."

Fear knotted Corran's stomach. "And then what?"

"Nothing that concerns you."

"Did you send the assassins?"

Damian smiled. "No, but I knew they were coming. I figured we could make the most of the opportunity."

"Same patrons?"

He shrugged. "I honestly couldn't tell you. Probably not. There's a lot more going on Above than you ever realized."

Corran looked up as footsteps sounded in the doorway. Another man entered.

"Message delivered. They know where and when."

So that's Alton. Corran sized up his captors. In a fair fight, he stood a good chance of taking either of them hand-to-hand; perhaps both of them, with a blade. But not when they had magic on their side. He swallowed. If Rigan knew he and Mir were prisoners, his brother would come. Might not even put up a fight. Corran was pretty sure Damian wasn't interested in an exchange. He had already made it clear that he cared nothing for Mir's life. Corran might prove a valuable hostage to keep his brother in line, but only for a while.

Corran could only guess how long they waited. The bells in the market tower were a distant jumble. He fervently hoped that Rigan and the hunters had run for their lives, taking Elinor and Polly with them. But he knew that his brother would never leave him behind, and he suspected the same was true of Aiden.

"You wanted me here; I'm here."

Rigan's voice came from the far corner of the room, not the doorway where Alton and Damian kept vigil. He stepped out of the shadows, and Corran took a moment's satisfaction in the shock on Damian's face. "There are many exits and entrances in Below. Might want to check that out, next time you decide to take hostages." Rigan's steady voice barely hid his anger.

"Don't mind me; I took the back way." Aiden's voice came from the doorway. Damian glanced away from Rigan, just for a moment, and everything happened at once.

Fire blasted from Rigan's hand, aimed at Damian's chest. Damian gestured, and the fire bounced from a translucent barrier that shimmered like a soap bubble. He made a fist and thrust out his arm, and Rigan flew backward across the room. Corran heard his brother hit the far wall.

Damian strode toward Rigan and Corran dove forward, grabbing at the witch's leg, wrapping his manacles around his foot. Damian responded with a vicious kick but Corran held on, wrapping the chain tighter, feeling metal grind on bone.

He heard a scuffle on the other side of the room, but could not spare his attention to see how Aiden fared against Alton. Damian kicked harder, landing a blow with his left foot to the side of Corran's head. Corran saw stars and tried to stay conscious, his focus narrowing to keeping the iron chain locked around Damian's ankle.

Rigan sent another blast of fire. Damian's hand jerked up to block the magic, but this time, he failed to stop the flames. Corran jerked backward as Damian's hair and clothing caught. "Corran, get away!" Rigan yelled.

Corran scrabbled backward, as Damian rose to his feet, a living, burning effigy. Fire wreathed his face—jaw set, eyes cold—and in two steps, he stumbled toward where Rigan had vanished into the shadows.

"Watch out!" Corran yelled as Damian grabbed for his brother, flames spreading, and then the two figures pitched backward as the ceiling came down, smothering them and the fire beneath it.

"Rigan!" Corran staggered to his feet, only to have Aiden catch him by the arm. Corran tried to shake loose of his grip. "Rigan's under there!"

Aiden's hand held him fast. "And so is Damian. Let me handle this."

Corran glanced past Aiden to where Alton lay in a bloody heap. Aiden gave a shake of his head. "Not now."

Corran relented, and the healer advanced carefully toward the pile of rubble. Corran swallowed hard, willing himself not to follow, straining to see anything in the gloom.

Aiden raised his arm and held out his hand above the mound. He murmured words that meant nothing to Corran, and a faint silvery glow slipped over the debris like moonlit spider webs, vanishing a heartbeat later. "Give me a hand," Aiden called.

Corran made his way across the garbage-strewn floor, chains clanking as he walked. Aiden looked up as he reached him, taking in the manacles as if noticing them for the first time. He placed a hand on each of Corran's wrists, and the cuffs fell away.

"Help me get them out," Aiden said.

Corran dropped to his knees, lifting away the stone, plaster, and wood. Aiden brought the lantern closer, and in its light, Corran could see a crimson rivulet snaking beneath the rubble. He caught his breath, fighting down panic, and kept digging.

Two beams and a large chunk of masonry trapped the bodies beneath them. "On three," Aiden said to Corran, who squatted to grab a corner of the stone. They worked together to tip it off and away; once it was gone, moving the beams was easy enough.

"Oh, gods." Corran groaned, now that they could see the damage. Damian's body lay on top. Charred clothing stuck to the skin on his arms. Most of his hair had burned away, and the skull was misshapen where a heavy stone had smashed in the back of his head.

Corran shoved Damian's body aside to get to Rigan. He reached for his brother's wrist, fingers pressing into the skin to find a pulse, steady but slow. Blood streaked Rigan's face and a shard of wood embedded itself like a dagger in his left arm. Blisters on Rigan's hands testified to holding off his burning attacker, but although his clothing was singed and blackened in places, it was clear Damian had not set them both afire.

"He's hurt, but he's alive," Aiden said after a rough triage.

"Damian and Alton?"

Aiden shook his head.

Corran looked back toward the wall where Mir lay slumped and still. "Mir's lost a lot of blood."

"I know. I could feel it when I neared the building. I'll do what I can for him, but I don't know if it will be enough." He rose stiffly, and gave Corran a hand up. "Come on. We need to get them back to the house."

Chapter Thirty-Six

"I'M GLAD YOU'RE on our side." Rigan looked up at Aiden as he entered the room they had turned into a makeshift library. "A little foresight is wonderful thing."

Aiden snorted. "Especially when it keeps you from running into a fight and getting blindsided."

Rigan shrugged and looked away. "That bastard took Corran and Mir. He had it coming." He paused. "Speaking of which—"

"You think you're up to this?" Aiden glanced at Rigan's hands, newly healed from the burns he had gained in his fight with the witch. Aiden had helped temper the headache from being thrown into a wall, but the rest of Rigan's body was bruised and aching from head to toe.

"I don't think we can afford to waste any time," Rigan said, "ready or not. Someone sent assassins after the hunters. Not guards—assassins. And Damian didn't betray the witches over a personal argument; he sold them out to someone important. The same someone wants us. I don't think he'll take 'no' for an answer."

"We could leave Below, go outside the walls," Aiden suggested. "We don't have to fight this battle."

"Or we could get our answers from the source, and know what we're really up against."

Aiden's skeptical glance spoke volumes. "Don't you think you should heal a little longer?"

"Do I have a choice?"

The healer closed the manuscript he had been reading. "Have you talked to Corran about what you want to do?"

Rigan's jaw tightened. He turned away, a cold fury settling over him. "No. And I'm not going to."

"He'll be seriously annoyed about it."

"Let him. It'll be over by the time he wakes up." Rigan took a deep breath and released the power that had begun to build as his anger rose. Aiden said nothing, but his raised eyebrow let Rigan know the healer had noticed the surge. "That son of a bitch betrayed our friends, tried to kill Corran, and intended to hand me over to his patron—" Rigan shook his head. "No. I'm doing this. You don't have to."

Aiden rolled his eyes. "I'm angry, too. I was there when Damian killed the others, remember? They were my friends for longer than you knew them." He sighed. "I just wish you wouldn't push it so soon after the fight."

"The assassins will come again," Rigan replied, barely recognizing the cold steel in his voice. "More of them, stronger. We need to root our enemy out, and his witch—stop the monsters, for good."

The look on Aiden's face told Rigan the healer knew he really could not argue with the logic, much as he wantd to do so. "All right, then. Where?"

"You've warded the house, and we've both put all the sigils and protections in place we can. We'll be best protected if we do it here."

"That's what I thought."

"Then let's do it."

Much as Rigan hated to admit it, Aiden was right to question the wisdom of doing the rituals now. They were both tired from the fight. Rigan's injuries hurt worse than he let on, though he doubted he could fool the healer. Worry over Mir and Corran's injuries gnawed at Rigan, part of what drove him to seek answers sooner rather than later. And despite everything, Rigan had insisted on properly preparing Dilin's body for burial. He was exhausted, heartsick and sore, but anger had kept him moving thus far, and he was counting on it to see him through this crucial task.

The rest of the house was quiet. Half of the hunters kept watch, while the others slept. Only Elinor and Polly looked up as they headed for the cellar.

"Surprised you're still awake," Elinor said. Her brows furrowed as she took in the rucksack Rigan carried. "And you're up to something."

"We're going to the cellar for a while," Rigan said, not eager to get into the details. "Can you make sure no one disturbs us?"

Elinor gave him a pointed look. "In other words, if Corran wants to know where you've gone, you want me to lie to him?"

Rigan winced. "Not lie. Just don't volunteer anything."

Elinor regarded him, eyes narrowing as if she could read his thoughts. "All right. But be careful. I'll strengthen the wardings, just in case."

Rigan gave her a tired, grateful smile. "Thanks." The only good thing to come out of their time Below, other than that he and Corran were still breathing, was his relationship with Elinor. *Not that I'm in any position to make any plans—or that I've got much of a chance of staying alive long enough to keep any promises.* He pushed those thoughts away as Aiden lit a lantern and led the way to the cellar.

Rigan hung lanterns, illuminating the low, dark space. "Here," he said, gesturing to the center of the room. "This will do nicely."

"I've never seen you work this kind of magic," Aiden said, unpacking their equipment.

"Until recently, I didn't even think of it as magic."

Rigan took the salt-aconite-amanita mixture and the pigments, and knelt in the middle of the floor. He drew in a deep breath and released it, grounding his power and stilling his thoughts. This work felt almost comforting in its familiarity. Banishing angry, restless spirits had been a regular part of their role as undertakers. For a moment, marking the sigils and connecting the salt lines felt so routine, so normal, that Rigan could almost fool himself into thinking that they were still Above, that Kell would be waiting for them with dinner at the end of the day. He closed his eyes, willing away the pain of loss, finding cold purpose as he finished the last of the lines and lit the candles.

Outside the circle lay a clipping of Damian's singed hair. It would help them in calling to his spirit. Rigan had questions that needed to be answered.

He chanted the invocation and sat back on his heels, waiting. Aiden stood in a small salt circle of his own, over in the corner, holding an iron sword.

I should have known you wouldn't let me rest.

Rigan looked up and saw Damian standing at the edge of the circle. He looked as he had before the attack, not the charred, unrecognizable corpse they had left in the abandoned building. Once, not long ago, Rigan had almost trusted this man. Now, the desire for vengeance burned so hot that his fists clenched, and he wished he could kill the traitor all over again.

"Who's your patron?" Rigan asked.

Why should I tell you? Even dead, Damian still sounded smug.

"Because grave magic is something I never needed your help to master. Because I can send your soul to the Dark Ones. You can either give me your confession willingly, or I can rip it from you word by word."

Damian's spirit glowered. *It no longer matters to me, and it won't help you, but I'll tell you. The Lord Mayor's blood witch sent me*, Damian said. *He was grateful when I took out the other witches, although they were a nuisance more than a threat to someone with his power. But you and the healer interested him.* He leered. *An undertaker with a powerful gift—that caught his fancy. He wanted you alive.*

Rigan's eyes widened, and Damian chuckled. *Did you think I'd been sent to kill you?* He shook his head. *Now your brother, that was a different matter. No use for him other than leverage against you. You've attracted the notice of people in high places. It didn't have to play out like this. If you had come willingly, done what they asked of you, they would have made it worth your while.*

Rigan's mouth tightened. "You mean, if I'd turned my back on Corran, forgotten that the guards and their monsters killed my brother, my mother, my father... if I'd abandoned my friends? What could they possibly give me to make any of that worth my while?"

Damian stared at him, as if he were a slow child. *Power. Influence. Wealth. Leverage with the men who run the city-state and the League itself—even the Crown Prince.*

"That's why you did it? That's what they promised you?"

"Men have been bought and sold for a lot less," Aiden said, his voice cold, his disdain for Damian clear.

"Is the Lord Mayor the one using the monsters, or is it his witch?" Rigan asked.

Damian shrugged. *I don't know—he didn't lay out his plans for me.*

"What else?" Rigan's patience was growing thin. "Tell me."

Damian paused as if wondering whether Rigan would make good on his threat. *The monsters are a tool. They keep the residents scared, make them accept the guards as a necessity. Can't go getting any ideas about conspiring against the Lord Mayor or the Guild Masters if they're always watching their backs. They keep the Balance.*

"The Guild Masters don't object, even when it's their own members dying?"

Damian shrugged. *Who cares what the Guild Masters think?*

"What's the Balance?" Aiden asked.

The source of the dark magic needs to feed on fear and blood, said Damian. *It's all about balancing the energy going in and the magic being worked. I'm not sure what exactly happens if the Balance isn't kept, but I don't think we want to know.*

"How do we stop the Mayor's blood witch?"

Blackholt? You can't. He's a lot stronger than you are, even than I was. And you lost your chance to come out ahead in this when you killed me. So now you get to die like the rest of them.

Rigan met Damian's eyes. "Maybe. But I can send you into the Darkness before I go." Rigan gestured, holding Damian's spirit in place as he began to chant. Damian's expression shifted from surprise to derision and then finally to panic. By then, it was too late. Rigan chanted loudly, ignoring Damian's promises and imprecations.

He kept on chanting as the temperature of the cellar plummeted, sending chills through his body, misting his breath, raising a sheen of frost on the stone walls. Intent on his purpose, Rigan barely noticed Aiden raise his hands in a gesture of warding and protection, eyes wide. Damian shrank back when one wall of the cellar vanished, opening into a limitless void from which no soul or light returned.

Rigan's chant rose in a crescendo. He thrust both his hands forward and Damian's spirit stumbled backward. The spirit cried out, struggled to free itself, and then tendrils of the darkness lashed at him, snaring him by the arms and legs, drawing him into the void. With a roar and a rush of wind, the darkness vanished, leaving behind it an ordinary cellar wall.

Rigan's head drooped forward and his arms fell to his sides. Damian was gone.

"Rigan?" Aiden's voice was steady, though the expression on his face told Rigan that the healer had not been fully prepared for what happened.

"I'm fine." Not quite true, but true enough.

"You don't have to finish this tonight."

"It won't be easier any other night. We might as well find out what we're really up against."

"Corran will have my ass if you get hurt."

Rigan snorted. "It'll be a while before he's up to thrashing you. I'll recover by then."

Rigan broke the circle and felt the wardings dissipate. He burned the lock of Damian's hair, feeling the last connection to his spirit wink out. He put a uniform button in the place where the hair had been, and completed the salt line once more. Protective energy sprang up anew from the markings.

"This shouldn't take long," Rigan said. Once again, he chanted the summoning spell. This time, the ghost outside the salt line was one of the assassins that had nearly killed Corran and Mir.

Where am I?

"You're a ghost. I'm an undertaker. Before I send your sorry soul into the After, I want to know who in the name of the gods sent you and your friend to kill us."

The ghost considered his words for a moment. *I was sworn to secrecy.*

"And now you're dead. You've done your duty."

Why should I tell you?

"Because I can send you on, trap you here, or redirect you to somewhere you really don't want to go."

All right. You want to know who sent me? Jorgeson, the Lord Mayor's head of security.

"Does he make a habit of sending assassins Below?"

The spirit barked a laugh. *Hardly. Most of the time, my comrades and I moved among the top levels of the League. This job was... unprecedented.*

"So why us?"

We were sent to kill the hunters.

"Why?"

The assassin shrugged. *I don't ask, and they don't tell. They give me a mark, I hit it. Best that way all around.*

"Are there other assassins after hunters who are still Above?"

The ghost frowned. *I think so. That's why I figured Jorgeson was using us instead of just having the guards do the job. The monsters have made the city folk restless. Half of them seem to think the hunters protect them, and the others think they're just another type of monster. Our orders were to take you out quietly, no fuss, no witnesses.*

Rigan was stunned. "How many assassins?"

Don't know. They don't give us the big plan, just our piece of it. If you mean, how many assassins are there in Ravenwood, in the League? He shook his head. *Dozens in the city. Hundreds, in the League. The higher-ups keep us busy. We're the soldiers in their private little wars. If we do our job, little problems don't get bigger.*

Rigan's lip curled in disgust. "Yeah, you're a real public servant." This time, he tired more quickly when he read the banishing spell and opened the gateway, but he felt nothing as the ghost gave a final scream and disappeared into the void.

Rigan panted with the exertion, and a sheen of sweat covered his forehead even though the air in the cellar was cold enough he could see his breath. His arm felt leaden as he reached out to smudge the salt line, and it took the last of his reserves as he canceled out the sigils and extinguished the candles. Only then did he give in to the weariness, slumping onto his hands and knees as Aiden broke his own wardings and rushed to catch him.

"Did you hear?" Rigan asked as Aiden checked his pulse and looked him over for any injuries.

"I heard." Aiden's voice was even. Rigan dared a glance at the healer, expecting to see judgment in his gaze. He was surprised by the flat, practical expression.

"I know we guessed that the Lord Mayor and his mages were behind the monsters, but I needed more than intuition," Rigan said.

"I can't lead the hunters against the Lord Mayor on just a hunch." He looked up to meet Aiden's gaze. "Taking the next step, it's huge. We're talking insurrection, treason. I had to be sure. This—this is real proof, right from the source."

Rigan dropped his gaze. "You're a healer. I figured you might have a problem with what I did," he said, so tired his words almost slurred. "Might think I misused my magic."

Aiden helped him lie down and went to fetch an elixir from his bag. "Drink this." He held a cup to Rigan's lips. "It'll replenish you."

He sat on his haunches. "As for misusing your magic, how do you think I took Alton down? I stopped his heart, before he even realized I was in the doorway. And then I put a knife through his chest, just in case."

Rigan must not have hid his surprise, because Aiden gave a rueful chuckle. "Technically, healers aren't supposed to do that. I imagine it's a stain on my soul. But Alton and Damian killed my friends, and I wasn't sure I could take Alton if it came to an all-out magic fight."

"Practical," Rigan said, arching an eyebrow.

"I could say the same about you." Aiden helped Rigan to his feet. "When you've gotten some sleep, I'd like to hear more about these 'soul confessions.' But right now, I'd best get you up to bed or your brother will have something to say about it."

Rigan thought about making a sarcastic retort, but he was too bone weary to come up with anything, and far too aware of how much help he needed just to climb the stairs. Corran's temper became one more thing on his list to face in the morning, right after killer witches and assassins.

"You're really struggling with this tonight." Elinor looked up as Rigan gave a disgusted sigh and turned his back on a shattered vase, a melted and charred candle, and an overflowing pitcher brimming with water that spread out across the floor in a large, growing puddle.

Rigan shook his head, utterly exasperated at himself. He hesitated, not wanting to take his anger at himself out on Elinor. "It's just... not coming. It isn't happening! And we don't have time for this shit."

Elinor watched him pace, saying nothing.

"I mean, Damian thought I had the kind of magic that would get me snatched by the Lord Mayor's guards," Rigan continued. "But look at the mess I make! It's almost as if the harder I concentrate, the worse it gets."

"Did you ever try *not* concentrating?" Elinor asked.

Rigan gave her a wide-eyed look of horror. "Are you kidding? I could collapse the street above us onto our heads, or flood us with the harbor! Or set us on fire. I've got to concentrate to keep from killing someone with my magic—I'm a danger, not an asset."

"Stop that." Aiden pushed away from the far wall where he had been observing the training session in silence. "You're doing no worse than any other witchling."

"Maybe not, but those other 'witchlings' didn't have assassins breathing down their necks, waiting for them to commit treason."

Aiden shrugged. "It's always something. Some reason why the world will end or terrible things will happen unless the student gains control of magic right this moment. And that's bullshit."

Rigan stared at Aiden, open-mouthed in astonishment. "How can you say that? You know what's at stake, how many people have already died!"

Aiden met his glare without flinching. "Yes, I do. But that doesn't change how the universe works, any more than it changes when the sun rises or the tide comes in. You have the ability to work powerful magic. You're disciplined, so you've come a long way to make up for lost time. But that doesn't change the fact that it still takes a lifetime to fully manage magic like this."

"We don't have a lifetime to wait for me to catch up."

"Stop it!" Elinor held up a hand to silence both men. "You're wasting what time we do have. And while we can't suddenly give you twenty years' worth of control in two months, that doesn't mean you can't gain important skills." Her glare kept Rigan and Aiden from interrupting.

"So here's what we're going to do," she went on, hands on hips. "We're going to stop working with big things and start getting small things perfectly right."

"I don't see—" Rigan started, only to have Elinor snap a warning finger in front of his face.

"It's like when I dyed cloth for the dressmakers," Elinor cut him off. "The apprentices would get so impatient to work on fancy gowns. But before they could do that, they needed to be able to put in a good hem, with fine, close stitches and even tension. If they couldn't do a good line of stitches for a hem, they couldn't sew a ball gown. You need to get your stitches right."

Rigan strained to keep a civil tone in his voice. "Time is running out. We're going to have to go up against the Lord Mayor's blood witch—who knows, maybe more than one—and I'm fucking useless!"

"Not useless," Aiden corrected, his voice sharp. "Distracted. I can sense your energy. It's all over the place. You're making me jumpy." He ran a hand through his hair. "For the gods' sake, sit down."

Rigan glared at Aiden, but did as he was told. Elinor sat down in front of him, crossing her legs at the ankles. Rigan mirrored her posture, and Elinor held out her hands. "Let's get you grounded again, and then we'll work on those 'stitches,'" she said with a smile. Reluctantly, Rigan took her hands. He felt Aiden kneel behind him and place strong hands on his shoulders.

"You're used to big, splashy magic, even as an undertaker," Elinor said quietly, closing her eyes and speaking in an even, calm voice. "Hearing the confessions of the dead and sending people into the

After. Most magic isn't like that. Most magic is just tweaks and flourishes. Nudges."

Her hands were warm, holding Rigan's fingers in a solid grip, steadying him. "When I would mix dyes for Parah, I often sang my magic," Elinor said, keeping her voice so low that Rigan had to concentrate to hear her. "Didn't matter what tune. Singing helped me concentrate, and the tune repeated itself, so I could get myself into a trance if I paid attention to my breathing."

"But I won't be in Parah's shop," Rigan countered; it was little more than a whisper, but he knew she could hear his fear. "It'll be a battle against a much more seasoned witch, and people's lives are going to depend on me. Your life. Aiden's. The hunters'. Corran's."

"Cast a smaller net with your thoughts," Aiden cautioned, gripping Rigan's shoulders more firmly. "Just you, just this moment, right here. Breathe. Focus. Feel."

Rigan strained to quell his fears and still the barrage of images crossing his mind's eye, each more horrific than the last. He tried to focus on the warmth of Elinor's hands, the strength in Aiden's hold on his shoulders, the pull of the muscles in his legs as he sat cross-legged on the hard floor. *Breathe in. Out. In. Out.* He focused on his breathing, gradually filtering the world out.

"Good," Elinor said, as if she could sense him stilling. "Now, ground yourself, and call a drop of water into your hand. Just a drop!" She turned his right hand palm-up and withdrew her grip to his fingertips.

Rigan allowed himself two more slow, deep breaths before he felt ready. He kept his eyes closed, aware of the pressure of Elinor's fingers against his and Aiden kneeling behind him. He sent his magic down into the ground beneath them, deep into the dirt and rock, then deeper still, seeking the ground water that fed the wells. He felt the cool water slip against his power, clean and wild.

Just a drop, he reminded himself. He recalled his training session with the witches when he had called blood instead of water. That seemed like a lifetime ago. He knew better, now. Yet while his magic rooted itself in the water far beneath them, the challenge lay in the control required to gather just a single precious drop. A cup-full, a bucket's worth—Rigan could twitch his magic and make it happen. But summoning a drop, a tear's worth of liquid, made him break out in a cold sweat as he struggled to create something so small.

Just a stitch. A single, perfect stitch, he told himself. And when he opened his eyes, he found a cold, clear bead of water in the center of his palm.

"You did it!" Elinor gave him a triumphant smile.

"And I feel like I've been hit with a wagon," Rigan replied, embarrassed at how tired he was, how much the control had taken out of him. "How can I hope to win a battle if I can barely shape a drop?"

Aiden dropped to sit down beside him. "Part of it is practice—you've done enough to know that it gets easier the more you do it. But Elinor's right—if you can do the little things perfectly, the big things fall into place. And sometimes, the little things are all you need."

Rigan stared at him. "That makes no sense."

Aiden gave him a patient smile. "We aren't going to win against this Blackholt by trying to match his power," he replied. "He'll be a master, and drawing strength from blood and death to go beyond his natural limits. We can't beat that with brute force. He'll crush us."

"Then it's over before it starts," Rigan said miserably, staring at the warming drop in his palm.

"Hardly," Aiden said with a laugh. "Because Blackholt can't imagine us doing anything except a frontal assault. He'll expect us to try to batter him into submission. And instead, we use small magics—concentrated, coordinated, carefully planned—and bleed him to death from a thousand cuts, so to speak."

"We can't fight him on his terms," Elinor said, closing her hand over Rigan's and bending his fingers around the drop in his fist. "So we'll use what we *can* do in ways he won't expect, to strike at the weaknesses he didn't think were important enough to safeguard. We'll hit him in dozens of little ways, all at once, ways he never anticipated, and cut him down before he has a chance to realize what's going on."

Part of Rigan's mind wanted to argue that the idea was ridiculous. But another part nurtured a spark of hope at Elinor's words. "You really think we have a chance, using small magic?" he asked.

Elinor and Aiden both nodded. "Enough that we're willing to bet our lives on it," Aiden replied.

Rigan managed a smile that he hoped looked more confident than he felt. "Then let's get on with it," he said. "What's next? A grain of sand?"

Chapter Thirty-Seven

MACHISON'S HANDS TREMBLED. Valdis had finished the new warding in the bedroom, requiring only the Lord Mayor's blood to activate it. The blood witch had seemed almost shaken at the darkness of the magic, even offering a prayer for the Lord Mayor's soul.

He couldn't trust Blackholt to protect him, that was certain. Blackholt couldn't even find and capture those bloody Valmondes, much less kill them. *Or maybe, he did find them, disobeyed my order, spirited them away where they can do the most damage for the highest bidder,* Machison's imagination supplied.

The secrets of the dead should stay in the grave. Machison had done what was necessary to ensure the success of the negotiations, enforce the peace, and keep the Balance. *The dead needed to keep their godsdamned mouths shut.* Yet the negotiations had faltered—Garenoth had balked at keeping Gorog's tariffs, let alone improving them—and Machison knew Gorog's patience was growing thin, and the Crown Prince's thinner.

Kadar got to them, Machison thought. *He must have bribed or threatened someone, damn him.* Garenoth refused to accept the terms, and Gorog remained adamant about them, leaving Machison the unappealing choice between disappointing the Crown Prince or a Merchant Prince, either of whom would send an assassin to register their displeasure. He had to turn the situation around. Find a way to please Gorog, satisfy Aliyev, and secure Garenoth's assent. Far too much was riding on the outcome.

Valdis had rolled back the carpet to clear a space on the floorboards. A line of salt and aconite ran around the perimeter of the room, but the Lord Mayor suspected that all the salt in the world couldn't keep the hag from his nightmares. "The intent is sealed in the gathering of the elements," Valdis had told him when he handed over the list of items needed to work the spell. Intent was the key. Machison paled when he read the list, knew that only a desperate man pushed to the edge would attempt the spell; only a man with nothing to lose could bring himself to gather the ritual's requirements.

Life blood from four different victims, drawn by the hand of the one who desires the spell, the final drops that bleed out, the richest blood because it holds the last dregs of life.

Machison's bodyguards obliged him in capturing the four victims and bringing them to him in an abandoned building far from the glittering palace. Whatever they thought of their master's request, they kept their mouths closed, their eyes blank, their expressions tightly shuttered. The bodyguards hadn't even flinched as Machison drew his knife down the victims' arms, collected their blood in jars, using a separate vessel for the last few cups as the skin paled, the final drops from a stuttering heartbeat.

All in all, it had been easier than Machison expected.

Finding the fresh body of a stillborn child took a bit more time, but one guard knew someone, and within a candlemark, the small, stiff, cold body was his.

Candles made from tallow from the fat of a hanged man's corpse might have taken longer, if Valdis had not steered Machison to a small shop in the darkest alleys of Below where such things could be purchased for the right price. Machison and his men had disguised themselves, hid beneath shabby clothes and dirty faces. It was essential that the beneficiary of the spell do the dirty work himself; proof of intent.

The other elements were just as grisly.

The severed hand of an unrepentant thief, cut while the victim was still alive. A brush made of bone and hair, taken from a virgin right after her maidenhead was forcibly taken. *Well that one wasn't quite so difficult*, he thought. Collecting the elements confirmed to Machison that the spellcraft not only assured intent but also gauged the darkness of the soul of the one for whom the spell was worked.

Some of the other elements were almost mundane in comparison: soot taken from a freshly burned body; bone powder from old remains newly disinterred; dried blood, now a dark red hue; dark blue powder made from monkshood and foxglove.

Valdis used a bone brush to paint sigils on the floor, consulting a crumpled parchment in his left hand. Machison watched, and his nose wrinkled with the smell of old tombs and rotting flesh.

The blood witch laid out the last of the components—two human finger bones lashed together with sinew. Machison had taken the bones from the hand of his victim, skinned them and peeled back the meat, stripped out the sinew. Now the bloody talisman lay in the center of the circle, waiting to be awakened as Valdis finished the ritual, creating both a refuge within the markings and an amulet to carry that power with the Lord Mayor beyond the walls of this room.

Valdis lit the candles at the four quarters of the circle, then thrust his thumb into the pots of thickened life blood and drew a red line down the side of each candle as it burned. Once again he dipped his thumb, and marked Machison with blood at the navel, sternum, throat, and between the eyes. Valdis consulted the parchment before lifting the amulet.

"I call to the discarded gods, to the powers of the hedge and byway, to the darkness of the crossroads and the forest. Hear me."

He dripped more blood at the circle's quarters, and then immersed the bone amulet in the bloody chalice.

"I call to the Elder Gods, and to Toloth, god of the Lord Mayors, heed my sacrifice. I have prepared a feast for you."

Valdis marked the dead man's hand with blood, and then nodded to Machison to recite the words he had memorized.

"I will be your hands and feet. I will do your bidding, if you grant me safety from my enemies."

Valdis took the shriveled infant's corpse and smeared it with blood before signalling to Machison again.

"I have done as the ritual demands. I have proven my intent. I prove it now, with my own blood." Machison's voice trembled and his hand shook as he set the edge of the knife against the tender skin of his forearm. He made one deep cut, sending a steady flow of bright red blood spilling over his palm, dripping to the floor.

If your plea is accepted, your life will be spared, Valdis had told him. Now came the fullest measure of proven intent, as he brought the knife down again, felt his own blood drain to seal his bargain.

Valdis walked slowly widdershins, letting the blood trail his steps as he flicked droplets from the knife.

Machison grew lightheaded, aware of his heartbeat thudding in his ears, his breath heavy in his chest. "Hear my prayer and deliver my enemies into my hand. Let me win the outcome I desire from the negotiations with Garenoth. Save me from the curse of the Wanderers, and shut the mouths of the dead against me."

Valdis completed the circle and stood watching the room, an uncertain expression on his face, as though he feared the outcome of the dark magic.

Machison's breath caught as he saw a silvery figure take form outside the circle. Toloth, whose oracle had spoken of fearful portents, stood before him.

"*I have heard your prayer,*" Toloth said in a voice like thunder rolling from the depths of a tomb. "*I will grant what I can, though not all of what you plead for is within my power to fulfill.*"

"But you are a god!"

"*To you. I do not control Eshtamon or the Elder Beings. Eshtamon has chosen his own champions in the struggle that is to come, and the Wanderers are his blood-bound. I cannot touch them. I can only give you my favor.*"

"And what will that do for me?" Machison spat, growing more lightheaded with the loss of blood. The cloying smell of incense made bile rise in his throat.

"*I cannot shut the mouths of the dead. Nor am I willing to waste my power manipulating so many minds for something as trivial as a contract. But I can deliver your enemies into your hand, allow you to face them on your ground, with the advantage.*"

Machison sank to his knees, relief mingling with growing weakness. "Thank you. I will give you sacrifice, make offerings, anything you demand—"

"*Be worthy of the wager I've placed on you.*"

"Wager?" Machison stared up into the god's gaze.

"*I find a game so much more interesting if I have a stake in it,*" Toloth remarked. "*The odds are against you, but I suspect you'll fight nonetheless. And I shall be watching.*" He gestured and Machison's wounds healed, leaving behind tracks of dried blood.

"This is a game to you?" Machison felt his sanity teeter on the edge. He had never stopped to ask why any of the gods might heed a mortal's prayer, bestow a miracle, or intervene for vengeance. The priests talked of chaos and primeval forces, of plans unknowable to mere men. Machison's life hung by a thread and Toloth spoke of gambling.

"*Did you expect more?*" Toloth asked, amused and incredulous. "*You don't have anything to offer me, except a distraction. Now make it worth my while.*"

With that, the figure vanished. A cold blast of wind swept through the room, extinguishing the candles and sending a chill through Machison that ran bone deep. Valdis appeared to be equally terrified, trembling and ashen as he stared at the spot where Toloth had stood.

The ritual had worked, but triumph tasted like ash in the Lord Mayor's mouth. *I have earned the support of a bored, jaded spirit who meddles in the affairs of creatures he clearly disdains*, Machison thought, forcing down his terror.

The reprieve was bitter, but even more so was the thought that Machison had played his last card, and Toloth's deal was the best anyone was going to offer him. He remembered the reproach of the Wanderer woman in his nightmares: the hollow words and veiled omens of the oracle; the tenuous support of his patron; the sidelong glances Jorgeson sent his way when he thought he wasn't looking. *Borrowed time. I'm running out of second chances. It's all falling apart.*

"Leave me," he ordered.

Valdis gathered his things and ran.

Alone in his room, door locked and surrounded by the grisly element of the spell, Machison swallowed hard.

I will not go out on my knees. I will not give Toloth or anyone else the satisfaction of seeing me beg. He lifted the bloody amulet and tied the leather strap behind his neck, sliding the talisman beneath his shirt. *I can turn this around. I can still win this. And if I can't, I will go down fighting and take as many of them with me as I can. Damn Aliyev and Gorog. Damn the Guilds. Damn Toloth and the Elder Gods, and damn Ravenwood. If I can't save myself, then I will burn and the world will be my pyre.*

"HAVE YOU DOUBLED the guard on the hostages?" Machison snapped.

"Yes, m'lord," Jorgeson replied.

"Their rooms are secure? The guards are trustworthy?"

"Yes, m'lord." He paused. "And I have the report from the spies that you wanted."

Five days had passed since the sleepless night Machison and Valdis spent working the bloody spell in his chambers. His servants were banished from his rooms to keep the secret of the warding he fed with blood each night; the circle in which he had slept the past two nights slouched in a chair. Even so, the nightmares still found him. Maybe the circle and the amulet would keep the Wanderer hag at bay in the waking world, but nothing barred her from his dreams. Machison swore he could feel the amulet beneath his shirt burning against his skin, and he wondered, if it came down to the wire, whether Toloth would actually give his protection, or leave the Lord Mayor on his own for the thrill of the game.

Just three days after they had worked the spell, he awakened from fitful sleep to see the salt circle blazing with unholy light—sickly green, like putrefying flesh. The memory burned fresh and hot in his mind, never far from his thoughts.

The candles had roared to life and the runes glowed. The blood had started to stink, but he used it to renew the markings, as Valdis said he must. And then Machison had seen the apparition, just beyond the warding: the hag from his dreams.

No longer content to harry him in nightmares, she had appeared in the waking world. Her wild eyes met his across the circle, foxfire light glinting from a knife in her hand.

"You can't reach me in here." Machison hated the way his voice shook, knew that the hag could sense his fear; yet the barrier held.

"You can't hide forever," the old woman had replied, scraping the blade gently across her thumb.

"I'm protected."

Her laugh was a hideous wheezing sound. "By those bits of bone on a strap around your neck? Or by a god who values your life as a chit in a game of cards? We've left our marks all over your city. When the time comes, they'll help avenge our murdered sons and daughters."

Her thin lips pulled tight across mottled teeth. "Our magic is older than your blood witch's tricks, older than your young gods. Nothing will save you."

"Is that so? Because the blood magic seems strong enough now, old woman. I'm in here, and you're out there." The Lord Mayor's bravado was all he had, and he clung to it, unwilling to let her see him cower.

"For now. I would have enjoyed making you bleed myself, but I have other ways of seeing things done. Won't be long until you're in the After."

"Leave me."

Her laugh left ice in the pit of his stomach. "I'll leave you, all right. I will leave you to fate."

A knock at the door jarred him from replaying the scene in his mind. Machison called out, "Enter," and Jorgeson strode into the room.

"What do your spies report?" Machison snapped, glad for the distraction of the briefing.

"You were right about the Guilds. There was a conspiracy," Jorgeson replied.

"Oh, there are so many conspiracies," Machison said. "Tell me."

Jorgeson began to pace as Machison settled into the chair behind his massive desk. "We were correct that the Guilds intended to play both sides when they 'disavowed' the hunters we caught," Jorgeson said. "The Weavers' Guild might have meant what they said, but not the smiths or the tanners, and after the fires, even Orlo and his undertakers weren't as reliable as they wanted to appear."

"Typical."

The attacks against the ambassadors had taken a toll. Progress had been bogged down in accusations and recriminations, and a simple solution no longer looked feasible. Jorgeson's men had dispatched one of the would-be assassins, though it was impossible to prove Kadar's involvement. The Itaran ambassador's abrupt return to his own city-state made the rest of the dignitaries skittish, and the Garenoth ambassador's latest instruction from his Merchant Princes at home recommended terms less favorable to Gorog's interests than had been previously discussed.

Despite all of Machison's efforts, the negotiations had come to a halt. Rumor held that Garenoth was making secret advances toward Kadar, that Crown Prince Aliyev had grown displeased with the delays. His last words to Machison had been curt and threatening. After all Machison had done to secure their fortunes, victory eluded his grasp.

I'm not out of the game yet. This isn't over, Machison told himself. *I can still win. But not if a godsdamned assassin puts a knife in my back*. All their efforts to soothe the ambassadors' jangled nerves and affronted sensibilities might be too little, too late. Which left Machison more intent than ever on victory and vengeance.

"Are the Guilds harboring the hunters? Have they hidden the Valmondes?"

Jorgeson shook his head. "No. The Valmondes and their hunter gang have gone to ground. If they're still Below, no one's getting close to them. I stopped sending assassins when the last lot didn't come back; it seemed a waste of good men."

"Damn."

"The Guilds aren't backing up their 'disavowal' in any meaningful way."

Machison barked a laugh. "We burned the Valmondes' godsdamned shop! What's left for the Guild to disavow?"

"There are other hunters besides the Valmondes. Blackholt's monsters have killed hundreds of people across Ravenwood. The Guilds have been pushed past their limits, and I'm not sure even hostages can keep the peace."

"Are they fulfilling the orders for their goods? So long as the ships sail full of merchandise..."

Jorgeson turned to face him, incredulous. "M'lord, it is not so simple! At first, yes, as the noose tightened, the Guilds were willing to turn a blind eye, absorb the losses from the guards and monsters and reap the profit, even if the coins were bloody. But of late, it's gone too far. The city is in flames and chaos. Merchant ships drop anchor at the edge of the harbor for fear their sails will burn. And even if the Guilds could keep discipline among their ranks, the city no longer functions as it should."

Jorgeson was a military man, not usually given to displays of emotion. Machison saw the truth in his eyes, that all was lost.

"And the Wanderers?"

Jorgeson gave a disbelieving laugh. "The Wanderers fled weeks ago. All they've left behind are their curses."

"We can fix this," Machison vowed. "We can force the Guilds to bring the hunters to heel."

"It's too late." Jorgeson stared at the Lord Mayor. "The Guilds haven't just turned a blind eye to monster hunters; they're letting them fight the guards, too. They don't blame the monsters for the fire—they blame the guards, and you."

"Then we'll use Gorog's private army to teach them respect."

"It's said that Merchant Prince Kadar has asked for the Crown Prince to amend the trade agreement to be more equitable, and to appoint a new negotiator and replace both you and Halloran."

Machison swallowed hard. "Aliyev wouldn't dare."

Jorgeson's gaze held truths he did not want to hear. "I have not heard whether Kadar received a response. But the asking is a problem in itself. Merchant Prince Gorog will not be pleased."

Machison ran a hand over his face. Gorog was far beyond displeased. His last, tersely-worded missive made that clear. Aliyev also threatened immediate consequences if Machison did not find some way to salvage the situation, and despite the problems, he had not recalled Blackholt. *Proving my suspicion that he wants rid of both of us*, Machison thought dourly.

"What does Garenoth have to complain about?" Machison demanded. "Their ambassador is safe. We stopped the attacks against the negotiators. Unrest from the rabble is not their issue. The terms we offered are as favorable as ever. What do they care how the profits are divided among our Merchant Princes? So long as the ships are full and the trade goes on, what is it to them how we handle our private matters?"

"From the rumors, I suspect Kadar and Tamas made additional concessions. Some of Garenoth's Merchant Princes would stand to benefit, if that's true. And then there's the problems with the hunters and the Wanderers. To a point, Garenoth might have overlooked the unrest. But the rest of the League is watching Ravenwood. I don't doubt other city-states have suggested better terms, and a more... stable trading partner."

Machison tried to steel his expression. "Spare me the economics lesson."

"I don't think you understand, m'lord. This won't be easy to fix."

"Everything can be fixed, for a price."

"In this case, the price will be high."

Machison's teeth ground together. "Surely the hostages will serve to remind the Guilds where the real power in Ravenwood lies. I'll wring concessions from them that will sweeten the pot for Garenoth, make him reconsider Kadar's offer." He glowered at Jorgeson. "In the meantime, make the consequences of further disobedience clear to the Guilds. And get the damned fires put out!"

Jorgeson opened his mouth to speak and closed it again. He straightened. "As you wish, m'lord."

FEW PLACES STILL gave Machison the chance for privacy. The garderobe was one of the last remaining bulwarks of personal space aside from his bed chamber. All his grand dreams, his lust for power, his desire to make a name for himself among the most important men in Darkhurst, and the list of enemies, the spectacular mistakes, had narrowed his world to these two inglorious havens.

He would take what he could get. Ravenwood, perhaps all of Darkhurst, seemed to be going to the Dark Ones, and prudent men did not take chances.

He finished his business and pulled up his pants, moving to fasten his belt, when he felt the poke of a knife between his shoulder blades.

One push, and the assassin had Machison pitching forward, catching himself on the back wall of the garderobe, bent over in a compromising position.

"My patron left the details up to me," the assassin hissed into his ear. "Just a few specifics. Bloody. Painful. Humiliating. I have a good imagination."

Machison pushed backward, ramming into the assassin and sending him stumbling back a step. The garderobe was too tight a space to allow the Lord Mayor to turn, so he kicked out, trying to catch the man in the knee and growling in frustration as the assassin dodged his strike. The second kick went for the groin; Machison's booted foot connected with his thigh instead, still eliciting a groan. The assassin fell backward another step, giving Machison the few inches he needed to turn.

His knife dropped into his palm from a sheath inside his sleeve. He'd expected an assassin, prepared for it. He thrust, aiming for the assassin's ribs, but the man blocked him with a wild swing of his arm.

Machison snarled and stepped forward. The assassin's knife sliced across the Lord Mayor's shoulder. The assassin thrust again and Machison parried. He brought his knee up hard, meaning to strike at the man's belly, but the assassin twisted away, wresting free and knocking Machison to one side with a punch that made him see stars. In the next breath, the killer's blade angled for Machison's chest, but the Lord Mayor turned at the last instant, so that the blade skimmed across his ribs.

Machison staggered, but he was tougher than he looked—the assassin would not be the first to underestimate him. The Lord

Mayor slashed across the assassin's belly, opening up a bloody gash that nearly spilled the man's guts to his garters. Machison followed the assassin down, dropping to his knees and using his momentum to drive his blade through the man's chest, hard enough to stick into the floorboards beneath him.

The assassin gulped, eyes open and glassy, breath coming in ragged puffs. Machison twisted the knife, and the man fell back, dead.

The Lord Mayor rocked back on his heels, shaking with adrenaline, hands covered in blood. He took a few deep breaths to gather his wits, and realized that little of the blood that slicked his arms and fouled his shirt was his own.

I need to find out how he got past the guards. Whoever sent him won't stop until he gets what he wants.

Machison got to his feet and walked to the washstand, rinsing away the blood. He knew from experience that he would never be able to scrub it all away from the creases in his knuckles, from beneath his nails.

It was such a good plan. Keep the Guilds sniping at each other so they don't consolidate their power, keep the ships full and the Merchant Princes happy, keep the rabble distracted, maintain the Balance. Favor Gorog while benefitting Ravenwood as a whole, and win Gorog's gratitude, the blessing of the Crown Prince, and make Ravenwood the envy of the League. I thought I had it all figured out.

And now it's falling to pieces. Ravenwood's no better off than Kasten, and my head will be on the block—or in the noose. Maybe Toloth is right, that it's all just a game of chance. I never asked whether he was betting for or against me.

Machison lifted his shirt to assess his wounds. They would need a healer's attention. Machison retrieved his knife from the assassin's body and walked to the door, cautiously peering out.

He found both guards dead on the floor, throats slit. Machison reached for the bell cord and pulled hard. *Someone needs to clean up the damn mess and get new guards up here. I'm going to bed.*

He was not surprised to see Jorgenson accompanying the servants when they entered. Jorgeson took one look at the blood and sent for the healer. It did not take him long to find the body near the garderobe. "I'll have that taken care of right away," Jorgeson said with a glance at the dead assassin. "Any idea—"

"Too many possibilities, and no proof."

"I'll have new guards assigned."

"Better ones, I hope." Machison scowled.

"I came to tell you that runners are reporting sightings of creatures throughout Ravenwood—more than usual, and even some here in the villas."

Machison ran a hand through his hair, desperation forming a cold knot in his stomach. "What in the name of the Dark Ones is Blackholt doing?"

"If he thinks you've lost Aliyev's trust, or if he believes the deal with Garenoth will fail and cost you—and him—your positions, he might have decided to bring everything down with him."

Machison snarled curses under his breath, shoving down panic and despair. "Tell Valdis it's time for the endgame. He'll know what that means. It looks like we're all going down in flames."

Chapter Thirty-Eight

"THAT'S THE MOST ass-backward plan I've ever heard." Calfon crossed his arms and stared at Trent and Corran as if they had lost their minds.

"Got a better idea?" Corran challenged. He had been awake for more than a day straight and his nerves were frayed.

"Not staging a suicide raid might be a better idea," Calfon snapped.

"Ravenwood is burning," Trent said.

"It's burned before." Calfon looked ready for a fight, arms crossed, fists clenched.

"Not like this."

"What would you prefer? That we sit down here and let the city burn to the ground while the monsters rampage through the streets?" Corran said. "Those people up there, they're our neighbors, our friends—"

"And they would have come to watch us hang as hunters." Calfon did not try to hide the bitterness in his voice.

"So what—we just turn our backs?" Trent said. "You plan to stay down here forever and just hide?"

"No," Calfon snapped. "Of course not. But I'm not so anxious to play the hero that I can't think straight. There might not be anything Above for me to return to, assuming we could win this fight, but I'd at least like to survive long enough to try my hand at being an outlaw beyond the gates."

That bleak future was the best the hunters had come up with. *Deal some justice, and then slip outside the wall and do what we do best: kill any monsters that cross our path*. Things like the strix existed beyond the gates, beyond the control of the Lord Mayor and his witch, but no less deadly. Their hard-won skills might be welcomed out there, maybe even earn them some coin. 'Killer for hire' was a long way from what Corran had always assumed would be his future. *That was before we swore our souls to Eshtamon,* he thought.

"We could do worse," Trent said. "Whether we fight now or later, we certainly can't stay in Ravenwood. If we stop the Lord Mayor and his witch, we can do one last service to our families and neighbors—get rid of the men who control the monsters and the guards."

"There'll be another Lord Mayor, and he'll have his own witch," Corran replied.

"Maybe. Maybe not. But we'll be long gone by then, and it'll be someone else's responsibility. We'll have done the best we could," Trent said.

Calfon shook his head. "That's dangerous talk."

Corran glared at Calfon. "And if it is? The Lord Mayor sent his guards after us, to kill our families, burn our shops. Sent his *assassins* after us more than once. And now we find out that the monsters are being summoned and controlled, maybe even created, by a witch that works for the Lord Mayor? Tell me where in there I owe *loyalty*, because I'm sure not seeing it."

Trent raised a hand, silencing both men. "Enough. Calfon wants a sound plan. He's still getting used to being a wanted man. And

Corran's right about why we fight; we can't sit on our hands forever. Me, I'd rather take the fight to the bastards that started it instead of waiting down here to take an arrow in the back. So I think we all basically agree. We just differ on the details."

Reluctantly, Corran conceded. "Yeah," he said. "But while we're arguing, Ravenwood burns. We don't have time to come up with a perfect plan, so 'good enough' is going to have to do."

"Agreed." Calfon's reply surprised Corran. "But can we go for something more in the order of 'insane' rather than 'suicidal'?"

"I think I could go for that," Corran replied, smiling. Trent rolled his eyes.

"The thing is, I can't come up with a plan to get an armed group of hunters into the Lord Mayor's palace so that three rogue witches can take out a blood mage that isn't *well* beyond 'insane,'" Corran admitted, running a hand through his hair.

The table the men sat at was littered with maps and scrolls. A tray held the scraps of dinner and a nearly empty flagon of wine. They had been at this for more than a day, ever since word came from Above that Ravenwood was in chaos.

"Now that you put it that way, I see your point," Calfon replied.

"Rigan and Aiden are certain they know how to fight the blood witch," Trent said. "We just have to get them inside."

"Doing this won't make the monsters disappear," Calfon said. "It just means that no one is controlling them. That should make them easier to fight, and maybe less of a threat. Of course, assuming we live through this plan, we'll have to run for our lives, so we won't be around to see what happens next."

"I'll take anything that feels like a win right about now," Corran admitted. "And that sounds like a big one."

"And we kill the Lord Mayor, since he's the son of a bitch who's been giving the blood witch his orders," Trent said. "But once we're done with all the killing, how do we get back out of the Mayor's palace? I'm fine with the killing, but not so much with the dying."

Corran looked to the wall where they had pinned the floorplan for the palace. They had pieced the map together from some of the old books Rigan and Aiden had found. Corran knew better than to assume the floorplan was completely accurate, but it was a damn sight better than wandering in with nothing.

He doubted they were the first assassins to try to breach the Lord Mayor's defenses. But the chaos overtaking the city provided a unique diversion, and a few strategically set fires near the palace might draw away the overtaxed guards long enough for the hunters to get past the outer defenses. After that, two stairways and a long corridor were all that separated them from their quarry, and all they would need to cover to make good their escape.

Corran suspected it would not turn out to be that simple. Calfon was right: the plan held too many assumptions and uncertainties.

"We've put out some feelers to our families, the ones who didn't disown us," Trent said, grimacing. *For those of you who still have families*, Corran thought, and pushed down the pain that rose in his chest.

"We can't completely trust the Guilds. In the past, they've disavowed hunters who were caught, washed their hands of us," Rigan warned. "They'd turn us over to Machison in a heartbeat."

"True enough, but the members don't often think like the Guild Masters, and enough people are angry about the spread of the monsters to take up arms, clearing the way for us, creating a diversion," Trent continued. "I'm pretty sure that if we can fight monsters, we can kill the Lord Mayor. But what about his witch? Do you think Rigan and Aiden and Elinor can take on a blood witch and win?"

"They think they can," Corran replied. "I'm not the one to ask. I know precious little about magic, if it doesn't involve banishing a spirit or sending a soul on to its reward. But from what they've said, it sounds possible. And we've got an advantage, because while we have some idea what a blood witch can do, he doesn't know what our team can do."

"Don't forget—Damian betrayed the witches that helped train Rigan," Calfon cautioned. "And if Damian was working for the blood witch, then he might have a very good idea of our strengths and weaknesses."

"It's possible," Corran admitted. "But Damian and Alton are dead. Rigan, Aiden, and Elinor have been working hard on their magic since they trained back at the witch house," Corran said. "I'm sure they'll give the Lord Mayor's witch a run for his money."

Or we all might be walking into a trap, rushing to our deaths.

"The unrest Above won't last forever," Trent pointed out. "If the Lord Mayor can't put things in order, the Merchant Princes will, or the Crown Prince will march an army into Ravenwood. So if we're going to seize the chance to do this while most of the guards are distracted, it needs to be soon."

"That's why it has to be tomorrow night," Calfon said.

"Do you think we're ready?" Corran met Calfon's gaze.

"The witches say they're ready. We have all the weapons we need. And we'll get some support from the Guilds—at least, from our friends. I think it's now or never."

"I agree," Trent said. "It's the best opportunity we're going to get."

"Then let's make it happen," Corran said, letting out a long breath.

Rigan was waiting when Corran returned to their room. "Is everything set?" he asked.

Corran nodded, sure the tight feeling in his gut would not ease until they had finished what they set out to do—assuming they survived. "Yeah. How about with you?"

"We're as ready as we're going to be."

"If you've had second thoughts, now is the time to mention it."

"You?"

Corran thought, then shook his head. "About needing to do this? No. About why the universe would pick a couple of undertakers and some tradesmen when there are plenty of trained soldiers available? Yeah."

"Do you think we can do it?"

"Gods, I hope so," Corran said. "I plan on living through this, Rigan. On *both* of us living through this. And on as many of our friends coming out alive as we can manage."

"I don't think I'll be sorry to leave Ravenwood behind, afterwards," Rigan replied. "There's nothing here for us now anyway."

Corran's dreams had been dark lately, filled with memories of their parents' deaths, of Jora's bloody body, of Kell's savaged corpse. He was certain his brother had heard him tossing in his sleep and knew what troubled him. Corran sat down on the edge of his cot, facing his brother. "I imagine with the unrest, they could use a couple of good undertakers out there."

Rigan snorted. "And by the time we're done, there'll be even more work for someone. But not us. At least, not the way it used to be. Whatever happens, I'm not expecting Eshtamon to save our asses."

Corran smiled. "The odds aren't exactly in our favor."

"Do you think the guards will come after us, once we're past the wall?" Rigan asked. The rest of his question, *assuming we get that far*, remained unspoken.

"It depends on whether or not anyone puts a bounty on our heads." Corran grimaced. "Or a higher one than we already have. Once you get out into the farms and forests, the Lord Mayor's guards are stretched pretty thin. That's where we head; we can't go home, and gods know we can't just sit here. And we seem to be the only ones who might have a shot of doing what needs to be done. So... no second thoughts. I'm in."

Rigan managed a sad smile. "Kell would be impressed."

"He'd have insisted on coming with us."

"Are you kidding? He'd have been the first one over the fence."

We haven't forgotten you, Kell, Corran thought. *We found out who's responsible, and we're going to kill the sons of bitches that did this to you. Maybe that will let you rest in peace.* He looked up and saw that his brother was watching him with concern.

"I miss him, too," Rigan said softly.

Corran swallowed hard and looked away. After a moment, he found his voice. "Yeah. Still can't really believe he's gone."

Rigan laid a hand on his brother's shoulder. "What we're going to do, it won't bring him back, but he'll be avenged. That's something important, something good."

"No argument from me on that," Corran replied.

Supper that evening was unusually quiet. Polly and Elinor served the last of what they had in the kitchen. "It's just going to waste if you don't eat it, since we won't be back," Polly told them, hands on hips, a spoon in one hand as if to smack anyone who dared disagree. *I understand why Kell liked her. They would have made a damn good team,* Corran thought.

"You have a plan for stealing that wagon tomorrow night?" Trent asked.

She huffed as if insulted. "I already stole the damn wagon. Which is why you're all going to haul your sorry asses and your gear up to it tonight, because I can't do it for you tomorrow when there are more important things going on."

Corran chuckled. Polly might be fourteen and a slip of a girl, but she managed to cow all of the hunters and three witches with a tone that brooked no disobedience. He had absolute confidence that she would have the wagon and a brace of horses ready for the getaway, even with the gods and Dark Ones arrayed against them. He shot a glance at Rigan, and saw the same amusement in his brother's expression.

What a houseful we would have been. Me with Jora, Rigan and Elinor. Kell and Polly. Corran looked back to his food, sobered at the loss of what might have been. Rigan, sensing the shift in his mood, elbowed him gently.

"We ought to have a destination in mind, for when we leave Ravenwood," Mir said. For days, they had talked battle tactics, weapons, magic, and spells. Aside from the need for horses and a wagon to put as much distance between themselves and the city, discussion of 'afterwards' had been vague.

"Fortunately for you, I'm amazing." Polly actually did smack Mir with the spoon then, lightly, but he still winced. "While the rest of you have either been shooting things or hocusing things, I've put some thought into escaping, since winning and then not getting away would be a pretty poor show." She gave a triumphant grin.

"Aiden gave me the maps he and Rigan used to locate the monasteries. There are a lot more monasteries, and since they were all abandoned back when the League seized their lands, I suspect they're prime for squatting. Narrowed it down to a couple to start with, because I figure we'll have to move around. The first one is a day's hard ride out, but it will be better than sleeping in the woods. The others are farther, but there's nothing to gain by staying close to the city. The more road we put between us and the wall, the better off we'll be."

Rigan laughed at the dumbstruck looks on the faces of the other hunters. Elinor stifled a smile, and Corran grinned broadly. "It's a great plan," he said, kicking Trent under the table, jarring him out of his thoughts and giving him a warning glare.

"Thank you, Polly," Trent said, clearing his throat. "Great work."

Polly rolled her eyes and gave a long-suffering sigh. "I'm not just a pretty face, you know. There's more to me than just my cooking." With that, Polly turned with a flounce and retreated to the kitchen.

After supper, Rigan, Elinor, and Aiden filled their rucksacks with scrolls. Corran packed weapons, clothes, and the essential tools of the undertaker's trade. Polly and Elinor squabbled over which of the battered pots and utensils to keep. Everyone else saw to their packing quietly, feeling the calm before the storm.

Corran slipped outside not long after the bells tolled eleven.

He leaned against the wall, and closed his eyes, missing the night sky and a chill evening breeze more than ever. Tomorrow night, there would be stars... and blood. He shivered.

Voices carried from one of the open windows. Rigan and Elinor. *Let them take a little comfort while they can*, he thought. He swallowed hard. Jora was never far from his thoughts, but her loss hit him so keenly at times that it felt as if no time at all had passed since her death. Maybe the sharp grief would fade with time, though he doubted it. He knew the hole in his heart where Kell had been would never heal, for him or for Rigan.

He took a sip from his flask, trying to quiet his thoughts. It was too early to sleep, too late to keep going over plans they had already memorized, and he was far too jumpy for cards or conversation. Despite the danger, the desperation of their plan, Corran found himself looking forward to the smell of fresh air, the feel of the wind, the sounds of a city that never slept.

If Eshtamon and Doharmu granted them favor and allowed them to survive the battle, Corran wanted nothing more than to put the past and its pain behind him and Rigan, to make a fresh start. It was the only thing that had kept him going through these past frantic days. Nothing grand or glorious, no dreams of becoming heroes or legends. Just a cold, quiet desire for vengeance for one brother, and a desperate hope of survival for the other, and perhaps for himself. It would have to be enough.

"It's time." Calfon looked at the men and women before him, awaiting the order to move out.

Polly had gone on ahead, to secure the horses. Trent and Calfon led the way, while Corran and Rigan followed, with Elinor and Aiden close behind. Mir and the rest of the hunters brought up the rear. All of them had weapons at the ready.

Already, Corran's pulse quickened in anticipation. A light sheen of sweat coated his forehead and his mouth was dry.

Sooner than he expected, they came to the alley door. He and Mir had scouted the route, which brought them out near the Lord Mayor's palace in a dark ginnel where no one was likely to see them emerge. There the teams would split up, the hunters going one direction while the witches made their own way.

Corran glanced at Rigan. He clasped his brother's forearm, and felt Rigan's hand tighten on his own. No words were necessary. A moment later, the battle began.

Chapter Thirty-Nine

Arson came easy. Learning to kindle flames quickly was part of hunting monsters. Few creatures could survive fire. Tonight, it would provide the distraction they needed to get inside the Lord Mayor's palace. Six guards paced the length of the building. Too many for Corran's taste.

Smoke drifted up from the wharf front, where Corran saw buildings burning; the hunters had nothing to do with them, but the conflagration—and subsequent riots—worked in their favor. The Lord Mayor's guards were scattered throughout the city, breaking up fights and hunting down other hunters. It presented a singular opportunity for setting things right.

Corran, Ross, Trent, and Mir slipped around to the back of the building, near the servants' entrance. Illir and Ellis headed toward the street on the far side, while Tomor and Calfon set out for a spot near the front gates.

Wait for it. Corran did not have to speak to see the warning in his companions' eyes. Shouts and screams rang from the west, as one of the Guild halls exploded in flame. The sight made Corran smile. Calfon and his team *had* set that one, to draw the guards away.

Nice job, he thought. *Must have taken most of the oil to go up like that.*

Fire erupted from every window and broke through the roof. The Lord Mayor's guards might not care about saving the Guild hall, but in a city as tightly packed as Ravenwood, they could not permit the blazes to spread.

A few minutes later, flames fountained into the night sky with a sound like thunder. This time, it came from the main street, the government building housing the exchequer; a fire set by Trent and Ross.

Soft footsteps close by made Corran raise his head, searching the shadows until he saw Illir and Ellis. Tomor and Calfon joined them a moment later, and they waited as more guards rushed to fight the new fires. Four of the guards ran toward the side of the palace, leaving only two at their post to watch the entrance.

Mir and Trent aimed their bows. Their arrows struck almost simultaneously, dropping the guards in silence. Corran and the others rushed to drag the bodies out of view.

At this late hour, the rear hallways were quiet and empty. Candles guttered in sconces in the walls, as the Lord Mayor's servants came and went out of sight of their master. Entering through the back avoided one set of hazards, and presented another—the threat of accidentally rousing one of the dozens of servants who kept the palace running.

They moved quietly, staying to the shadowed side of the hallway, slipping forward in pairs. Corran reached the end of the passageway first; an unlocked door yielded to his touch, and he signalled the others to follow. The narrow, winding steps were dark, and Mir lit a single candle to light their way, shielding the flickering light with his hand to hide their position.

Footsteps sounded nearby. The hunters drew back into the darkness, flattened against the wall. In the narrow confines of the hallway, anyone with a lantern would be sure to see them immediately. Corran watched as a thin, stooped man carrying a tray rounded the corner.

Mir grabbed the man from behind, putting a hand over his mouth and a knife to his throat. Trent dove forward to catch the tray and its contents before they could fall.

"Make a sound louder than a whisper and I cut your throat," Mir growled with his mouth beside the man's ear. "Do you understand?"

The servant nodded. He was a sharp-faced man past his middle years, stoop-shouldered and balding. He looked terrified, staring at the hunters with wide eyes, rigid with fear.

"I'm going to ask you some questions," Mir said. "You'll answer in a whisper. Nothing else. Understood?" For emphasis, he pressed the flat of the blade against the man's throat. The servant blanched.

"How many servants are in the palace?"

"Thirty-two," the man stuttered. "But they're nearly all asleep now."

"Where are their quarters?"

"To the left," the servant replied. Corran glanced in the direction the man indicated and saw another darkened hallway stretching off into the distance.

"How many are awake?"

"Just me. The Lord Mayor rang for me to bring him some tea. I took it to him, and brought back his dinner tray."

"Is the Mayor alone?"

"Yes."

"Tell us how to get to his rooms."

Corran listened as the servant gave directions, squaring what was said with the floorplan he had memorized. "How many guards at his doorway?"

"Two."

"All right. How many inside?"

"None."

"What's the layout of his apartment?" Mir asked.

"There's a parlor inside the front doors. The bedroom is behind that. No one but the Lord Mayor is allowed in there."

Trent eased open the door at the end of the hallway, and in the dim light, Corran could see a butler's pantry. He set down the tray and returned with a napkin, which he rolled up and stuffed into the servant's mouth. Then Trent unbuckled the man's belt and used it to tie his wrists. A tablecloth served to bind his ankles.

"Make any noise, try to summon help, and we'll come back and kill you," Mir said. It was a lie, but the servant blanched and nodded. Trent closed the door behind him, and the three men exchanged a relieved glance. Corran saw Calfon peeking out from the stairwell, and gestured for the others to catch up.

"We know where Machison is," Mir said when they regrouped. "Let's do this and get out of here."

Illir and Ellis stayed below to ensure their way out remained clear. Calfon, Ross, and Tomor would guard this stairway, keeping their route open. Mir, Trent, and Corran all had their own reasons for wanting to see Machison dead, although Corran had claimed the first strike.

He moved through the corridors alert and tense. *Just another hunt for a different kind of monster*. His heart quickened and all his senses felt painfully alert. As they neared the turn to the Lord Mayor's quarters, he signaled for the others to wait.

Bows were unwieldy indoors, but still best for a silent strike at a distance. The wide hallways helped. Bowstrings thrummed and the guards dropped, blood bubbling from their throats. Corran ran to scout the connecting corridor, but it was empty.

Alert for traps, he turned the knob to Machison's chambers, unsurprised to find it locked. He pressed an amulet Rigan had made for him against the lock, and heard the bolt slide back of its own accord.

Corran and Mir opened the doors slowly. A shuttered lantern provided enough light to make out the furnishings of the parlor, and to assure them that no one was inside. Corran gestured, and the two hunters dragged the dead guards inside. That got rid of the bodies, but they could do little to hide the bloodstains on the floor.

Mir took up a position outside the doors, and waved Corran and Trent on. Corran slipped noiselessly to the door to the bedroom and gently tried the knob. Locked.

Cursing silently, Corran again withdrew the amulet Rigan had given him, which he said would open any door. The bolt drew back and the lock opened with a quiet click as the double doors inched open. Trent's bow was ready, arrow nocked, and Corran had a sword in one hand and a knife in the other. They burst into the room.

A four-poster bed dominated the room. On the nightstand sat a pitcher of water and a darkened lantern, and at the foot of the bed, the rug lay in a heap. To the left, on the other side of the room, Lord Mayor Machison stood in the middle of a green, glowing circle, surrounded by shimmering runes and guttering candles. The chamber stank of old blood and stale sweat. Too late, Corran realized it might have been wise to bring a witch with them.

"You can't hurt me." Machison's voice was low and even, angry but not afraid.

Trent let his arrow fly. It bounced harmlessly against the phosphorescent shimmer rising from the circle to the ceiling. The Lord Mayor smiled. "I told you it wouldn't work."

Now that he stood face to face with the man, Corran's anger dulled to a low hum, replaced by a cold determination. *Mama. Papa. Jora. Kell. Bant and the hanged hunters and the dead witches. He's as guilty for their deaths as if he had murdered them himself. Tonight, he dies.*

The runes at the quarters of the circle flared, the light almost blinding. Machison did not even bother to draw a weapon, though Corran was certain any man desperate enough to invoke death magic for protection would certainly be armed.

"I don't care what magic you've meddled with," Corran said. "We're going to kill you."

"You won't be the first to try." Machison's smile was infuriating.

They couldn't afford to linger. Someone would notice the missing guards even if the hastily-mopped-up blood did not catch their attention. Corran doubted that a palace this size would truly be deserted for long, even in the middle of the night. It would only take one servant on a late night errand, one guard carrying a message, to sound the alarm.

Trent flicked his wrist and a knife flew from his hand, aimed for Machison's heart. The point stalled at the green curtain of energy and dropped to the floor.

"You can't cross the barrier," Machison said. "I'm safe in here."

Corran and Trent exchanged a glance. "Do it." Corran ordered.

Trent dug into the rucksack for the wineskin of oil, and then grabbed a bottle of whiskey from the nightstand, soaking the mattress and sloshing the liquids liberally on the bed curtains, the draperies, and the carpet.

"Are you insane?" Machison roared. "You'll burn with me!"

Something familiar, yet tainted, tugged at the edge of Corran's senses. "Wait," he told Trent as the man moved to light a candle from the banked embers in the fireplace.

Corran had none of Rigan's witch powers, but the grave magic of all the Valmondes who had ever been Wrighton's undertakers flowed in his blood, along with the legacy of his mother's Wanderer heritage. Long experience banishing unruly spirits and chanting over the bodies of the dead had attuned him to the singular magic of their craft. And it was a twisted echo of grave magic that Corran felt when he extended his senses toward the sickly green glow of the warding circle.

His gaze fell on the elements that worked the protection. Through the shimmering curtain of power, he saw a small shriveled corpse and a dead man's hand, along with what looked like finger bones.

Dried blood caked the floor and the candles. An iron knife lay next to the corpse's hand. The glowing sigils were perverted versions of the runes Corran and Rigan marked to afford the dead safe passage to the Golden Shores, and he recoiled from them instinctively, knowing their essence to be infernal.

"I know how to beat you."

Machison stared at him, loathing clear in his expression. "You're not a witch. You're not a Wanderer. You're nothing but trash."

"No, I'm an undertaker. A hunter. And my mother's people—*they* were Wanderers." Corran smiled as he saw fear in Machison's eyes at the last. "My brother has heard the confessions of the dead. They accuse you. They told us the truth about who's been controlling the monsters and making people disappear. Your guards killed our brother the night they went after the Wanderers, and I'm here to get justice—for Kell, and for all of them."

He turned to Trent. "Cover me."

Trent gave a curt nod and raised his bow.

"The dead convict you," Corran said, closing his eyes and focusing on the souls of those from whom the blood had been harvested, on the spirit of the owner of the severed hand, the ghost of the stillborn child, the person whose bones had been taken without permission, the corpse burned into ash. He did not attempt to summon them against their will, but asked for their help, reminding them of how they had been misused.

The spirits came. One by one, they materialized outside the green fire of the circle, regarding Machison with dark, baleful eyes. Kell was not among them. "Don't you want to come out and meet them?" Corran taunted the Lord Mayor. "They've come for an audience with you."

"You'll have to do better than that," Machison said, a smile creeping across his lips. He closed his hand around his amulet, and lightning flashed from the green curtain, blazing through the spirits. Whenever the energy touched a ghost, the spirit vanished with a shriek.

Corran dove for the pitcher of water on the night stand, and sluiced the liquid across the floor to erase the circle of protection. A bolt of energy struck him and he went tumbling across the room. Corran's shoulder burned and a shock ran through his body, making his heart skip a beat, freezing his chest for a moment so that he could not draw breath. Panic filled him as he gasped and the room spun. His back and head throbbed from the force of hitting the wall. Gritting his teeth, Corran pushed himself up to stand.

Trent had managed to stay out of the way of the arcing energy, and he grabbed the bellows from beside the fire, before crawling back towards the circle. He set the nozzle against the floor and pumped hard, scattering the line of salt and aconite.

The ghosts rematerialized on the other side of the warding. Machison kept his grip on the amulet, but Corran saw the toll the borrowed magic took on the man. A pained expression crossed the Lord Mayor's face. *Guess he never asked his blood witch where the energy came from that makes the amulet work. It looks like he's just started to figure it out.*

The sickly green glow of the warding dimmed and the ghosts rushed towards the Lord Mayor.

This time, the energy that crackled in response was a feeble echo of the first attack. Trent adjusted the angle of the bellows and pumped it once more, just as Machison gathered his waning magic for one last salvo. A single brilliant arc lanced from the curtain of green fire, striking Trent squarely in the chest and throwing him hard enough against the far wall to crack the plaster. The hunter slid down the wall just as the air from the bellows drove the spilled water across the floorboards, dislodging the last of the salt circle.

The phosphorescent shimmer winked out.

Smoke filled the room, rank with the smell of a funeral pyre. Machison gave a feral cry and launched himself at Corran, and Corran closed with him, kicking aside the trappings of the warding.

"Cur," Machison spat. Corran parried, narrowly fending off Machison's advance.

"Murderer." Corran watched for an advantage. Despite his age and paunch, Machison could move like a coiled snake. Corran gasped as the man's blade slashed down his forearm, soaking his sleeve with blood.

"You're no match for me, boy. Kneel and I'll make it quick."

"Go to the Dark Ones." Corran ignored the pain and thrust forward, scoring a hit to Machison's thigh.

The Lord Mayor cursed and returned a string of attacks with the deadly grace of long practice, and all Corran could do was hold off the worst of the blows. Rage and pain sent him back at Machison, wielding his sword two-handed, making up for the training he lacked with the unpredictability of his strikes.

To Corran's satisfaction, his blade bit into flesh more than once, opening gashes on Machison's face, chest, and arms. The ghosts did not try to interfere, but drew back to the shadows, silent observers.

Corran stumbled, and Machison stepped forward, sliding his blade under Corran's guard, sinking the point into his side. "You're losing."

Corran gasped, but he managed a backhand slash that opened a cut across Machison's ribs deep enough to reveal bone. "You're bleeding."

They circled each other like bloodied predators, panting for breath, eyes wide with pain. Sweat ran down Corran's face, mingling with blood. Machison paled, but he gave no indication of faltering.

"All this, and for what?" Machison's voice was thick with contempt. "You won't escape. Maybe I'll let Blackholt have you for a while. What should it be? Drawn and quartered, or flayed alive?"

"Dark Ones take your soul." Corran's mouth was dry, and his words slurred. He was fuelled by anger alone now, but as long as he could stand, he would fight.

For Kell, for Jora, for all of them.

Machison came at him with a flurry of strikes which Corran managed to deflect. The Lord Mayor sent him sprawling with a roundhouse punch to the jaw, landing him amid the debris that had been the circle of protection. He caught Machison with a kick to the knees as he fell, sending the Lord Mayor onto his ass.

Corran licked the blood from his lips, tried to ignore the ringing in his head, and nursed a loose tooth with his bleeding tongue. With a growl, he pushed himself to his feet, one hand swiping through the salt and aconite as he dragged himself to his feet.

Machison was already standing, bloodied and wounded, but swaggering. "Admit that you're beaten."

"Not yet."

With the last of his strength, Corran surged toward the Lord Mayor, hurling a handful of the salt mixture into the man's eyes, blinding him for a moment and sending Machison's swing wide. Corran lunged, angling his sword to take Machison in the heart. Machison's arm swung to block the blow, letting the blade sink bone-deep, then he jerked back, tearing the sword from Corran's blood-slick grip.

Corran rammed Machison with his shoulder, taking them both to the floor, and slammed his opponent's wrist against the wood until he knocked Machison's sword from his hand. Corran was younger and fit, but Machison was heavier and experienced. Corran raged at him, drawing from the well of anger that was all he had left, each bone-jarring hit signed with vengeance. *Kell. Jora. Jott and Pav and Bant. Mama. Papa. Dilin. The Wanderers. Even the murdered witches from Below.*

He landed more blows than he missed, but Machison was still scrabbling to get free. The Lord Mayor dug his thumb into the open wound in Corran's side, giving him the opening he needed to wrestle Corran onto his back and straddle him, pinning him.

Blood filled Corran's mouth and ran from his ears and his nose. One eye was swollen shut, his lip split. Everything hurt, and blood soaked his clothing.

"Time to end this." Machison's meaty fist smashed into Corran's jaw, snapping his head to one side. The Lord Mayor's hands closed around Corran's neck, throttling him. Corran's hands clawed at

Machison's arms, trying to break the grip, but Machison had the weight advantage. Corran's right hand fell away, dropping to the floor. The world faded, but he heard a dull clink as his hand thumped against the floorboard, and in desperation, he reached toward the sound.

His hand closed over cool iron. Corran brought his arm up with all his remaining strength, angling the blade through Machison's back, between the ribs, hilt deep—a killing strike.

Machison jerked back as blood poured from his mouth and splattered across Corran's face and chest. The pressure eased on Corran's throat, and he brought his arms up inside the Lord Mayor's reach, pushing the hands away. Gasping for air, Corran shoved the dying man away and into the center of the ruined warding.

Machison's breathing gurgled wetly. "Toloth. Should have known... you'd bet against me."

Corran stared into the darkness at the edge of the room. He could see the ghosts much better now. *Probably because I'm almost dead myself*, he thought.

Well done.

The voice made Corran startle, and he looked around the room, fearing someone had entered. Instead, he saw the spirit of an old Wanderer woman standing at the forefront of the crowd of apparitions. She gave him an approving look. *Your blood calls to me, telling me you are kin. Eshtamon was right to favor you. I feel his hand on you. Blood calls to blood. Just like the sigils we left in the city, before we fled or died, cursing the Lord Mayor, praying for vengeance. The sigils's magic stirred tonight, awakening the curse.*

"He had it coming," Corran panted. "For killing Kell and Jora, and all the others." He looked to the ghosts that crowded behind the Wanderer. "He's all yours. Enjoy yourselves."

He turned away, trying to shut out the last, terrified scream that tore from Machison's throat as the spirits swarmed over him and took their vengeance.

The spirits left as abruptly as they came, their need for revenge sated. Corran lay face up on the floor, wondering how much more blood he had left in his body.

"Looks like I missed the party." Trent knelt beside him, but the levity in his voice died as he looked over Corran's wounds. "Gods, Corran. I'm so sorry—"

Corran grunted, cutting him off with a gesture. "Thought you were dead. Glad I'm wrong. Help me up."

"I figured I would have to carry you out of here."

"Not leaving," Corran said, trying to turn on his side to raise himself. "Got to help Rigan. So give me a damn hand up or get out of my way."

"You're bleeding from a dozen wounds. By all rights, you shouldn't still be breathing. And you want to fight?"

"No, I want to make sure Rigan gets out of here in one piece." Corran's voice was hoarse after the damage Machison had done to his throat. He wiped a sleeve across his mouth, smearing blood.

"You're a fool."

"Didn't say you had to come with me." He met Trent's gaze. "Set the fire. We need to go."

Trent turned toward the oil-and-whiskey-soaked bed and tossed the lantern onto the sheets. Flames blazed, licking at the bed curtains. Cursing under his breath, Trent crossed to where Corran struggled to get to his feet, trying to figure out the least painful way to help him up. "I'll get under your shoulders and lift. On three—"

Corran growled as Trent hauled him upright.

"Get the others," he said. "Rigan's in the dungeon. Let's go."

Chapter Forty

"HE KNOWS WE'RE here." Rigan whispered.

Aiden's mouth set in a grim line. A hastily-healed cut above his eyebrow was one of many reminders of the fight to secure the stairway, and a trail of dried blood marked the side of his face. Rigan knew they'd both have bruises to show for the fight, since they had elected to reserve their magic for the real battle, and not tip their hand to Blackholt until absolutely necessary.

Rigan glanced at the still bodies of the guards that lay bound and gagged in the shadows to one side of the passageway. A few steps away, Elinor spread out her potions on the smooth stone floor in the small alcove of a sentry station. She chalked sigils as she laid down a circle of salt and aconite, but did not yet complete the line, unwilling to trigger a flare of power that might alert Blackholt to their plans.

She set out a chalice, a crudely-made stuffed poppet, and a mortar and pestle, and then laid out the materials for the night's work—garlic, turmeric, red pepper, castor beans, sweet clover, apple seeds, crab's eye, belladonna, and a flagon of wine. Next to the items lay a long thin knife with a razor-sharp blade imbued with Elinor's magic.

"Blackholt bolsters his own abilities through the blood he takes from his victims," Aiden had told them. "Weaken the power in the blood, and Blackholt is left with his own magic, nothing more."

The poisons that Elinor had assembled thinned or tainted the blood, some of them deadly in even the smallest doses. She could afflict the poppet with her poisons and have Blackholt feel the effects, giving Rigan and Aiden a fighting chance.

Rigan was still unhappy that Elinor insisted on joining them instead of remaining with Polly and the wagon. They had argued about that, but she had stood her ground.

Rigan pulled himself out of his thoughts. He did not miss the worry in Elinor's eyes as she prepared the items. This was the first time she had set out to use her abilities to kill. She wanted vengeance for Parah's son just as surely as Rigan did for Kell, and Aiden did for the witches Damian had betrayed.

"Sure you're all right with this?" Rigan said. Elinor met his gaze. He saw the hesitation she tried to hide, felt it himself.

"I'm not much of a fighter, but I can do this. Give us to the count of two hundred, then start the working. And be careful."

"You too." He bent to kiss her, a brief, unspoken goodbye, and turned to join Aiden.

Aiden and Rigan headed down the stairs, deeper into the dungeons. Both wore amulets to mask their magic, but that would only work at a distance. The closer they got to Blackholt, the less the amulets would deflect his attention.

The coppery tang of blood mingled with the sickly sweet smell of rotting flesh.

Is this how Corran and the hunters felt, going into a monster's lair? He wondered whether Corran and the others had managed to reach Machison, and how they had fared. *Eshtamon, if you're listening, this is what we traded our souls for. I'm calling you on those 'gifts' you gave us. You'd damn well better have meant what you said, because we're in the thick of it now.*

As they descended, the air grew thick with corrupt power, heavy with malice. Sweat beaded on Rigan's forehead. A glance at Aiden told him that the healer was equally rattled.

Neither man expected to survive the fight. Even Elinor did not know the lengths Rigan and Aiden had agreed to go to stop Blackholt, and Corran still less. *I don't imagine he'll forgive me. I wish it could be different. Maybe we'll get lucky. But I'm not counting on it.*

"They're all dead," Aiden's said as they reached the cages where Blackholt held his victims. The stench was overpowering. Rigan fought to keep his stomach under control, and bile rose in the back of his throat. Aiden's expression was grief-stricken, and Rigan knew that the healer could sense the torment of those who had perished here.

"They were all killed recently," the healer said. "He's been preparing for our arrival."

Adrenaline thrummed through Rigan's body; his blood sang and his taut muscles screamed for action. His magic strained at its constraints, so ready for release that he was sure his amulet could not hide the power that welled up, as if it would burst through his skin.

Restless spirits crowded around them as they made their way deeper into Blackholt's lair. The temperature plunged, dropping from suffocatingly close to frigidly cold, and Rigan could see his breath misting before him.

The spirits did not speak, but their anger required no words. Hollow eyes followed the two witches, urging them to avenge their deaths, excoriating them for remaining among the living, coveting the warmth of their blood.

"They're all here, all the ones he's killed. He's siphoning their souls the way he drained their blood, and he'll keep them here until they're used up," Aiden said.

As the passageway opened into a workroom, they saw Blackholt standing in between two blood-soaked tables.

A naked man lay spread-eagle on one of the tables. Deep cuts had opened the arteries in his neck, arms, groin, and legs, allowing the victim's blood to drip into ceremonial bowls on the floor.

"Valdis thought he could hide his treachery," Blackholt greeted them with a twitch of his head toward the dying man. "He and Machison sided against me, thought they could undercut me. I saved him for last. He was a blood witch, and that makes his blood particularly potent. A fitting final sacrifice."

Blackholt's gaze flickered from his victim to Rigan and Aiden. "You shouldn't have come." Rust red stains smudged Blackholt's gray robes. He was a thin man in his middle years, unremarkable in appearance, with a high forehead and receding chin, someone Rigan might have mistaken for a worker at the counting house had he not been so utterly at home in this abattoir.

A deep growl sounded from a corridor off the far side of the workroom. *Of course he would have monsters at his beck and call*, Rigan thought. *That's what he does.*

Crimson nearly hid the whites of Blackholt's bloodshot eyes, and a thin line of blood ran from the man's nose. Aiden's right hand came up and Blackholt staggered, gasping for breath. The healer's gaze fixed on the blood witch, focusing his power to still Blackholt's heart and steal the air from his lungs. The blood witch fought for air, a terrible rasping sound, and he stumbled, one hand going to his chest.

Rigan chanted the banishing ritual. *If I can send the ghosts away, Blackholt can't draw on them for power anymore,* he thought. *They'll be free, and he'll be weakened.*

Blackholt forced himself to straighten, eyes burning with rage. He brought his hands together and pushed out, sending a shockwave through the room. Rigan and Aiden hit the far wall, hard enough that Rigan's vision blurred and pain exploded through his skull. He reached up and tore away the amulet, fearing that it might dampen his power now that the need for secrecy was gone. He struggled to his feet, as Aiden pushed himself up, ready to return to the fight.

Four *hancha* scrabbled from the far corridor, their blood-black faces slowly turning to Aiden and Rigan.

Hancha, Rigan thought. *Useful to clean up the bodies.*

"Son of a bitch." Rigan unsheathed his knife an instant before the first two *hancha* were on him, tearing at his skin with their icy fingers. Teeth snapped close to his neck, raising gooseflesh.

A yelp let Rigan know that Aiden had gone down under the other two monsters, but at the moment, it was all he could do to keep his attackers away from his own throat. He tumbled across the floor in a tangle of bony arms and skeletal legs, biting back a cry as the *hancha* scored his skin with their sharp nails, drawing blood.

The creatures were thin as famine victims, but unnaturally strong. One of them wrapped its arms around Rigan's chest and squeezed. He struggled to breathe, bucking and twisting to free himself from the hold. The second *hancha* sank its teeth into Rigan's thigh, and he cried out in pain as the monster tore at his flesh.

Rigan slashed at the *hancha* by his leg, sinking his blade deep between the thing's ribs. The creature reared up, almost ripping the knife from his grasp. Rigan held on, twisting the blade. The *hancha* gave an inhuman shriek as ichor flowed from the wound, soaking his hand. More foul-smelling black liquid bubbled from the monster's mouth. Its teeth were red with Rigan's blood. He ripped the knife from the *hancha*'s cold flesh and stabbed again, just below the creature's ribs, close to the spine, pulling the blade down through dead flesh. The *hancha* trembled, clawing at air, and fell backward, still twitching and trembling.

At the scent of blood, the first *hancha*'s attention shifted to the open wound on Rigan's thigh. He seized the momentary distraction, grabbing the *hancha* by the throat with his left hand and squeezing hard. The *hancha*'s clawed hands dug at Rigan's chest and arms, but he kept the creature pinned with one hand as he sank his blade into its heart. Syrupy ichor welled from the wound, spraying Rigan's face and shoulders as the blade tore through the monster's chest.

His thumb dug into the *hancha*'s windpipe, crushing it. He tossed the body aside, desperate to help Aiden and get back to the fight against Blackholt.

He dragged himself to his knees, and saw that while he'd been fighting the *hancha*, the spirits of Blackholt's victims had gathered. Dozens of ghosts stood against the walls. Controlled by Blackholt's will, they watched the struggle with baleful eyes.

A groan brought Rigan's attention back to Aiden, though he dared not ignore the threat posed by the malevolent dead. The healer was buried beneath two *hancha*, his face tightened with pain and concentration, ignoring the creatures' attacks in order to maintain his own assault on Blackholt and keep the blood witch from coming after his companion.

Rigan ripped into the *hancha* feasting on Aiden's leg, slashing the blade across the creature's neck until the throat gaped. Blood and ichor fountained down the front of the *hancha*'s chest. He grabbed the creature's forehead, forcing the nearly severed head away from his friend, wincing as the sharp teeth tore away from Aiden's skin, leaving raw, bloody tracks.

With a growl, Rigan turned his knife of the second *hancha*, and this time his swing had enough power to take the creature's head clean off. Jaws clamped on Aiden's shoulder, and Rigan sank his knife into the *hancha*'s cheek, forcing the blade back against the molars, prying the mouth open until he could kick the head away.

Through it all, the healer's eyes remained shut. Rigan knew that Aiden was focused on inverting his healing power, breaking his vows as he used the one ability he possessed in a desperate gamble against a far stronger opponent.

Trickles of blood started from Blackholt's ears, and his breath wheezed as Aiden's magic froze the muscles of his chest. His skin glistened with sweat, and his cheeks reddened with fever. Elinor's magic had poisoned Blackholt's blood, and Aiden's had ravaged the mage's body. Boils rose on the blood witch's arms and neck. The growing gush of blood from Blackholt's mouth suggested organs cut or crushed, and the wet coughs gave Rigan to imagine lungs torn and inflamed.

The effort to kill Blackholt took a deadly toll on Aiden. He lay, corpse-pale, breath coming in short, harsh panting gasps, eyes darting desperately beneath his closed eyelids.

The ghosts surged closer, keening as they swept toward the two witches. Rigan took a step forward, putting himself between Aiden and the spirits. He gathered his magic, ignoring his injuries, and once more began to chant the banishing spell.

The spirits washed over Rigan and he fought to keep on chanting, though the press of wraiths stole his breath, chilled his blood and threatened to freeze his heart. In all the times he and Corran had dispelled malicious revenants, he had never faced them without the barrier of a warded circle. *This had better work.* As his grave magic rose to his call, power flowed through him. Beneath his shirt, the sigil he had drawn in ochre on his abdomen began to glow, bright enough that the orange-red light shone through the fabric. The chalk sigil on his chest flared with brilliant white light. The angry ghosts drew back, shrieking as the stark light burned.

Searing pain made Rigan gasp as the blue sigil on his throat glowed brightly, nearly cutting off his air. He staggered, but kept on chanting, his voice falling to a whisper. He'd had no idea whether marking himself with the sigils of the banishing spell—effectively making his body the quarters of a banishing circle—would work, but it was a decision made in desperation, knowing that they would not get the chance to lay down a true circle as the ritual required. He wondered whether the runes would tear his soul from his body, or whether he would forfeit his hold on the world of the living by virtue of the magic's power. If so, he accepted his fate.

His throat closed as the pain grew more intense, and he continued the chant inwardly, moving his lips though no sound came. Light bathed his body, radiating from the three marks of power. Blackholt's horde of ghostly attackers dimmed and withdrew. He sensed that he and the blood witch were locked in a contest of wills to control the spirits, even as Aiden kept up his relentless assault against Blackholt's failing body.

Blackholt's skin paled to translucence, eyes bloodied, lips stained with blood. Racking coughs alternated with harsh, raw gasps, and blue-black lesions mottled his face and stretched from his neck past the line of his tunic. Rigan wondered just how much damage Elinor and Aiden's magic had inflicted; if he could banish the spirits from which Blackholt drew his reserve of power, he could destroy his last defense.

Even as Rigan mustered the courage to draw on the final sigil, he knew his own body was also failing. *Grave magic was never meant to be worked on the living.* It would be a lesson bequeathed to survivors, a cautionary tale. A flash of sorrow constricted his heart, knowing that Corran would be left to deal with his body—assuming he ever learned his fate.

Thumps and clatters sounded behind him, but Rigan was too far gone, too consumed by the spell to care. *If this works, if Blackholt falls, it should take the* hancha *with him.*

He forced the words of the banishing spell past his burning lips, little more than a painful croak. The black sigil on his forehead took on a muted golden glow around its edges as a blinding headache staggered him. Rigan almost fell to his knees, but a hand closed on his arm, steadying him, and a familiar baritone voice joined his in the banishing chant.

Corran stood beside him, battered and bleeding but alive. Rigan could see in his brother's eyes that there would be hard questions to answer if they both survived, that Corran would take him to task for the risks he had taken, but for now, they stood shoulder to shoulder. And in that moment, Rigan imagined that he heard a third voice, Kell's voice, joining in the chant, and he found the will to keep going, although his breath hitched and his heart stuttered and the pain behind his forehead felt as if it would blow his skull apart.

Blackholt stumbled and swung toward Rigan, Corran, and Aiden. His lips drew back in a snarl, and he thrust out a splayed hand, summoning his waning power for a final, fatal strike.

Before he could invoke the words of power, a dark shape swept behind Blackholt in a single, fluid movement and steel glinted in the torchlight. Trent's blade swung with two-handed force, sending Blackholt's head toppling from his shoulders as his ravaged body dropped to the floor.

Freed from the blood witch's will, the vengeful spirits could no longer hold out against the strength of the brothers' grave magic, and the banishment spell rolled through the dungeon like a storm, casting the malevolent ghosts through the gates of Doharmu and into the After. Their screams echoed from the stone walls and the cold wind whipped into a maelstrom that guttered the torches and lanced across bare skin like shards of ice. Incorporeal fingernails dug into the hard floor, leaving gouges as the void beyond pulled them to eternity.

Rigan heard Corran shouting at him, but the voice was far away, the words indistinct. He found himself on the floor and looked up, saw his brother's panicked expression, but could only focus on how much blood was soaking through Corran's shirt and that he should feel more worried about that, should feel... something, before sight and sound failed him and the darkness folded around him.

Blackness receded. Rigan felt strong arms lifting him, dragging his unresponsive body up the stairs. Everything hurt, and if the banishment spell had not succeeded in ripping his soul from his body, then his spirit nonetheless felt tethered by a fragile thread.

"Stay with us, Rigan," Trent said. "We've still got to get out of here."

"Corran—"

"Mir's got him. Damn both of you for cutting it too fucking close."

"Aiden and Elinor?" Rigan managed.

"Calfon's got Aiden. Elinor's still standing. You're all crazy, brave, stupid, sons of bitches and I've just lost ten years off my life because you've scared me out of my wits, damn you," Trent replied.

Rigan tried to laugh, but it hurt too much to breathe. "Oh, shit," Trent muttered as the witch's legs buckled and the hunter took his full weight. Once again, Rigan's world faded to black.

"STAND UP, RIGAN. You've got to stand up." Trent's voice sounded close to his ear, barking an order that Rigan knew meant life or death. He grunted in response and forced his knees to lock, realizing that only the rough wall behind his back kept him upright.

Memories ghosted through his mind, of the palace burning and of fighting their way through the scattered guards who had not already fled the flames. Although Rigan knew he had taken part in that fight, had fresh blood on his bruised knuckles to prove it, he could not remember the details.

"We're pinned down," Trent said. "The city's in chaos. Can't get to the meeting point for Polly to pick us up."

"Corran—"

"Behind you," Trent replied. Rigan turned his head to see his brother propped against the same wall, just as bloodied and battered. As Rigan's head cleared, he saw the rest of their group huddled in the shadows of a building a few blocks from the Lord Mayor's palace. The palace itself had become an inferno.

"Plan?"

"Nothing yet," Trent replied.

Tomor came around the corner, eyes wide, hair sweat-soaked. "Everything between here and the harbor is blocked," he reported breathlessly as the others gathered closer to hear. "Too many burning buildings, and between the falling timbers and the people trying to fight the fire, we'll never get through."

Trent and Calfon cursed under their breaths. "Polly can't keep circling for long," Calfon said. "Someone will notice."

Ellis joined them a moment later from the other direction. "There's a riot off to the right," he said, pointing. "Couldn't make out faces, but I'm guessing it's at least a hundred people, maybe more, fighting with the guards. Good news is that it's pulled guards away from the street in front of the palace. I think they've given up on fighting the fire."

"How about to the left?" Mir asked over his shoulder, keeping his gaze trained on the street, watching for threats.

"Small fires, and a mob of bystanders like it's some damn holiday festival," Ellis told them. "We'd get separated in the crowd, and there's no good way around to where Polly's supposed to meet us."

"North?" Trent asked.

"Most of the guards are that way, standing watch over the villas," Tomor said. "We'll get caught for sure."

"Take the cemetery road." Corran's voice was a harsh rasp, but it carried over the noise from the street. "Runs along the wall. No one's going to be guarding the dead."

Rigan met his gaze. "If we run into monsters—"

"Then we fight," Corran replied. "But it's better than standing here, waiting to get caught."

Rigan mustered his strength and a little of his magic, enough to let him push away from the wall and stand without swaying too much. Elinor came up beside him, putting a steadying hand on his elbow. Corran joined them a moment later, a signal that it was time to move out.

They circled to the north, anxious to avoid the opulent homes of the Guild Masters and Merchant Princes, with their guards and high fences. Illir and Tomor went ahead to scout. Calfon and Mir took point, with Elinor, Rigan, Aiden, and Corran in the middle. Ellis, Trent, and Ross brought up the rear.

Rigan strained to hear the bells from the tower. He already knew they were late to meet Polly. *She's resourceful, and ruthless. She'll be there. We just have to make it to the meeting point,* he told himself.

A glance behind him told Rigan that Corran probably felt as bad as he did. His lips were pressed into a bloodless line, his face looked paler than normal in the moonlight, and blood streaked his shirt and cheek. Not that Rigan looked any better himself. The others were worse for the wear as well, injured from the fight in the palace, except for Elinor. They just had to make it to the wagon.

Of all the problems the guards had this night, enforcing curfew was the least of them. Behind Rigan, he heard the shouts and chants of an angry mob, and the roar of flames. Smoke hung heavy in the air, stinging his eyes and burning in his throat. Even in the alleys and side streets, people jostled shoulder to shoulder, anxious to see what was going on, or to flee the unrest.

Illir and Tomor did their best to clear the path for the rest of them, shouldering aside the frantic city-dwellers, trying to keep from getting separated in the press of bodies. Half of the people were trying to get away from the city; the rest wanted to see what the fuss was all about.

The flow of the crowd suddenly shifted, and Rigan caught the panic in their faces as shouting and the clatter of weapons sounded in the distance. A line of guards blocked the plaza at the end of the alley, leaving them nowhere to go.

"Go back to your homes. Clear the streets." The guard's manner made it clear he expected to be obeyed.

Frightened and angry, caught up in the adrenaline rush of the mob and the fires, the energy of the crowd changed in a heartbeat.

"Shouldn't you be down there, fighting the fires, instead of up here getting in our way?" The speaker, a broad-shouldered man with muscles toned by hard labor, bent and threw a chunk of stone from the gutter, striking one of the guards in the chest.

The soldiers surged forward, just as angry and scared as the crowd. Civilians hurled rocks and debris, while others pulled down bricks and wood from the walls of nearby buildings to wield as weapons.

"Shit," Illir muttered. "Those people are going to get themselves killed."

Three of the townspeople had already fallen to the ground, bloodied from the guards' swords. The crowd roared its anger and came at the guards again, blind with rage. More guards appeared behind the first group, and Rigan counted over a dozen.

"No choice," Calfon said. "We've got to fight our way through."

"We've got the six on the right," Aiden said, with answering nods from Rigan and Elinor.

"We'll go left," Illir, Tomor, and Ellis volunteered. That left Mir, Trent, Ross, Calfon, and Corran for a frontal assault.

They plunged into the fray without a battle cry, already bloodied and exhausted from the fight at the palace. Aiden focused his magic on two of the guards: boils sprang up on their faces and arms, swelling their eyes shut and forcing them to drop their swords to claw at the lesions. Elinor's expression of concentration had the next two clutching at their hearts, sagging to their knees as she worked the same magic that had weakened Blackholt.

Rigan's power lacked Aiden's control or Elinor's finesse. He grounded his magic in the energy of the burning buildings all around them and sent a wave of fire that killed his two targets, along with two new guards just joining the fight from behind them.

"I think that's it for me," he gasped, staggering until Elinor got under his shoulder and pulled him back against the wall. Aiden went to join Corran's group, holding their own in a pitched battle in the middle of the plaza.

Most of the civilians had fled. The bodies of half a dozen of the unlucky ones littered the paving stones or slumped over the shallow wall of the fountain in the center of the plaza. A hardy few fought on, and Rigan wondered if they were also hunters, because they managed to hold their own with just knives and improvised weapons.

Rigan turned toward the group on the left just as Ellis's opponent lunged forward, sinking his blade through the hunter's chest. Ellis staggered, then his knees buckled before his killer could withdraw the blade. Rigan's choked shout barely carried above the noise of the fight. Elinor gripped his arm tight enough to bruise, holding him back from rejoining the fray.

"Rigan, no!" Elinor pulled him back.

Rigan felt his anger snap, although he knew she was right. He sent his fury in a stream of fire that caught Ellis's killer in the back, setting him ablaze. "Serves him right," he muttered, then gasped and sagged against the wall.

"Idiot," Elinor muttered under her breath, but her grip on his arm never wavered, and he could feel her sending tendrils of her power through the contact to sustain him.

The world wavered in his field of vision as Rigan fought vertigo, and then Elinor and Trent were pulling him to his feet and dragging him forward. "Move! Go!" Trent urged.

Rigan oriented on Corran, alive but injured, supported with an arm over Aiden's shoulder. He guessed that the healer was also using the opportunity to replenish what he could of Corran's strength, although his brother still looked pale and drawn.

The guards lay dead, bodies scattered across the bloody paving stones of the courtyard. Mir had Ellis's body slung over his shoulder, while Tomor carried Illir. Rigan had not seen Illir go down.

"Are they—?" he asked.

"Keep moving," Elinor replied, giving his answer in what she did not say.

By the time they reached the cemetery by the outer wall of the city, the crowds had thinned, just the occasional thrill-seeker heading toward the ruckus, or wide-eyed refugees fleeing the flames, too frightened to pay the bloodied stragglers any notice. The guards did not bother coming out to the wall. They did not expect trouble from the dead.

"We can double back on the other side of the cemetery," Calfon said, pointing. "From there, we should only be a few blocks away from where Polly's waiting."

If she's still there. The words went unspoken, but Rigan felt certain he was not the only one thinking it.

Halfway past the cemetery, a low growl raised the hair on the back of Rigan's neck, and a distinctive stench assaulted his nose. He saw the horrified recognition on Corran's face a heartbeat before a huge, bat-faced black beast sprang over the iron fence. The creature swatted Tomor out of the way with its heavy paw, sharp claws opening furrows across his chest and belly, sending him sprawling on top of Illir's body.

The creature bared its sharp teeth, drawing back blackened lips and crumpling its squashed face even further. It stood as tall as a boar, large as a hog, covered in coarse black hair. Red eyes sized them up and it lowered its head to charge. Before the others could move forward to meet the threat, an answering growl sounded from behind them.

Two beasts. Rigan remembered the fight he and Corran had put up to kill just one of the monsters, and a smaller one at that. This time, they had more men to face the threat, but all of them were hurt. He and Corran were barely standing; Trent and Ross looked equally spent, and the others were a mess of blood, bruises, and burns.

Trent, Ross, and Corran went forward, while Calfon and Mir turned to face the threat from behind. Aiden and Elinor dragged Rigan back, knowing the best they could do was to stay out of the fight.

"Aiden, can you help Tomor?" Rigan asked, watching as their friend slumped against the iron fence. Illir's and Ellis's bodies lay beside him, dropped in the fight.

Aiden shook his head. "Even if I could get to him, he's dying. The damage is too great. More than I could fix, even at full strength."

Corran's group came at the monster all at once, striking from three directions. The creature howled in rage, snapping its teeth, striking out with its long claws, and throwing its heavy head side to side with enough force to shatter bone. Still, Trent and Ross baited it, lunging in and out, distracting it so Corran could score with his sword.

Behind them, Mir and Calfon had their hands full. Against two fighters, the creature could better keep track of its attackers, dodging their blows and managing to get in more than one solid hit with its teeth and claws.

They aren't going to make it, Rigan thought in despair, cursing his injuries for keeping him out of the fight.

Just then, he saw Tomor drag himself up against the fence. His blood-soaked shirt and the smell of shit made the extent of his injuries clear as he pressed one hand to his abdomen, holding his entrails inside.

He tied his ruined shirt tightly across his belly and moved stiffly to grab one of Illir's arms, dragging him through the cemetery gate. He returned a moment later, staggering painfully, to drag Ellis away as well.

"What is he doing?" Elinor whispered, eyes wide with fear.

"Hey, ugly!" Tomor shouted, his voice trembling with pain. "Easy pickings. Fresh meat."

"Sweet Oj and Ren, he's playing bait," Aiden groaned.

"Tomor, get out of there!" Calfon yelled, but the creature caught the scent of blood and hurtled forward, nearly knocking Mir over in its haste to reach the cemetery grounds. Tomor took off at a limping run, trying to draw the monster deeper into the graveyard.

"Go!" Tomor yelled. "Make this count!" A moment later they heard a heavy thud, then Tomor cried out in pain, broken by the unmistakable crack of bone.

That left the second beast, which remained fixed on the three hunters who were fighting it—and losing.

Calfon and Mir ran to help just as a loud clatter echoed from the high stone city wall. A shadow loomed in the night, screeching and wailing, thundering closer.

"Run, you son of a bitch!" Polly yelled as her brace of horses barreled down the street straight for the monster. The horses she had stolen were large and fast, closing the distance as she bore down on the creature.

Corran and the others had to throw themselves out of the way as Polly rode straight for the monster, forcing it to flee. With an enraged howl, the monster vaulted the fence, and a moment later they heard it fighting with its companion over the spoils of the dead hunters' corpses.

"Come on!" Polly shouted, reining in the horses. Rigan managed to crawl into the back of the wagon on his own; Aiden and Elinor pulled him forward and secured him. Corran dragged himself in, looking as if it required the last of his strength. The others scrambled up into the wagon, but Calfon hesitated, staring toward the cemetery.

"I hate leaving them behind," he said, his voice raw with grief.

"Let them go," Trent urged quietly. "Tomor knew what he was doing. Honor the sacrifice and let it go." Calfon's expression hardened and he turned, dragging himself into the wagon as Polly cracked the whip and sent the horses galloping into the night. Rigan felt the sharp turn as Polly changed direction, heading for the gate in the city wall. Ahead of them lay shadow, and behind them, flames leapt into the sky as Ravenwood burned.

The next time Rigan woke, pain dragged him from the darkness as something hard beat him across the back and shoulders. Each jolt made him gasp, and when his head thumped against unforgiving wood, he barely bit back a cry of pain.

"Easy," Trent coached. "Sorry about the rough ride. Last damn time we let Polly drive. Can't stop now; guards are after us. But damned if she isn't widening the gap."

It hurt too much to concentrate on the words, and Rigan was too disoriented to fit the pieces together. Cold, fresh air broke over him, air that smelled of grass and horses and fresh dirt, no longer filled with the stench of potions and death. *Out? Are we out? Free?*

"You're in the wagon. Outside the wall. Running for our lives, but for now, we're safe."

Rigan stopped fighting the pain and surrendered, embracing numbness as consciousness retreated.

Chapter Forty-One

Corran groaned. He opened his eyes and stared up at an unfamiliar ceiling, before trying to sit up. The movement made him gasp and set the world spinning, so he dropped back, panting against the pain.

"You need to lie still." Trent's voice held an edge of exhaustion, but it was damn good just to hear him, to know both of them were alive.

"Where?" Corran forced through parched lips. Trent slid a hand under his shoulders and lifted him just enough to hold a cup to his lips. Corran sipped the water greedily until Trent withdrew the cup.

"Take it slowly, or everything will come back up," he warned, lowering him to the bed. "We're two days' ride out of Ravenwood, at one of those deserted monasteries Polly and Elinor found on the map. We'll go further as soon as we can get everyone patched up, but you and Rigan in particular were both in a bad way and we couldn't risk it."

"How long?" Corran rasped. "How long since..."

"Three days. We damn near lost both of you."

"Rigan?"

"Alive. Aiden's with him. I won't pretend to understand what in the name of the gods he and Aiden did to Blackholt, but by rights, both of them cheated Doharmu. You, too."

"The others?" Corran inventoried where his body hurt the most—sharp pain in his side, not as bad as it had been; dull ache in his bones, probably from being thrown around. He was sore everywhere, with bruises from head to toe.

"We lost Illir, Ellis, and Tomor."

"I remember."

"Everyone else is healing," Trent continued. "Can't promise the damage won't scar, but Aiden doesn't think anyone will be permanently crippled."

"We need to get moving," Corran said, swallowing hard. "Can't let them catch us."

"If Aiden says the two of you are healed enough for it, we'll move out tonight," Trent replied. "There's another monastery three days from here that should be remote enough to take us off the map for a while. We could all use time to recover."

Gods, Trent looks awful. I have the feeling it was worse than he's let on.

"What about Ravenwood?"

Trent let out a long breath. "From what we could see as we went through the gate, the fires were contained around the Lord Mayor's palace. With Machison and Blackholt dead, there should be no one to summon the monsters. The other hunters can take care of the ones still remaining. The only beasts they should have to worry about after that are the ones that crop up naturally. And the guards are going to be too busy putting out the fires to worry about killing people and collecting bribes."

"There will be a new Lord Mayor eventually."

"Yes, but maybe he won't have a pet blood witch. And if he does, if it starts again, we know how to stop it. We've gotten justice for all the people we lost. Ravenwood's as safe as we can make it—at least for now."

Corran felt himself fading then, and did not have the energy to fight the tide.

When he woke, it was dark outside. With consciousness came pain. He gritted his teeth and tried to shift on the bed, only to choke back a cry.

"I guess the story you told me about Eshtamon was true."

Corran turned to see Aiden sprawled in a chair beside his bed. The healer looked like death warmed over, wan and hollow-eyed.

Corran swallowed hard and looked away. "Yeah. It's true."

"It had to be," Aiden said, exhaustion seeping into every word. "Because there's no other reason the two of you aren't dead. You lost so much blood. That wound in your side, you should have bled out. By the time we got you to the monastery, you were barely breathing. Almost no heartbeat. Cold."

He sighed. "Rigan wasn't in much better shape—in and out of consciousness, banged up pretty badly. I won't say that I felt great, either, but I wasn't in as much danger as the two of you. Rigan panicked thinking that you were going to die, and did some kind of binding spell to keep your soul in your body until I could heal you." The healer shook his head. "I thought we were all going down for good."

"Thanks."

Aiden shrugged. "Thank Eshtamon. I just patched you back together. I couldn't have saved either of you; I know my limits. The damage was too bad."

"Where's Rigan?"

"Next room over. Trying to badger me into bringing him over to see with his own eyes that you're alive—"

"Help me up," Corran said, and this time he managed to get to a seated position before the room swam and his ears buzzed.

"Gods, you're stubborn. The two of you will be the death of me yet." Aiden glared at him. "Lie down. For now, you'll just have to trust me. Trent says we're moving on tonight, so you and Rigan will have three days in a wagon to trade stories. Believe me, you haven't missed anything. Both of you have been unconscious for most of the time, except for the bleeding and the swearing, and the nearly dying."

"How about you?"

Aiden looked away. "I'm drained. Got some bruises, from where that bastard Blackholt tossed me into the wall, and some nasty gashes from the *hancha*. Overdid my magic. Taking on those guards after Blackholt was too much: I've got a headache like someone hit me with an iron rod." He shifted uncomfortably. "I'm a healer, and I used my magic to kill. I broke my vows. That's something I've got to find a way to live with. I found out what I'm capable of doing—what sort of person I am—and I'm not sure I like him."

Corran regarded him in silence for a moment. "I've killed men," he said quietly. "I did it because I believed it had to be done. But knowing I could do that... it changes how you see yourself. Even when it is the right thing to do."

Aiden met his gaze and held it for a moment before looking down. "I'll have to figure out how to make peace with it. It probably won't be the last time."

"Probably not."

"You're awake." Rigan stood in the doorway, leaning against the frame as if it alone held him up. He looked like shit, and Corran had never been quite so happy to see him in his life.

"Sit down before you fall down," Aiden growled. He vacated the chair next to Corran's bed, and gestured for Rigan to take a seat. To Rigan's credit, he managed to cross the few feet from the door to the chair without falling on his face.

"I'll be back with some food," Aiden said, giving them both a warning look. "And you'd both better be ready to eat and sleep while you can. I don't imagine the wagon ride will be pleasant. Mir and Calfon went to see if they could steal us a few more horses."

Rigan and Corran stared at each other in awkward silence after

Aiden left. "Aiden says you did some kind of magic when we were in the wagon. Kept me from dying."

"Guess it worked," Rigan said, managing a tired grin. He looked away and the grin faded.

"Yeah, imagine that." Corran's appraising gaze took in his brother's bruises, his pallor, the pinched set of his lips. He realized that Rigan was making the same assessment of him. "What you did in the dungeon, and on the way out of the city, and then saving me... I don't understand how, but I know it cost you something."

"You showed up looking like you'd taken on an army single-handedly," Rigan replied. "Cost you something, too."

"How many?"

Rigan frowned in confusion. "What?"

"How many threads of your soul did you use?"

Rigan stared at the floor. "I don't know. Haven't figured that out. Even Aiden doesn't know how to reckon that."

"Dammit, Rigan," Corran growled. "That's not good enough."

"No," Rigan conceded, "it isn't. Maybe once we can stop running, Aiden and I can find something in one of the old books. I'm not suicidal, Corran," he said, raising his gaze. "But we made our bargain with Eshtamon to avenge Kell and I had my part to play."

Corran swallowed hard. "He was there. Just for a moment. Did you—?"

"Yeah. I felt him too. But I don't know how it could be real. We were working a banishing spell. It should have driven off every spirit, even his." He ran a hand back through his hair. "I hope it was, though. I miss him."

"Me, too. Think he'll move on now?" Corran asked, his voice tight as he blinked back tears.

Rigan shrugged. "Maybe. For being undertakers, Doharmu's acolytes all these years, there's so damn much we don't know."

They sat in silence for a few moments. Corran did not know what was going through his brother's mind, but his own thoughts were a raw, painful blur. *So many people, dead. So much destruction. How did we end up in the middle of this?*

"Was it worth it?" he asked finally in a harsh whisper. "Did we do the right thing?"

Rigan shook his head slowly, and Corran's heart clenched. "I don't know," he admitted, staring off into the distance. "I just don't know. But I think... maybe. Because it wasn't just for Kell, although that was the breaking point. *Our* breaking point. But there were Mama and Papa, Jora, all the others, people we didn't even know who were killed by the monsters or the guards, the Wanderers, the other witches Below... Kell's death might have been the spark, but the kindling had been laid long ago, was already smoldering."

"And now?" Corran pressed. "We're outlaws. Fugitives. Criminals. And while I figure there'll always be bodies to bury, and we'll do what we can where we can, that's not really who we are now. We're Eshtamon's hunters, until he decides to let us die."

Rigan met his gaze. "We're alive. We're together. We have friends and we have a plan, maybe even a place to live. A purpose. And I think... I'm all right with that. You?"

Their world had been turned upside-down. When their home and shop burned, he and Rigan had gathered only the essentials and fled. Now, Corran thought, they had done it again, seized what really mattered from the fire as Ravenwood and their past burned to ashes.

"Yeah," Corran replied. "I am. I really think I am."

Epilogue

"I HAVE A job for you," Crown Prince Aliyev said, staring down at the injured, broken man who knelt before him in chains.

"What pleases m'lord?" Hant Jorgeson kept his head bowed. When the jailers came to drag him from the dungeon where he had languished since the uprising, he guessed his execution was nigh. Someone needed to take the fall for the disaster, and Jorgeson had the dubious honor of being the last man standing.

Machison and Blackholt had died in the uprising.

Gorog committed suicide, although reflecting on the details of his death, Jorgeson suspected the Merchant Prince had help. His son inherited the role, duly chastened by his father's disastrous overreach.

Jorgeson had no way to know exactly what transpired with Garenoth, but Crown Prince Aliyev salvaged the agreement. Jorgeson suspected Kadar and Tamas achieved the improved terms they wanted. One look at Gorog's shabby heir made it clear at whose expense their turn of fortune had come.

Hunters had broken into the Lord Mayor's palace, committed arson and murder, and some of them lived to escape. Jorgeson's failure would be a cautionary tale for generations to come.

"How badly do you want vengeance on those hunters?"

"With all my being, sir."

Jorgeson could feel the weight of the Crown Prince's attention on him. Evaluating. Calculating. Maybe even wagering with himself. "You've failed me badly. I should have you killed as a warning to others."

"Yes, m'lord." Jorgeson could make no other response. 'I'm sorry' seemed woefully inadequate.

"Yet before this... debacle... you served admirably. You can't redeem yourself; you know that. I can't reinstate you. Who would trust you, when you failed so... memorably?"

Jorgeson tried not to wince at Aliyev's words, but he could not dispute them. He had gone to help the guards fight back an altercation in the street that night, a riot he now realized was a distraction to the real threat. No apology sufficed.

"I can give you a chance to be useful," Aliyev added. "To win your freedom and your life. I will supply the weapons, men, mages, and money you need. You'll have to leave the city, but if you achieve your goal, I'll know."

Jorgeson bit his lip, willing himself to stay still, afraid to look too hopeful, too desperate. Aliyev deserved his reputation as a hard son of a bitch, not known for second chances. Whatever might be offered would come because it suited the Crown Prince's needs, not out of any sort of mercy. And Jorgeson would accept whatever Aliyev gave him, because dead men could not be choosey.

"How may I be of service, m'lord?"

"I need to know what Itara and Sarolinia are up to," Aliyev said, and Jorgeson looked up with surprise.

"M'lord?"

"Our spies suggest that they're plotting, planning a move against us, but we don't know what. Maybe you can learn something they can't."

"I will not fail you."

Aliyev's bitter grimace suggested that Jorgeson's promise was already too little, too late. "Find the hunters who broke into the palace. We know two of them were Valmondes. Shouldn't be hard to identify the others by who's gone missing. We need to make an example of the hunters, keep the commoners out in the village from joining up. Hunt them. Punish them. Kill them."

"And if I am successful, m'lord? What then?"

"If you succeed, I will not do the same to you."

Acknowledgements

Thank you, readers! Because you read, I write. Whether you're just discovering my books or whether you have been with me from the start, I deeply appreciate each and every one of you.

Many thanks also to my agent, Ethan Ellenberg, and his team. I appreciate everything you do.

Lots of gratitude and appreciation for my editor, Jon Oliver, and the whole Solaris crew, including Ben Smith, David Moore, Rob Power and all the other folks who work hard to make my books a reality.

Big thanks to my beta readers: Vikki Ciaffone, Trevor Curtis, Nancy Northcott, Jean Rabe, and of course, Larry, Kyrie, and Chandler Martin. Your input helped a lot!

Conventions are the heart of the sci-fi/fantasy community, where readers and authors meet. Thank you to Arisia, Illogicon, Ad-Astra, Capricon, Mysticon, Awesomecon, Capclave, Marscon, Lunacon, Chattacon, Libertycon, Ravencon, Balticon, ConCarolinas, ConGregate, Dragon*Con, Atomacon, Philcon, World Fantasy, Contraflow, Confluence, Origins Game Fair, GenCon, and the Arizona and Carolinas Renaissance Festivals who always make me feel at home and who have welcomed me as a guest author—as well as the new conventions I have yet to experience. I am very grateful for the opportunity to be part of convention programming, meet wonderful people and give back to a community I truly appreciate.

Thank you to my Thrifty Author Publishing Success Network Meetup group, an awesome group of writers. We have so much fun and have all come so far.

Many thanks also to my author, artist, musician, performer and reader convention friends and Renaissance Festival regulars who help me survive life on the road, to the fantastic bookstore owners and managers who carry on a valiant fight on the front lines of this crazy publishing industry, and to my social media friends and followers who are always up for some online mayhem.

And most of all, thanks to my husband, Larry Martin who plays a huge part in bringing all the books and short stories to life. He's my best first editor, brainstorming accomplice, proof-reader extraordinaire, and now official co-author of our steampunk series, *Iron & Blood: A Jake Desmet Adventure*. The books wouldn't happen without him, and I'm grateful for all his help and support. Thanks also to my children, who are usually patient with the demands of the writing life, and for my dogs, Kipp and Flynn, who are experts at dispelling writer's block. It takes a village to write a book, and I am grateful to each and every one of you!

About the Author

Gail Z. Martin is the author of *Scourge: A Darkhurst novel*, the first in a brand new epic fantasy series from Solaris Books. Also new are: *The Shadowed Path,* part of the Chronicles of the Necromancer universe (Solaris Books); *Vendetta: A Deadly Curiosities Novel* in her urban fantasy series set in Charleston, SC (Solaris Books); *Shadow and Flame* the fourth and final book in the Ascendant Kingdoms Saga (Orbit Books); and *Iron and Blood* a new Steampunk series (Solaris Books) co-authored with Larry N. Martin.

She is also author of *Ice Forged, Reign of Ash* and *War of Shadows* in The Ascendant Kingdoms Saga, The Chronicles of The Necromancer series (*The Summoner, The Blood King, Dark Haven, Dark Lady's Chosen*); The Fallen Kings Cycle (*The Sworn*, *The Dread*) and the urban fantasy novel *Deadly Curiosities.* Gail writes three ebook series: *The Jonmarc Vahanian Adventures, The Deadly Curiosities Adventures* and *The Blaine McFadden Adventures. The Storm and Fury Adventures,* steampunk stories set in the Iron & Blood world, are co-authored with Larry N. Martin.

Her work has appeared in over 35 US/UK anthologies. Newest anthologies include: *The Big Bad 2, Athena's Daughters, Heroes,*

Space, Contact Light, Robots, With Great Power, The Weird Wild West, The Side of Good/The Side of Evil, Alien Artifacts, Cinched: Imagination Unbound, Realms of Imagination, Clockwork Universe: Steampunk vs. Aliens, Gaslight and Grimm, Hath No Fury, Journeys, #We Are Not This, The Baker Street Irregulars, and *In a Cat's Eye.*

Find her at www.GailZMartin.com, on Twitter @GailZMartin, on Facebook.com/WinterKingdoms, at DisquietingVisions.com blog and GhostInTheMachinePodcast.com, on Goodreads https://www.goodreads.com/GailZMartin and free excerpts on Wattpad http://wattpad.com/GailZMartin.

RETURN TO THE WORLD OF *THE SUMMONER*

GAIL Z. MARTIN

THE SHADOWED PATH

A JONMARC VAHANIAN COLLECTION

"ADVENTURE WITH WHOLE-HEARTED PASSION" - *SFX*

Soldier. Fight slave. Smuggler. Warrior. Brigand Lord. You may have encountered Jonmarc Vahanian in the *Chronicles of the Necromancer* but you don't really know him until you walk in his footsteps. This is the start of his epic journey. A blacksmith's son in a small fishing village before raiders killed his family, Jonmarc was wounded and left for dead in the attack. He tried to rebuild his life, but when a dangerous bargain with a shadowy stranger went wrong, he found himself on the run. Gail Z. Martin returns to the world of her internationally best-selling books with these thrilling tales of adventure and high fantasy, collected together here for the very first time.

WWW.SOLARISBOOKS.COM

Follow us on Twitter! www.twitter.com/solarisbooks